YOU CAN'T ESCAPE

Husair Zein

BLUEROSE PUBLISHERS
India | U.K.

Copyright © Husair Zein 2024

All rights reserved by author. No part of this publication may be reproduced, stored in a retrieval system or transmitted in any form or by any means, electronic, mechanical, photocopying, recording or otherwise, without the prior permission of the author. Although every precaution has been taken to verify the accuracy of the information contained herein, the publisher assumes no responsibility for any errors or omissions. No liability is assumed for damages that may result from the use of information contained within.

BlueRose Publishers takes no responsibility for any damages, losses, or liabilities that may arise from the use or misuse of the information, products, or services provided in this publication.

For permissions requests or inquiries regarding this publication, please contact:

BLUEROSE PUBLISHERS
www.BlueRoseONE.com
info@bluerosepublishers.com
+91 8882 898 898
+4407342408967

ISBN: 978-93-6783-822-8

Cover Design: Shubham
Typesetting: Sagar

First Edition: November 2024

Author's Note

Hello, dear readers!

First, let me say how grateful I am that you've chosen to pick up my very first novel in this fast-paced, modern world. I want to take a moment to express my immense gratitude for each of you who has chosen to read You Can't Escape.

This book holds a special place in my heart, not only because it's my debut novel but because it represents countless hours of dedication, late nights, and a journey filled with passion and perseverance. In an age where there are so many ways to experience stories, I am truly honored that you've picked up this book. Thank you for allowing my words to become a part of your world—I couldn't be more grateful.

A special thank you goes out to the people who were there with me at every step of this journey:

Raza, you have been my greatest pillar throughout this process. Your support during my toughest moments made this book a reality— If you hadn't been there in my moments of need, this novel wouldn't be here at all.

And to Razi, thank you for lending your editing talents and guidance; you turned this work into something far beyond what I could have achieved alone.

To Arjun Pandit and Pritham Pandit, your encouragement drove me to finish this novel with efficiency and passion and your kind support made it possible for me to complete this novel with greater speed and focus.

I also extend my heartfelt thanks to Rahil, Thabsheer, Shafeeq, Afraz A., Masroor, Aman, and Hadin for your unwavering support. And to AL-FUTHOOH members, thank you for inspiring me and keeping me focused.

And to my family, whose encouragement and love have been my foundation, and most of all to my mom and dad—you are my biggest supporters and my inspiration. Thank you for always believing in me and for your endless support and guidance.

To Sakfun Nawaz, you have been a tremendous help to me—thank you very much. Rafi, Nizar, Noushi, Junni, and Hazara, Unais and Raula, thank you all for your kind support throughout this journey.

To every reader holding this book, thank you for sharing in this journey. This story now belongs to you, and I hope it brings you as much meaning and emotion as it did to me in its creation.

And I poured my heart into each page. I'm incredibly grateful that, in this fast-paced world, you chose to spend your time with my words. I hope you find meaning, emotion, and a connection within these pages, just as I found joy in crafting them for you.

With this, now you can finally embark on a journey to You Can't Escape.

Contents

Prologue 1

Chapter One
A Journey to Escape 5

Chapter Two
Back to Mumbai 45

Chapter Three
Six Years Back 85

Chapter Four
Endless Confinement 291

Prologue

The night was thick with tension as I reached the college backyard. I found Aliya and the others huddled together at the far end, their faces etched with fear. I couldn't understand why they had come here or what was going on.

As I approached them, the tension in the air was palpable. "What happened, guys? Why are you here?" I asked, but before anyone could respond, Vikram, Rahul, Arjun, Raj, and a few others I didn't recognize, but clearly weren't from our college, emerged from the shadows and positioned themselves between me and my friends. Vikram's cruel smile sent a shiver down my spine.

"Now let's see how you save your friends," Vikram said, his cruel smile cutting through the darkness.

"Galath wakth par galath jagah pahonch gaya hei tu." You've ended up in the wrong place at the wrong time. Remember, this time I won't show any mercy, I retorted, trying to hide my fear.

"Today, fate might be on my side," Rishab. This time, I'm the one who won't show any mercy," Vikram blurted back.

"After I take care of your men, we'll see whose side fate is on," I shot back defiantly.

One of the new faces stepped forward, ready to attack. Three of them came at me simultaneously. The first one swung a punch, but I dodged. The other two were faster, their blows landing hard and strong, sending me staggering backward.

Aliya and the others tried to intervene, but Rahul, Arjun, and Raj held them back. Vikram's malicious laughter filled the air. "Looks like someone's getting a proper beatdown," Vikram jeered.

"You managed to land a blow on me—impressive," I said, gritting my teeth. My eyes caught sight of a wooden log lying on the ground. With a burst of adrenaline, I grabbed it.

As one of them lunged at me again, I swung the log and hit him on the head. He collapsed, blood oozing from his wound, his screams of pain piercing the night.

"One down," I said, panting as I turned to face the other two. They charged at me together, but I used the log as a shield, deflecting their kicks. I quickly steadied myself and struck them both with the log. They fell to the ground, howling in agony.

"Go, you three! What are you waiting for?" Vikram shouted at his men.

"I don't want to get hospitalized," Rahul said, clearly frightened.

"Me neither," Arjun added.

"And you, Raj?" Vikram's voice was laced with frustration.

"I'm not going to the hospital!" Raj declared.

"You scaredy cats! You're all morons!" Vikram cursed, his anger boiling over.

He charged at me. I was ready to block his attack, but Vikram was quicker. He pulled out a canister and sprayed it directly into my eyes. The intense burning sensation told me it was pepper spray. I staggered back, rubbing my eyes desperately but unable to see clearly.

"Now attack!" Vikram yelled.

I struggled to see through the searing pain. Blinded and in pain, I stumbled, trying to regain my vision. I could barely make out a figure approaching me, but before I could react, he struck a metal rod hard on my head. I turned to face the attacker, but his face was obscured by a mask. The eyes peering out from behind the mask were filled with hatred—a look I felt I would never forget. The pain overwhelmed me, and I collapsed to the ground.

Amidst the chaos, I heard Aliya's panicked voice. "Catch her! Don't let her go!" Vikram ordered.

"Leave me, please! Let me go!" Aliya's voice pleaded.

"Beat him and kill the others except her. I want both of them alive," Vikram commanded.

I felt the blows landing on me, the pain becoming almost unbearable. My senses began to fail. I tried to focus, but the pain in my head and my blurring vision made it nearly impossible to focus. My friends' cries filled the air. The last thing I saw was a red substance—blood—flowing from my friends as they fell, and then everything went black.

I was unconscious....

Chapter One

A Journey to Escape

"Move quickly, you fools! Catch him, or I will have all your heads!" he said in a stern voice, echoing through the dimly lit basement. Riya and I stayed close together near a staircase, hiding in the shadows. I had quietly given Riya a sleeping pill to keep her safe from the chaos around us.

The basement felt like a prison, and desperation filled every thought. Escaping from this frightening place seemed nearly impossible. The risk of getting caught grew with each passing moment, and fear gripped me.

"How can we escape?" I thought, my mind racing for a way out of the clutches of our captors and their constant chase. The darkness seemed suffocating, and I desperately wished for a miracle to save us.

In this dangerous moment, every breath felt hard, and every corner seemed to conceal a threat. Yet, I refused to give in to hopelessness. My determination to survive surged as I held onto the hope of freedom and safety.

My heart raced as I reminded myself that Vikram was more than just a name; he was a person with his own secrets and fears. Discovering his true identity might be the key to finding a way to escape.

In the depths of the basement's darkness, my mind began to piece together a plan, a daring escape that could lead us out of this nightmare. I looked at Riya, her peaceful face giving me strength and resolve.

I knew it wouldn't be easy, but we had to try. Risking everything, I whispered to her sleeping form, "We'll get out of here, Riya. I promise."

With each passing second, the urgency intensified. It was time to face our fears and seize any opportunity that presented itself. The basement may have been a dreadful place, but I was ready to confront the unknown and break free from its suffocating grasp.

As I took a deep breath, I knew that this was the moment when our fate would be decided. We would either escape into the light or remain trapped in the darkness forever. It was time to make a choice – to fight for our lives, for our freedom, and for a chance to live beyond the confines of this terrible nightmare.

The basement air felt thick and oppressive as I cautiously peered around, desperately searching for any means of escape. Suddenly, my eyes locked onto a wooden crate, its lid barely closed, revealing a chilling cache of grenades and revolvers. Fear mingled with a glimmer of hope as I realized these weapons could be the key to our freedom.

Riya's slumbering form weighed heavily in my arms, but I knew I had to act swiftly. Setting her down gently on the floor I prepared myself for the daring move ahead.

As the thugs' attention shifted to another room, I seized the opportunity and quietly emerged from the shadows. My heart raced like a thundering drum as I crept closer to the box, every step feeling like an eternity.

Hiding behind pillars and staying close to the walls, I moved with the stealth of a hunter stalking its prey. My breaths were shallow, my senses heightened, and every creak of the floor beneath my feet seemed to echo like a gunshot.

Just as I approached the crate, the hairs on the back of my neck stood on end - one of the thug unexpectedly reappeared. Panic surged through my veins, but there was no time to retreat. I had to think fast, my mind racing like a whirlwind.

I pressed myself against the pillar, praying he wouldn't notice me. The seconds stretched into an eternity as he lingered nearby. My heart pounded in my ears, drowning out all other sounds. There was no other choice - I had to act.

Summoning every ounce of courage, I lunged at him without a moment's hesitation. My hands found his neck with a vice-like grip, determined to end his threat without a single sound. He struggled, gasping for air, but I refused to relent. The gravity of the moment weighed heavily on me, but this was survival - a brutal dance of life and death.

The encounter was over almost as quickly as it had begun. His body slumped lifelessly to the floor, and the weight of what I had done settled upon me like a leaden shroud. I had taken a life, even if it was to protect our own.

In the deafening silence that followed, my mind wrestled with the choices I had made. This dark basement had changed me, forcing me into a role I never imagined. But amidst the turmoil, I knew that there was no turning back. My actions had bought us a chance, however slim, to defeat our captors and escape from the clutches of this nightmarish prison.

The adrenaline surged through my veins as I quickly moved the thug's lifeless body behind the pillar and took off his clothes. My heart pounded with each second, knowing that time was of the essence. With the clothes and mask on, I now looked like one of them, armed with a suppressed assault rifle in my hands.

As I rushed toward the box of weapons, my heart sank when two thugs unexpectedly entered the hall. I was trapped between terror and deception, but I knew I had to stay composed. My life and Riya's depended on it.

"Hey! Where are you going?" one of them questioned, and my mind raced to find a convincing answer.

"No... No... I was just looking around this room," I said, my voice shaking, trying to sound like one of them.

They seemed to buy my response, and I let out a sigh of relief. "OK. Come with us," the other one instructed, and I nodded, trying to suppress the fear that threatened to consume me.

As we walked together down the empty hall, my heart pounded loudly in my ears. Suddenly, Riya woke up and started crying. Panic surged through me; we couldn't afford any attention.

"Did you hear anything?" one of the thug asked,

"No... sorry, I didn't hear anything," I replied, attempting to divert their attention. and I tried to keep my voice steady.

"I heard something, sounds like crying," the other one remarked, and my heart sank.

They turned towards Riya, who was standing with her hands on her eyes, her cries echoing through the hall. Fear clenched at my throat; we were on the verge of being discovered.

In a split second, I made a desperate decision. Without hesitation, I aimed the suppressed gun at one of the thugs' head and pulled the trigger. The silence was shattered by the deafening gunshot as his body collapsed to the floor, blood pooling around him.

The second thug's eyes widened in shock, but before he could react, I fired again, silencing him forever. The room was now painted with a macabre scene of violence and death.

I quickly removed the mask and rushed to Riya, who was still trembling and crying. I tried to soothe her, my heart breaking for what she had to witness.

"Riya, look here, everything is okay," I said gently, wiping away her tears and holding her close. "You have to be strong, my little one. We can't stay here."

She nodded, still in shock, and I knew we had to move quickly. "If you want to get out of this place, then you have to stop crying," I told her softly.

"Okay, Daddy," she whispered, trying to control her sobs.

With my heart heavy from the violence we had just encountered, I cradled Riya in my arms and made a silent promise that I would protect her at all costs. We were embarking on a dangerous journey, but the will to survive burned brightly within us.

With Riya in my arms, we hid in the room, safe from danger. I gently placed her beneath a table to keep her secure and then looked around.

There were three doors ahead of us, each leading to a different place. I peeked through the first door and saw a straight path that seemed endless. I decided to leave that door closed and locked. I moved on to the second one.

As I carefully opened the second door, my heart raced. There, I saw Vikram, he had three tough-looking bodyguards with him, and it made me shiver. Quickly, I closed and locked the door, not wanting to take any chances.

Now, just the third door remained, and I prayed it would be our way out. Peeking through the gap, I spotted a line of rooms with a bright "EXIT" sign above one of the doors. A glimmer of hope lit up inside me, but that hope dimmed as I noticed two armed guards stationed by the exit.

Returning to Riya's side, I whispered, "Baby, do you want to get out of this place?"

Her eyes filled with a mixture of fear and determination as she softly replied, "Yes, Daddy."

"Okay, now when a loud noise is heard, you have to stay quiet, alright?" I instructed her, my voice steady despite the anxious rising in my chest.

She nodded, understanding the gravity of the situation. I knew that our only chance at escaping this hellish place was to seize the moment, no matter how dangerous it seemed.

Taking a deep breath, I formulated a plan in my mind. We had to act quickly, but with caution. If we were to survive, I needed to eliminate the guards and make our way to the exit undetected.

Gently kissing Riya's forehead, I whispered, "Stay here and hide yourself."

I moved toward the door, my heart pounding like war drums in my ears. With every step, my resolve strengthened. This was the moment we had been waiting for – a chance to break free from the chains of our captivity.

In a flash, I reached into my pocket and pulled out a grenade. It was do or die, and I knew I had only seconds to make a move. With my heart pounding, I yanked the pin and tossed the grenade towards them. The room seemed to hold its breath for a moment, and then chaos erupted.

The explosion was incredibly loud, like a thunderclap, and it shook everything around us. It blew bits of broken stuff into the air, and the room quickly filled with smoke and chaos. My ears were ringing, and it was hard to see clearly because of all the smoke around.

The room filled with a loud explosion, and things got really messy afterward. Smoke went everywhere, the explosion was so strong that it broke the windows, and the air smelled funny, like something was burning.

As the smoke cleared from the grenade blast, everything turned chaotic. I think the loud noise had alerted everyone in the base, and the thugs were now on high alert,

"Riya, it's okay now," I reassured her, my voice shaking with a mix of relief and fear. She opened her eyes and cautiously came out from under the table. She looked scared, just like me, but I understood that we needed to continue moving if we hoped to stay alive.

However, in that moment, suddenly Vikram entered the room with two armed thugs. My heart sank because escaping now wouldn't be simple. Vikram was clever and ruthless, and he wouldn't let us escape easily.

"Aim at him," Vikram commanded his men, his cold eyes fixed on me. "You should have stayed hidden, Rishabh. But now, you will pay for your defiance."

The two thugs obeyed their leader without question, their guns now trained on me. The odds were stacked against me, but I couldn't back down. I had come this far, and I would do whatever it took to protect Riya and avenge all those innocent lives that had been lost.

Then he quickly grabbed Riya by her arms, "Please, let her go," I pleaded, trying to appeal to any trace of humanity that might remain in Vikram. "She's just a child. Let her go, I'll surrender myself."

Vikram's lips curled into a cruel smile, and he tightened his grip on Riya. "I don't think so," he taunted. "You took everything from me, you killed my brother Rishabh. Now, I will take everything from you."

My blood boiled at his heartless words, but I had to keep my emotions in check. Riya's safety was my top priority, and I couldn't risk anything that might hurt her.

"Stay calm, Riya," I said, my voice gentle but resolute. "Everything will be okay. Just trust me, okay?"

Riya nodded, her eyes still filled with fear, but she knew that she had to trust me. I took a deep breath, my mind racing for a plan. I had to create a diversion, something that would give us a chance to escape.

As Vikram kept talking, my eyes spotted a knife on the floor. A daring idea crossed my mind. It was a dangerous move, but it might be our only way out.

Vikram stared at me when I picked up the knife. He quickly told his guards to shoot me. My heart raced, and I moved fast, barely avoiding the bullets. I was in survival mode, and I dodged their gunfire, narrowly escaping a terrible fate.

With the knife in hand, I moved forward with determination. In an instant, I made deadly, accurate strikes, taking down two of Vikram's guards. They were clearly shocked in their final moments.

Without any delay, I picked up one of the guns dropped by the fallen guards. The situation had changed significantly, and I was now in control of the situation.

I took a deep breath and pointed the gun at surprised Vikram. The room was filled with tension, as the once-confident mastermind now found himself at the mercy of an unexpected twist of fate.

"Stay back! Don't come any closer," I warned him, my voice firm and unwavering. "Let Riya go, or I won't hesitate to end this right now."

"Step away from Riya," I commanded, my voice quivering with a mix of fear and determination. I kept the gun aimed at him, my hands steady despite the surge of emotions coursing through me. "Don't even think about moving," I warned, my eyes locked onto him, unwilling to let my guard down.

Vikram's eyes burned with anger and frustration, but he realized that he was now at my mercy. He carefully released his grip on Riya, but then suddenly, she collapsed to the floor, her eyes closed, and her body weak. My heart sank as I screamed, "Riya...!"

Riya's unconscious state hung heavily in the room, adding an extra layer of tension to the already charged atmosphere.

He began to stammer, his voice tinged with desperation. "Don't shoot, please... don't shoot. Listen, Rishabh..."

I maintained my focus, keeping the gun trained on him as he pleaded for his safety.

"Kneel down," I ordered, my tone firm as I pointed the gun towards him.

He complied quickly, his hands raised in surrender. My heart raced, the weight of the situation sinking in.

"Okay, okay, I will," he said, his voice tense with submission.

As he knelt before me, his hands in the air, my attention shifted to Riya. I tried to gently wake her, my concern growing as she remained unconscious. With a mixture of relief and responsibility, I carefully lifted her into my arms, ensuring her safety above all else.

"You may have underestimated me, Vikram. But now, you're under my control," I said, my voice holding an edge of determination.

Vikram's expression shifted from surprise to arrogance as he spoke, "You may have defeated me, Rishabh, but your escape won't be so simple. My people are waiting outside. How do you plan to get past them?

My resolve deepened. "I know they won't harm us."

He scoffed, his voice filled with doubt. "And how can you be so sure of that?"

"Because you're coming with us," I declared, changing the situation against him.

His confidence weakened, and he looked uncertain. "What..." he began, his voice trailing off in disbelief.

"Get up, you go first," I said in a firm voice. He reluctantly rose to his feet, and I followed closely behind, my gun trained on his head. With caution, he slowly opened the exit door, and we stepped outside, surrounded by hundreds of armed men, all waiting to kill me and Riya.

Vikram, under my control, made sure they couldn't make a move. "Tell them to throw their guns away," I ordered him.

Vikram stammered, "Th-Th-Throw your guns!" Fear evident in his voice, his men complied, they dropped their weapons in a heap. The tension was thick as we moved through the line of parked cars.

"Hurry, move!" I urged, and as we neared a car, I commanded him to drive. "Get in the driver's seat, now!" I shouted.

"P...Please, let me live. I won't do anything," he pleaded, but I cut him off mid-sentence.

"Step on it!" I snapped. He demanded his men to hand over the car key, which they quickly did. After opening the car door, he got in, and Riya and I settled into the back seat, the gun still trained on him.

Riya was still unconscious, showing how dangerous our situation was.

"Drive!" I ordered, and the engine roared to life as we sped away from the base.

The rush of adrenaline made my heart beat faster, but I stayed concentrated. "Go to the hospital," I instructed, pressing the gun against his head to show I was in charge.

As we drove, everything outside our car looked like a jumble of confusion. I had to be really careful at every street corner because I never knew what danger might be waiting there.

We kept driving for almost half an hour, but we still hadn't reached the city. I was starting to feel really confused and had no clue about where we were or where we were going. The road ahead seemed to go on forever, and it was surrounded by thick forests on both sides. We didn't see anyone else on the road; it felt really creepy and deserted.

As I looked at Riya I couldn't help but wonder, she shared an almost identical appearance with her mother Aliya. It was like looking at a mirror image. Riya's skin was soft and had a glow like the moon. She had the twinkling blue eyes, and her nose was shaped nicely, making her look elegant.

Her lips had a gentle curve, and her hair was as smooth as black silk, making her even more charming. Every action she took had a graceful quality, just like her mother.

The similarity was astonishing, and it made my heart ache. Aliya's heart-breaking death was a wound that never seemed to heal, and seeing Riya brought back a rush of sadness and anger.

"Vikram!" I whispered angrily, my grip on the gun getting tighter. He was the person who had ruined our lives, who had taken Aliya away from me.

"He killed Aliya!" I muttered, the words heavy with pain and anger. The memories flooded back - the sinister smile on Vikram's face as he snatched away our happiness, the cruelty in his eyes, and the heartlessness that shattered our world.

I held the gun tightly, determined to make Vikram pay for what he had done. The road seemed to go on forever, just like the pain inside me.

Suddenly, a voice echoed in my mind, a voice I hadn't heard in a long time - Aliya's comforting words that used to soothe me in times of distress. "Don't let hate consume you," she would say. "Remember, love and forgiveness are stronger than any darkness."

Tears welled up in my eyes as I struggled to regain composure. I knew Aliya wouldn't have wanted me to become a harbinger of vengeance, but the pain was so intense that it threatened to consume me. I took a deep breath, trying to find strength amidst the turmoil.

"I will make him pay, Aliya," I whispered to the memory of my aliya, as if she was still alive with me.

"Stop the car!" I said in a stern voice.

"What?" he asked, taken aback by my sudden command.

"I said, stop the car!" My voice was filled with anger and determination.

He complied, pulling the car over to the side of the desolate road. I stepped out, my face burning with rage, and aimed the gun at him.

"Get out of the car!" I spat, my emotions overwhelming me.

Reluctantly, he stepped out, his expression a mix of fear and surprise. "Kneel down," I ordered, my grip on the gun unwavering.

He tried to reason with me, "Rishabh, I know that I messed up. I'm sorry. Please, forgive me. I'll surrender to the police, but please don't kill me."

"I had told you back then that 'Galath wakth par galath jagah pahonch gaya hei tu,' but you still dared to kill my friends and imprison us," I retorted, my anger boiling over. "You dragged us into hell, killed innocent people, and took away the love of my life, Aliya!"

Tears welled up in my eyes as the pain of losing Aliya resurfaced. "If only she were alive, I'd spare you. But you can't bring her back, can you? You're not a god!"

He pleaded for mercy, speaking of his family waiting for him at home. But my wrath only grew stronger. "What about Riya, that little girl? Her mother, Aliya, died because of you!" I shouted, my body trembling with rage.

As he continued to beg, I closed my eyes, trying to gather my thoughts. I remembered Aliya's smiling face, and the pain inside me intensified.

With a deep breath, I opened my eyes, my resolve clear. "You will die today, Vikram. You deserve no mercy for the pain you've caused!"

Before he could utter another word, I pulled the trigger, and the bullet hit him in the head. He fell to the ground, but my rage was not quenched. I emptied the entire magazine into his body, consumed by my emotions.

As I stood there, surrounded by blood, I let out a heavy sigh. Aliya's face appeared in my mind, and I felt a mixture of grief and relief.

Regaining my composure, I threw the gun away and returned to the car and sat in the driver's seat. Looking back at Riya, pale and weak, my heart ached for her. She had suffered enough because of Vikram's actions.

Starting the ignition, I drove the car forward, leaving the horror behind. My journey for justice wasn't over, and I vowed to protect Riya and ensure that no more innocent lives were lost because of Vikram's sins.

After a few minutes of driving, we finally reached the city. I slowed the car down and searched for someone who could direct me to the nearest hospital.

Spotting a person nearby, I urgently asked, "Excuse me, can you please tell me where the nearest hospital is?"

"The hospital? Go straight ahead, then take a right turn, and another right. You'll reach the hospital," he replied, pointing in the direction.

"Thank you so much!" I said with gratitude and quickly drove the car. Following directions to the hospital, keeping a close eye on Riya. She needed immediate medical attention. My heart pounded with worry as I drove as fast as I safely could, hoping we would reach the hospital in time.

Finally, we arrived at "Noora Hospital," and I parked the car in front of it. Without any delay, I carefully carried Riya in my arms and made my way inside, seeking medical assistance for her.

The hospital staff acted swiftly, and they took Riya to the examination room. I provided them with details about her condition, stressing that she required prompt attention.

After what felt like a long wait, a doctor finally came to speak with me. My heart pounded as I awaited updates on Riya's condition.

"Will she be all right?" I asked, trying to keep my voice composed.

The doctor looked at me with a reassuring smile. "We're taking care of her. She's stable, but she needs proper care and observation," he said calmly.

Relief washed over me, but I couldn't help but remain anxious about Riya's well-being. "Can I see her?" I asked, wanting to be by her side.

The doctor nodded and led me to Riya's room. She looked fragile as she lay on the hospital bed, she was sleeping. I gently held her hand, willing her to be strong and recover soon.

"You're going to be alright, Riya," I whispered softly. "I'm here with you, and I won't leave your side."

I stayed by Riya's bedside, assuring her that I was there for her, just as she believed me to be her guardian. I hoped and prayed for her swift recovery, vowing to protect her and ensure that she had a safe and secure future.

I was gazing at her innocent face as she slept peacefully. Despite the circumstances, she looked beautiful when she slept, reminding me of the love I held for her and the responsibility I had taken on as her protector.

My thoughts went back to the past when we had a happy life before Vikram ruined it. We had lost six years of our youth in his captivity, and now that we were free, I felt a mix of relief and uncertainty about our future.

As I caressed Riya's hair gently, my heart ached, thinking about the countless nights she spent in captivity, robbed of her childhood. The pain of not being able to see my parents for six long years weighed heavily on my shoulders. Would they even recognize me now? What would they think of the person I had become after being subjected to such a heart-breaking experience?

Vikram, the man who had caused us so much pain, had ruined our lives in terrible ways. I couldn't stop thinking about Aliya, the woman I loved and lost. Her memory, especially her smiling face, was something I held dear in my heart.

After the doctor assured me that Riya was going to be alright with some rest, I had her admitted to the hospital room. She slept peacefully, and I remained by her side, gently caressing her hair. She looked so fragile, but I knew she was a strong girl, suffering six years of captivity with me.

"After six years, we finally escaped from that place," I murmured to myself, feeling a mix of relief and anxiety. "But now, we are in an unknown location, and I have no idea where we are. The last time we were kidnapped, we were in Mumbai, at our college annual day, with Aliya."

The memories of our life before the kidnapping weighed heavily on my mind. Six long years of imprisonment had separated us from our loved ones and the world we once knew. I longed to reunite with my parents, but I feared what they might think of me after such a traumatic experience.

As frustration and anger surged within me, I muttered, "Vikram ruined my entire life. Damn him!"

My stomach growled, making me realize I hadn't eaten since morning. However, the reality of our situation hit me hard—I had no money to buy food.

"I'm starving, but I don't have a penny," I sighed in despair. Then it struck me—I still had the car, and perhaps there was something I hadn't checked. I hurriedly stepped out of the hospital room and went to the car. As I searched every corner, I found nothing until I opened the dashboard. My eyes widened in astonishment as I discovered two bundles of five-hundred-rupee notes—a significant amount of money that I had never seen in my entire life.

After securing the money from the car, I went to a nearby hotel with a sense of relief and hunger. Entering the restaurant, I ordered some food for myself and made sure to parcel a meal Riya.

While waiting for the food to be prepared, my thoughts whirled around Riya and the responsibilities that now rested upon my shoulders. She had become my sole priority.

Once the food was served, I ate silently, and bought a parcel— for Riya. I hurried back to the hospital with a heart full of concern and love.

While I was walking back to the hospital, something caught my eye— a café on the street corner. Inside, there was a young couple, a guy and a girl. The guy seemed really nervous as he reached into his pocket, pulled out a small box, and got down on one knee. It was obvious that he was about to ask her to marry him. But things took an unexpected turn when she reacted by slapping him right in front of everyone. She left the café in a hurry, leaving the guy looking stunned and embarrassed.

My thoughts drifted to a similar memory, a cherished moment from my past. It was the day I proposed to Aliya, the woman I loved more than anything else. Her eyes had sparkled with joy, and she had accepted my proposal with a smile that could have brightened the darkest room. That memory was a precious one, forever etched in my heart.

As I witnessed the scene, it stirred up painful memories of what I had once shared with Aliya. Tears welled up in my eyes, and I hastily brushed them away. My journey to the hospital continued, my heart heavy with the weight of my emotions. Right now, my focus had to be on Riya. She depended on me, and I had to set aside my feelings and be strong for her.

Arriving at the hospital, I once again sat beside Riya's bed, keeping a watchful eye on her as she rested. The memory of the rejected proposal still lingered in my mind, reminding me of the fragility of love and life. Life was unpredictable, and my life was changed after six years of captivity.

As I looked at Riya, I felt a deep sense of responsibility and love for her. I couldn't change the past or undo the pain we had experienced, but I could promise her a future filled with care, affection, and support. Riya is my family, and I would protect her with all my strength.

With a determined resolve, I held Riya's hand, feeling a sense of comfort in her presence. As we faced the uncertainties of the past together, I knew that my love for her would guide us through the darkest moments and help us discover a path of healing and hope.

"Riya, wake up!" I gently nudged her, trying to wake her from her nap.

Riya stirred, rubbing her eyes sleepily. "Huh? Daddy?" she asked, looking up at me with drowsy eyes.

"Yes, Riya, it's me!" I beamed, ruffling her hair affectionately. "Are you alright sweety?"

Riya didn't say anything, she was still in a sombre mood,

Look here I bought you food, here eat it, I said. But she refused to eat.

I gently cupped her face with my hands and said, "Please, sweetheart, you need to eat something. You haven't had anything since morning. It's important to keep your strength up."

She hesitated for a moment, her eyes downcast. "Look, sweetheart," I said, a soft smile playing on my lips. "I have a special plan for you. How would you like to meet your mommy?"

Riya's eyes widened in surprise and excitement at the mention of her mother. "Really, Daddy? Can I meet Mommy?"

"Yes, you can," I replied, trying to keep my emotions in check. "But to meet her, you need to eat something first. If you have the strength, we can go and visit her."

Riya's face lit up at the prospect of meeting her mother. "Okay, Daddy, I will eat," she said, determination creeping into her voice.

With that, I picked up the food parcel and started to feed her, albeit slowly at first. Encouraging her with each bite. "That's it, Riya. You're doing great!"

As I fed her each bite gently, my heart ached at the truth I was hiding from her. Her innocent trust in me made it difficult to reveal the painful reality. I couldn't bear to see her hurt, so I decided to shield her from the truth forever.

"You're doing so well, Riya," I praised, seeing her finishing the meal. "Almost there!"

With every bite, her mood seemed to brighten, and by the time she finished, a sense of accomplishment filled her. "There you go, sweetie," I said, wiping her mouth with a napkin. "You did it!"

Daddy when we going to meet mommy? She asked instantly.

"We will leave from here tomorrow morning, and I promise, you will meet your mommy," I said with a soft smile, brushing a strand of hair away from her face.

Her eyes lit up with joy, and she hugged me tightly. "Really, daddy? Can I really meet mommy?"

"Yes, sweetheart," I replied, trying to hold back my emotions.

Riya's excitement was contagious, and for a moment, I allowed myself to believe in the possibility of a miraculous reunion. I knew the truth would be difficult to face, but I couldn't bear to see her hopes crushed.

"Now, sleep tight, my little angel," I said, tucking her in. After tucking her to sleep I settled on the couch, my heart felt heavy with the weight of the promise I made. My mind was filled with uncertainties and the guilt of hiding the truth. But seeing Riya's innocent smile, I couldn't bring myself to break her heart just yet.

I whispered to the silent room, "I don't know how or when, but I'll find a way to keep that promise to you, Aliya.

With a mix of determination and apprehension, I closed my eyes, ready to face whatever challenges lay ahead in our journey

I tried hard to sleep, tossing and turning on the couch, but my mind was restless, haunted by memories of Aliya and the weight of the truth. Frustration gnawed at me as I felt the coldness of the night seeping into my thoughts.

Finally, unable to find peace on the couch, I decided to step out onto the balcony. The cold breeze hit my face, awakening my senses and momentarily distracting me from my swirling thoughts. The serene night sky, dotted with stars, seemed to be a canvas of memories.

"Why did you leave me, Aliya?" I whispered, as if she could hear me from the beyond. "I miss you so much."

The night embraced me with its calm, but my mind was filled with turmoil. The burden of keeping the truth from Riya weighed heavily on my heart. She was just a little girl, innocent and full of hope. How could I break her spirit by revealing the painful reality of her mother's death?

A part of me wanted to protect her from the truth forever, but I understood that someday she will come to know. The challenge was when and how to talk about it in a manner that wouldn't break her young heart.

As I stood there, staring out into the night, a mix of strong feelings surrounded me. The memories of Aliya, the love we had shared, and the guilt I felt about keeping the truth from Riya all swirled around in my mind.

The cold breeze brushed against my face, making me shiver slightly. It was as if the night itself was trying to calm my troubled thoughts. The stars in the sky sparkled like tiny beacons of hope, and for a moment, I felt a sense of peace wash over me.

But beneath that peace, the weight of the truth still pressed on my heart. I knew I couldn't hide it forever, and the thought of revealing it to Riya filled me with worry. It was a difficult situation I couldn't escape, and it kept me restless even in the calm of the night.

After spending some time on the balcony, lost in my thoughts, I eventually decided to head back inside. The cold night air had managed to soothe my troubled mind to some extent, but I knew I need some rest. Riya was still peacefully sleeping on the bed, and I didn't want to wake her up.

As I settled down on the bed next to Riya, I found myself in that strange state of exhaustion mixed with restlessness. The emotions of the day had taken a toll on me, and my mind was a whirlwind of memories about Aliya, Riya, and the future.

I tried to close my eyes and clear my mind, but sleep didn't come easily. The room was silent, except for the occasional sounds of the night outside. I stared up at the ceiling, my thoughts drifting between memories of Aliya and the weight of the truth I had yet to share with Riya.

Gradually, as I lay there, a sense of fatigue washed over me. I don't exactly remember how it happened, but sleep must have claimed me in that moment. I found myself in a strange state of half-consciousness, tangled between dreams and reality, with Riya peacefully sleeping beside me, her presence a source of both comfort and turmoil.

"Daddy... Daddy, wake up..." Riya's voice woke me up.

I groggily opened my eyes and saw her sweet face looking at me with curiosity. "You woke up early," I said, trying to gather my thoughts.

"Daddy, when are we going to meet mommy?" she asked innocently.

I paused for a moment, my heart sinking at the question. "Soon, sweetheart," I replied gently, not wanting to reveal the truth yet.

"Oh! God," I whispered to myself, feeling the weight of the situation. "We will go, but first, let's freshen up," I suggested, trying to divert her attention. "Come on, let's wash our faces."

I took her hand and led her to the bathroom, splashing water on my face to wake myself up. "It's cold, Daddy," Riya exclaimed, feeling the chill of the water.

After washing her face, Riya, with her tiny hands, playfully splashed water on my face. I couldn't help but smile at her mischievousness.

"Alright, alright, you got me," I chuckled, wiping the water off my face.

As I looked at her innocent face, I couldn't help but feel a mix of emotions—love, protectiveness, and a deep longing for Aliya's presence. But for Riya's sake, I would do whatever it took to shield her from the harsh realities of life, at least for a little while longer.

"We'll go and meet mommy soon, I promise," I said, holding her close.

"Let's go, Daddy!" she was excited again, her previous disappointment erased. "Ok, ok, let's go," I replied, determined to make this day special for her. But first, we had to see the doctor.

I carried Riya in my arms. She seemed a little apprehensive now, not wanting to meet anyone except her mother. I tried my best to reassure her with a comforting smile.

"Please sit down," the doctor said, motioning towards the chair. "Now, tell me how is she doing?"

"She's better," I replied, my gaze fixed on Riya, who was holding onto me tightly.

The doctor observed her for a moment and then looked at me. "It's not uncommon for children to have difficulty opening up after going through a traumatic experience," he said softly.

I nodded, understanding the impact of what Riya had been through. "Yes, she doesn't seem to want to talk to anyone."

"It's alright," the doctor reassured me. "She needs time to heal. Just be patient with her."

He then turned to Riya, trying to engage her in conversation. "Hey, little girl, what's your name?" he asked kindly.

"I won't tell you," Riya replied, turning her head away.

The doctor smiled, understanding her feelings. "That's alright. You don't have to tell me if you don't want to."

After discussing her condition with the doctor in private, he suggested taking Riya out and spending quality time with her. "Go out with her for some days, play with her, make her happy. That's all she needs right now," doctor advised.

"Thank you, doctor," I said gratefully, feeling a sense of hope that spending time together might help Riya overcome the trauma.

As we left the doctor's chamber, Riya held onto me tightly. "Come, Riya, let's go," I said, guiding her towards the exit.

"Say goodbye to the uncle," I whispered to her.

Riya turned her head and shook it, but I could see a small smile forming on her face. The doctor chuckled behind us, understanding Riya's reluctance to say goodbye.

Then We left the hospital and came out and headed towards the car, I placed Riya in the front seat, fastening her seatbelt securely. I settled into the driver's seat, starting the ignition to drive the car.

But the problem was that I didn't know where to go. This place didn't look like Mumbai, where I had spent my college days. Confusion filled my mind as I tried to recall any familiar landmarks, but nothing seemed recognizable.

"No, it's not Mumbai," I said to myself, trying to figure out our location.

Riya looked upset, and my heart ached seeing her like this. "Riya," I called her name gently, "why are you sad?"

"I want mommy," she said, her voice filled with longing.

Her innocent plea tugged at my heartstrings, and I knew I couldn't tell her the painful truth. I lied to comfort her, "Riya, we are going to meet mommy."

Her face lit up with curiosity, and I wished with all my heart that it could be true. "Really?" she asked.

"Yes," I replied, trying to sound convincing, "very soon."

I continued to drive, my mind clouded with thoughts of the uncertain future and how to protect Riya from the truth.

I suddenly noticed a mobile shop nearby and had an idea. Maybe if I bought a mobile phone, I could call home and talk to my parents. Without hesitation, I stopped the car and took Riya with me, heading straight to the mobile shop.

"Daddy, where are we going?" Riya asked with curiosity.

"Just wait for a few minutes, Riya," I replied, trying to keep the surprise.

At the mobile shop, the shopkeeper greeted us, "Yes, how can I help you?"

"I want to buy a mobile phone," I said, scanning the options he presented. Not knowing which one to choose, I decided to involve Riya. "Riya, select one among these," I said.

She carefully considered her choices and pointed to an Oppo mobile. "This one," she said with a smile.

"Alright, give me this one," I said to the shopkeeper, then inquired about the cost.

"Twenty-five thousand," he replied.

I also needed a sim card, so I requested one. However, the shopkeeper asked for my Aadhaar card for registration, and I realized I didn't have it with me.

"Sir, if you don't have your Aadhaar card, you can't get a sim," he informed me.

I didn't want to give up on the idea, so I made a request, "Please register it with your Aadhaar number. I'll pay extra."

"How much?" he asked.

"How much do you want?" I inquired.

"One thousand," he replied.

"Okay, done. But with recharge," I agreed, and promptly paid the bill.

After a few minutes, he handed me the mobile phone along with the sim card.

"Thank you, sir," he said as we left the shop.

Returning to the car, we both sat inside, ready to start the next phase of our journey with the new mobile phone in hand. Riya looked at the mobile phone in my hand and asked, "Daddy, what is it?"

"It's a mobile phone, sweetheart," I replied, showing her the device.

"What does it do?" she inquired, her eyes filled with curiosity.

"It's a special device, sweetheart," I replied, trying to explain it in a simple way. "It helps us stay connected with our loved ones, even if they are far away. We can send messages, pictures, and even talk to them, just like magic!"

"Wow!" Riya exclaimed, fascinated by the idea of this magical device. "Can I try it, Daddy?"

"Sure," I said, handing the mobile phone to her. "Be careful with it, okay?"

Riya took the mobile phone in her hands, her eyes filled with wonder. She explored the touch screen, tapping on icons and discovering its features.

"Daddy, look!" she said excitedly, showing me a funny sticker, she had found.

I chuckled at her enthusiasm. "That's great, Riya! You're already a pro at using the mobile phone."

As we continued driving, Riya played with the mobile phone, exploring its different functions. It brought a sense of joy and distraction to her, which I was grateful for, considering the difficult circumstances we were in.

In the back of my mind, I knew that I would eventually have to face the truth and find a way to tell Riya about her mother. But for now, I wanted to protect her innocence and keep her happy.

In the bright afternoon sun, the car's air conditioning fought valiantly against the summer heat. Riya's eyes fixed on the mobile phone in her hands. It was her first encounter with such a device, and her curiosity manifested in the gentle taps and swipes on the screen.

"Be careful, Riya," I cautioned, stealing a quick glance from the road. "Hold it properly, don't drop it."

Her small nod indicated that she heard me, her grip on the phone tightening as if it held the secrets of a magical realm. Her fascination was both amusing and a stark reminder of the innocence that life's challenges hadn't yet extinguished.

Amidst the hustle and bustle of the city streets, Riya's excitement gradually gave way to a yawn. As her eyelids grew heavy, and her once-energetic tapping slowed.

Chuckling softly, I glanced at her as she dozed off. The mobile, now a prized possession, slipped from her fingers and nestled comfortably on her lap. It was a sight that filled me with a mix of emotions – relief that she could find respite in the midst of our tumultuous journey, and a renewed sense of purpose that tugged at my heart.

The road stretched ahead, the bright sunlight casting long shadows on the pavement. The rhythm of the car's engine and the soft breeze through the windows provided a soothing backdrop to Riya's slumber. Her innocence was a beacon of hope, a driving force in my quest to provide her a better life.

Quietly, I took the mobile from her lap and opened Google Maps. As I glanced at the mobile screen, my heart sank, and a sense of disbelief washed over me. I couldn't believe what I was seeing, the location on the map clearly showed that we were in Srinagar, KASHMIR!!!.

How is this even possible? I thought to myself, trying to comprehend how we had ended up so far away from Mumbai. My mind raced with questions, but there were no immediate answers. The weight of the situation weighed heavily on my shoulders. I needed to find a way to get back to Mumbai

I don't know where to go, so I kept driving, hoping to find a peaceful place. Suddenly, I spotted a park and decided to stop the car. Riya was sleeping peacefully.

"Riya, wake up! Look where we are," I said, gently shaking her awake. Her eyes slowly blinked open, adjusting to the world outside the car.

"Where are we, Daddy?" she asked, her voice still drowsy from sleep.

"Look outside," I replied, pointing towards the vibrant scene beyond the car windows.

As her gaze fell upon the scene outside, her eyes widened and a gasp escaped her lips. Before us lay a park, a vast expanse of greenery adorned with colourful playground equipment. It was a sight that must have seemed like a fairy-tale to her, a place she had only heard about in stories.

"Wow, is this the park you told me about?" she exclaimed, her voice tinged with awe.

I smiled and nodded. "Yes, Riya. This is the park I mentioned to you."

Her face lit up with pure excitement, and a sense of joy swelled within me. It was the first time she was experiencing the world outside the walls that had held her captive for so long. The park was her portal to a realm she had only heard stories about.

As we stepped out of the car, she hesitated for a moment, her eyes darting around as if trying to take in every detail at once. The colourful playground equipment, the open grassy spaces, and the children playing freely were all a feast for her senses.

"Daddy, can we play here?" she asked, her voice a mixture of hope and uncertainty.

"Absolutely, Riya," I assured her with a warm smile. "We can play and explore as much as you want."

With that reassurance, her excitement bubbled over, and she practically skipped towards the swings and slides. I watched as she gingerly touched the slide, her fingers grazing its surface in disbelief. This tangible reality was beyond her imagination.

As she climbed onto the swing, I gently pushed her, and her laughter rang out like a melody. The sheer innocence and happiness in that moment were a stark contrast to the dark years we had endured.

As Riya and I played in the park, we had an absolute blast. She ran around, full of energy, while I tried to keep up with her enthusiasm. At one point, Riya spotted a group of pigeons near the fountain.

"Daddy, look! What's that!" she exclaimed, her eyes wide with wonder as she pointed at the pigeons.

I smiled at her fascination. " Riya, those are pigeons," I said, kneeling down to her level.

Her curious gaze turned towards me, and she asked, "What are pigeons, Daddy?"

"They're birds," I explained. "They're quite common in cities, and you can often see them in parks like this one."

Her face lit up with excitement, and I could see her brain working to process this new piece of information. But then, her mischievous side took over.

"I'm going to catch one!" she declared with determination.

I chuckled at her boldness. "I don't think you can catch a pigeon, Riya. They're pretty fast."

She didn't seem discouraged at all. Instead, she saw it as a fun challenge. She looked determined and started moving her tiny arms like bird wings. "Come here, little pigeon!" she exclaimed, giggling all the while.

I watched in amusement as she ran after the pigeons, her giggles echoing through the air. Her happiness and innocence were a breath of fresh air, reminding me of the simple joys life could bring. Following her, I felt a sense of lightness I hadn't experienced in years.

Of course, the pigeons were far too quick for Riya, and they flew away as soon as she got close. She turned back to me, pouting, and said, "They're too fast, Daddy!"

"It's alright, sweetheart," I said, trying to hold back my laughter. "Pigeons are meant to fly, not be caught."

Riya huffed but then quickly her eyes widened with curiosity as she observed the colourful cart with a large umbrella nearby. "Daddy, what's that?" she asked, pointing at the ice cream vendor.

I smiled at her curiosity and said, "That's an ice cream vendor, Riya. They sell a yummy frozen treat called ice cream."

Her face lit up with intrigue. "Ice cream? What's ice cream, Daddy?"

"It's a sweet and cold dessert," I described. "It comes in various flavours like chocolate, vanilla, strawberry, and many more. People enjoy it, especially on warm days."

Riya's excitement was palpable as she processed this new information. She turned her attention back to the vendor, her eyes scanning the different flavours on display.

"Can we try some, Daddy?" she asked, her anticipation evident in her voice.

"Of course, " I replied with a grin. "Let's go get some ice cream."

We went to the vendor, and Riya couldn't decide which flavour she wanted.

"Do you want chocolate, strawberry, or vanilla?" I asked.

"Can I have all of them, Daddy?" she asked with big, hopeful eyes.

I chuckled at her innocent request. "How about we get a scoop of each? That way, you can try them all!"

Riya's face lit up with joy, and we got a cone with three different scoops of ice cream. We found a nearby bench and sat down, enjoying the warm sun and the anticipation of savouring the ice cream. Riya took her first bite, and her eyes widened in delight. She let out a happy giggle, relishing the sweet and chilly treat.

"It's so yummy, Daddy!" she exclaimed, her face adorned with chocolatey delight.

I couldn't help but smile at her joy. Watching her experience something as simple as ice cream for the first time reminded me of the magic in life's little pleasures. In that moment, I realised that this journey was not just about escaping the past, but also about embracing the present and creating beautiful memories together.

The sun was slowly going down, casting a warm, golden light all around us. After our tasty ice cream treat, we started heading back to the car. Riya, who had been so full of energy earlier, now seemed a bit tired but still had a happy look on her face. As we drove along, I was thinking about where we should go next. Then, just as the sun was getting lower in the sky, Riya asked, "Daddy, where are we going?" I looked at her in the rear-view mirror and couldn't help but smile at her innocence. "Well, sweetheart," I began, my eyes going back to the beautiful scenery, "I've got a fun idea. How about we go to a place called a hotel? We can stay there for one night. What do you think?"

Riya blinked, a look of confusion crossing her face. "Hotel? What's that, Daddy?"

I chuckled at her innocence. "A hotel is like a big house where you can stay when you're away from home. They have comfy beds, and it's like a little adventure."

Riya's eyes lit up, her curiosity piqued. "Adventure? I like adventures!"

I smiled. "Well, then, staying in a hotel is going to be an adventure for us tonight."

I instantly googled nearby hotels, and it showed that there were rooms available in Ghaziabad. Without thinking twice, I drove straight to Ghaziabad.

We arrived at the hotel, and I took Riya inside. At the reception, I requested, "I want a room for one night, please."

"Certainly, sir," the receptionist replied cheerfully, handing me a key card. "Room number 013, second floor."

"Thank you," I said, taking the key card.

We made our way to the second floor, and at the end of the hallway, we found room 013. As we stepped inside, Riya's eyes were instantly drawn to the television mounted on the wall. "Daddy, what is this?" her voice was filled with curiosity as she pointed towards the screen. With a smile, I decided to show her. I reached for the remote control, turned on the TV, and tuned in to a classic Tom and Jerry cartoon. "Watch it and enjoy, " I said, gently seating her on the sofa.

She looked at the screen with wide-eyed wonder as the colourful characters of Tom and Jerry began their antics. I watched her expression shift from curiosity to pure delight as she laughed at the cartoon's playful humour. It was a simple moment, yet so precious, as Riya experienced the magic of television for the very first time.

While Riya was engrossed in the show, I took the opportunity to enter the room. I realized I needed to freshen up, but I had left all my clothes behind during our escape.

I need new clothes, "I have money, so I can buy anything we need." I called Riya to come along, but it seemed she was too captivated by the show. Eventually, I left her watching TV and went to a nearby clothes shop to buy clothes for both of us.

After purchasing the clothes, I returned to the hotel as quickly as possible. Upon entering the room, I found Riya still engrossed in the TV show. I placed the new dresses on the bed and called her.

"Riya," I called her softly.

"Hmm?" she replied, not taking her eyes off the TV.

"Turn off the TV now, it's time to take a bath," I said gently.

"No, Daddy, little more, please!" she pleaded.

I smiled at her enthusiasm but insisted, "No, that's enough for today. Come, let's go to the bathroom and have a bath."

As Riya and I stepped into the bathroom, the excitement in her eyes was contagious. She giggled and splashed water with her tiny hands, creating little ripples in the bathtub. I couldn't help but smile at her innocent joy

"Daddy, look!" Riya exclaimed, trying to make the water splash higher.

We spent almost an hour playing and splashing water in the bathroom, having a great time together. As our bath time fun came to an end, I wrapped Riya in a soft towel, and she gave me a big, wet hug.

Then I dressed Riya in the new dress I had bought for her, she looked absolutely gorgeous in it.

After dressing up and sharing a delicious meal at the hotel's restaurant, Riya and I returned to our cozy room. As the night drew closer, the tiredness from the day's adventures began to catch up with Riya. She yawned and rubbed her eyes, a clear sign that she was ready to rest.

"Are you feeling sleepy, dear?" I asked with a soft smile.

"hmm...," she replied, nodding sleepily.

I picked her up in my arms and carried her to the bed. With a gentle kiss on her forehead, I tucked her under the warm blankets. Riya's eyes fluttered closed, and her breathing softened as she drifted into a peaceful slumber.

I settled down beside her, gazing at her innocent face. The weight of the past six years had lifted, and I marveled at the strength and resilience my little girl had shown. Despite the darkness that had surrounded us, she had kept her spirit alive, and it was a testament to the indomitable nature of a child's heart.

I reached out and brushed a strand of hair away from her face, feeling a surge of love and protectiveness. I vowed to be her guiding light, her shield against any hardships that might come our way.

As I lay beside her, my thoughts drifted back to the moment we had escaped from that dreadful place. Aliya, with her unwavering love and sacrifice, had given Riya the chance for a better life. Her memory lingered in my heart, a constant reminder of the love we had shared.

Tears welled up in my eyes as I whispered, "Thank you, Aliya. You gave me the most precious gift in the world—RIYA."

Feeling a mix of sorrow and gratitude, I leaned in and kissed Riya's forehead once more before closing my eyes. The weight of the day's events and the surge of emotions caught up with me, and soon, I too collapsed to sleep.

The first rays of sunlight gently streamed through the curtains, filling the room with a warm glow. I woke up to find Riya still peacefully asleep, her small form curled up beside me.

Careful not to wake her, I slowly got out of bed and made my way to the window. Opening the curtains, I looked out at the world beyond. The city of Ghaziabad was waking up to a new day. I went to the bathroom to wash my face. I observed my face in the mirror, dark circles under my eyes showed the signs of many sleepless nights and exhausting days.

I splashed water on my face, fully waking myself. Feeling refreshed, I returned to the room, and there she was, still sleeping peacefully. I smiled at the sight of Riya, her small form curled up under the covers, her face serene in sleep. I gently sat down on the edge of the bed and softly called her name.

"Riya, it's time to wake up, sweetheart," I said, running my fingers through her hair.

Riya stirred, her eyes fluttering open. "Good morning, Daddy," she said, rubbing her eyes with her tiny fists.

"Good morning, my little angel," I replied, brushing a kiss on her forehead.

"Did you sleep well?" I asked, as she stretched and yawned.

"Hmm...," she replied, rubbing her eyes.

"Well, first, let's get ready and have a yummy breakfast," I said, helping her out of bed.

I guided her to the bathroom to wash her face. She rubbed her eyes sleepily, blinking in the soft morning light. After a refreshing splash of water, I carried her back to the room.

Riya, still half-awake, perched herself on the edge of the bed, her eyes gradually lighting up with curiosity. "Daddy, what are we going to do today?" she asked, her voice a mix of excitement and drowsiness.

I smiled at her eagerness and patted her head affectionately. "Well, sweetie, today holds some fun plans for us. But first, how about we start it with a delicious breakfast?"

Riya's eyes widened, and her sleepiness seemed to vanish at the mere mention of food. "Breakfast? Yay!" she cheered, her joy infectious.

With a sense of purpose, I reached for the phone and dialled the hotel's restaurant. A friendly voice answered, and I placed our breakfast order. "Could we have a serving of those pancakes and a delightful fruit platter, please?" I requested.

As we waited for our morning feast, Riya and I settled by the window. The city beyond was slowly waking up, and the soft sunlight painted everything with a warm hue. Riya's face was adorned with a serene smile as she gazed out at the view, a view that held the promise of a brighter future.

Soon, there was a knock on the door, and our breakfast was delivered. Riya's eyes widened with wonder as she laid her gaze upon the stack of fluffy pancakes and the vibrant assortment of fruits on the platter. The colours and shapes seemed almost like a magical display to her innocent eyes. We settled around the small dining table in our cozy room, the anticipation of our morning meal filling the air.

"Daddy, what are these?" Riya asked, pointing at the pancakes and then the fruits, her curiosity piqued.

I smiled warmly at her curiosity. "Well, sweetie, those are pancakes," I said, pointing at the soft, golden discs on the plate. "And this is a fruit platter, with lots of different fruits for us to enjoy."

Riya's eyes lit up with understanding, and a sense of excitement dawned upon her. "Pancakes and fruits?" she repeated, as if savouring the words.

"Yes, exactly!" I replied, a hint of amusement in my voice. "You're going to love them."

As we started eating, Riya hesitated for a moment, unsure of how to go about it. She watched me take a bite of the pancake and then followed suit, taking a small piece in her little hands. Her eyes widened with delight as she tasted the sweetness. "Daddy, it's yummy!" she exclaimed, her mouth full.

"I'm so glad you like it," I said, my heart warming at her joy.

Once we finished breakfast, I packed our belongings, and we headed to the reception to check out. Riya held my hand tightly as we walked, and I could sense her excitement about meeting her mom, but unfortunately it was not possible to meet Aliya.

Back in the car, I fastened Riya's seatbelt and made sure she was comfortable. As I started the engine, she looked at me with her innocent eyes.

We have to go back home as quickly as I can. I haven't been home in six years, so many years have passed without seeing my parents, I thought with a heavy heart. The memories of my family flooded my mind, and I longed to reunite with them.

Then I took out my mobile and set the location to Mumbai. My jaw dropped as I saw the distance—it showed forty hours of driving, almost two full days on the road. Instantly, I realized that driving for two days straight was not a feasible option, especially with Riya beside me.

"What if we go to Mumbai by train?" I thought. It seemed like a better and more practical idea.

"Daddy, where are we going?", Riya asked

"We are going to Mumbai," I replied, trying to focus on the road.

"Mumbai? Where is that, Daddy?" she asked, puzzled.

"It's very far from here," I said, glancing at her. "But don't worry; we'll get there soon."

After half an hour of driving we reached to the station, I parked the car, taking Riya in my arms.

Inside the bustling station, I purchased two tickets to Mumbai, keeping a close eye on our surroundings. The fear of being discovered weighed heavily on my mind. I held the tickets tightly in my hand, a lifeline to our escape, and made my way towards the platform.

As we boarded the train, the clatter of wheels and the hum of conversation surrounded us, I couldn't help but contemplate the situation we were in.

I gazed out the window, my mind filled with the memories of our captivity, the torment we endured for years, and the constant fear that followed us. And It was time to break free and return to the safety of our home.

As the train journeyed on, I felt a mix of emotions—fear, hope, and determination. I knew that Riya relied on me for protection, and I would do whatever it took to keep her safe. Together, we faced the problems hand in hand, as the train carried us towards our destination—*Mumbai*, and hopefully, once again a new beginning.

As the train chugged along its way to Mumbai, A man in his fifties took a seat across from us, his presence drawing my attention. Riya's voice interrupted my reverie, her innocence shining through as she asked, "Daddy, when will I meet Mommy?"

"We're going to meet your mommy," I assured her gently, hoping to ease her longing heart.

While I observed the passing landscape, I sensed the man's gaze lingering on Riya. It felt unsettling, as if he was sizing her up with unsettling intentions. Yet, when he noticed my watchful gaze, he attempted to initiate a conversation.

"Hi," he ventured.

I responded with a cautious, "Hello," my tone carrying a hint of scepticism.

"Delhi?" he inquired about our destination.

"No, Mumbai," I clarified.

As the conversation continued, his focus on Riya didn't go unnoticed. Her unease was palpable, and she clung to me for comfort. "Daddy," she murmured, seeking solace.

"It's okay," I whispered back, holding her close in a protective embrace.

"Is she your sister?" he probed, and I could sense his prying nature.

"No, she's my daughter," I answered firmly, wishing to assert our boundaries.

"How old is she?" he continued, his questions becoming more invasive.

"What does her age matter to you?" I retorted, my patience wearing thin.

"Nothing, just curious," he replied, trying to sound innocent. "I have a seven-year-old daughter like her."

His inquisitiveness was testing my patience. "So what?" I replied curtly, irritated by his line of questioning.

"Sorry to say, but you look too young to have a daughter like her," he remarked casually.

My annoyance grew, and my frustration spilled over. "You know what, you look too old to have a seven-year-old child," I shot back, my words laced with sarcasm.

Chapter Two

Back to Mumbai

The train came to a halt at Mumbai's central railway station, and the clock struck midnight. Riya was fast asleep in my arms as I carefully stepped out of the train, ensuring not to wake her. The platform was bustling with activity, but all I could focus on was getting Riya and myself to safety.

I held her close, her tiny frame a constant reminder of my responsibility to protect her. With Riya in one arm and our bag in the other, I made my way through the crowded station. The familiar sights and sounds of Mumbai brought back a flood of memories, both bitter and sweet.

Outside the station, I headed towards the taxi parking lot and hailed a cab. "Arabian Hotel," I said to the driver, the name rolling off my tongue with a sense of familiarity. The car set off on its journey, and I couldn't help but steal glances at the city passing by. The roads, the buildings, and the surroundings all felt like they had missed me during the long six years I was away.

As we drove through the streets of Mumbai, a mixture of emotions filled my heart. It was a bittersweet homecoming, knowing that my parents were somewhere in this vast city, waiting to see me after all these years. The weight of our experiences in the past lingered, but being back in my hometown brought a sense of comfort and hope.

The taxi finally stopped at the Arabian Hotel, and I carefully lifted Riya and our luggage out of the car. I paid the taxi driver with a grateful smile and headed towards the entrance of the hotel. The air inside was warm and welcoming as we stepped in.

At the reception, I asked for a room and checked us in. Riya remained asleep. As I made our way to the room, I couldn't help but think of the journey that had led us here—escaping from the clutches of our captors, facing unknown dangers, and finally finding our way back home.

Inside the room, I gently laid Riya on the bed, tucking her in with care. She stirred slightly in her sleep, and I brushed a strand of hair away from her face. Exhausted but relieved, I laid beside Riya and fell into a deep sleep.

"You cannot run forever, Rishab," Vikram's voice echoed through the air, the gun in his hand pointing menacingly at me. His lips curled into a cold smile that sent a chill down my spine.

"Please, Vikram, spare me," I pleaded, my words almost a whisper as fear gripped my throat. The weight of the gun's muzzle felt like a mountain on my chest, suffocating me.

"Ha hah haha," his laughter echoed, a dark melody filling the air. The sound carried a sense of wickedness that wrapped around me. His gun pointed at me, a chilling reminder of the danger that surrounded me.

Abruptly, I snapped awake, my body drenched in cold sweat, heart racing like a galloping horse. I scanned the dimly lit room, my eyes searching for any sign of the haunting dream. Beside me, Riya slept peacefully.

Running a shaky hand through my hair, I took a deep breath, attempting to steady my racing heart. The room felt like a cage, trapping me with the remnants of that nightmare. With a determined step, I rose from the bed and made my way to the bathroom.

Under the shower's cool embrace, I closed my eyes, the water's cascade a soothing balm against the heat of my fear. Each droplet that slid down my skin was a promise of cleansing, a symbolic release from the grip of the nightmare.

While the water cascaded over me, I allowed my thoughts to drift away from the disturbing remnants of the dream. I imagined a future where fear no longer controlled us, where Riya and I could discover peace. The steady flow of the water created a soothing backdrop to my dreams, and in that fleeting instant, a spark of hope ignited within me.

After what felt like an eternity, I turned off the shower and stepped out, wrapping a towel around myself. The remnants of the dream slowly fading away, I glanced at the clock, the red digits blinked steadily, indicating that it was nine A.M in the morning. The early light seeped through the curtains, casting a gentle glow over the room. It was a new day, a chance to leave behind the terrors of the night.

My gaze turned towards Riya, her innocent form sprawled across the bed. With a tender smile, I approached her and sat down beside her. Her soft, chestnut hair spilled over the pillow like a halo, and I couldn't resist the urge to gently caress it with my fingers.

As my fingers continued to trace the silky strands of her hair, I reflected on the journey that had brought us here. The trials and uncertainties had forged an unbreakable bond between us. Riya was not just a little girl I was responsible for—she was my anchor, my reason to fight against the darkness that threatened to engulf us.

With a sigh, I leaned down and placed a gentle kiss on Riya's forehead. Her eyelids fluttered, as if sensing my presence even in her sleep. "We'll face whatever comes together, Riya," I whispered, my voice carrying a promise of determination.

As the day's light continued to grow, I rose from the bed, silently resolving to make the most of this new beginning. Riya's well-being was my priority, and I was ready to confront the challenges ahead with unwavering strength.

Leaving her to her peaceful slumber, I made my way to the window and drew back the curtains. The world outside was waking up, and I felt a surge of hope. With a deep breath, I let go of the lingering shadows of the night and embraced the possibilities that lay ahead.

The city beyond the window seemed different now, though not entirely unfamiliar. Six years had passed since I had last walked its streets, and it was as if the landscape had changed to accommodate the passage of time. Buildings had risen, roads had shifted, and life had evolved in ways I couldn't have anticipated.

Mumbai, my hometown, had once been a labyrinth of memories, both beautiful and painful. It was here that I had laughed with friends, celebrated milestones, and dreamed of a future that felt within reach.

And yet, it was also the place where the shadows had deepened, where I had faced challenges that had tested my strength and resilience.

But now, as I stood at the window, I felt a renewed sense of connection to this city. The air held a familiarity, and the sights and sounds carried a sense of homecoming. The honking of horns, the aroma of street food, the vibrant colours of market stalls—all of it felt like a part of me.

With each passing moment, I embraced the realisation that I was no longer the same person who had left Mumbai six years ago. The experiences I had gained, the lessons I had learned, and the strength I had discovered had transformed me. I was no longer defined by the challenges I had faced, but by the resilience that had carried me forward.

The gentle rustling of bedsheets and the soft sounds of awakening drew me back from my daydream at the window. I turned my attention to Riya, who was stretching and blinking as she woke from her slumber. Her eyes, still drowsy with sleep, widened with surprise as they met mine.

"Daddy, where are we?" she asked, her voice tinged with curiosity and wonder.

A smile tugged at the corners of my lips as I shifted my gaze from the outside world to Riya. "We're in Mumbai, sweetheart," I replied, my voice filled with warmth.

"Mumbai?" Riya repeated, her eyes now fully awake and sparkling with curiosity. "Is this where we coming?"

I nodded, and her face lit up with excitement, as if a magical realm had been unveiled before her. The morning sunlight filtering through the window bathed her in a soft glow, emphasising the innocence and joy that radiated from her.

I walked over to the bed and sat down beside her. "Yes, my dear," I said, brushing a strand of hair away from her face. "This is Mumbai, my hometown."

Her eyes widened in amazement as she walked over to the window, her small steps filled with curiosity and wonder. With her hands pressed against the glass, she took in her surroundings with a mix of awe and fascination. The cityscape beyond the window seemed to captivate her, and I could see her imagination spring to life as she absorbed the vibrant colours, the moving vehicles, and the bustling streets.

I watched with a tender smile as Riya's eyes darted from one detail to another, her face reflecting a childlike wonder. Her innocence and genuine excitement were like a breath of fresh air, rekindling my own appreciation for the beauty of Mumbai.

"Daddy, look!" Riya exclaimed, her voice a joyful whisper as she pointed at the bustling scene outside. "There are so many cars, and people, and... and look at those big buildings! They're like giants!"

I joined Riya at the window, standing next to her and enjoying the view together. "See, Riya," I explained, using simple words, "those really tall buildings are called skyscrapers. They're like giants among buildings and you can find them in big cities like Mumbai. They touch the sky, and they look amazing, especially when the sun sets and the city lights up."

Her eyes sparkled with excitement as she listened to me, and she kept her focus on the captivating view outside. The city's bustling sounds, the steady beat of people walking on the sidewalks, and the vibrant colours created by passing cars all came together to form a beautiful picture of city life. Riya was taking it all in, savouring her first experience of the urban world.

"Are those the clouds, Daddy?" she asked, her finger tracing an imaginary line towards the sky-scraping towers.

I chuckled softly at her innocent question. "No, sweetheart, those aren't clouds," I explained. "Those are the tops of the buildings. The real clouds are up in the sky, far beyond our reach."

Riya nodded, her curiosity increased. "I want to see everything, Daddy. Can we go out and explore?" she asked.

"Of course," I replied, ruffling her hair warmly. "We'll go down and explore the city together. Mumbai is a place full of stories and adventures waiting for us to discover."

"But first, let's get you refreshed. How about washing your face and then having breakfast? After that, we can head out and start exploring."

Riya's eyes lit up at the idea of exploring the city, and she nodded enthusiastically. "Okay, Daddy! I want to see everything!"

I chuckled, delighted by her enthusiasm. "We'll see as much as we can. Now, let's go to the bathroom, and you can wash your face.

In the cozy bathroom, Riya stood on her tiptoes in front of the sink, her eyes sparkling with excitement. I turned on the tap, letting the water run until it was the right temperature. Cupping my hands, I filled them with water and gently splashed it on Riya's face. She giggled, the sensation of water making her laugh.

"Close your eyes, sweetie," I advised, grabbing a soft washcloth and wetting it with water. She obediently closed her eyes, her small face scrunched up in concentration. I carefully ran the damp cloth across her forehead, down her cheeks, and over her chin, cleansing away the sleep from her skin.

With her eyes still closed, Riya let out a content sigh, enjoying the sensation. Her trust in me, warmed my heart. As I softly dried her face with a fluffy towel, she opened her eyes, a wide smile on her lips.

"All clean now?" I asked with a grin.

"Yes, Daddy!" Riya replied, her voice bubbling with happiness.

I ruffled her damp hair playfully. "Great! Now, let's head to the dining area for some delicious breakfast."

As Riya stepped out of the bathroom, her face still damp from washing, I reached for a soft towel hanging nearby. Gently, I patted her face, absorbing the excess moisture and leaving her skin refreshed. She looked up at me, her eyes twinkling with innocence and trust.

"Feeling better?" I asked, a warm smile on my lips.

She nodded, a radiant smile spreading across her face. "Yes, Daddy."

I continued to pat her face, my touch light and caring. It was a simple act, but it carried a sense of comfort and connection that words couldn't convey. Riya's presence, her happiness, it all felt like a new beginning, a chance to create beautiful memories together.

"Alright, all dry," I said, gently folding the towel and placing it back in its spot. "Now, how about breakfast?"

We made our way down to the hotel's restaurant, hand in hand, our steps echoing in the quiet hallway. Riya walked beside me, her excitement palpable. As we entered the restaurant, the aroma of freshly brewed coffee and delicious food filled the air.

We found a cozy corner table with a view of the city beyond the large windows. Riya hopped onto a chair, her eyes scanning the menu with curiosity. I smiled as I sat across from her. "So, little explorer, what caught your eye?"

Riya looked up from the menu, her face lighting up. "Daddy, can we have those pancks we had yesterday?"

I chuckled. It's not pancks Riya it's pancakes. "You really love them, don't you?"

She nodded enthusiastically. "Yes, they're so yummy!"

"All right, pancakes it is," I agreed, flagging down a waiter to take our order.

As we waited for our food to arrive, I couldn't help but marvel at how Riya was embracing every new experience with such enthusiasm. It was as if the world was an uncharted territory, and she was ready to explore it all. I watched her gaze wander from the bustling restaurant to the panoramic view outside. The city was alive with the hustle and bustle of people, cars, and life in motion.

When the pancakes were served, Riya's eyes lit up with excitement. The stack of golden pancakes, glistening with a drizzle of maple syrup, looked absolutely delicious.

Riya's little hands delicately picked up a piece of pancake, her fingers covered in a sticky layer of syrup. With careful precision, she brought the bite-sized portion to her mouth, her eyes lighting up with anticipation. I watched in amusement as her small mouth opened to accommodate the pancake, and her eyes closed in sheer delight as she savoured the sweet and fluffy treat.

As I savoured my breakfast, my attention was drawn to a newcomer entering the hotel. There was something strangely familiar about his gait, the way he carried himself. I tried to place where I might have seen him before, racking my brain for clues.

He approached the receptionist with a familiarity that suggested he was a regular here. My curiosity was piqued, and I watched their interaction with a growing sense of intrigue. *Who was this man, and why did he seem so familiar?*

Yet, before I could puzzle out his identity, Riya's voice broke through my thoughts. "Daddy, I'm full," she announced, her face a delightful mess of pancake cream. I turned my attention to her, my heart warming at the sight of her innocent satisfaction.

"Eat a little more, Riya," I urged gently, my eyes twinkling with amusement. She shook her head in protest, showing me her stomach with a playful exaggeration. "See, Daddy? My stomach is already full!"

I laughed at her antics, unable to resist her infectious energy. As I leaned back in my chair, my gaze once again drifted toward the man at the reception.

While Riya and I enjoyed our breakfast, the unfamiliar yet strangely familiar man engaged in conversation with the receptionist. Their exchange seemed amiable, as if they shared a long history of familiarity. I observed their interaction, my curiosity growing with every passing moment.

As the conversation drew to a close, the man flashed a smile and nodded politely to the receptionist. With a final wave, he turned and walked towards the exit. My gaze followed him, and for a moment, our eyes met. There was a flicker of recognition, a shared moment of acknowledgment that hinted at a connection from the past. But before I could dwell on it, he was gone, leaving me with a sense of intrigue and a flurry of unanswered questions.

With a contented sigh, I signalled to the waiter for the bill. As we prepared to leave the restaurant, I glanced once more towards the entrance, where the enigmatic man had made his exit. Though his identity remained a puzzle, I couldn't help but wonder if our paths would cross again, weaving our lives together in ways yet to be discovered.

After settling the bill, I made my way to the hotel receptionist, determined to uncover the mystery surrounding the stranger who had caught my attention earlier. I approached the receptionist, a courteous woman with a warm smile.

"Excuse me, could you tell me the name of the gentleman who was just here?"

She looked at me cautiously before answering, "Of course, sir. He is Mr. Arora." I furrowed my brows, the name Arora, sending a faint jolt of recognition through me. It felt like a distant memory trying to resurface.

"Mr. Arora... Do you know his full name?" I insisted

The receptionist nodded, a touch surprised by my request. "Yes, sir. His full name is Karthik Arora."

Suddenly, it was like a curtain lifted from my past. Karthik Arora - the name sounded so familiar and brought back memories. My mind was filled with a rush of thoughts, and it was hard to believe that the person I had just seen was actually my childhood friend.

A smile tugged at the corners of my lips as I thanked the receptionist and headed towards the lobby, lost in a whirlwind of emotions. Karthik Arora, my college buddy, was here after all these years. The realisation hit me like a wave, and I couldn't wait to reconnect and reminisce about our shared past.

thoughts of our mischievous school days played in my mind. The pranks we pulled, the laughter we shared - it all felt like it had happened just yesterday. And now, fate has brought us back together in the most unexpected way.

Lost in my own thoughts, the bustling sounds of the city outside seemed distant and hazy. Riya's voice broke through my reverie, bringing me back to the present moment.

"Daddy, can we go out?" she asked, her eyes wide with anticipation.

I looked down at her, her innocent eagerness infectious. A smile tugged at the corners of my lips. "Of course, sweety," I replied, ruffling her hair affectionately. "Let's go out and explore more of this wonderful city."

With Riya's hand securely in mine, we walked out of the hotel and into the lively streets of Mumbai. The city was buzzing with its energetic vibe, and I felt a blend of anticipation and a touch of nostalgia. While we strolled, I glanced at the people around us, hoping to spot a familiar face.

Riya was wide-eyed, taking in the sights and sounds of the city. Her small hand held tightly onto mine, and I could feel her curiosity radiating off her. "Daddy, this place is so big!" she exclaimed, her voice filled with wonder.

"Yes, sweetheart, Mumbai is a big city with lots of things to see and do," I replied, squeezing her hand gently.

As we walked down the busy streets, I kept an eye out for any glimpse of Karthik. Memories of our college days flooded back to me. Karthik and I had shared many laughs, adventures, and secrets during those years. I hoped that he would recognize me too. Riya tugged on my hand, her eyes gleaming with excitement.

"Daddy, look at that!" she said, her little finger pointing excitedly towards a street vendor selling a vibrant array of balloons.

I couldn't help but smile at her infectious enthusiasm. "Would you like a balloon, Riya?" I asked.

She nodded eagerly, her face lighting up even more. I bought her a bright red balloon, and her happiness was contagious. As we continued our walk, I couldn't help but feel a growing sense of anticipation.

Would I be able to reconnect with Karthik after all these years? The city was vast, and the chances of running into someone you knew were like finding a needle in a haystack. But the idea of reuniting with an old friend from childhood was both exciting and heart-warming.

As we walked along, Riya's small hand still in mine, I wondered how life had shaped Karthik in these six years, and I hoped that somewhere in this bustling city, our paths would cross again.

Flagging down a passing taxi, I helped Riya into the backseat and settled in beside her. As I closed the door, I leaned forward and gave the driver the directions. "Infinix Mall, please."

The driver nodded, and our taxi drove into the busy but organized traffic of Mumbai. I looked out the window. The tall buildings turned into bustling markets, and the sound of car horns stayed in the background.

"Daddy, what's a mall?" Riya's curious voice broke through the noise of the street.

I turned to her, glad for the opportunity to explain something new. "A mall, Riya, is a big building with lots of different shops, restaurants, and even a movie theatre. It's a place where people come to shop, eat, and have fun."

Riya's eyes widened in fascination. "Wow, that sounds amazing! Are we going to have fun there, Daddy?"

I smiled at her enthusiasm. "Yes, sweetheart, we're going to have a lot of fun. We can explore the shops, maybe have some ice cream, and even do a little shopping if you want."

Her face lit up with excitement, and she clapped her hands. "Yay, I want ice cream!"

"Sure thing," I said, chuckling. "We'll definitely get some ice cream."

While we were en route, Riya's enthusiasm got the best of her, and she playfully pressed her balloon against the car's window. It burst with a comically loud pop, startling us both. But instead of being scared, we burst into laughter, finding the unexpected surprise quite funny.

The taxi ride went on, and before we knew it, we reached Infinix Mall. The sight of the enormous mall, its welcoming entrance, and all the people bustling around filled Riya's eyes with amazement once more.

I paid the bill to the taxi driver and helped Riya out of the taxi. Holding her hand tightly, we made our way into the mall. The air conditioning was a welcome relief from the heat outside.

As we walked through the mall's corridors, I watched as Riya's eyes darted around, taking in the colourful displays and the variety of shops. Her excitement was contagious, and I found myself looking forward to the day's adventures just as much as she was.

"Daddy, can we have ice cream now?" Riya asked, tugging at my hand.

"Absolutely," I replied with a grin. "Let's find an ice cream parlour."

We navigated through the mall until we found an ice cream shop. Riya's eyes sparkled as we stood in front of the ice cream counter, the array of flavours was almost overwhelming. Riya's eyes widened as she took in the colourful display, her excitement palpable.

"Daddy, there are so many of them! How do I choose?"

I chuckled, sharing her enthusiasm. "Well, why don't you try a few samples and see which one you like the best?"

Riya nodded eagerly, and the ice cream attendant handed her a tiny spoon with a sample of chocolate ice cream. She took a small bite and her face lit up. "Mmm, this one is really good!"

Encouraged by her reaction, Riya started sampling more flavours. She tried strawberry, vanilla, and even a funky blueberry cheesecake flavour. With each taste, her expressions ranged from delight to thoughtful consideration.

After a few minutes of sampling, Riya turned to me with a grin. "Daddy, I want to try something different!"

I raised an eyebrow, intrigued. "different, huh? What do you have in mind?"

Riya scanned the options once again before pointing to a bright orange scoop labelled "Mango Madness." "I want that one! She pointed toward the mango madness."

I couldn't help but chuckle at her enthusiasm. "Alright, Mango Madness it is!"

The attendant scooped a generous helping of the vibrant orange ice cream onto a cone, and Riya's eyes widened at the sight of it. It was topped with colourful sprinkles and even a small piece of mango.

As Riya took the first bite, her face lit up with a mix of surprise and delight. She looked at me with wide eyes, her mouth full of ice cream. "Daddy, this is soo... good! You have to try some!"

I couldn't resist her excitement, so I ordered a scoop of Mango Madness for myself too. As I took a bite, the burst of mango flavour was indeed so good, just as Riya had described.

We found a table near the ice cream counter and sat down to enjoy our unconventional choices. With each bite, Riya's laughter and joy were infectious. It was as if the vibrant flavours had infused us with a burst of happiness.

"Daddy, we should try different things more often!" Riya exclaimed, wiping away a drip of ice cream from her chin.

I smiled at her, heartened by the simple yet profound truth in her words. "You're right, Riya. Sometimes, trying something different can be a lot of fun."

As we walked through the vibrant mall, Riya's eyes sparkled with curiosity. Her gaze landed on a shop adorned with an array of dolls in different sizes, colours, and outfits. She tugged at my hand, her voice filled with intrigue, "Daddy, what's that?"

I glanced at her and realized that she hadn't experienced these simple pleasures in her life before. "That's a doll shop, Riya. Dolls are like little figures that you can play with. They often look like people or characters from stories."

Riya's brows furrowed as she processed the information. "Play with? Like toys?"

I smiled and said, "That's right, darling. Dolls are toys you can play with. You can pretend they're your friends and create all sorts of exciting stories for them."

Her eyes lit up with curiosity, and she asked, "Stories?"

"Yes," I replied. "You can make up your own stories and act them out with your dolls. It's a fun way to use your imagination and have a great time."

Riya's curiosity was piqued even further. "Can we go inside, Daddy? Please?"

Her eagerness was infectious, and I couldn't resist her genuine enthusiasm. "Of course, Riya. Let's go explore the doll shop."

With her hand still in mine, we entered the shop filled with dolls of all kinds. Riya's eyes darted around, taking in the colourful displays. She moved from shelf to shelf, examining each doll with wonderment. I watched as her fingers hovered over the dolls, as if she was deciding which one to interact with first.

"Daddy, they're so pretty," she whispered, her voice filled with awe.

I chuckled softly. "Yes, they are, Riya. Each one has its own unique look and story."

Riya's gaze settled on a particularly large doll dressed in a vibrant red dress. She pointed at it, her eyes shining. "What about this one, Daddy?"

I followed her gaze, a smile tugging at my lips. "That's a beautiful choice, Riya. It's a big doll, isn't it? If you like it, I can get it for you."

Her face lit up, and she looked at me with a mixture of excitement and gratitude. "Really, Daddy? Can I have it?"

I nodded, my heart swelling with happiness. "Absolutely, Riya. It's all yours."

As she clutched the big doll in her hands, a sense of pure joy radiated from her. In that moment, surrounded by dolls and her innocent excitement, I couldn't help but feel immensely grateful for this newfound freedom and the opportunity to witness Riya's happiness bloom.

Riya's eyes practically danced with delight as she held the big doll in her arms. Her smile was infectious, and I couldn't help but share in her happiness. The doll's vibrant red dress seemed to match the newfound joy that had lit up Riya's face.

"Daddy, thank you!" she exclaimed, hugging the doll tightly as if it was the most precious thing in the world.

"You're welcome, sweetheart," I replied, my heart swelling with warmth. Seeing her so happy was worth every bit of effort it had taken to bring her to this point.

Riya's fingers traced the doll's dress, her eyes sparkling with wonder. "She's so pretty, Daddy. I'm going to call her Zoya!"

"Zoya, that's a lovely name," I said, nodding in approval. "Now, Zoya will be your new friend, and you can take her on all sorts of adventures."

Riya's imagination was already in full swing. "Yes, Daddy! Zoya and I will have so much fun together.

I chuckled, utterly captivated by her enthusiasm. "I'm sure you will, Riya. Zoya seems like the perfect companion for you."

As we left the doll shop, Riya held Zoya close to her heart, her happiness radiating through her every step. We continued our exploration of the mall, and I couldn't help but feel a deep sense of satisfaction. This moment was a small victory—a reminder that despite the challenges we had faced, there was still so much beauty and joy to be found in life.

"Daddy, can Zoya come with us wherever we go?" Riya asked, her eyes earnest.

"Of course, she can," I assured her. "Zoya is now a part of our journey, just like you are."

Riya's smile widened, and she held Zoya up to her face, as if sharing a secret with her new friend. The bond between a child and her toy was a simple yet profound thing, a symbol of innocence and the power of imagination.

With Riya's hand in mine and Zoya tucked under her arm, we continued to explore the mall, our hearts light and our spirits high. And as we walked, I couldn't help but be grateful for this moment of pure joy that had found its way into our lives once again.

Amid the hustle and bustle of the mall, a familiar face caught my attention. It was Karthik. My heart raced as I tried to make my way through the crowd, but by the time I reached the spot where he had been standing, he was gone.

"Daddy, what's wrong?" Riya's voice brought me back to the present. She looked up at me with concern in her eyes.

I shook my head, my mind still processing what I had just witnessed. "It's nothing, Riya. I thought I saw someone I know, but it seems like they've left."

Riya's brows furrowed, clearly curious about the situation. "Who was it, Daddy?"

"Just someone from a long time ago," I replied, my gaze still lingering on the spot where Karthik had been. "Come on, let's go."

Riya nodded, but I could tell she was still puzzled. As we walked through the mall, I kept stealing glances around, hoping to catch another glimpse of Karthik. I couldn't shake the feeling that this unexpected encounter meant something, that our paths crossing again after all these years was significant in some way.

As we stepped out of the mall, the vibrant cacophony of the city engulfed us once again. The taxi we hailed seemed to blend seamlessly into the flow of traffic. Riya settled into the back seat, her doll cradled in her arms like a cherished companion. I took the seat next to her, lost in thought as the cityscape passed by.

The hum of the engine and the rhythm of the road were strangely soothing. With each turn and curve, I couldn't help but feel like we were navigating the twists of our own story—a story that had taken us from captivity to the expanse of Mumbai.

Riya's voice broke through the silence, her innocence a refreshing interruption. "Daddy, I like this doll so much. Thank you."

Her words warmed my heart, and I turned to her with a smile. "You're welcome, sweetheart. I'm glad you like it."

Her eyes sparkled as she held the doll up to show it the world outside the window. The passing scenes seemed to dance across her imagination, creating a bond between her and the doll that was both endearing and magical.

As we journeyed through the streets, I found myself gazing outside, lost in the ebb and flow of the city. I couldn't help but wonder about the people who walked these streets, the dreams they held, and the stories that unfolded within the walls of these buildings.

"Daddy, why are you looking outside so much?" Riya's voice brought me back to the present.

I smiled at her, my thoughts returning to the present moment. "I was just thinking about our journey, Riya, and how sometimes unexpected things happen."

Her eyes widened with curiosity. "Like what?"

"Like meeting old friends," I said, glancing out the window once more.

"Old friends?" Riya echoed, her interest piqued.

"Yes," I replied with a smile. "Sometimes life brings back people we haven't seen in a long time."

The taxi came to a smooth stop in front of the hotel entrance. I settled the bill with the driver and stepped out, the weight of the day's adventures clinging to me. Riya, clutching her new doll, hopped out beside me with an energy that never seemed to wane.

The hotel lobby greeted us with its familiar warmth. The receptionist acknowledged our return with a smile, and I couldn't help but feel a sense of comfort as I crossed the threshold into the familiar space.

As we made our way to the elevator, Riya chattered excitedly about the dolls and toys she had seen in the mall. Her enthusiasm was infectious, and I couldn't help but smile as I listened to her animated tales of discovery.

Reaching our room, I inserted the key card into the slot, and the door swung open with a soft click as we stepped into our hotel room, the quiet familiarity of the space felt like a gentle embrace. Riya's face lit up as she clutched the doll she had chosen, her eyes dancing with delight. She settled on the bed, her small fingers exploring every detail of the doll's attire and features.

I smiled tenderly as I watched her completely absorbed in her play. The innocence and happiness she radiated washed away the years of hardship and uncertainty we had faced.

As Riya's laughter filled the room, I found myself lost in thoughts of my own family—my mother who had always been a pillar of strength, my father whose wisdom had guided me, my brother with whom I had shared countless childhood adventures, my sister whose laughter had been a constant melody in our home.

My heart ached with the absence of their presence in my life. Six long years of separation had etched deep voids within me, a longing that never truly faded. Memories of shared moments, of birthdays and festivals celebrated together, of whispered secrets and shared dreams, played like a bittersweet reel in my mind.

I glanced at Riya, her pure laughter a stark contrast to the weight of my emotions. She looked up at me, her eyes sparkling with curiosity. "Daddy, look!" she exclaimed, holding the doll up for my inspection. "Isn't she beautiful?"

My heart filled with love as I agreed, playing along with her. Riya's happiness was a precious treasure, a balm for wounds that were still healing. In her, I discovered a fresh motivation, a cause to continue despite the pain of our history.

Lost in my thoughts, I could almost hear my family's voices, feel their embraces, and see their smiles. It was as if they were beside me, offering silent reassurance and unwavering support. I closed my eyes, allowing their memory to envelop me like a warm embrace.

"Daddy, look, she's dancing!" Riya's voice brought me back to the present. I opened my eyes to see her twirling the doll with a contagious enthusiasm. I couldn't help but chuckle, joining her in the momentary escape from reality.

As I watched Riya and her doll, I realised that while I couldn't change the past, I could shape the present and the future. The ache of separation might always linger, but the love I had for my family and the newfound bond with Riya were sources of strength.

With a deep breath, I let go of the heaviness that had settled in my heart. Riya's laughter and innocence filled the room, washing away the shadows of my thoughts. I found solace in the simple yet profound joy of being with her.

The midday sun cast a warm glow over the room as Riya played contentedly with her doll. My thoughts drifted toward the place I had once called home. A mixture of anticipation and anxiety stirred within me as I reached for my phone, my fingers tapping in the familiar digits of the only number I knew by heart.

but it was met only with an automated voice stating, "The number you have dialled is not reachable."

This call was a lifeline, a connection to a world I had been separated from for six long years. A shadow of unease began to creep in.

The call ended abruptly, the line going dead. A sense of disappointment and frustration washed over me. I stared at the phone, willing it to ring back, to establish a connection that would bridge the gap of time and distance. Yet, the silence that followed was a stark reminder of the challenges that lay ahead.

"Daddy, are you okay?" Riya's innocent voice broke through my reverie, her eyes filled with concern.

I forced a smile, though my heart was heavy with the weight of uncertainty. "Yes, Riya, I'm fine."

As she returned to her play, I clung to the phone as if it held the answers to all my questions. It was a device that had once connected me to the familiar voices and faces of my family, a lifeline that had now been severed. I stared at the screen, grappling with the harsh reality that I was on my own, disconnected from the world I had left behind.

The unanswered call had left me feeling a mix of frustration and helplessness. As I stared at the phone, a new thought began to take shape in my mind.

What if I went home? The idea hung in the air like a fragile thread, both tempting and terrifying. A wave of conflicting emotions surged through me. Would they recognize me after all these years? Would their faces light up with joy, or would I be met with a mixture of shock and disbelief?

I shut my eyes briefly, picturing the scene in my head. I could nearly hear the laughter, the tears, the talks that would fill the room if I entered that door. A sharp sense of desire tugged at my heart, a longing for the warmth of family, the solace of being part of something.

But doubt crept in too. Would I be an intruder in their lives, an unexpected guest from the past? Would the years of absence have created an insurmountable gap, leaving me a stranger in a place that was once my home? The uncertainty gnawed at me, a reminder that time could change anything.

The noon sun filtered through the curtains, casting a warm and gentle light across the room. The tranquillity of the moment wrapped around me as I glanced at the clock. The hands pointed to 1 o'clock, and a sense of calm settled within me. Riya, nestled in her sleep, held the doll close, her chest rising and falling in a peaceful rhythm.

A soft smile tugged at my lips as I observed her innocence, the doll serving as her constant companion. With careful steps, I moved closer, ensuring she was comfortable and content in her dreams. The sight of her stirred a deep sense of protectiveness within me, a commitment to shield her from the uncertainties that life could bring.

The decision to go home lingered, a choice that had grown from a mere thought into a resolute plan. I settled down beside Riya, mindful not to disturb her peaceful slumber.

Closing my eyes, I allowed the weariness of the past days to catch up with me. The world outside faded as sleep gently wrapped its arms around me,

Karthik walked into the hotel lobby, his steps echoing softly against the marbled floor. The golden glow of the chandeliers cast a warm ambience around him as he made his way to the reception desk. There she was, Isha, his friend and the receptionist who had shared many moments with him during his stays.

Hey, Isha," Karthik greeted her with a warm smile.

Isha's eyes lit up as she looked up from her work. "Oh, hey Karthik! Back here again?"

Karthik nodded. "Yeah, I just wanted to say bye before I leave for America tomorrow."

"Ah, the big trip!" Isha grinned. "Have a fantastic time, Karthik."

"Thanks, Isha. I'm going to miss this place," he replied.

As the conversation settled, Isha's expression turned curious. "Oh, by the way, something interesting happened earlier. Someone was asking about you."

Karthik raised an eyebrow. "Really? Who?"

Isha leaned in a bit, her voice lowered. "It was a guy with a little girl, about six years old. He was asking about you, your visit today."

Karthik's interest was piqued. "A guy with a little girl?"

"Yeah, and there was something odd about it," Isha said, a tinge of surprise in her voice. "He was here and rented a room yesterday around midnight. Still in his room, I think."

"Midnight?" Karthik mused. "That's strange."

Isha nodded, her eyes widening. "And guess what, I found his name in the records. His name is Rishab."

Karthik felt a sudden jolt of shock at the name. Memories he thought were buried deep resurfaced. "Rishab? Are you sure?"

Isha frowned, sensing his reaction. "Yeah, why? Do you know him?"

Karthik hesitated, his mind racing. "No, not really. Just a name that sounds familiar."

Isha studied him for a moment. "Are you okay, Karthik?"

He managed a smile. "Yeah, just surprised. Thanks for letting me know, Isha."

As he turned to leave, Karthik couldn't shake off the weight of the name Rishab. It was as if a door to the past had been opened, revealing fragments he thought he had moved on from.

"Cancel the trip to America?" he muttered to himself, the words hanging in the air.

With a resolute sigh, he reached for his phone and dialled the airline's number to cancel his trip. The voice on the other end asked for a reason, and for a moment, he hesitated. How could he explain this sudden change?

"I... I have a personal matter to attend to," he finally replied, his voice steady. It was true, after all.

He dialled another number and told the person on the other line, "I think he's back."

I woke up to the soft glow of the setting sun streaming through the window. Glancing at the clock on the wall, I realised that it was already evening.

Beside me, Riya was still asleep, her small form curled up with her favourite doll clutched tightly. The world outside seemed quieter at this hour, as if time itself had slowed down. I took a moment to watch her, a sense of calm settling over me in her presence.

Silently leaving the bed, I walked quietly to the bathroom. I flipped the switch, and the bright light revealed my face in the mirror. I turned on the tap and splashed my face with cool water. The drops woke me up a bit, making me more alert.

After leaving the bathroom, I saw that Riya was still asleep. She looked so innocent compared to the complicated world outside. I kneeled by her bed and brushed a strand of hair away from her forehead.

Then I went straight to the window and looked out at the city. The evening view was mesmerising as the urban landscape glittered beneath the darkening sky. The city seemed to have a life of its own, bustling with stories hidden behind each window.

As I stood there lost in thought, a rustling sound behind me caught my attention. I turned around, and there was Riya, her eyes still heavy with sleep but curiosity shining bright.

Riya's eyes blinked open, the sleep gradually dissipating as she adjusted to being awake. Her gaze met mine, and a soft smile tugged at the corners of her lips. "Hi, Daddy," she murmured, her voice still carrying traces of drowsiness.

"Hey there, sleepyhead," I replied, matching her hushed tone. "Did you have a good nap?"

She nodded, rubbing her eyes with her little fists. "Mm-hmm. I dreamt about the doll."

"That's nice," I said, ruffling her hair gently. "Are you feeling hungry now?"

Her stomach answered for her, emitting a soft growl that made her giggle. "I guess so."

"Alright, let's go get some food," I said, holding out my hand to her.

Riya took my hand, her small fingers fitting perfectly in mine. We made our way to the hotel's dining area together.

At the restaurant, I helped Riya settle into a chair and took a menu. Knowing that she couldn't read yet, I quickly glanced through the options and then turned to the waiter. "We'll have two servings of pasta, please."

Riya looked at me with a mixture of curiosity and excitement, unaware of the order I had placed. The waiter nodded and headed to the kitchen.

As we settled into our chairs, waiting for our food to arrive, I couldn't help but notice a flicker of movement from the corner of my eye. My gaze shifted inadvertently to the receptionist's desk. She seemed occupied with her tasks, yet her eyes were fixed on me with an intensity that I couldn't ignore.

Minutes passed, and the receptionist's gaze remained fixed on us. It was as if she held a secret, a piece of information that I was not privy to. Then, in a swift motion, she reached for her mobile phone and dialled a number. I watched her discreetly, my curiosity growing with each passing second.

Leaning against the counter, talking quietly with changing expressions, sometimes surprised and sometimes looking urgent. I noticed she kept looking in our direction, suggesting that our presence was the topic of her conversation.

After a satisfying meal, Riya and I returned to our room, Riya's eyes sparkled as she clutched her doll, her tiny fingers carefully brushing against the fabric. With a bright smile, she settled down on the floor, creating a small world of her own.

"Daddy, look!" she exclaimed, her voice filled with enthusiasm.

Riya started playing with the doll, creating imaginative stories in the peaceful room. Her happy laughter echoed around, pulling me into a world of my own thoughts. I sat on the bed's edge, lost in memories and reflection.

The next day, I stood at a rental car counter, feeling excited. Riya, my young companion on this journey, stood with me, her eyes filled with curiosity.

"I'd like to rent a car for one week," I said to the attendant, the words carrying a sense of purpose that had been absent for far too long.

After a brief exchange of details, we were handed the keys to our temporary vehicle. Riya's excitement was palpable as we stepped towards the sleek car waiting just outside.

With Riya in the passenger seat, I settled into the driver's seat, the engine humming to life beneath my touch.

I drove the car, and with every turn, we got closer to our destination. After about half an hour, we reached the streets of Gandhi Nagar, where I used to live. It felt like the streets remembered us, like a silent greeting from the past.

Soon, as I parked the car in front of the house that was filled with memories. Looking at the house, a rush of emotions overcame me. Memories flooded my mind like an unstoppable tide, creating a mix of both happy and sad thoughts.

"Quick, Rishab! Come down, we are leaving!" my dad's voice rang through the house, urgent and tinged with a hint of frustration.

"Coming, dad!" I shouted back, feeling a bit sad about leaving our home. I looked around the room, taking in all the things I knew so well. We were about to leave the place where we had lived for a long time, and it made me feel a little emotional.

The news that we were moving to Mumbai had a big impact on me. We were going to a new house there, and even though Mumbai seemed exciting, But I had deep connections here. Part of me didn't want to leave.

My dad's work at the bank forced us into this situation. He was transferred to Mumbai, and we had to move along with him. I knew he had a lot of responsibilities, but it was hard to leave behind the memories, the familiar streets, and the friends I had known for so long. It was a tough situation to accept.

As I reached the door, I paused to take a final look around, as if trying to etch the scene into my memory. With a deep breath, I bolted the door, the sound resonating in the silence. The chapter of my life in this house was closing, and a new one was set to begin in Mumbai.

"Why are you always late?" my dad's voice snapped like a rubber band stretched too far.

I ignored his remark and got into the car, sitting between my brother Roshan and sister Rishika. The car felt like a capsule of tension, the front seats occupied by my parents—Mom up front, Dad in the driver's seat.

"Can't you ever get things done on time?" Dad's irritation grew as he turned the key in the ignition.

"Whatever," I muttered, my gaze fixing on the outside world, as if the road could offer an escape.

"Look at this behaviour, Shanthi," Dad's voice flared, now directed at Mom.

"Listen to your father rishi," Mom chimed in, her voice a soft plea for calm.

"He's always like this," Roshan took the opportunity to taunt me.

I shot him a glare that could melt steel. "Shut up," I warned.

"Why are you guys arguing now? Let's just go," Rishika's voice cut through, wanting to bring calm to the situation.

The car began to move, carrying us away from the house, from the arguments. Yet, the air inside remained thick with unspoken words. It wasn't just about our argument today; it was also about us moving to Mumbai. I had argued against it, but my dad had a strong point: he had secured my admission at Mumbai's M.M.K. College, making sure my future would be much better.

As the car embarked on its journey to Mumbai, I settled into my seat, ready for a different kind of journey—one involving the latest episode of Game of Thrones. The screen flickered to life, pulling me into the fantasy world of dragons and kings.

"Still watching this nonsense series?" Roshan's voice cut through, dripping with his usual disapproval. He never understood why I liked it, especially because it was meant for adults.

I gave him a stern look, my loyalty to the show unwavering. "What's your problem if I watch it? Can't you just focus on your own business."

He didn't back down. "If you spent as much time studying as you did watching that, you might actually get a decent rank."

I rolled my eyes, quick to defend myself. My rank was low because I had a fever during the exams. Couldn't study properly. Besides, this is a lot more better than texting your girlfriend *"mere babu ne khana khaya"*.

Rishika laughed and gave me a playful pinch. "Your funny behaviour might get us into trouble," she joked.

"Ouch, that hurt," I complained, rubbing the spot where she had pinched me.

After hours of driving, we finally arrived at our new home in Mumbai's Gandhi Nagar. The car came to a halt just as the G.O.T episode I was watching reached its conclusion. I tucked my mobile into my pocket and stepped out of the car, feeling the rush of Mumbai's air against my skin.

Taking a deep breath, I sighed, letting the weight of our new beginning settle in. Rishika, my sister, was the first to voice her excitement. "Wow, it's such a beautiful house!"

I couldn't resist teasing her. "You say that about everything you see. 'Wow, it's so wonderful.' 'Wow, it's so amazing.'"

Her response was swift—a pinch that took me by surprise. "What's your problem if I say that?" she retorted.

"If you pinch me again, I'll give you a reason to complain," I warned playfully.

"Go on, go do your useless work," she dismissed me with a grin.

Ignoring her playful comment, I went outside where my dad was calling for help. "Rishab, come over and lend us a hand with this wardrobe!"

"Coming, Dad," I responded, leaving our playful conversation behind as I joined my family outside to start working on the tasks that needed our attention in our new home.

Among all the boxes and the busy moving activities, I finally got a chance to relax in my room. I lay down on my bed, feeling a sigh escaped my lips—a sigh that carried both tiredness and a sense of relief.

Our new house has two floors. The first floor has a big living room, a dining area for eating together and having fun, a kitchen that smells like we'll cook great meals, and four bedrooms. Three of the bedrooms are on the first floor, while I had taken one on the second floor for myself.

My fingers automatically reached for my phone, and I opened WhatsApp. There, in the midst of the digital chatter, was a message that caught my attention. It was from Karthik, my childhood comrade,

I opened our chat history. As I scrolled through our past messages, I came across his latest one, a straightforward yet intriguing statement:

-"I have two good news for u

- Call me when u reach Mumbai."

Without wasting a moment, I dialled his number. The phone rang, and on the third ring, he answered.

"Hey, bro, are you reached?" he asked eagerly.

"Yeah, I got here a little earlier," I replied.

"So, tell me, how's your new home? Do you like it?" he inquired.

"Just like always, useless. I don't like it," I confessed.

"Don't say that, bhai," he chided gently.

"Why? Do you have a problem if I don't like the place?" I retorted.

"You're gonna love Mumbai," he said with conviction.

"How can I love this place when all my friends are in Kalyan?" I protested.

"I bet that by now you'll fall in love with Mumbai," he asserted.

"Whatever. Hey, you said you have good news. Tell me what it is," I urged.

"Are you ready to listen?" he asked.

"I'm always ready for everything," I assured.

"Okay, then listen carefully."

"Hmm..."

Stepping out to the balcony, I felt the evening's cold breeze brush against my face. As he spoke, his voice carried through the phone:

"The first one is, I told you I was arguing with my parents when you mentioned you were shifting to Mumbai next month."

"Yeah, what happened?"

"My parents agreed to let me shift to Mumbai too."

My jaw dropped as he revealed the news. "Are you serious?" I asked, still in disbelief.

"Yeah, I swear to God, and I'll be leaving for Mumbai in two days."

"Yeahhhh!" I screamed in excitement, and my loud scream probably reached everyone in the house.

"Why are you screaming?" my mom's voice rang out.

"Sorry, Mom," I quickly responded.

"I can't believe my ears! You're coming to Mumbai, holy shit!"

"Yeah, me too! When my parents agreed to let me shift to Mumbai."

"Wait, where will you stay? At a hotel?"

"Are you mad? How can I stay in a hotel for so long?"

"Right, then where?"

"I don't know exactly, my mom said it's somewhere in Gandhi Nagar, at my aunt's house."

"No, that's not possible. Are you kidding me?"

"No, seriously, I swear to god. Why?"

"Because we're living in Gandhi Nagar too."

"WTF, are you serious?"

"Yeah, bro."

"OMG, is this a coincidence?"

"I think so," I answered with excitement.

"Okay, okay, now listen to the second one."

"Tell me, tell me, I'm pretty curious."

"What's the name of the college you joined?"

"Smt. M.M.K. College. Why?"

"I'm joining there too," he revealed.

I was so surprised that I couldn't say anything. "Oh my gosh, are you serious, Karthik?"

"I'm telling the truth."

"You've made my day, Karthi."

"It's nothing; it's just the beginning. We're going to have a blast in Mumbai," he said confidently.

I laughed heartily. "Okay, Karthi, I have some work to do, have to go. Bye, call you later." I said and hung up the call.

I looked out from the balcony, feeling the cool evening breeze on my face. Suddenly, a grey Toyota parked across the street, right in front of our neighbour's house. A man in his forties got out of the car, followed by a woman who appeared to be his wife. The man's eyes landed on me, and he seemed slightly surprised.

"Are you shifted here from Kalyan?" he asked.

"Yes," I replied.

"Whenever you're free, come over and visit us. My wife makes a wonderful coffee; you should taste it."

"Of course, Uncle," I agreed.

In that moment, Mumbai felt a little warmer, a little more welcoming. A sense of connection was beginning to weave itself into my new surroundings, just as the bond with my old friend was finding a place in this bustling city.

The happiness of Karthik's news still lingered within me, a spark of excitement in my thoughts.

"Daddy, what are you thinking?" Riya's innocent voice broke through my reverie.

I smiled at her and shook off the thoughts. "Nothing, dear. Come, let's go to the house," I said, helping her out of the car.

I knocked on the door, the echoes of my knocks resonating in the air. No response. I knocked again.

"Coming," an unfamiliar woman's voice drifted through the door.

When the door opened, I was taken aback by the sight before me— a woman in her thirties stood there. This wasn't the face I was expecting.

"Sorry, is Raj Shekar Sahab home?" I inquired about my dad, my confusion evident.

"No, sorry I think you're in the wrong house," she replied.

"No, I'm not in the wrong house," I insisted, confusion gripping me. This was my home, my address. How could it be wrong? But as I stood there, the reality began to sink in. This was my home, but it was different now. It was as if the timeline had shifted, leaving me in a state of disbelief. *Where were my parents?* Where was the life I knew?

A question slipped from my lips before I could even think, "When did you begin living here?"

"Five years ago," she replied straightforwardly.

"Five years." Those two words echoed in my mind, and I couldn't believe what I had just heard. It was almost too much to understand.

"Daddy, up, up," Riya's voice brought me back to the present. I lifted her in my arms, making sure I was balanced even though it felt like the world was tilting around me.

"You're probably looking for the people who lived here before us," she pointed out.

I nodded, my heart heavy with realization. "Yes, I am."

"They must have shifted to another house," she suggested.

"Do you know where they went?" I asked, my hope rekindling.

"Sorry, I don't know where they went," she answered apologetically.

"Okay, thank you, and sorry to disturb you," I managed to say, my mind racing.

"It's okay," she assured, closing the door behind her.

Back in the car, the reality of the situation was like a weight on my shoulders. I couldn't believe what had just happened. It was my home, but now it's not.

With a heavy heart and a mind swirling with confusion, I made my way back to the hotel, Riya by my side. The weight of the unexpected encounter still hung over me, leaving me feeling disoriented and upset. Each step felt like a struggle, as if the ground beneath us had shifted.

As we entered the hotel room, the familiarity of the surroundings offered a momentary respite from the whirlwind of emotions. I sank onto the bed, Riya's presence a small comfort in the midst of the turmoil.

While Riya played happily with her doll, I found myself tangled in a web of thoughts that became increasingly confusing. The heaviness of my recent experiences, the long years in captivity, weighed down on my mind. The memories of those difficult times mixed with the uncertainty of my current life, creating a complicated blend of emotions that I struggled to understand.

I watched Riya's innocent joy as she played, her laughter a bittersweet contrast to the turmoil within me. She was a reminder of the life that had been taken away from me, a life that I had fought hard to reclaim. But the reality was harsh—I had returned to a world that had moved on without me, a world where my family's whereabouts remained a mystery.

The room's quietness made me think more about my difficult journey. I leaned against the headboard of the bed, closed my eyes, and tried to remember everything that had happened. I was held by Vikram for six painful years, and escaping from them felt like a miracle. The scars on my body and my heart reminded me of the terrible things I went through.

However, the joy of being free was overshadowed by the loneliness that surrounded me. Knowing that my family had moved to an unfamiliar place added more confusion to an already complicated situation. I couldn't stop thinking about where they were, if they were safe, and if there was a way to reconnect after all the time apart.

As Riya's laughter faded into the background, frustration welled up within me. My family, who had always been my anchor, now felt like a distant puzzle. The years of separation had created a gap that seemed impossible to close. I yearned to hear their voices, to see their faces, but the road ahead was unclear and filled with unknowns.

With a heavy sigh, I opened my eyes and looked at Riya. She glanced back at me, her innocent eyes filled with curiosity and trust. In her presence, I found a glimmer of hope—a reminder that despite the challenges, there was still a chance to build a new chapter in our lives.

After dinner, I lovingly tucked Riya into bed, her small form nestled beneath the covers. As I watched her sleep peacefully, a sense of contentment washed over me. Her innocent slumber was a reminder that amidst the chaos and uncertainty, there were moments of tranquillity and joy.

I waited by her bedside, the soft glow of the nightlight casting a gentle illumination across the room. Slowly, the rhythmic rise and fall of her chest indicated that sleep was beginning to claim her. With a final glance, I turned away, leaving the door slightly ajar to ensure her comfort.

Stepping out to the balcony, a flood of memories rushed to my mind. The cool breeze brushed against my face, carrying with it fragments of the past—That day when Karthik arrived at the Mumbai railway station marked a significant moment in our friendship. We had shared so many good times together. But then, our lives took a dark turn when something sinister happened that changed everything.

Chapter Three

Six Years Back

I waited at the train station, feeling excited and a little nervous. My eyes were glued to the train tracks, hoping to catch a glimpse of the approaching train. The minutes dragged on, and my heart raced.

Then, like magic, the train appeared in the distance, getting closer until it pulled into the station. Passengers poured out, creating a lot of noise and commotion. I strained my eyes to spot a familiar face in the crowd.

Amidst the chaos, I felt a tap on my shoulder, and I turned around. It was Karthik! He wore a big, friendly smile, just like the one I remembered.

"Rishab!" he exclaimed loudly, without hesitation, he pulled me into a tight hug, and for that moment, it felt like time had stopped.

"Karthik, you're here at last," I said, relieved and thrilled as we let go of the hug. He laughed, that familiar sound I had missed. "Of course, I couldn't let you explore this city all by yourself."

As we stepped out of the station, the bustling energy of Mumbai greeted us like a wave of anticipation. The honking horns, the rush of people, and the city's vibrant rhythm—it all felt like a whirlwind of new experiences. Karthik and I managed to hail a taxi, and as we settled into the backseat, a sense of adventure filled the air.

"Man, can you believe we're actually here in Mumbai?" Karthik said with a mix of excitement and disbelief, his eyes wide as he gazed out the window.

I chuckled, sharing his sentiment. "I know, right? It's like stepping into a whole new world."

He nodded eagerly. "Absolutely. The sights, the sounds, the vibe—it's unlike anything I've ever experienced."

I leaned back, taking in the view as the taxi navigated through the bustling streets. "And to think, this is just the beginning."

Karthik grinned. "Exactly! I mean, we've heard so much about Mumbai, seen it in movies, and now we're finally here."

"We're about to create our own stories in this city," I said, my voice tinged with excitement.

He chuckled. "Oh, I have no doubt about that. We're going to explore, discover, and make the most of every moment."

"Do you have any must-visit spots on your list?" Karthik asked, turning to me.

I pondered for a moment. "Well, I've always wanted to see the Gateway of India up close. And of course, indulge in some local street food."

Karthik's eyes lit up. "Yes! You can't be in Mumbai and not have Vada pav or pav bhaji."

I laughed. "Absolutely. And what about you?"

"I've heard Marine Drive is a must-see, especially during sunset. And I definitely want to explore the local markets," he replied.

As the taxi continued its journey, our excitement grew. The unfamiliar streets held the promise of new discoveries, friendships, and memories waiting to be made.

"This is going to be one unforgettable adventure," I said, my voice filled with anticipation.

Karthik grinned, a sense of camaraderie binding us even closer. "You bet. Mumbai, here we come!"

After a short ride, we reached Karthik's home. As we entered the house, a sense of warmth and hospitality welcomed us. Karthik's aunt, a kind and cheerful woman, greeted us with a warm smile.

"Welcome, welcome!" she exclaimed, her arms open in a gesture of hospitality. "You must be Karthik's friend."

I smiled warmly, extending my hand. "Yes, I'm Rishab. It's a pleasure to meet you."

Karthik beamed with pride. "Aunt, this is the friend I've been telling you about—Rishab."

His aunt's eyes twinkled with a mixture of curiosity and friendliness. "Well, Rishab, it's wonderful to have you here. Karthik has spoken about you a lot."

I was filled with gratitude for Karthik's warm reception. "Thanks so much, Aunty."

As we made ourselves comfortable in the living room, Karthik's aunt kindly served us some refreshments. She soon returned with two cups of hot coffee, and the air carried the delightful aroma of the freshly made coffee.

"Here you go, boys," she said with a warm smile, placing the cups on the table in front of us.

"Thank you, aunt," Karthik said, taking a cup with appreciation.

I expressed my thanks and savored the warmth of the cup in my hands.

"You're most welcome," she replied. "Make yourselves comfortable and enjoy the coffee."

Karthik's aunt turned to me with a smile. "Rishab, where do you live?"

I considered for a moment. "I live near your house, just a short distance away."

Her eyes lit up. "Oh, that's wonderful! We're practically neighbours then. I would love to meet your parents."

"Next time you come, bring your parents along. It would be lovely to get to know them," she said warmly.

I nodded in affirmation. "Definitely, I will."

After our friendly exchange, Karthik's aunt excused herself and headed to the kitchen. Meanwhile, Karthik and I moved upstairs and sat on his bed. As we settled in, he turned to me with a curious smile.

"So, tell me, Rishab, what's your plan for the weekend?" he asked, his eyes filled with anticipation.

I leaned back, considering his question. "How about going to a club?" I suggested.

His face lit up with excitement. "That's a great idea! I'm totally in."

I grinned in response. "Awesome. I thought it would be fun to spend the evening."

Karthik nodded enthusiastically. "Absolutely. We'll have a great time."

After our friendly chat, I excused myself and stood up, ready to head out. As I reached the door, a thought struck me, and I turned around to face Karthik.

"Hey," I said with a smile, "let's meet up this weekend, alright?"

Karthik grinned and gave me a thumbs up. "Definitely! It's a plan."

With that, I nodded and headed out, the excitement of the weekend plans filling me with a sense of anticipation.

I was getting dressed to go to the club with Karthik when, out of nowhere, Roshan stormed into my room and sat down on my bed. I felt quite irritated by his sudden entrance, and I wondered why he hadn't given me any heads-up or knocked on the door.

"What do you want now?" I snapped, not bothering to hide my annoyance.

He looked at me with a typical smirk and cut straight to the point. "Where are you going?"

"I'm going wherever I want. Why do you want to know?" I replied, sounding a bit defensive.

"Just tell me," he insisted, clearly not backing down.

I sighed, momentarily taken aback by his persistence. "Fine, I'm going to a club."

He leaned in, his curiosity evident. "With whom?"

"Karthik," I responded, straightforward as always.

A confident smile stretched across his face. "Ah, so that's the deal! Karthik, huh?"

I continued getting ready, trying my best to ignore him. "Yeah, now if you're done interrogating me, kindly leave me be."

"Wait, wait, wait!" he exclaimed, as if he had just stumbled upon some juicy gossip. "Is he already here in Mumbai?"

I nodded, not surprised by his reaction. "Yeah, he shifted here, in Gandhi nagar."

His astonishment was palpable. "You're going out with him?"

"Yes, Roshan, you got it right. Now, can you please get out of my room?" I asked, my patience was wearing thin.

But he wasn't about to let this go without a few more remarks. "You can't just go anywhere with that bastard."

I shot him an angry look, my irritation growing. "Mind your words, Roshan."

"I'm serious," he insisted. "I'll tell Dad."

I rolled my eyes, his threats having no effect on me. "Go ahead, tell him. See if I care."

"I'll stop you." He said in a threatening way,

"Why are you so interested in ruining my day?" I shot back, outraged. "What's your problem if I go out with Karthik?"

Without another word, Roshan abruptly stood up and left the room, leaving my questions hanging in the air. I finished getting ready, a mixture of irritation and defiance bubbling within me. Nothing Roshan said was going to stop me from enjoying my plans with Karthik, even if it meant dealing with his drama along the way.

After I finished getting ready, I made my way downstairs. As I entered the hall, I couldn't ignore the intense gaze of my father fixed on me. Roshan was seated beside him, and I could already sense that this wasn't going to be a pleasant encounter. Determined to stay focused, I tried to walk past them towards the door.

But my father's voice halted me. "Where do you think you're going?"

I turned to face him, not thrilled about the upcoming conversation. "It's the weekend, Dad. I'm heading out."

"With whom?" he inquired, his tone more serious than usual.

"Karthik," I replied, keeping my tone steady despite the rising tension.

My father's expression darkened. "That troublemaker is here too?"

I could feel my frustration simmering beneath the surface, but I remained composed. "Yes, he's here."

"You can't go out with him." My father's words ignited a fire within me.

"Why not?" I shot back, my voice tinged with defiance. His warning made my blood boil. "What if I decide to go? What's the big deal?"

"I'll cut your pocket money if you go out with him." His response caught me off guard.

I could feel the anger rising inside me, my fists tightening on their own. "What's the matter, Dad? Please, just let me go. Why do you both have to complicate things so much?"

My plea seemed to hang in the air, but my father's resolve remained firm. "I won't say it again."

I felt trapped, a mess of emotions inside me. I gave up and went back to my room, feeling a deep sense of shame that was tough to forget. Their rules felt heavy, like I couldn't breathe. I was left feeling sad that I couldn't enjoy my time with Karthik.

A storm of emotions swirling within me, making me feel all mixed up. I lay on the bed, looking up at the ceiling, as if I could find comfort in the midst of the chaos. After a while, the door opened slowly, and my mom came into the room. Her presence was soothing, and she sat down at the edge of the bed, speaking to me in a gentle voice.

"Rishi, look at me," she said, her tone soothing.

I let out a sigh, my frustration still lingering. "What do you want now, Mom? Please, just let me be."

She spoke with a hint of hope. "I understand Roshan messed up your weekend plan, but I can help you with it."

I looked puzzled. "Really?"

She extended Roshan's bike key towards me. "Take it."

I examined the key in her hand, feeling doubtful about her intentions. "Mom, this is Roshan's bike key. Why do you want me to have it?"

Her gaze softened, a smile playing on her lips. "Because I want you to go out and enjoy yourself."

A rush of gratitude surged within me, and I reached out to take the key. "Thanks, Mom." I pulled her into a tight hug, relief washing over me.

I couldn't help but voice my concerns. "But, Mom, I can't go out. Dad's in the hall."

Her response was full of reassurance. "You've learned martial arts, haven't you?"

I nodded, recalling the countless hours of training. "Yes."

She got closer and whispered quietly, "Can't you jump from the window or the balcony?"

I suddenly realized, and I felt a spark of hope. "Oh, right. I didn't think of that."

I made my way to the balcony, standing on the edge, I hesitated for a moment. "Is this even safe?" I wondered.

"Come on, what are you waiting for?" My mom's voice encouraged me.

Taking a deep breath, I jumped from the balcony. Time seemed to slow down as I hung in the air for a fleeting moment, a mix of excitement and nervousness. And then, as if in an instant, I landed on solid ground, the world around me resuming its pace. I glanced up at the balcony, feeling proud of what I'd done.

"Good job, Rishi!" my mom's voice echoed from above.

"Thanks, Mom," I whispered with gratitude. I carefully pushed the bike away from the house, trying to be as quiet as possible to avoid making any noise that could alert Roshan and Dad.

Once I had moved a bit farther away, I cautiously got on the bike and started the engine. It roared to life, and I couldn't help but feel a surge of excitement tinged with a hint of nervousness.

I wasted no time and immediately rode towards Karthik's house. The wind brushed against my face, and the thrill of overcoming challenges pushed me forward.

After what seemed like an eternity, I finally pulled up in front of Karthik's house. I quickly called him, and without a moment's delay, he emerged from his house and hopped onto the back of the bike.

"Why are you so late?" he asked as he settled onto the bike.

"Roshan created a scene at home, and they're aware that you're here," I explained, the engine humming beneath us.

"What does it matter if they know?" Karthik questioned,

"Have you forgotten what happened with Roshan? You beat him up so badly that he was hospitalized for a week," I reminded him.

"I did that because he slapped you right in front of me. I couldn't stand that," he justified.

"He slapped me because I asked his girlfriend for a date," I confessed, memories of the incident flooding back.

"I didn't know that part. I just saw him hit you and reacted," he explained.

"Let's not think too much about what happened before," I suggested, as I changed gears and concentrated on navigating through the busy streets of Mumbai.

"So, tell me, have you found any nice girls in our neighbourhood?" Karthik asked, a mischievous smile on his face.

I chuckled, shaking my head. "No, yaar, not a single girl. What about you?"

Karthik's expression changed, a mischievous twinkle in his eyes. "Well, yeah, I found one."

"Really? What's her name?" I inquired eagerly.

Karthik scratched his head. "I don't know her name yet. I've just seen her hanging out with her friends. I'm still working on gathering information."

We both laughed. "You're quite the detective, aren't you?" I teased.

Karthik shrugged playfully. "Gotta be prepared, you know?

"Guess what? King is performing at the Downtown Club," Karthik exclaimed.

"Seriously?" I responded, surprised.

"Yeah, let's go catch the show," Karthik suggested.

"Sure, sounds exciting," I agreed, and I pulled out my phone to open Google Maps for directions to the Downtown Club.

After a few minutes of driving, we finally arrived at the Downtown Club. As I parked the bike and stepped out, Karthik turned to me with a concerned look.

"Hey, did you bring your ID?" he asked.

I let out a frustrated sigh. "Oh, damn! I forgot it at home."

Karthik's eyes widened in disbelief. "What? How could you forget your ID, yaar?"

I ran a hand through my hair, feeling the tension rise. "Roshan created such a scene at home that I think I left it on my bed."

Karthik shook his head in exasperation. "Well, now what? We can't get in without IDs."

A sudden idea struck me, and I turned to Karthik. "Do you have a lighter?" I asked, my mind racing with possibilities.

Karthik looked puzzled. "Why would I carry a lighter? You know I don't smoke," he replied with a quizzical expression.

I explained my plan to him, my voice hushed with the excitement of a risky idea. "I was thinking of making a Molotov cocktail," I confessed.

Karthik's eyes widened in shock. "Are you serious?" he asked, his voice laced with tension.

I nodded, my determination unwavering. "We need a way to distract the guards and we will sneak inside the club. This might be our best shot."

Karthik hesitated, clearly unsure about the plan. "What exactly is your plan then?" he inquired cautiously.

I laid out the details. "We'll create a Molotov cocktail and throw it to the edge of the building. When the guards rush to see what's happening, we slip in and enter the club."

Karthik let out a deep breath, his gaze fixed on the ground as he contemplated the audacious scheme. The gravity of the situation was clear, and the weight of our decision hung in the air.

I looked at Karthik, waiting for his response. The seconds felt like minutes as he finally met my gaze. "Alright," he said, a mixture of excitement in his voice. "Let's do it."

Karthik's eyes sparkled with a mischievous glint as he gestured toward a nearby shop. "Looks like we've got a solution," he said with a grin,

I couldn't help but chuckle at his resourcefulness. "Well, this just got interesting," I replied, feeling a mixture of excitement and nervousness.

We found a quiet place near the edge of the building, hidden in the shadows created by nearby structures. In the distance, the music and laughter from the club invited us, as if challenging us to go ahead with our different plan.

Karthik purchased a lighter and a bottle of beer from the nearby shop. With our newfound supplies, we were ready to proceed with our makeshift Molotov cocktail.

"Now, we need something that can catch fire easily to ignite this," I said.

Karthik thought aloud, looking around where we were. He noticed a thrown-away piece of paper on the ground and folded it into a makeshift material that could easily catch fire.

With our ingredients in hand, I held the beer bottle steady while Karthik prepared the Molotov. He soaked a piece of cloth in the beer, careful to leave enough at the end for a makeshift wick. The beer-soaked cloth would serve as the fuel for our Molotov cocktail.

As we worked on assembling the makeshift Molotov cocktail, I couldn't help but notice a group of girls nearby, their curious gazes fixated on us. Karthik stayed cool as ever, but the feeling of being watched by them made our secret task even more challenging.

"Hey, look, what are they doing?" I heard a female voice from the group.

Karthik's jaw tightened, a hint of annoyance flashing across his face. He shot a quick glance towards the girls, his expression a mix of irritation and determination.

"Ignore them and focus on the Molotov," he instructed, his voice firm and steady.

I nodded in agreement, trying my best to block out the distraction and maintain my concentration on the task at hand.

"Ready?" he asked, his eyes locking onto mine.

I agreed and felt a rush of excitement. Our task was serious, and the weight of what we were doing was clear, but there was also an exciting feeling in the air that was hard to ignore.

Karthik used a lighter, and a little flame appeared. He carefully put the flame to the cloth. The cloth started burning, and the fire was dancing at the bottle's edge.

"Time to make our grand distraction," Karthik said, a mix of exhilaration and tension in his voice.

We both knew that once we tossed the Molotov, there was no turning back. The heat of the moment held us captive as we stared at the flames, flickering and crackling in the night air.

"Ready?" I asked, my heart pounding.

Karthik's gaze met mine, his expression a mix of determination and resolve. "Let's do this," he replied.

With a swift motion, I threw the flaming Molotov towards the edge of the building. The bottle broke when it hit, and flames burst out, making the dark area glow strangely.

With the blazing distraction we had created getting everyone's attention, Karthik and I took the chance to quietly leave the area. While the crowd, including the guards, hurried toward Molotov's fiery impact, we moved swiftly toward the club's entrance.

Our hearts were pounding with excitement as we got closer to the entrance. We felt a mix of nervousness and anticipation from our daring plan, but our strong desire to have a good time that night kept us moving forward. Without any hesitation, we went inside the club, and the booming bass from the music welcomed us as we stepped in.

Inside, it felt like being in a place buzzing with energy. Imagine bright lights flashing all over, music thumping loudly, and lots of people dancing to the beat. Everyone seemed really excited and looking forward to a fun night. I could smell fancy perfume, drinks, and the excitement of having a great time in the air.

Karthik and I exchanged a glance, a silent acknowledgment that we had successfully sneaked inside the club.

As the DJ's music played loudly through the crowd, we got lost in the lively dance floor's energy. All our worries and the outside world's limits faded, replaced by the joy of the here and now.

I walked up to the bar, the low hum of conversations and the rhythmic beat of music enveloping me. The bartender, a skilled multitasker, was busy attending to various orders, he looked confident and skilled as he moved between the bottles and glasses. I leaned against the polished counter, waiting my turn as I watched the bartender in action.

As he finished crafting a cocktail and placed it on a coaster, he glanced in my direction, acknowledging my presence with a nod. "What can I get you?" he asked, his voice projecting over the ambient noise.

"Vodka," I requested, my tone calm and composed. It was a simple order, but in the midst of the club's liveliness, it felt like a brief respite from the energy around me.

He reached for a glass, his movements fluid and practiced, and began preparing my order. The hiss of a can opening filled the air as he poured the vodka over ice. I watched as he worked, his hands moving with precision and familiarity.

In the midst of the lively club, a girl came and stood beside me, her sweet perfume lingering in the air. I stole a glance at her from the corner of my eye, and my eyes widened in awe as I took in her presence. Her hazel eyes sparkled like stars, reflecting the vibrant colors that bathed the club in a mesmerizing glow. Her silky hair flowed gracefully over her shoulders, a cascade of dark silk that framed her face like a beautiful painting.

Her lips had the softness and allure of strawberries, a temptation I could almost taste without even touching them.

A soft blush adorned her cheeks, adding a touch of innocence to her striking appearance.

She was dressed in a stunning red sheath dress, her stunning beauty that caught my attention instantly. There was no denying that she was absolutely gorgeous.

Suddenly, she looked at me, our eyes met, and my heart skipped a beat. Feeling a rush of nerves, I quickly looked away, hoping to avoid any embarrassment.

As I stood there, my mind raced with questions. Should I start with a friendly "hello" or jump right into asking her name? A rational voice in my mind told me to take a moment. "Hold on, Rishab. This isn't how you go about it. What's your plan?" I scolded myself inside, realizing the importance of a more considerate approach.

While I was thinking about what to say, I think she might have sensed my hesitation. In response she smiled, her cheeks turned a bit red, making her even more attractive. We looked at each other briefly, and there was an unspoken connection between us. I quickly looked away but kept stealing glances at her to admire her without being too obvious. The club's noisy atmosphere seemed less important as we had this silent moment, and it left me feeling a bit flustered and very interested.

But just as I was lost in my thoughts, Karthik's voice interrupted my thoughts. "Hey, Rishab, what are you doing there? Come over here and dance!" he called out, His words snapped me out of the dream the girl's presence had put me in.

"Yeah, coming," I replied, even though I felt a bit unsure about leaving. It wasn't just about the dance; it was the captivating moment I had shared with the girl that held me back.

Seeing that I hadn't joined the dance floor, Karthik took charge and came over to me. He playfully grabbed my arm and led me to the energetic dance area. However, I couldn't fully enjoy or appreciate the experience. My thoughts kept returning to that brief meeting with the mysterious girl. Her presence was etched in my thoughts, and I couldn't forget the moment when our eyes locked.

As the music's rhythm pulsed around me, my eyes automatically searched the area for a glimpse of the girl. Sadly, she was nowhere to be seen, and I couldn't help but feel increasingly disappointed.

Feeling disappointed to catch another glimpse of her, I decided to leave the dance floor. Karthik's voice cut through my thoughts as he questioned my departure, "Hey, Rishi, where are you going?"

Thinking on my feet, I quickly responded, "Toilet," a weak excuse I had made in a split second. I needed a reason to get away, to look for her once more.

As I made my way toward the bar, my heart raced with a mixture of anticipation and anxiety. I searched the area, hoping to spot her again, but no matter how hard I looked, she remained elusive, as if she had vanished into thin air.

And then, as if destiny had played a role, I saw her. She was heading towards the exit, and it felt like my heart skipped a beat. I couldn't resist the urge to approach her.

My legs seemed to move on their own accord, carrying me toward the exit as well. I stepped out of the club, the cool night air hitting me. I looked around, my heart pounding with a mixture of excitement and apprehension. Unfortunately, luck wasn't on my side this time either, as she seemed to have disappeared once again.

Feeling a sense of defeat, I headed towards the parking lot, hoping to catch one last glimpse of her. The parking lot was huge, and I had no idea how to find her.

I got more and more frustrated as I looked around for her. I couldn't figure out what to do next. I couldn't find her, and time was running out. After a few minutes of searching with no luck, I sadly realized I might not see her again. With a big sigh, I decided to head back to the club.

I was walking when I suddenly heard a cry for help. "Help me, please! Someone, please help me!" I quickly turned around to see who was calling for help. To my surprise, it was the girl I had been looking for. She was running toward me, and when she reached me, she hid behind me, clutching my shoulder tightly.

"Please help me," she pleaded, her voice trembling with fear. "They are harassing me."

Four people were in front of us. Their appearance left no doubt in my mind that they were indeed " Chapri's".

Just a minute ago, I was searching for her, and now she was standing behind me, seeking help. How could I possibly refuse her plea, especially since she was the very girl I had been looking for? Even though I didn't know her name or anything about her yet, I felt a strong connection and a readiness to do anything to help her in this moment.

"Hand her over to us," one of them said.

I straightened up and stared back, my voice firm, "What if I don't?"

I could feel her trembling, her grip tightening on my shoulder. "Please, save me from them. They're very dangerous," she whispered, her fear palpable.

I turned slightly toward her and offered a reassuring smile. "Don't worry, I'm here."

"If you want to live the rest of your life peacefully, hand her over to us," another one sneered.

"Who the hell are you to decide whether I'll live peacefully or not?" I retorted.

"You're new here, aren't you? Haven't seen you before. You don't know who you're dealing with. Leave her and get out of here," one of them said, a wicked grin on his face.

"You're right, I'm new here, and I don't know you guys. But one thing is clear – if anyone tries to touch her, I'll break his hands," I declared.

"They're very dangerous people. Let's get out of here," she pleaded, pulling my hand in fear.

I stood my ground, not moving an inch. "Don't worry. You're with me," I assured her, gently squeezing her hand. It was incredibly soft, like delicate fabric in my hand.

One of them stepped forward, nunchuk in hand. "Oh... nunchuk? Are you kidding me?" I said with a teasing tone.

"Come on, let's get out of here," she urged once more, her voice tinged with concern.

But I ignored her words, my focus on the approaching threat. He sprinted towards me, showing his nunchuck skills, aiming to strike me.

In an instant, I reacted. With a swift movement, I delivered a kick to his face. He fell to the ground, he screamed loudly feeling the pain. The unexpectedness of my action left everyone shocked. It was clear they didn't know that I was a national-level martial arts player.

"What... what did you do to him?" one of them asked, fear evident in his voice.

"Just a sidekick, nothing more," I replied calmly, maintaining my composure amidst the tension. Her eyes widened as she looked at him lying on the ground.

"Hey, Rishi!" I heard Karthik's voice from behind. He was accompanied by three more girls, strangers to me.

The girl behind me rushed towards the three girls and embraced them, relief evident in her actions.

Karthik took charge, calling the security to handle the situation. The guards came to help and took the troublemakers away.

Karthik pulled me aside, his tone filled with frustration. "What are you doing here, Rishi?" he questioned, his voice raised.

I didn't pay much attention to his words, my gaze fixed on the unfolding events.

"You'll pay for it," the guy I had knocked down said before leaving, his threat hanging in the air.

"Let's see who pays and who doesn't," I said firmly, refusing to back down.

"Come on, Rishi, why are you creating such a scene here?" Karthik asked, attempting to reason with me.

"I'm not the one who created the scene, they did," I replied resolutely, my frustration palpable.

"Alright, enough now. Let's go from here," Karthik insisted, trying to defuse the tension.

As we began to leave, I glanced at the girl. She was engaged in a conversation with her friends. It felt like our paths were separating once more.

Karthik pulled up with the bike, "Come on, let's get out of here." he said, I took my place on the back seat, and soon, the engine roared to life, and we sped away.

"Why did you get into a fight with them?" Karthik questioned, curiosity etching his voice.

"The girl who came to me for help," I replied, a hint of urgency in my tone, "that's why I got involved."

"The girl in the red dress? Do you even know her name?"

"No, I saw her at the club, and before I could talk to her, you pulled me away into the crowd," I explained, a bit frustrated.

"I apologize for that, but why did you follow her out of the club?" Karthik continued to inquire.

"My mind was fixated on her. I couldn't shake off the thought of her. I had to talk to her," I said, the memory still vivid in my mind. "I searched for her and saw her leaving, so I followed her out of the club. And you know the rest."

"If the guy with the nunchaku had managed to hit you, what would you have done?" he inquired with a smirk.

"You know me better than my parents do, Karthik. You know I can defend myself and fight back," I replied with a grin, the strong friendship bond between us clear.

Our laughter filled the air, releasing the tension of the previous encounter.

"So, you really like the girl in the red dress?" Karthik asked.

"A lot. It's like the feeling of love at first sight," I confessed.

"Finally, you're a believer in love at first sight too," Karthik teased, his grin growing wider.

Aliya

After dropping me off at my house, Lilly said goodbye, "Bye, Aliya. Let's meet tomorrow."

"Sure, let's catch up tomorrow. Bye, Lilly," I responded with a smile.

As I pushed the creaky door open and entered my house, I couldn't help but feel a slight shiver. The sound of the door sometimes gave me the creeps.

Inside, I tossed my bag onto the bed and headed to the wardrobe, searching through its contents. After about five minutes of searching, I finally located what I was looking for. I picked it up and went to my desk, dragging a chair along.

It was a diary, a gift from Lilly on my nineteenth birthday last year. It's strange how time flies; I can't believe a whole year has already gone by.

Opening the diary, I pondered on where to start. Writing a diary was a new quest for me, I never even considered keeping one before, not even in my wildest dreams. But today was different. Something significant happened in my life, something that felt both strange and exciting. And that's why I've decided to give this diary a shot. Who knows, maybe writing things down will help me make sense of it all.

Hello, Diary,
DAY-1

This is a bit new for me—I've never really written a diary before. In fact, I'm not entirely sure how to go about it. But hey, there's a first time for everything, right?

Let's start with an introduction. My name is Aliya, I hail from Ahmedabad, but right now, I'm living in the bustling city of Mumbai, in a cozy little house in Govind Nagar. It's just me here—living alone.

Life hasn't always been smooth sailing for me. About five years ago, something really sad happened. My parents died in a car crash. That event changed everything for me. I had to leave behind my old life and move in with my uncle for a while. But two years ago, I decided it was time to stand on my own feet, so I moved to Mumbai.

Now, let me tell you about Lilly. She's my best friend, my confidante. When I arrived in Mumbai from Ahmedabad, she was one of the first people I connected with. And over time, our friendship has grown stronger. In fact, Lilly has become a pillar of strength for me. She's been there for me through thick and thin, and I can't imagine what life would be like without her.

I am studying in Smt. MMK College. To support myself and maintain the lifestyle I want, I work part-time as a waiter at a restaurant. It's not exactly the most glamorous job, but it helps me pay the bills and keep things running smoothly. Sometimes, you've got to do what you've got to do, right?

I think you'll be the place where I can share my thoughts, feelings, and experiences. Maybe writing them down will help me understand this thing called life better.

Alright, that's all for now. Now it's your turn, dear diary. I've been thinking of a name for you, and one name that resonates with me is

Rishi. I hope you like it; somehow, I believe you will because I certainly do.

Do you want to know why I've chosen this name for you? Well, there's quite an interesting story behind it, and I'm excited to share it with you. Just promise me you'll keep it between us, alright? After all, you're going to be my confidant from now on.

I was lying on my bed in the evening, feeling incredibly bored, when the sound of my phone ringing interrupted the dullness. I looked at the screen and noticed it was Lilly calling. Without any second thoughts, I picked up the call.

"Hello?"

"Hey, birthday girl! Where are you?" she asked with palpable excitement.

"I'm at home. Why?" "It's your birthday, Aliya! Why are you just staying at home?" Her enthusiasm was infectious. "I don't know, Lilly. I just felt like staying in tonight."

"Well, listen up. I'm heading to the Downtown Club. Do you want to come? Sara and Rita are joining too."

My heart raced at the mention of a club. I had never been to one before. "Yeah, I'll come," I replied eagerly.

"Great! Get ready. I'll pick you up in thirty minutes." With those words, she ended the call.

As soon as I hung up, I sprang out of bed and headed straight to the bathroom for a quick shower, once refreshed, I stepped out, wrapped in a towel, and approached my wardrobe, hoping to find the perfect outfit. After scanning through my collection for what felt like ages, I couldn't settle on anything better. Spending almost twenty minutes in this quest, I eventually settled on wearing a red sheath dress for the occasion.

When I was finally ready, I received a call from Lilly, informing me that she was waiting outside. Quickly locking the house, I made my way to Lilly's car and took a seat. "Looking gorgeous," Lilly exclaimed as I got in. "Thanks, Lilly. Let's go," I said with excitement in my voice.

I could feel the excitement in the air as she accelerated the car. After a few minutes of driving, we arrived at the downtown club where Sara and Rita were already waiting for us.

"You're late," Sara and Rita chimed in together.

"Sorry, guys," Lilly said and motioned for us to move. "Come on, let's go."

"Hey, wait, did you bring your IDs?" Sara inquired.

"Yeah, I brought it. How could I forget that?" Lilly responded.

"Guys, I think I didn't bring mine," I said tensely.

"What? All of them said simultaneously.

"How could you forget your ID, Aliya?" Lilly asked.

"I didn't know I needed an ID for a club. I've never been to one before," I admitted.

"Oh God, what do we do now?" Rita sighed in frustration.

"We have to find a way to get inside the club," Rita said, her brows furrowed in thought.

I surveyed the scene, my mind racing for a solution. Suddenly, my gaze fixated on two boys near the building's edge, their figures hidden by the shadows cast by the surrounding structures.

"Hey, look, what are they doing?" I said aloud, prompting everyone to shift their attention to the spot I was pointing at. It seemed like they heard my voice, and one of the boys shot us an annoyed glance before we turned away, attempting to ignore them. However, I couldn't shake off the feeling that they were up to do something crazy.

My mind raced with questions as I continued to observe them from the corner of my eye, avoiding direct eye contact to evade detection.

One of the boy, dressed in a grey jumper and cargo pants, held something in his hand. The darkness prevented me from identifying what it was. Suddenly, he flung the object away, my heart pounding with a mix of curiosity and apprehension at the unexpected action.

In an instant, burst of flames erupted from the spot where he had thrown the object, accompanied by a faint but distinct sound.

The pieces of the puzzle fell into place as realization struck me. It was clear now - what they had thrown was a Molotov cocktail.

The fire attracted a lot of people. Some were from the club, and the guards too who usually checked IDs and kept order at the entrance. They all came to see what was happening because of the flames and the noise.

The sudden burst of activity created a chaotic atmosphere as people tried to understand what had just occurred. The guards began questioning a few individuals about what had happened, my attention was still fixated on the two boys.

I couldn't believe my eyes when I saw them taking advantage of the chaos to sneak into the club without permission.

"Hey, look, they're sneaking inside," I whispered urgently. An idea suddenly struck me, and I shared it with the group. "Guys, I have a plan to get in."

Everyone turned to me, intrigued. "What is it?" they asked in unison.

I shrugged casually. "Nothing much, just follow those two boys discreetly."

"That's actually a clever idea. Let's not waste any time," Lilly agreed enthusiastically.

And just like that, we discreetly followed the two boys as they entered the club. Before we knew it, we found ourselves inside the club as well, seated comfortably on a couch.

"they probably didn't bring their IDs either, just like Aliya. Their plan to distract the guards seemed clever," Lilly said and took a casual sip of her vodka.

My thoughts were captivated by the man who had thrown the Molotov cocktail. I couldn't shake off the memory of that incident. The dark setting, the fiery object flying through the air - it was etched in my mind. Questions swirled around - who was he? Why did he resort to such a risky move? The thoughts consumed me, drowning out the party sounds around.

I was lost in my own world, fixated on the mysterious figure. The chaos of the club faded, leaving only the image of that mysterious guy and my burning curiosity inside me.

The image of the man in the grey jumper and cargo pants was imprinted in my mind, and I found myself lost in a daydream. Lost in thought, I imagined him navigating through the crowd towards the bartender. It felt almost enchanting, like a scene out of a magical story.

And in a surprising twist, I suddenly realized that the guy I had been lost in thought about was actually the one making his way towards the bartender.

I was determined to talk to him, yet I had no idea how to approach him. A plan popped into my head—I could take another round of drinks. Swiftly, I emptied my glass and rose from my seat, heading towards the bartender.

"Leaving already?" Manvi questioned.

"Need another drink," I replied, showing her my empty glass. It was a quick excuse to get closer to the bartender.

As I neared the bartender, my heart raced, torn between whether to strike up a conversation with the guy or not. I mustered the courage and stood beside him.

I couldn't help but sneak glances at him from the corner of my eye. As I took in his appearance, my eyes widened as I took in his appearance. He was utterly handsome, incredibly good-looking, in a way that was different from the other guys in the club. He had a unique charm that drew me in.

His eyes, oh my, his eyes were a stunning shade of blue that I can't describe properly. They were like two sapphires, shiny and captivating. I'd never seen such a colour before, and it left me completely fascinated.

But what truly caught me off guard was the fact that he was looking at me. Again, I cut a quick glance in his direction, and there he was, his gaze fixed on me. I couldn't believe it. He was actually watching me. I couldn't resist the urge to look at him again, and to my surprise, I saw that he was staring right at me. My heart skipped a beat, and I quickly looked away, pretending to be deeply interested in my drink. But when I cautiously stole another glance, I realized that his gaze was still on me.

A surge of nervous excitement ran through me. Let me just say it plainly: he was hot. When a non-hot guy stares at you relentlessly, it's awkward at best and irritating at worst. But when a hot guy does it... well, I don't have to say it.

My heart kept beating fast, and my thoughts were all over the place. What was the right thing to do now? Should I approach him and talk? Or should I wait for him to make the first move? I was in an exciting but nerve-wracking situation, my attention firmly fixed on this hot guy.

In the end, I settled on what seemed like the most sensible approach – I would stare back. Why should boys have a monopoly on the staring game, after all? I decided to give it a shot.

I focused my attention entirely on him, looking at him with complete concentration. Our eyes locked for the very first time, and for a brief moment, it seemed like everything else around us vanished. In that second, it was only him and me.

But then, as he realized that I was looking back at him, something unexpected happened. His captivating blue eyes, which had been locked onto mine, eventually shifted away, and he looked away.

He looked like he wasn't sure, maybe a little nervous, as if he wanted to do something but couldn't decide. I couldn't help but smile at him, sensing his hesitation. He glanced at me again, and this time, he saw me smiling at him.

However, just when it seemed like he might make a move, his friend called out to him, breaking the spell. "Hey, Rishi, what are you doing? Come here!" he shouted.

It was the first time I had heard his name, "Rishi." It suited him well, but despite his friend's call, he didn't move an inch. His friend seemed to notice and came over, and literally he pulled him back into the crowd.

As I turned to get another drink, my heart sank when, four boys came up to me. They were my college seniors. I didn't know their names yet and hadn't met them before. But the whole college knows them as the "chapri gang." but I chose to ignore them, hoping they would leave me alone.

"Hey babe, what's your name?" one of them asked, but I remained silent, "You're new here at this club, aren't you?" another one chimed in.

My frustration was building, but I bit my lip and tried to keep my composure.

Then, one of them went too far. He put his arm around my shoulders, and I immediately shrugged it off. "Don't even think about touching me," I warned,

But then, things took a turn for the worse. As I turned to leave the place, one of them slapped me on my butt, a deeply disrespectful act that crossed all boundaries. I couldn't control my fury any longer. In an instant, I turned around and slapped him back as hard as I could.

He held his hurting cheek, clearly surprised by my reaction. "How could you, you...!" he started to say, but I didn't stick around to listen. I had already left, heading for the exit. Their rude actions had completely spoiled what should have been a fun day.

As I exited the club, my mind was a whirlwind of thoughts. I had been enjoying the moment, and their behaviour had completely ruined it. However, to my utter surprise, they were waiting for me outside. I couldn't fathom how they had managed to exit the club faster than I did.

I tried my best to ignore them and walked towards the parking lot where Lilly had parked the car. To my dismay, they began to follow me, their presence feeling increasingly menacing with each step.

I started to run across the vast parking lot, my heart pounding with fear as I saw them still chasing after me. Suddenly, two of them appeared right in front of me, and I came to an abrupt stop.

"You slapped me, you bitch, you know what, now, it's payback time," one of them sneered, his words sending shivers down my spine.

My body began to tremble, and my hands shook with fear. Without thinking, I turned and tried to run, but the other two quickly blocked my escape.

"One way or another, we've got you, sweetheart," one of them taunted with a malicious grin.

The parking lot felt like a trap, and I desperately searched for a way out. In my panic, I sprinted to the left side of the parking area, running as fast as I could, my heart pounding.

I crouched behind the car, gasping for breath, hoping that I had managed to evade them. But fate had other plans. As I pressed myself against the cold metal, the car's alarm suddenly blared loudly.

Their cruel laughter filled the air, and one of them taunted, "Haha, we've got you now!"

Without a second thought, I sprang to my feet and bolted toward the club, my heart racing faster than ever. The pounding in my chest matched the rhythm of my hurried footsteps.

I felt desperate and screamed for help, but it seemed like no one was coming except for these four scary guys. I shouted again, hoping someone would hear.

Then, I saw a guy standing near the parking lot entrance. I looked closely and realized it was the man with the amazing blue eyes.

Without thinking, I ran to him and hid behind him, trembling with fear. I begged, "Please help me, they're bothering me."

The air was tense, and I clung to this stranger, hoping he could save me from the chaos.

"One of them demanded, 'Hand her over to us.' He turned and looked at me, his voice firm as he responded, 'What if I don't?'

Tears welled up in my eyes as I pleaded, 'Please save me.' A droplet rolled down my trembling cheek.

He turned to me and offered reassurance, 'Don't worry, I am here with you.'

Then, they threatened him, 'If you want to live the rest of your life peacefully, hand her over to us.'

Defiantly, he retorted, 'Who the hell are you to decide whether I'll live peacefully or not?'

They taunted him, 'You're new here, aren't you? We haven't seen you before. You don't know who you're dealing with.'

With unwavering resolve, he declared, 'You're right, I'm new here, and I don't know you guys. But one thing is clear – if anyone tries to touch her, I won't hesitate to break his hands.'

Even though he barely knew me, he was willing to argue and stand up to them to protect me."

"Go and teach him a lesson about crossing us," he commanded. Then, one of them stepped forward with a nunchaku in hand, ready to attack him. But, before the attack could land, he swiftly kicked the man in the face, and the man fell to the ground, screaming in pain.

I couldn't believe my eyes. He had just taken down a man to protect me. Who was this guy, and why was he defending me from these troublemakers, I wondered.

The others were equally astonished by his unexpected and expert move. His kick had the precision of a professional. Just then, Lilly, Sara, and Rita arrived with his friend. I hurried to them and hugged them tightly. His friend decided to call the guards to resolve the situation.

Lilly asked me, "Aliya, what are you doing here?"

I replied, "They were bothering me, but thanks to him, he saved my life."

However, before I could even get a chance to meet him properly, he and his friend had already left the place, disappearing as mysteriously as they had arrived....

So, that's the story behind the name I chose for you. Now, tell me, did you like the name? Of course, you will because I liked it too.

"That's it for now. Life has its surprises, and today, I found help from a stranger, Rishi, who has these amazing blue eyes. It's nice to see that kindness and good manners are still around.

"Goodnight, diary," I said, closing it, and then I lay down on the bed, my thoughts consumed by those captivating blue eyes.

I lay on my bed, my mood quite sombre as I couldn't get the image of the girl in the red dress out of my head. I couldn't help but replay the scenario in my mind repeatedly. Regret began to wash over me like a heavy wave, a feeling that was growing stronger by the minute. Why hadn't I talked to her when I had the chance? I asked myself over and over again.

The weight of my missed opportunity seemed to hang heavily in the room. In an attempt to distract myself from these thoughts, I reached for my mobile phone and dialled Karthik's number. I needed a friend to talk to, someone to help me get out of this funk. To my dismay, Karthik didn't pick up. Frustration welled up inside me, and I tossed the phone onto my bed, where it landed with a soft thud.

I continued to lie there, still staring at the ceiling. It felt as if I were trapped in a never-ending loop of thoughts, all revolving around that girl in the red dress.

I could almost hear my inner monologue: "Rishab, stop dwelling on this. It's just a chance encounter. You didn't even know her, for heaven's sake!" Yet, despite the rational arguments, I found myself lost in the maze of her memory, unable to break free from its grip. The girl in the red dress kept occupying my thoughts. I wanted to stop thinking about her, but I couldn't shake it off, no matter how hard I tried.

My dad's voice interrupted my thoughts, snapping me back to reality. "Rishi, come over here," he called out.

"Yeah, coming," I replied, as I rose from the bed and made my way downstairs and stood before my dad.

"Yeah, Dad, did you call me?" I inquired, a bit puzzled.

Dad had a stern expression as he asked, "Why are you stuck inside the house like a girl?"

I felt a bit embarrassed and mumbled, "Well, Dad, I don't have any friends here, and it's kind of boring."

"Is that your problem?" he inquired.

I nodded in agreement, feeling a bit awkward.

"Uff... you're a boy, not a girl. You should go out, explore the city, and make some new friends," he advised, trying to sound encouraging.

Once again, I nodded in agreement, still feeling somewhat reluctant.

"Okay, now go out and take a ride around the new city," he firmly ordered, pushing me to take action.

I hesitated for a moment, muttering, "Not now, Dad. I'll go later."

But he was determined. He firmly stated, "No, now."

"Uggg... okay," I said and turned to head towards the door. As I opened it, my eyes widened in shock and awe. Right there, before me, stood a brand new YZF R15, my favorite bike.

I couldn't believe what I was seeing. I had to pinch myself to make sure I wasn't in a dream. Ouch! The pain was real, so this wasn't a dream; it was all happening for real! I couldn't believe it! It was actually real.

"Dad! Dad!" I screamed.

He looked up at me and asked, "What happened?"

"Whose bike is this?" I asked, my excitement pouring out.

"Oh, I think it's Rishi's bike," he replied.

"Are you serious, Dad? Is this bike for me?" I questioned.

"No, it's not for you. It's Rishab's," he said with a laugh.

I couldn't contain my excitement, so I ran up to him and hugged him tightly.

"Ouch, it's hurting," he said as he hugged me back.

"Thanks, Dad. Thank you so much for giving me my dream bike!" I exclaimed.

"I'm your dad, Rishi. It's a small gift from me to you. Do you like it?" he asked.

"Like it? No, I love it, Dad! Thank you so much!" I said, planting a kiss on his cheek.

"Enough, leave him," Rishika said and pinched me.

"Ouch! That hurts! Why are you always pinching me?" I protested.

"Because I love pinching, and if I pinch Roshan, he will hit me. His behavior is so rude. That's why I only pinch you. I know your behavior; you're not like him. You're sweet, and you're my lovely brother," she explained and pinched me again.

"Ouch!!"

"Hey, give me a ride on your bike," she asked.

"I'm not going to give you a ride," I replied.

"Please, Rishi."

"No," I said and came out of the house. I touched the bike for the first time; it felt like touching the clouds as I climbed on it. But then I realized that I didn't have the key.

"Dad... Dad, where is the key?" I asked.

"It's with me," Rishika said, showing the key in her hand.

"Give me the key," I said.

"If you want the key, promise me you'll take me on a ride."

"Ugh... Fine," I said reluctantly. As I agreed, she instantly climbed onto the bike.

"Can you give me the key now?" I asked.

"Oh, here," she said and handed me the key.

I put the key in its place and turned it. The bike roared to life, making a loud noise. Slowly, I revved the engine and pulled onto the road.

"So, where do you want to go?" I asked.

"I don't know the places around here; it's all new to me," she replied. "Let me check something on my phone."

After a moment, she suggested, "It shows there's an Infinix Mall about 10 kilometres away. We can go there."

"A mall? No way! I'm not taking you to a mall. Remember the last time you spent my five thousand on your silly shopping?" I protested.

She pinched my shoulder, making me wince. "Ouch! Why?"

"We're going to the mall. If you don't take me there, I'll keep pinching you until you agree," she said with a grin.

"Alright, alright! Tell me the directions," I sighed, hoping this time she wouldn't empty my wallet on shopping.

After a thirty-minute ride, we arrived at the Infinix Mall. I parked the bike in the parking lot, and as we entered the mall, the cool blast of air conditioning hit our faces.

"Wow, it's so beautiful," Rishika commented as she took in the surroundings. The mall was filled with people, and there were many ice cream vendors lined up one by one.

As we strolled through the mall, Rishika suggested, "Hey, let's watch a movie."

I thought it was a good idea, "Not a bad plan." I replied we both started looking for the theatre, but suddenly, a girl collided with me, and her head hit mine.

"Ouch!" I exclaimed, feeling the pain in my head.

"Ah," she said, also feeling the pain.

"I looked at the girl who collided with me, putting a hand on my forehead.

'Are you okay?' Rishika asked.

'Yeah, I'm okay,' I replied.

My eyes widened as I looked at the girl. It was the same girl I met at the club last night and saved.

'Can't you see?' Rishika shouted at her.

'It's you!' we both said simultaneously, surprised."

"Do you guys know each other?" Rishika asked, somewhat surprised.

Neither of us responded to her question. I was already engrossed in watching her. Our eyes met for the second time since the last time. Her hazel eyes locked onto mine, and something was building deep inside me. I couldn't quite put my finger on what it was exactly."

"Rishi... Rishi!" Rishika patted my shoulder, but I was not in a state to respond to her words.

The girl had captured me with her beauty. I was looking deep into her eyes, lost in her hazel gaze. The whole world seemed to stop, and there were only the two of us - me and her. Now, I understood why people called it eye contact.

Suddenly, Rishika pinched me hard enough to break our eye contact.

"Who is she?" Rishika asked.

"Oh! I forgot to introduce myself," the girl said. "I am Aliya. Nice to meet you." She stretched her hand towards Rishika.

So, her name is Aliya. What a lovely name, just like her, I thought.

"I am Rishika. Nice to meet you too," she said and shook her hand.

"Hi, I am Rish...," I began, but before I could finish my words, she interrupted me.

"I know your name is Rishi," Aliya said, her voice carrying a touch of amusement.

"Do you guys know each other?" Rishika asked, her curiosity evident in her tone.

"Sort of," I said, glancing at Aliya and recalling our encounter.

"What do you mean by 'sort of?'" Rishika questioned, her eyebrows furrowing.

"Actually, we met last night at the club," Aliya said, her voice soft yet confident.

"Club? When did you go to the club? You didn't tell me," Rishika asked firmly, crossing her arms.

I stayed silent, somewhat guilty about not sharing that part of my evening with my sister.

"Thank you, Rishi," Aliya said sincerely, her eyes meeting mine. "You saved my life yesterday. If you hadn't been there in time, I don't know what they would have done to me by now."

Her words brought back memories of that chaotic night. I nodded, acknowledging the truth of her statement.

"It's okay; there's no need to say thanks," I replied, trying to downplay my actions from the previous night.

Rishika's curiosity and concern grew. "What is she saying, Rishi? What happened yesterday?" she asked tensely.

I hesitated, searching for the right words to describe the events of the previous night. "Well, you see...," I began, but Aliya chimed in.

"He saved my life from some bad guys," Aliya explained in one swift sentence. "He fought with them to protect me."

Rishika's eyes widened as the truth sank in. She looked at me, her expression a mix of surprise and concern.

"Is that true?" Rishika asked, her tone firm.

I nodded, and she immediately pinched me. "Why didn't you tell me about that?"

"Ouch! It hurts," I said, rubbing the spot where she had pinched me. A small smile formed on the corner of Aliya's lips.

Then, out of nowhere, Aliya's friend joined us. Aliya introduced her, "It's my friend Lilly."

"Hey, Lilly. Do you remember him? He's the one who saved my life last night," Aliya said.

"Oh, it's you. Thank you for saving Aliya's life. I'm Lilly," she said, extending her hand towards me.

I shook her hand and replied, "I'm Rishab."

Lilly smiled and said, "I know your name; Aliya has talked a lot about you since you saved her last night."

I was taken aback, never expecting Aliya to mention me in conversation. I glanced at Aliya, who looked down shyly.

"And she?" Lilly inquired.

Oh! She is my... Before I could complete my sentence, Rishika interrupted me abruptly. "I am Rishika, his girlfriend," she declared, taking my hand in hers.

I was stunned by what she had just said and looked at her in surprise. Rishika pinched me discreetly and signalled me to remain silent.

I turned toward Aliya, and as soon as she heard Rishika calling herself my girlfriend, her face fell. The sparkle in her eyes vanished, and her face lost its earlier glow. An uncomfortable silence hung in the air between us.

Breaking the silence, Aliya spoke up, "Oh, we have to go now. Come on, Lily, let's leave." she said and without uttering another word, they both turned and left the place, disappearing into the crowd.

"Why did you say that?" I asked, my tone stern.

"What if I said that? Do you have any problem?" she retorted.

"I don't have any problem, but it's still not right. You're my sister, not my girlfriend," I replied.

"I know, but you like her," she said after a pause.

"Who said that I like her?" I questioned.

"The way you both looked at each other, there's no doubt that she likes you too," she answered confidently.

"How can you be so sure of that?" I asked.

"I'm a girl, and girls can feel these things. And when I said that I'm your girlfriend, did you notice how her face fell? I noticed all of that," she said with certainty.

"And what if she doesn't?" I inquired.

"She will, I bet. You wait; she will definitely fall for you," she said.

"Whatever, let's see," I replied, trying to sound like I wasn't too interested.

I began to walk away, "Hey, wait for me!" Rishika blurred out.

Dear Rishi,
DAY-2

It's the second day of sharing my secrets with you. Today, something crazy happened. Lily, my best friend, and I went to Infinix Mall. She had some work to do, so she left me, saying she'd be back soon. I was hungry, so I decided to go to a restaurant. As I was walking, a boy bumped into me. Our heads hit each other.

"Ouch!" I growled in pain.

When I looked at the boy, my eyes widened in surprise. It was the same guy who saved my life from my college seniors!

"Are you okay, Rishi?" the girl who came with him asked at Rishab.

"Can't you see?" the girl shouted at me!

"It's You!" we both said simultaneously.

"Do you guys know each other?" the girl asked, somewhat surprised.

I didn't respond to her question, and neither did he. We were both too busy watching each other. Our eyes met for the second time, this time longer than before, and I was totally captivated by his blue eyes.

Something was building deep inside me, and the whole world seemed to stop. There were only two of us: me and him. Now I know why people call it "Eye contact."

Suddenly the girl pinched Rishab. We deprived our eye contact.

"Who is she?" the girl asked at Rishab.

"Oh! I forgot to introduce myself, I am Aliya. Nice to meet you," I said and extended my hand towards the girl.

"I am Rishika, nice to meet you too," the girl said and shook my hand.

"Hi, I am Rishi..." Before he could complete, I cut him midway.

"I know your name is Rishab," I said.

"Do you guys know each other?" Rishika asked.

"Sort of," he said.

"What do you mean by sort of?" Rishika questioned him.

"Actually, we met last night on a club," I said.

"Club! When did you went to club? You didn't tell me about it," Rishika said in a firm voice.

He didn't say anything; he kept quiet.

Thank you, Rishi, you saved my life yesterday. If you wouldn't be there on time, I don't know what will be they done to me by now, I said.

It's okay, no need to say thank, he said.

What is she saying, Rishi? What happened last night? Rishika asked tensly.

Nothing happened, it's just a... he paused, searching for the right word to describe.

He saved my life from bad guys. He fought with them to save me, I said in one shot.

Rishika looked at him, eyes widened.

Is that true, Rishab? she asked sternly.

He nodded in silence.

Why didn't you tell me about it? she said and pinched him.

Ouch! It hurts!

By then, Lily arrived and joined me.

"Hey, Lily, do you remember him? He's the one who saved my life from those guys," I said.

"Oh! It's you. Thank you for saving Aliya's life. I'm Lily," she said, extending her hand toward Rishab.

"I'm Rishab," he replied, shaking her hand. "I know your name. Aliya talks about you a lot since you saved her."

I felt embarrassed when she mentioned that, and I looked down shyly.

Who is she? Lily asked, pointing to Rishika.

"Oh, I forgot. She's my..." Rishab began, but Rishika interrupted him.

"I'm Rishika, his girlfriend," she said, taking his hand in hers.

I didn't know he had a girlfriend, and I felt really upset hearing that. An awkward silence lingered among us.

"Sorry, guys, but we have some work to do," I finally said, breaking the silence, and I left them without uttering another word.

So, this is what happened today. It seems luck wasn't on my side. Rishab already had a girlfriend, and you know what? I think I have feelings in my heart for Rishab. It was like love at first sight, but it seems that kind of love isn't meant for me. I don't know why I'm telling you all these stuffs, but sharing something with you lightens my heart...

"Rishab... Rishab... wake up! Look at the clock, it's 9 in the morning," Mom shouted.

I instantly jumped out of bed, rubbing my eyes. "What happened? Why are you shouting, Mom?"

"Why am I shouting? Look at the time! It's 9 am, and you forgot to go to college. You're already a month late, and you're still in bed," Mom scolded.

I cursed under my breath. "Oh, shoot, I forgot," I said as I rushed to the bathroom. I took a quick shower and came out, wrapping a towel around myself. In no time, I dressed up and searched for my mobile. There were several missed calls from Karthik.

I hurriedly grabbed my bag and rushed downstairs. Snatching my bike key, I swiftly stepped out of the house.

"Rishi, dear, have some breakfast," Mom's voice called out from the kitchen.

"No, Mom, I'm running late," I said. I quickly mounted on my new R15, accelerated the engine, and sped away

I quickly reached Smt. M.M.K. College. As I entered the college gate, a bunch of people stared at me with wide eyes. After all, I had arrived on my brand-new bike. I parked the bike, turned off the ignition, and got off. Just then, I heard my name called from behind. It was Karthik. I walked over to him.

"Why are you so late?" he asked.

"Sorry, I was lost in deep sleep," I replied.

"You're always late for everything," he teased.

"Sorry, buddy. It won't happen next time," I assured him.

"Alright, come on, let's go meet the principal," he said, hurrying towards the office.

"May we come in, sir?" we both asked at the same time.

A man in his fifties looked up and smiled, saying, "Yes, please."

We entered his office and stood before him.

"New admissions, right?" he asked.

"Yes, sir," we both confirmed.

"What are your names again? I seem to have forgotten," he said, trying to remember.

We introduced ourselves. "Ah, I remember now. Have a seat," he said, pointing to some chairs.

We took a seat, and he noted, "You guys are two months late."

We remained silent.

"You'll need to catch up on your syllabus," he told us.

We nodded.

"Alright, come with me," he said, standing up and leading us.

We silently followed him to the second floor. He suddenly stopped in front of a classroom.

"This is going to be your classroom," the principal announced.

We both nodded, glancing at the door of the classroom. As I looked inside, I saw a woman in her forties, who appeared to be the teacher, engrossed in the ongoing class.

The principal called the teacher, and they exchanged a few words. The entire class turned their attention toward the door, eyeing us with curiosity.

Then, the principal called us inside the classroom, and we entered the room, standing beside him, feeling like the centre of attention as the class continued to watch us with curiosity.

"Dear students, today you have two new buddies joining your class, and these two will be your new friends," the principal announced, addressing the class with a warm smile.

He then turned to us and encouraged, "Come on, boys," waving his hand to prompt us. "Introduce yourselves to the class," he requested, indicating that it was our turn to make our introductions to our new classmates.

"Hello, everybody," I began, addressing the class with a friendly smile. "My name is Rishab. I'm originally from Kalyan but recently shifted to Gandhi nagar."

Both of us introduced ourselves to the entire class, sharing a bit about our backgrounds and where we were from.

"Now, since you guys are two months late, you'll need to work hard to catch up on your syllabus. I'll choose two students to help you," the principal declared.

We nodded, acknowledging the need for assistance.

"Aliya," he called out.

"Wait a minute, I know this name,"

"Yes, sir," a girl responded and stood up.

I couldn't believe my eyes as I looked at her. To my amazement, it was Aliya, we were not only in the same college, but we were also in the same class.

"You'll help Rishab catch up on the syllabus, okay?" the principal instructed.

"Okay, sir," she agreed, her hazel eyes captivating my attention.

"Shreya, you'll help Kartik, okay?" the principal asked, turning to another girl.

"Okay, sir," she replied.

"Enjoy your class," the principal said before leaving the class.

Our teacher then addressed us, "Rishab, Kartik, go ahead and take your seats."

We obeyed, making our way to the last row. I wished I could get a seat next to Aliya. As the class began, my attention remained focused on her, unable to take my eyes off her.

With each passing minute, it seemed like every boy and girl in the class was glancing in my direction, leaving me feeling a bit startled. I couldn't help but wonder why they were all looking at me like that. Did I look that bad, I wondered to myself.

"Hey, Karthik, why are they looking at me like that?" I whispered, feeling curious and slightly self-conscious.

"Why are your eyes blue?" he asked instead of answering my question.

I shrugged, unsure how to answer. "How can I answer that? It's natural," I said.

"You know it's very rare to have blue eyes."

"Yeah, I know, that it's a rare phenomenon, but why are they all looking at me?"

"It's because of your eyes. They're blue, and I think they're attracted to your eyes," he explained.

"Attracted to my eyes? That's weird,"

"You know what? I'm getting jealous of you." he confessed.

"Why are you getting jealous of me?" I asked in astonishment.

"Because everyone's watching you, not me," he replied.

"What will happen if they watch me, Karthik? I blurted out loud enough for everyone to hear my voice.

"Quiet, the one with the blue eyes," the teacher scolded.

I felt embarrassed and quickly apologized, "Sorry, ma'am."

Karthik leaned in and whispered, "Even the teacher is captivated by your eyes."

I shook my head, insisting, "Stop. No more talks on this matter."

I tried to concentrate on the lecture, but I couldn't. I kept looking at Aliya. She was so engrossed in the lecture, I couldn't help but stare at her. I don't know why, but it felt like I was watching someone who was most important to me.

I didn't even realize when the class ended. I was still lost in watching Aliya. The way she casually moved a strand of hair away from her face was awesome.

"Rishi... Rishi..." Karthik's voice finally brought me back to reality.

"Ah! What happened?" I asked, a bit disoriented.

"Who are you staring at?" he inquired with a playful grin.

"No one," I lied, trying to conceal my curiosity.

Karthik didn't believe it. "Yes, you are. You're staring at someone."

I hesitated for a moment, then decided to share with him. "Do you remember the girl I saved at the club?"

Karthik's eyebrows furrowed as he recalled the incident. "Yeah, why?"

"Look," I said, pointing my finger towards Aliya, "there she is."

"I need to talk to her," I said with determination, and I stood up. However, due to my lack of courage to approach a girl overwhelmed me, and I ended up sitting back down.

"Ha ha ha. You don't even have the courage to talk to a girl." he teased.

"Shut up," I replied, feeling a mix of embarrassment and frustration.

Then, to my surprise, Aliya stood up from her seat and started walking towards me. Karthik pointed it out with excitement, "Hey, look, she's coming over here."

"Yeah, I see," I replied, my heart racing.

I stood up as she approached me, although I wasn't entirely sure why.

"Hey... um... can we talk?" Aliya asked, her words filled with hesitation.

"Yes, of course," I responded instantly, and I looked over at Karthik, who furrowed his eyebrows as he overheard our conversation.

With her hesitation, she started walking, and I followed her out of the classroom, aware of the entire class's curious gazes fixed upon us.

"Thank you, Rishab, for saving me that day," she said.

"You've already thanked me," I remembered.

"I know, but still, thank you," she insisted.

"You're welcome," I replied warmly.

"Ah..., and I wanted to talk about your syllabus," she continued.

"Tell me, I'm listening," I said, ready to hear what she had to say.

"The principal assigned me the job of helping you catch up on your syllabus. So, I'm going to take your classes twice a day," she explained.

I nodded in silence, appreciating her willingness to support me.

"One session will be before our regular classes start in the morning, and the other will be in the evening," she explained.

"Alright, but where are you taking the classes?" I inquired.

"Come to the college backyard, and remember, time punctuality is very important. Please be on time," she instructed, her tone turning teacher-like.

"Okay, ma'am," I responded.

"Your class starts tomorrow morning, so be on time,".

"Yes, ma'am," I agreed.

Why are you calling me ma'am, "Call me by my name,"

"Okay, ma'am, I mean Aliya,"

"Let's meet tomorrow then," she said.

"Can't we meet before tomorrow?" I asked playfully.

"Unfortunately, we can't," she replied with a smile at my request, and went inside the class.

As Aliya left, Karthik approached me, eager to know what she had said.

"What did she say?" he asked instantly.

"Nothing interesting. She mentioned she's going to take my classes to help me catch up on the syllabus, that's it."

"You're so lucky that she's going to teach you," Karthik exclaimed.

I shrugged, "Let's see."

Soon, the next period's teacher arrived, and we took our respective seats. The lecture began, immersing us in the dull world of academics.

After what felt like an eternity, the lunch bell finally rang, signalling the much-needed break.

"Come on, let's go eat something," I suggested.

"You go. I'm not hungry." he declined.

"You're sure?" I double-checked,

"Yeah, you go and have some food. I don't want anything," he confirmed.

"Okay," I replied, respecting his decision.

My eyes scanned the class for Aliya, but she had already left. As I exited the class and entered the corridor, a group of four students - two pairs of girls and boys - noticed me and called me over.

I walked toward them and greeted, "Hey, guys," even though I wasn't sure what to say.

"What did you say your name was?" the girl in the group asked,

"Rishab. already forget my name?" I replied with a chuckle.

"Actually, when you were introducing yourself in class, my mind was more focused on you than your words." She responded with a playful tone,

Her comment made me feel a bit embarrassed, and I lowered my gaze.

"Hey, don't be shy. I'm just kidding. Anyway, I'm Seema. Nice to meet you." She extended her hand.

"Nice to meet you too," I said, shaking her hand. The others introduced themselves as Anika, Varun, and Aadhi.

"Have you had lunch?" I asked,

"Not yet. We're planning to eat out. Would you like to come with us?" Anika replied,

I inquired, "Is your plan to bunk the afternoon class?"

"Ah... you got it right." Anika confirmed,

"Are you scared about bunking class?" Varun chimed in.

"Scared? Not in my wildest dreams." I said with confidence.

That's the spirit. Come on, let's go, then." Seema blurted out.

As we walked along the corridor, my eyes widened in surprise as I spotted the same troublesome group, the Chapri Gang. I couldn't believe my eyes.

"Who are they?" I whispered to Seema,

"Stay away from them. They're very dangerous people. Every student in this college trembles in fear if they call them. They're the college seniors, and not a single student in this college dares to cross their path."

Do you see the tall man in the center with long hair? He's their leader, and his name is Vikram. The person on the left is Arjun. Standing next to him is Rahul. On the right side of their leader is Raj. she said in a hushed tone,

Quickly, I covered my face with a towel, attempting to avoid being noticed by them.

"Why are you covering your face?" Anika asked, puzzled by my actions.

I gestured for her to stay silent. Just as we were about to pass by them, they called out, "Hey, you guys, come over here."

All of us stopped, standing there like statues. Not a single one of us dared to move an inch.

"What do we do now, Rishab? I'm so scared." Seema said.

"Stay calm." I tried to reassure them.

"Hey, you guys, come over here!" The gang called us again,

Reluctantly, we turned around and found four pairs of eyes staring at us. We walked towards them and stood in front of them. All four of them looked at us with intimidating gazes, making us feel like we were about to be swallowed by them.

"Seema, why didn't you answer my love letter?" one of them asked.

However, she remained silent, not even looking at him.

"Why aren't you talking to me?" he asked, placing his hand on her shoulders. He appeared to be their leader, standing at six feet with long hair and a chubby face that looked like a pumpkin.

"Don't even dare to touch me," Seema said, forcefully throwing his hand away.

"Why are you guys irritating her? Just leave her alone," Varun raised his voice against the gang's leader.

In an instant, the leader slapped Varun hard, causing Varun to fall to the floor by the force of the blow.

"Who the hell are you to talk to me like that?" he roared, held Varun's collar and raised his hand to strike him again. When the attack was inches away from landing, I quickly grabbed his hand, preventing the blow from hitting varun again.

All of them were surprised by my unexpected move.

"How dare you hold our leader's hand?" another one said, grabbing my shirt.

But my focus was fixed on their leader, who was looking at me astonished.

"Leave his hand, Rishab," Seema insisted, coming to my defence.

However, I gestured for her to remain silent. I wasn't afraid of this confrontation.

"Why are you covering your face?" he demanded, moving forward to remove my towel.

In an instant, I reacted, punching him on his face, and he fell to the floor, screaming in pain.

Everyone was startled by my swift reaction, and the pumpkin face removed his hand from Varun's collar.

"You are interesting. After a long time, it will be fun to teach you a lesson," the pumpkin face declared.

"Grab him," he ordered his men, and without hesitation, they grabbed me tightly. Then he came forward and removed my towel. His eyes widened as he looked at me.

"It's you," he blurted out. "That day your friend interrupted our fight midway, but that won't happen today. You will pay for what you've done before."

I formed a sly smile on my lips and responded, "Let's see who will pay." and pushed all three of them hard, they all fell to the ground by my strong push.

Instantly, I ran. "Catch that bastard!" pumpkin face shouted to his men, and now all of them were chasing me. I ran and ran, coming to the backyard of the college. Everyone in the college was watching us with interest.

My gaze fell on a small building, though I didn't know what it was. I ran towards it as fast as I could and entered the building. It turned out to be the college canteen, and when I entered, everyone in the canteen was startled by my sudden entrance.

A moment later, the four of them entered the canteen too.

"What will you do now? You're trapped here, and you can't run anymore. I'll crush you this time," Pumpkin Face said.

I didn't say anything. Instead, I smiled at him. Looking around, I noticed that everyone was watching us with curiosity.

"You're done," another one said, coming at me. He raised his hand to hit me, but I simply held his hand. He was shocked, I tightened my grip on his hand as much as I could. He screamed in pain. Then, I punched him in the stomach, he fell to the floor, by my powerful punch, screaming in pain.

I looked at Pumpkin Face, and his face was burning with rage, turning bright red. Everyone had now surrounded us, and they were all surprised, stunned by the fact that I had managed to knock one of them down.

Another one approached, and I remembered him. He was the man with the nunchaku whom I had beaten at the club.

"Oh, not again," I said as he neared, taking his nunchaku out of his pocket. My gaze fell on a tray on a nearby table. I quickly grabbed it, and when he swung his nunchaku towards me, I managed to dodge his attack and hit the tray hard against his head. The tray shattered into pieces, he put his both hands on his head, groaning in pain.

"Do you remember me?" I asked him.

He nodded, still holding his head.

"Do you remember the night when I hit you for the first time?"

"Yes," he managed to utter.

"You know, right? Then why did you dare to confront me? Come here," I said, putting my hand on his shoulder. I walked with him to a nearby chair. "Sit down here and enjoy the next scene.

Someone, please give him juice or something," I said loudly.

Out of nowhere, someone emerged from the crowd and handed me a can of Pepsi. "Thank you," I said, then I gave the Pepsi to the man I had hit.

"Who's next?" I asked with certainty.

"Go and teach him a lesson," Pumpkin Face said to the last man.

I looked at him, and he was shivering with fear.

"What the hell are you thinking? Go and hit him!" Pumpkin Face said again.

"No, I don't want to break my hands or anything. You go if you want to break your hands," he said to him.

"You bloody rascal!" he blurted out loud. He came forward to attack me.

He seemed strong, and it was going to be a tough fight. As he neared, I tried to hit him, but he blocked my punch and hit me on my stomach. I took a few steps back from his punch. I stumbled backward, trying to catch my breath. A sinister smile curled his lips.

This is what I needed – a strong opponent.

He charged at me again, but this time I was ready. I blocked his punch and countered with a swift kick to his head. I didn't let up, I unleashed a barrage of punches and kicks that I had learned during my time in martial arts. Finally, he fell to the floor with his face covered in blood, grumbling something.

His men rushed to his side and helped him to his feet. They glared at me for a moment, then turned and fled.

The canteen was silent. I stood there, catching my breath, my chest heaving. I had done it. I had defeated them all.

Everyone was shocked that I had taken down their leader and his gang. and they began murmuring among themselves as I stood there.

"Sorry to disturb you guys," I said, trying to defuse the situation. But then, my eyes fell on the corner of the canteen. There was Aliya, watching me. When she realized that I was looking at her, she quickly sat down at her table.

By then, Seema, Anika, Varun, and Aadhi came over to me.

"Wow... how did you beat them all?" Aadhi asked, his eyes wide with curiosity.

"You fight very well, where did you learn to fight?" Anika inquired.

"Yeah, the way you hit them, it was awesome," Seema added.

"Guys, firstly, I'm very hungry. I need something to eat," I said.

"You guys take a table. I will fetch food," Varun said and left to get food.

We sat at a window-side table, Aadhi couldn't contain his curiosity. "Tell me, how did you manage to fight with them all?"

"Guys, I need to tell you something," I said.

"What are you waiting for? Tell us!" Seema urged.

"The thing is, I am a national-level martial arts player," I declared.

Everyone's jaws dropped in surprise.

"What... Are you a national-level martial arts player?" Seema said.

I nodded.

"That's why you managed to fight with them," Anika chimed in.

"Right. And you know what, this is the second time I'm fighting with them," I said.

"Second time... You already fought with them before?" Seema asked.

"Yes," I said and narrated the whole story of the night when Karthik and I snuck into a club, and I fought with them for the first time over a girl.

"You fought with them for a girl?" Aadhi asked.

I nodded.

"Can you tell us who that girl is?" Seema asked.

Instead of answering her question, I looked straight at Aliya, and everyone followed my gaze, fixing their eyes on her.

"Is that the girl, Aliya?" Anika asked.

"Yes, I fought with them for Aliya," I admitted.

By then, Varun arrived with a tray full of food.

"Basically, you like her, then," Aadhi asked.

I remained silent, and my silence answered his question.

"So, you like her. There's no doubt about it," Anika chimed in.

"Did you tell her that you like her?" Seema asked.

"Not yet. It's too quick to express my feelings to her, and what will she think of me if I said that?" I wondered.

"That's right, it will be too quick to express your feelings to her. We need a plan to bring you and Aliya together," Seema suggested.

"Wait a minute, the principal told Aliya to help him with the syllabus, right?" Varun reminded.

"Yes, that's going to be a good opportunity for you, Rishab," Aadhi said.

"Oh, yes, I didn't think of that," I admitted.

"Don't miss a chance, Rishab," Seema added.

"I will give my best for that," I assured them.

After that, we had our lunch, and returned to our class. and our plan to bunk the class was cancelled because of the chapri gang. Karthik didn't know of my earlier fight with the chapri gang, and I decided it was better not to tell him about my fight with the chapri gang.

Our class for the day had ended, and now everyone was rushing to go home. Karthik had to leave for some reason, so he left earlier. I looked at Aliya, who was packing her bag to leave as well.

I made my way towards Aliya. She looked up at me while packing her bag.

"Ah... I began," but she interrupted me.

"Why did you fight with them again?" she asked.

"I didn't want to fight with them. They forced me to do it, and they even slapped Varun and irritated Seema. I had to step in," I explained.

"You've already made friends? That was quick."

I looked deep into her eyes. Our eyes met, and we held eye contact longer than before. Her eyes were gorgeous, and they had something that captivated me deep inside. I didn't know what it was, but it was building something deep inside me.

I felt my heart pounding in my chest. I had never felt anything like it before. It was like she could see right through me, into the very depths of my soul.

I didn't know what was happening between us, but I knew that it was real. And I knew that I wanted more.

If Seema hadn't interrupted us, I don't know how long we would have looked at each other.

"Hey, Rishab, are you daydreaming?" Her words snapped me back to reality.

And automatically, the eye contact disconnected.

Aliya stood up, preparing to leave.

"Aliya, we're planning to go to Marine Drive. Would you like to come?" Seema asked.

"Sorry, Seema, I can't come. I have some work to do back home," Aliya replied.

"Oh, okay. Then next time. Rishab, you're coming, right?" Seema turned to me.

"Ah!...yes." I said, hesitated.

"Bye, Aliya. Let's meet tomorrow," Seema said and left.

"Tomorrow morning, 7.30," Aliya reminded me.

"I know. Uh... Can you give me your number?" I said, hesitated.

"Why do you want my number?" she asked.

"If I have doubts in any subject, I need someone to help me clear them," I quickly made an excuse.

"You just joined the college today, and I'm taking your class. If you have any doubts, ask me when I teach you in the morning or evening," Aliya responded confidently.

"If in the future I have any doubts..."

"Then I'll give you my number in the future," she said with a smile.

She indirectly said No to my request.

"I need to go. Bye. Let's meet tomorrow morning," Aliya said and left.

Seema came to me as Aliya left, accompanied by the gang.

"Why are you both staring at each other like that?" Anika asked.

"You don't know that simple thing, you silly girl? It's called eye contact," Seema teased me.

"Shut up," I grumbled.

"Ah... look at him, he's getting angry."

"Stop bothering him," Aadhi said, taking my side.

"When did you guys plan to go to Marine Drive?" I asked, trying to change the topic.

"Sorry, we didn't tell you about it. We had planned it a week ago," Varun said.

"Oh!..."

"You're coming, right?" Seema asked.

"I don't have any work to do, so I'm totally in. Plus, this is my first visit to Marine Drive, so it's going to be exciting," I said.

"What are we waiting for? Let's go, then," Anika said.

All of us came out of the college, and Varun and Aadhi went to bring their bikes. In an instant, they returned with the bikes.

Seema hopped onto Aadhi's bike, and Anika settled on Varun's bike.

Come fast Rishab, Seema said. "Tripling," Varun added.

"I have my own bike," I said.

"You have your own bike?" Aadhi asked, surprised.

I nodded and left them to retrieve my bike. Everyone's eyes widened when they noticed my Yamaha R15.

"Wow... holy shit, you have a sports bike," Aadhi exclaimed excitedly.

Suddenly, Seema jumped from Aadhi's bike and quickly hopped onto my bike. Everyone burst into laughter.

Dear Rishi,
DAY-3

It's the third day of sharing my secrets with you. I hope you find them interesting. The thing is, we never really know what life and fate have in store for us in the future.

I don't know if it's a coincidence or if fate has a hand in it. The first time I met him was at the club, and he saved my life. The second time, we crossed paths unexpectedly at the mall. And today, on the third day, he joined the same college I attend. Damn, he's in the same class as I am. It's quite astonishing how our paths keep crossing.

This morning, Smrithi Ma'am was teaching our class. Unexpectedly, the principal walked into our class and had a conversation with her. Then, he turned to us and said, "Two new students have joined, and they will be studying in our class."

And finally, he called them inside the classroom. I couldn't believe my eyes when I saw that Rishab was studying in our class.

I tried to hide, but unfortunately, the principal called my name loudly and asked me to help Rishab catch up on the syllabus. I think Rishab was surprised to see me in the classroom.

And you won't believe what happened in the canteen in the afternoon. Rishab suddenly walked in, and his unexpected entrance surprised everyone in the canteen.

Then, the four people who had misbehaved with me in the club also entered the canteen. I wasn't sure what was going on, but I could tell that Rishab had confronted them, and that's why they were all after him.

One by one, they started attacking him, but he didn't back down. He fought them all and defeated them. It was the first time anyone had managed to defeat them. Everyone in the canteen was shocked by how this newcomer had defeated them.

Then, after the fight, his gaze landed on me. I felt nervous as he looked at me. I couldn't tear my eyes away from his captivating blue eyes. But I managed to look away, reminding myself that he already had a girlfriend.

And when our class ended, he came up to me. "Hey," he began, but I interrupted him midway, "Why did you fight with them again?" I asked directly.

"I didn't want to fight with them, but they forced me to. Plus, they slapped Varun and irritated Seema," he confessed.

"You already made friends, too quick," I added.

He didn't answer that question. Instead, he looked straight into my eyes. Our eyes met, this time for longer than before, and again, the same sensation built inside me. His captivating blue eyes were amazing. The more I saw them, the more I fell in love with them.

No matter how hard I tried to look away from him, I couldn't take my eyes off him. But thanks to Seema, she finally came to us, and he looked away from me. Seema asked me to join them as they were going to Marine Drive.

However, I declined because I knew Rishi would be going with them. I was afraid that if I stayed with him, I wouldn't be able to control my feelings and prevent myself from falling for him. That's why I said no to Seema.

And when Seema left, he asked for my number. My mind was screaming at me to give it to him, but I managed to control myself and didn't share my number with him.

So, that's what happened today... And, one more thing, please promise to keep everything we talked about just between us, okay?

"It's been 9:30 when I reached home. 'I'm back,' I said, entering the house.

'Where have you been?' my mother shouted at me.

'Sorry, Mom. Went out with friends,' I said.

'Where did you go?' she insisted, not letting go.

'Marine Drive,' I said.

'You went to Marine Drive?' Rishika said, coming out of her room.

'Yeah, it's a lovely beach,' I said, recalling my experience.

'Did you bring chocolates?' she asked.

Roshan was working on something with his laptop. When he heard Rishika asking about chocolates, he began, 'Are you still a kid, eating chocolates like children?' he said in a rough voice.

'Do you have any problem if she likes chocolates?' I raised my voice, defending my sis.

'Why are you both arguing? Just let it go,' Mom said.

"Did you bring it?" she whispered so that Roshan couldn't hear.

'Why would I bring chocolates?' I said, although I had brought her favorite Ferrero Rocher.

Her response was a pinch.

'Ouch! That hurts,' I grumbled.

'I hate you,' she said and rushed to her room. Mom and I burst into laughter."

'Go and take a bath,' she said. 'I will prepare dinner.'

I nodded and made my way upstairs to my room. Grabbing a towel, I entered the bathroom for a refreshing shower.

After the bath, I wrapped the towel around me and came out. My eyes widened as I noticed Rishika on the bed, holding the box of Ferrero Rocher.

"What are you doing in my room?" I blurted out.

"I came for this," she said, showing the box in her hand.

"Give it back to me," I said.

She shook her head. "If you gave me this before, when I asked; I would definitely give it to you, but now it's impossible!" she replied playfully and ran downstairs.

I changed into my regular night clothes and sank onto my bed, feeling the tiredness of the day. Just as I was getting comfortable, Rishika called my name.

"Rishi... Rishi!" Rishika called my name.

"Look what I have found," she said, holding her phone in one hand and chocolates in the other, her mouth full of Ferrero rocher. She came and sat on the edge of the bed.

I looked up at her, "What did you find?" I asked with curiosity.

With a mischievous grin, "I found Aliya's Facebook account!" she said, a triumphant smile on her face.

"Really? You found Aliya's Facebook account? Show me!" I urged eagerly.

She chuckled, "Ah...ah...ah... If you want to see, promise me you'll get another pack of Ferrero Rocher tomorrow."

"Okay, okay. Can you show me now?" I agreed.

"Look here," she said, handing me her phone.

As I scrolled through Aliya's profile, I was astonished. "You really found Aliya's Facebook account?" I said.

"Took me five hours of effort." she mentioned casually, popping another Ferrero Rocher into her mouth.

Without wasting any time, I searched for Aliya's ID on my phone and sent a friend request.

"I hope she accepts it," I said, a mix of excitement and anticipation in my voice.

"Don't forget your promise, you have to complete it," she reminded me with a playful smirk.

"What if I don't?" I teased, wanting to see her reaction.

She leaned in, a sly smile on her face. "I already thought of that. I have your FB account on my phone. If you don't keep your word, I'll spill all the naughty stuff to Aliya."

A wave of surprise washed over me, "How did you get my FB account?"

She shook her head, a secret smile playing on her lips. "I won't say. Let's just say it's my secret weapon for some friendly blackmail."

"That's not fair," I protested.

She chuckled, "Everything is fair in the game of blackmail, it's all in good fun," she said, laughing.

"This is the last time I'm promising to buy Ferrero Rocher. Next time, it won't happen," I declared confidently.

"Oh, so confident. Remember, overconfidence is not good," she responded with a playful smirk.

"Let's see how you'll blackmail me next time. I might change my account password. What will you do then?" I challenged.

"I've prepared for that too. I know you'll change your password, and I have a plan for it as well," she replied confidently.

"And what is it?" I insisted.

"I'll tell Dad that you went to the club that night, even though he prohibited you from going out with Karthik. I'll also spill the beans about the fight you had with those guys," she declared in one shot.

I couldn't help but wonder how she always seemed to be a step ahead in this playful game of sibling banter. I was left speechless, realizing that she had a counter-move for every step I took.

"No... no... please don't reveal it to Dad. If he finds out, he'll kill me," I pleaded.

"Then you have to do what I say," she stated matter-of-factly.

"Huff... fine," I reluctantly agreed.

"From today on, I am your queen. Now kneel down before your queen," she declared.

"Kneel down to you? That's never going to happen," I retorted.

"Dad..." she screamed aloud.

"Shh... ok, ok, I will," I said quickly, realizing the gravity of the situation, and reluctantly kneeled down before her.

"That's my boy," she said triumphantly and left.

"Why does this happen to me every time?" I muttered to myself as she walked away, leaving behind the sound of her laughter.

The next day I woke up early in the morning; the clock was ticking at 6:30 AM. After washing my face, I headed downstairs. Dad was already there, engrossed in the morning newspaper.

"Good morning, Dad," I greeted.

"Ah, good morning. You woke up early," he observed.

"Yeah, I have a special class," I explained.

"I forgot to ask, how's your new college?" he inquired.

"Good," I replied.

"You made new friends, right?" he continued.

"Yeah, and yesterday I went out with them," I shared.

"Really?" he raised an eyebrow.

I nodded, confirming the little adventure from the day before.

Then Mom arrived, holding two cups of coffee, and placed them on the table in front of us. I gratefully took one of the cups.

"Are you okay? You woke up early," Mom asked, a hint of surprise in her voice.

"I'm fine, Mom," I reassured her. "I have a special class."

"A class this early?" she questioned.

"Yeah, I'm two months late, and I need to catch up on the syllabus," I explained.

"I should make breakfast quickly," she said and headed into the kitchen.

"Where is Rishika?" I asked Dad.

"Still sleeping, I think," he replied, glancing in the direction of Rishika's room.

An evil plan crept into my mind. I grabbed a vessel filled with cold water and stealthily entered her room. With a mischievous grin, I spilled it onto her face.

Suddenly, she jolted awake, clearly startled and confused. "Have you lost your mind? What on earth was that for?" she erupted in fury.

"I was just waking you up," I innocently replied.

"Is that the way of waking someone?" she asked angrily.

"I thought it was a brilliant idea to wake you up," I defended with a smile.

"Why are you irritating me?" she questioned, clearly annoyed.

"Because I love to irritate you," I admitted with a mischievous grin.

"Fine, you're done. I will definitely take revenge for this," she declared and headed toward the bathroom, leaving me chuckling at the success of my early morning prank.

I headed back to my room, taking a quick shower and selecting an outfit for the day. Once dressed, I descended the stairs to find the dining area ready, breakfast neatly laid out. I took a seat opposite to Dad, and we had a strict rule not to speak while eating.

After finishing breakfast, I slung my bag over my shoulder, glancing at the clock - 7:15 AM. Grabbing my bike keys, I made my way toward the exit.

"Don't forget to complete your promise," I heard Rishika's voice behind me.

I turned, a smirk playing on her lips. "Promise? Oh, you mean the Ferrero Rocher pact."

She nodded, the mischievous glint in her eyes. "Exactly. Don't think I'll forget."

I chuckled, giving her a casual salute before heading out, the morning sun casting a golden hue over the day.

A few minutes into the drive, and I arrived at the college. Surprisingly, not a single person was in sight. I must have come too early, I thought. Parking my bike,

I went to the backyard of the college. It was deserted; not a soul in sight. As I took a few steps ahead, I found Aliya sitting on a bench under a tree.

"Good morning," I greeted as I reached her.

"You're ten minutes late," she pointed out.

"Sorry, I tried my best to reach on time," I apologized.

"Anyway, take a seat," she said, tapping on the bench. I sat down, leaving only a few inches of gap between us.

"So, tell me, what's your favorite subject?" she asked.

"You"

"What?!" she exclaimed.

"You know what, I don't have any favorite subject," I quickly corrected.

"Which subject do you want to study first?" she inquired.

"How to fall for you," I whispered.

"Did you say something?"

"Anything," I replied.

"What about statistics?" she suggested.

"Statistics? No, I hate it. Perhaps we can go with another subject."

"Then it is statistics," she declared with certainty.

"Oh, no..."

"Do you know what statistics is?" she began, taking on a teacher-like tone. I shook my head.

"Let me explain," she said. "Statistics is a bunch of mathematics and a scientific method that involves collecting, analyzing, interpreting, and organizing data." Her words floated around me, but it was hard to focus on the subject with her sitting beside me.

The cool morning breeze made her hair flow, and strands of it washed over my face. Her hair felt soft like fabric, distracting me from the complexities of statistics.

I was lost, my eyes fixated on her, unable to look away. No matter how hard I tried, I couldn't break free from the spell she unknowingly cast.

"Hey... hey, Rishi!" she tapped my shoulders, snapping me back to reality.

"Are you daydreaming? Where are you, Rishab?"

"I am right here in front of you," I replied.

"No, you're not. You were here, but your mind is somewhere else."

"Sorry, it won't happen next time," I assured her.

"Don't let your mind wander. So, where were we? Ah, got it. Now, you have to study these matters:

. Mathematics complexity

. Data analyzing

. Hypothesis testing

. Multivariate analyzing

. Statistical software

Did you get my point?" she asked.

I nodded, though I didn't exactly know what those terms meant. The complexities of statistics seemed to blur in the background as her words and the gentle breeze created a unique melody, creating a special moment, no matter how confusing the terms were.

I lost track of time, still captivated by her presence. She glanced at her watch, breaking the spell.

"Oh, it's already 8:30 AM. Okay, that's enough for today," she said.

"Thank God," I let out a sigh of relief.

"I only taught you for forty-five minutes, and you're acting like I taught you for two hours," she remarked.

"I hate statistics. If I open a statistics textbook for five minutes, it feels like an hour," I complained.

She laughed at my remark. "Why are you laughing? I'm not joking," I said.

Her laughter made her even more beautiful. She was already beautiful in her normal form, but when she smiled, she became even more elegant. like a crescent moon lighting up the night. I found myself enchanted by her smile.

"Why are you looking at me like that?" she asked, noticing my stare.

I shook my head, unable to explain why. It was like I was watching my soulmate. I blurted out without thinking.

Her cheeks turned a shade of red, a sudden flush of embarrassment. Without uttering a single word, she hastily got up and left the place, leaving me there with a perplexed expression.

"What have you just done, you jerk?" Now regret it, my mind scolded me.

Feeling disappointed, I stood up from the bench and walked towards the classroom. My eyes scanned the classroom for Aliya, but she was nowhere to be seen. Feeling disoriented, I sat at my desk, unsure of what to do next. Did I hurt her by saying that?

Running my hand through my hair, I pulled out my mobile and called Seema. On the fourth ring, she answered the call.

"Hey Seema," I began, but she cut me off midway.

"Why are you calling me at this time?" she asked first.

"Something happened," I said.

"Is everything okay?" she asked tensely.

"Where are you right now?" I inquired.

"En route to college," she replied.

"Okay, then come fast."

"Is everything okay? Where were you?" she asked.

"Everything's fine. I am in college. Can you come fast?"

"Okay, I will be there in ten minutes," she said and hung up.

Now, slowly, the corridor started to crowd with students, my eyes fixed on the corridor, searching for Seema's appearance. Each passing moment made my heart race like a bullet train.

Finally, Seema came running into the class and approached me. "Rishab, what happened?" she asked, breathing heavily, her voice filled with tension. I narrated the whole incident.

"This is why you called me? Oh, yaar, I thought something happened to you."

"Didn't you get it? Aliya left me there, and her face turned red with rage," I blurted.

"Why are you being so stubborn? She left you not because of anger; she left because of shyness, hearing you call her your soulmate.

Do you really think that she left me because of shyness?" I asked, surprised.

"If you don't trust me, let's wait for a few more minutes. When Aliya comes, let's see whether she is angry or not," Seema suggested.

"It's a good idea. Okay, then let's wait for Aliya," I said.

I locked my eyes on the class entrance, hoping Aliya would arrive soon. Finally, my waiting came to an end as Aliya walked into the classroom.

"Look, she is not angry or upset," Seema said as Aliya entered the classroom. I let out a sigh of relief upon hearing that she wasn't upset about what I had said.

"So, Mr. Fighter, do you agree now?" Seema asked.

"Can you do me a favour?" I asked.

"Now, what do you want to know? Anyway, tell me what I need to do."

"Can you talk to Aliya?" I requested.

"This is the last time I am doing you such things. Next time, you have to do it," she said.

"Done," I agreed instantly.

Seema stood up and went to Aliya. They spoke, and I didn't know what they talked about, but Aliya was smiling as she conversed with Seema. A wave of relief washed over my entire body. Thank God, she's not angry with me.

By then, Karthik arrived. "You came earlier," he said, sitting beside me.

"Yeah, Aliya took my classes a little bit earlier," I explained.

"Oh, yaar, you are so lucky she is teaching you. Does she have a boyfriend?" he asked.

"I don't know yet, still figuring it out," I replied.

"What if she had a boyfriend?" Karthik asked.

"Aliya is single," Seema said, coming to us.

"See, fate had already decided that I will be her soulmate," I said with a grin on my face. By then, the teacher entered the class, and the class continued.

I was waiting for Aliya in the backyard of the school, the same place where she took my class in the morning. The evening sun rays hit my face directly, and I slid from the bench, seeking refuge in the shadows.

Unlike other places, this spot was quite different. My eyes searched for Aliya's appearance, and as she neared, my mind raced, thinking about how to start the conversation after what happened in the morning.

"Sorry for the delay," she said as she reached out to me.

"It's okay. You waited for me in the morning, and I waited for you now," I replied, smiling.

I slid from the bench and gave her space to sit. She smiled and sat on the bench a few inches away, her perfume lingering in the air.

"Can we go with statistics, or do you want to change the subject?" she asked.

"Let's complete statistics first, then move on to the next subject," I suggested.

"Good. Let's start then," she said, taking out the book from her bag, and I did the same.

"Where did we stop this morning?" she asked, trying to remember.

"Mathematical complexity," I said.

"Ah, right. Do you know what mathematical complexity is?" she asked, looking at me.

I shook my head.

"Okay, let me explain it. Listen intently," she began, turning her tone teacher-like. She was engrossed in taking the class, and I found myself falling in love with each passing moment.

Her hair flowed in the evening breeze, caressing my face. It was as soft as fabric. The surroundings faded away, and I lost track of time, completely absorbed in her words and presence. The gentle breeze carried her voice, and for a while, the only thing that existed was the world we created in that moment. When she eventually wrapped up the class, I was startled, realizing that I didn't even know how the time had passed. Aliya's smile brought me back to the present.

"Enough for today. Let's continue tomorrow," she said as she closed the book and tucked it inside her bag.

The sun was setting behind the horizon. I opened my mobile and saw several missed calls from Rishika, reminding me that I needed to buy her chocolates. I tucked the mobile inside my pocket.

"Hey, Aliya... ah... I am sorry for what I said in the morning," I apologized.

"Huh... it's okay," she said, smiling. "I shouldn't have left you without saying anything."

"So you didn't feel angry about what I said in the morning?" I asked.

"No," she said, smiling again.

"Then why did you leave me all of a sudden? Is it because I called you my soulmate?"

Again, her face reddened. Was she angry, or was she blushing? Damn, understanding these girls is more difficult than learning coding.

After a pause, she spoke, "I think I should leave; it's getting late." She said and started walking without waiting for my response.

I watched her as she walked away, but then she suddenly stopped walking. Wondering why, I soon spotted Vikram and his men - that explained why she had stopped. They surrounded her.

"I will make them pay if they even touch her," I cursed under my breath. My fists clenched tight as I made my way towards Aliya.

"You didn't pay for what you did at the club. No one was here. Now it's the right time to take back revenge," I heard Vikram's voice.

Aliya was trembling with fear, "Please leave me." I heard her pleading with them for mercy.

"I think you should keep an eye on the surroundings before abusing her," I said sternly.

"Huh... where did you come from?" You guys didn't tell me he is here. Vikram yelled at his men.

"Leave her, or I won't regret to do what I don't want to do now," I said sternly.

"Bhai let's get out of here" Rahul said, fear evident in his voice, Yeah let's leave the place Arjun added, And all of them pulled Vikram's hand and went aside,

Aliya rushed towards me and took refuge behind me. As she held my arm tightly, memories of the day I first helped her at the club flooded back.

And one more thing "Don't even dare in your wildest dream to irritate her."

Vikram's eyes burned with rage. "It's not over Rishab. We will take revenge for what you have done to us," Vikram blurted behind us as we left the place.

When we reached the college entrance. I said, "I will drop you home,"

"Thanks, but I can go home," she said.

"And what if they come back?" I asked cautiously. She fell silent, contemplating my words. I shrugged.

"It's already 7 PM. What will you say at home if you get late?"

"I have an excuse for that too," I said confidently.

"But..." she started to protest.

"No 'Buts.' I will drop you home," I asserted, my voice firm with determination, and I headed off to retrieve my bike.

"When I returned to her, she seemed kind of astonished.

'You have a sports bike,' she said, surprised.

I smiled at her and replied, 'Come, sit.'

She climbed on, holding my shoulder. Her touch sent a current shock through my entire body. As she settled on the pillion, she removed her hand from my shoulder.

'Let's go,' she said, and I accelerated. 'Where do you live?' I asked her while navigating through the road.

'Govind Nagar,' she replied.

I accelerated the bike, and after a few minutes, we reached Govind Nagar. 'Take a right from here,' she instructed, and I drove the bike as she told.

'Stop... stop...' she said suddenly.

I pulled the brake, and the bike came to a halt.

'I live here,' she said, stepping out of the bike. I looked around—it was a small, cozy house.

'You live here alone?' I asked.

'Ah, yeah,' she said, facing me. 'And your parents?' I inquired.

"They died in a car accident," she confessed, her words laden with sorrow and loss.

'Oh... sorry to hear that.'

"Thank you, Rishab. Once again, you saved my life,"

I muttered to myself, "A girl who can't even give her number to a friend... why should I even listen to her?" I turned my gaze away from her,

'Give me your mobile,' she said.

'Why do you want my mobile?' I asked, surprised.

'Just give it,' she insisted.

I took out my mobile and gave it to her. She typed something in it and returned it.

'Here,' she said, handing me the mobile.

I looked at the screen. To my surprise, she had typed her number into my phone. Instantly, I saved it.

'Good night,' she said and entered her house. I couldn't tear my eyes away from her, captivated by her presence. Just before the door closed, she turned and looked back at me, a silent exchange that held the promise of something yet to unfold.

Again, I was late when I reached my home, "Why are you late today?" my mom questioned as I stepped through the front door, her eyes filled with curiosity. "Did you go out again?"

I offered a quick explanation, tossing my bag onto the couch. "Special class, Mom," I replied, trying to sound casual.

My dad, seated with his laptop nearby, looked up at me with a glimmer of interest in his eyes. "How did it go?" he inquired.

In that moment, the events of the evening flooded my mind. I paused, for a moment before answering, "Good."

Dear Rishi,
DAY-4

It's day four of sharing my experiences with you, and today has been a different and, I dare say, the happiest and the scariest day of my life. Describing it is a bit challenging, but I'll do my best to convey what I went through.

I know you're curious to hear all about it, and I'm excited to tell you. But, promise me, this will stay between you and me.

Today, I went to college early in the morning to take a special class for Rishab. We found a quiet spot in the backyard, sitting under a tree. With just a few inches between us, I started the class.

After about half an hour, I noticed Rishab sighing in relief. "Why are you acting like I've lectured for two hours?" I teased.

He confessed, "I hate statistics. If I open the textbook for five minutes, it feels like an hour." His voice took on a childish tone, and I couldn't help but smile.

As I continued, he started watching me with full attention. "Why are you looking at me like that?" I asked.

He shook his head and said, "I don't know why, but it's like watching my soulmate."

"Oh my God, did he just say that I'm his soulmate?" My cheeks flushed with embarrassment, and I couldn't stand there after hearing his confession. I grabbed my bag and left without saying another word to him.

I couldn't understand why I left so abruptly. It was the first time someone had called me their soulmate, and it made me happy. But the reality struck hard - Rishab was already committed to someone else.

Now, accepting the truth, I felt a pang of disappointment washed over me leaving me grappling with conflicting feelings.

Then, as I entered the classroom, Seema approached me – a surprise in itself. Our conversation started casually, but in an instant, her tone shifted to seriousness.

"Did Rishab say anything unusual or weird to you?" she asked abruptly.

I was taken aback. "What... no, he didn't say anything weird," I replied. "Why do you ask?"

Seema explained, "He thinks you're angry with him for something. He mentioned that you left him abruptly."

Now it made sense. Rishab must have sent her to find out why I left so suddenly. I decided to be direct. "Did Rishab send you?" I asked.

Seema hesitated for a moment before confirming, "Well, yes. Fine, let me tell you why he sent me. Did you leave him because he called you his soulmate?" she inquired.

I didn't know what to say. "Yeah..."

Seema continued, "Now listen, he thinks you left him angrily, and he also said that your face turned red when you left. But I know you didn't leave because of anger. Did you?"

I admitted, "You see, it's the first time someone called me like that, and I didn't know how to react, so I left."

"Oh yaar, you are a fool! Are you mad? Look at him, he is so handsome, plus he is interested in you. Don't miss the chance," Seema exclaimed, surprising me with her boldness. It was the first time she spoke like that.

I stammered, "I don't know what to do."

She reassured me, "You don't have to do anything; he will do everything."

"But he's committed; he already has a girlfriend," I pointed out.

"Does he really? Think about it," Seema said and left, leaving me utterly bewildered.

"Do you think he doesn't have a girlfriend? No, he does have one. I saw her with my own eyes. When we met at the mall, I saw his girlfriend standing beside him. Plus, she told me herself that she is Rishab's girlfriend.

It's a false hope to think he is single. I think I am going off track. Let me tell you what happened in the evening after taking a special class for Rishab.

"Hey, Aliya, uh, I am sorry for what I had said in the morning," Rishab apologised.

"It's okay," I said. "It's my fault too. I shouldn't have left you abruptly."

"So, you are not angry for what I had said?" he asked.

"Of course not," I said.

"Then why did you leave me all of a sudden? Is it because I called you my soulmate?" he asked again, using that word that made my cheeks burn.

Though I didn't say anything, I fell silent, and after a pause, I said, "I better leave; it's getting late," and started walking.

I don't know why, but my mind was fixated on his words — soulmate. Does he really mean what he said, or is he saying it because I remind him of his girlfriend?

"Where are you going, darling?" Vikram's voice snapped me back to reality. I stopped midway, wondering where I was, and before I could do anything, the four of them surrounded me. I was trapped, unable to do anything.

"That day, Rishab saved you. What will you do now?" Rahul said.

"You will pay for slapping me, you bloody bitch!" Vikram roared.

"Please, leave me alone," I said, trembling.

"I think you should keep an eye on the surroundings before bothering her," I heard Rishab's voice from behind. Suddenly, relief washed over me.

"Where did you come from?" Vikram barked.

"Leave her," Rishab said. Then Rahul, Arjun, and Raj pulled Vikram's hand and stepped aside, saying, "Let's go, bhai, or he will tear us apart."

Quickly, I ran towards Rishab and took refuge behind him, holding his shoulder tightly, my whole-body trembling with fear.

"Come on, let's go," he said, and we both walked past them.

"It's not over; we will take revenge," I heard Vikram's voice behind us as we walked to the college entrance.

"I will drop you home," he said as we stood face to face in the entrance.

"Thanks, but I can manage," I said, trying to sound normal.

"And what if they come back?" he said instantly. I fell silent hearing that. I think he noticed my silence and added, "I'll take it as a yes." He went to the parking area nearby, and when he returned, I was shocked to see he came back with a sport bike.

"Come, sit," he said, and I hopped on the back seat. Within minutes, we reached my home. When I stepped down from the bike, he looked around and asked, "You live here alone?"

"Yeah," I said.

"And your parents?" he asked.

"They died in an accident," I said in a low voice.

"Oh... sorry to hear that," he replied.

I ignored that and said, "Thank you, Rishab. You saved me again," looking into his blue eyes.

"Why should I accept your thanks when you can't give your number?" he said, looking away. I couldn't control my emotions anymore and said, "Give me your mobile."

"Why do you want my mobile?" he asked, somewhat surprised.

"Just give it," I insisted. He handed me his mobile, and I typed my number on it, handing it back to him. He looked at the screen perplexed.

"Good night," I said and entered the house. Before I closed the door, I took a quick glance at him, his eyes fixated on me.

So, this is what happened today. Each day, no matter how hard I tried to stay away from him, he got too close, and each time, he was there for me when those four tried to abuse me. I don't know what to do. I think I'm going to fall for him, but I don't want to. Knowing he already has a girlfriend, what should I do? Every day when I see him, my heart starts to pound like a thundering drum, and with each passing moment, my feelings for him grow stronger and stronger.

Does he really like me, or does he just want a one-night stand like the others did when they saw a girl? I don't know about that, but one thing is clear: I am really going to fall for him.

And now that I gave him my number, what will happen next? Damn, why can't I keep my mind from thinking about him? Is it wrong to fall for someone who is already committed to someone else? Oh, God, why didn't I meet him before his girlfriend did?

Let's hope I don't fall for him. I will try my best. Anyway, I think it's enough for today. See you next time. Until then, pray for me not to love him. Okay, bye. Good night.

I glanced at the clock; it was ticking at half-past nine. I didn't even realize how quickly time had passed. My stomach grumbled, reminding me of my hunger. I took out my mobile and ordered food from the Just Eat app, an online food delivery service. The app promised that the food would arrive within twenty minutes.

I tossed my mobile onto the bed and grabbed a towel, heading to the bathroom for a shower. The cold water flowed over my body, sending shivers down my spine. After the refreshing bath, I wrapped the towel around me, emerged from the bathroom, and slipped into my usual nightgown. Sinking onto the bed, I awaited the arrival of my ordered food.

Automatically, my thoughts drifted to Rishab. What is he doing now? Is he thinking of me like I am? I took my mobile and opened WhatsApp. I saw that Rishab was online. Why the hell did I check that? I looked at his display picture; he had put a girl's photo as his DP–the very same girl I met at the mall with Rishab, his girlfriend.

"Hi," it was a message from Rishab. My heart raced fast; did he get to know that I was thinking of him?

"Hello," I replied back, my heart beating fast.

"What are you doing?" he messaged.

"Thinking of you," I wanted to tell, but instead, I typed, "Nothing special, just waiting for my dinner to arrive," I said.

"You order food from outside?" he asked.

"Yeah," I said,

"You don't know how to cook?" he inquired.

"Of course, I can, but today my mood is off since what had happened, and it's a bad evening," I replied.

"I don't think so, to me, it's the best evening of all time," he replied.

"What?! Are you insane? They almost caught me, and you are saying it's the best evening," I shot back.

"I think I am insane. I have got your number, though," he said along with a smile emoji.

"What does that mean? Is he flirting with me?" I thought.

"Don't overthink; I just gave it because you helped me, that's it," I said.

"Believe me, I am not overthinking it; I am just beyond happy that you gave me your number.

Anyway, what are you doing?" I asked.

"I am now chatting with you," he said.

"Ha ha ha, a bad joke," I replied.

"Can I ask you one question?" he asked.

"Go on," I said.

"If I wasn't there when they surrounded you, what would you have done then?"

"Hello, mister, you are not the only one who knows fighting; I know too," I lied.

"Is that so? Then why did you take refuge behind me and hold my shoulder tightly?" he questioned.

Suddenly, I heard someone knocking on the door.

"One sec," I said to Rishab and went to the hall and opened the door. It was the food delivery man.

"Your delivery, ma'am," he said and handed me the bag. I paid him and came inside, shutting the door. I took my mobile and went to the dining table, sitting on a chair. I looked at the screen.

"What happened?" he messaged.

"Food delivery," I said.

"Oh! I thought something happened."

"What?"

"I thought Pumpkin Face and his men came to you."

"That's odd," I said.

"It is possible. Think, what will you do if they really come?"

"Don't scare me like that," I replied along with a scary emoji.

"Sorry, just kidding," he said.

"I will tackle you tomorrow morning. Be on time and no excuses," I said.

"I won't come to college tomorrow," he said.

"Why?"

"Tomorrow is Sunday," he said along with a laughter emoji.

"Oh, I forgot about that."

"Dad is calling, gotta go. Bye, good night and sweet dreams," he said along with several hug and *zzz* emoji.

"Why did he send that hug emoji and in what context?" I thought and started eating.

Three weeks had passed since I joined the college, and every day it felt like my feelings for Aliya were growing stronger and stronger. We became more closer than before, especially during the classes she taught me.

Initially, she strongly opposed me looking at her, but as time passed, she no longer resisted. Instead, she smiled and playfully punched me on the head. We started spending more time together, talking and enjoying each other's company.

One day, I decided to ask her directly, "Do you have a boyfriend?" To my surprise, she replied with a simple "No." This revelation sparked a new level of curiosity and excitement within me.

However, there was a twist. Aliya seemed to think that I had a girlfriend. She teased me every day about this imaginary girlfriend. I wanted to clarify and tell her the truth, but I couldn't find the right opportunity. Instead, I decided to play along a bit and. Sometimes, I would flirt with her, and in response, she would blush. The connection between us was growing, and I was enjoying every moment of it.

Aliya was conducting my class in the evening, and naturally, my attention was fixated on her rather than the subject matter.

"Can you stop staring at me like that and try to focus on the class?" she said, breaking my trance.

"Trust me, I am trying my best to focus on the class, but I can't. Your beautiful face has captured my attention. I think I'm attracted to you," I replied in a flirtatious voice.

"Stop flirting with me," she scolded, delivering a playful punch to my head. "If your girlfriend finds out what you're doing, she will not only kill you but also me."

"Trust me, she won't," I said confidently.

"Stop it, that's enough for today. Let's leave," she declared, standing up to go.

I rose too, agreeing, "Okay, let's go."

As we walked in silence, only a few inches separated us. My hand brushed against hers, and a sudden urge to hold her hand gripped me. A voice in my head encouraged, "Hold her hand." For a moment, my hands trembled as I neared them to hers. She sensed the intention and subtly moved an inch away from me.

"We've reached the college entrance. I'll drop you," I said.

"Thanks, but I can go myself," she replied.

"Oh, okay then. See you tomorrow," I said and went to the parking area to fetch my bike. I knew she wanted to come with me, and it wasn't the first time she had said something like that.

I hopped onto my bike, started the ignition, and rode it outside the college gate. I glanced at Aliya in the mirror, and she was watching me. I stopped the bike and said, "Are you coming or not? I'm leaving." Before I could finish my sentence, she had already sat on the back seat.

"Wow, that was fast!" I exclaimed, accelerating the bike.

At first, she didn't hold onto my shoulder; instead, she gripped the rod attached to the back seat. I drove a bit faster, hoping she would hold my shoulder, but she didn't. I raced the accelerator even faster.

"Go slow, Rishab!" she screamed in my ear. Before I could slow down, we approached a speed breaker. I drove the bike over it, making us jump from our seats.

"Sorry, I didn't notice that," I apologized. Then it struck me—Aliya was holding onto my waist tightly. I felt the warmth of her body against mine, and she rested her head on my shoulder.

I didn't say anything after that; I wanted to savour the moment. I slowed the bike, not wanting to reach her house too soon. It was the first time she was holding me so tightly. Glancing at her through the mirror, she had closed her eyes, her warm breath sending shivers down my spine. I slowed the bike even further, relishing the sensation.

After what seemed like an eternity, I stopped the bike in front of her house. When she didn't immediately step down, I looked at her. Her eyes were closed, and I thought she might have fallen asleep.

"Aliya," I gently called her name. Suddenly, she sprang up and stepped down quickly.

"Sorry, I didn't mean to..." she started, but I interrupted her, "It's alright. It felt good, though," I said, making her blush.

"Go home or you'll get late," she said.

"You go first," I insisted.

"I'm not ten kilometres away from my home. You go home," she insisted.

"No, you go inside, and then I'll go," I said.

"You're always this type," she asked.

"What type?" I asked, puzzled.

"Nothing," she said, smiling, and went inside her house. She looked back at me before closing the door. I smiled and drove to my home.

Dear Rishi
DAY-24

Time is like a bullet train, and it has been three weeks since I started taking classes for Rishab. With each passing moment, I feel our connection growing stronger, and I believe he senses it too.

Now, we've begun spending more time together, and our bond is becoming even more profound.

Today, when he was dropping me home on his bike, he drove fast. I told him to go slow, but he didn't listen. Suddenly, a speed breaker appeared in our way. He sped over it, causing both of us to jump from our seats. I was scared at that moment and quickly held onto him from behind, tightly.

It felt so good to hold someone who is most dearest to you. I didn't let go of him as if someone might steal him away. I rested my head on his shoulder, feeling the warmth and the wonderful connection between us.

I wanted to express my feelings for him, but I couldn't. He already has a girlfriend. Why can't she break up with him, so I could be with him? I think I am jealous of his girlfriend because she has Rishab. He is so kind and caring about everyone. Every girl wants to be with him.

Day by day, my suspicions about Rishab's relationship status grew. Despite having a girlfriend, he continued to spend an increasing amount of time with me. Strangely, I hadn't noticed any calls or messages from his girlfriend when I was around. And whenever he's on the phone, if I ask who he's talking to, his answer is always the same – his sister.

Could it be that he and his girlfriend broke up? The thought brought a mix of emotions – hope and confusion. Hope, because it might mean he's available, and confusion, as I couldn't understand why he would spend so much time with me if he was already committed.

Does he really have a girlfriend, or is he just avoiding the topic? Is he genuinely interested in me, or am I misinterpreting his actions?

I'll share more of my thoughts with you soon. Until then, good night.

"I was watching the latest episode of G.O.T Lost in the intense drama. I was completely absorbed as Daenerys Targaryen commanded "Dracarys," her dragon unleashed its fiery wrath upon King's Landing. The tension in the scene held me captive, my attention fixated on the unfolding spectacle.

Suddenly, Rishika burst into the room, her hurried steps echoing against the walls. She rushed over to where I sat, her presence catching me off guard amidst the intense moment of the show.

"Rishab, did you hear? There's a new mall opening today. Come on, let's go check it out," Rishika exclaimed, breaking my concentration from the intense scenes unfolding on the screen.

Without tearing my gaze away from the television, I responded, "I don't really feel like going. Why don't you go with Roshan?"

"What? You don't want to come?" Rishika's voice carried a hint of disappointment. "I thought Aliya mentioned you were going. Now I'll have to go alone," she muttered to herself, clearly puzzled by my reluctance.

"Aliya's going too?" I inquired, my curiosity piqued.

"Yeah, she's the one who told me about it," Rishika confirmed.

"Aliya told you?" My interest heightened as I processed this new information, wondering why Aliya hadn't mentioned it to me directly.

"Yep, anyway, I'm getting late. I have to head out," Rishika said, already making her way to the door.

"Wait, wait. I'll come too," I called out, suddenly changing my mind. I quickly rose from my seat, determined not to miss out, though my true motive was to see Aliya rather than explore the mall.

"You said you didn't want to come," Rishika pointed out, surprised by my sudden change of heart.

"Well, I've changed my mind," I replied with a hint of hesitation, masking my true intentions.

"Alright, then I'll wait outside. Come quickly," she urged before heading downstairs.

With a swift motion, I adjusted my attire and hair before heading downstairs to meet Rishika. "Let's go," I said as I reached her, ready to embark on this unexpected adventure. As I climbed onto my bike, Rishika settled in behind me, and with a roar, we set off towards the mall.

I revved the engine, propelling us towards the mall. With Rishika directing me, we navigated the streets until we arrived at our destination, half an hour later.

As we reached the mall's entrance, Rishika turned to me with a smile. "You know, I actually tricked you about Aliya coming," she confessed, her eyes twinkling mischievously.

"What? Aliya isn't coming?" I asked, feeling a sudden pang of disappointment.

"Yeah, sorry. I just wanted to make sure you came along. I know you like her, so I thought it would be a good way to convince you,"

My heart sank at the realization that Aliya wouldn't be here. The excitement I felt about exploring the mall with her vanished in an instant. Despite the dazzling decorations and lights, the whole atmosphere seemed to dim with my dashed hopes.

Rishika led me on a whirlwind tour of the mall, darting from one shop to another with boundless energy. We explored every nook and cranny, not skipping a single cozy-looking shop along the way. With each step, my legs grew heavier, the ache in my feet a constant reminder of our marathon journey through the bustling corridors.

As we reached the far end of the floor, my weary eyes caught sight of the theatre. The idea of sinking into a comfortable seat and losing myself in a movie sounded like a welcome respite from the fatigue.

"I'm going to watch a movie. Do you want to come?" I asked Rishika, hoping for some company to ease the fatigue.

But she declined with a wave of her hand. "Nah. You go ahead. I'll take this chance to browse for some new dresses," she replied, her eyes already scanning the nearby stores for fashion finds.

"Alright then. I'll call you after the movie," I said, giving her a nod before making my way towards the theatre, grateful for the chance to rest my tired legs and immerse myself in a different world for a while.

I approached the ticket counter and exchanged some cash for a ticket. The movie currently playing was a horror flick called "Dark Rising."

Stepping into the theatre, I found a seat near the middle, about the fourth row from the front. As the lights dimmed and the screen flickered to life, the movie began.

However, about half an hour into the film, I realized it was a poor choice. The storyline felt forced, the jump scares were predictable, and overall, it was just plain awful. I couldn't understand why the theatre manager didn't opt for something more captivating, like a series or movie similar to "Game of Thrones."

Disappointed, I left the theatre and headed back into the mall, pondering the strange choices in entertainment.

I pulled out my phone and dialled Rishika's number, the anticipation building with each ring until she finally answered on the fourth.

"Hey, where are you?" I inquired eagerly.

"Did the movie finish early? It's only been half an hour," she replied, sounding surprised by my call.

I chuckled, "The movie was so boring that I couldn't stand it anymore. So, I decided to bail. Anyway, where are you now?"

"Actually, we're heading to the food court," she replied, her excitement palpable even through the phone.

"We?" I echoed, immediately intrigued. "Wait, is someone else with you?"

"Well, yeah..." she trailed off,

"And who is it?" I pressed, unable to contain my curiosity.

"Come and see for yourself," she teased, then abruptly ended the call, leaving me with a sense of mystery lingering in the air.

I stared at my phone, pondering who could possibly be joining her. With a mix of excitement and curiosity, I decided to head to the food court to find out for myself.

Putting my swirling thoughts aside, I focused on making my way to the food court. Having explored every inch of the mall earlier with Rishika, I had a clear idea of where to find the food court. With swift strides, I navigated through the bustling corridors until I arrived at the entrance of the food court.

"Hey, Rishab," and As I heard Rishika's voice behind me, I turned around and was taken aback to see not just her, but also Aliya and Lily standing there. Aliya greeted me with a broad smile,

"Hi, Rishab," Aliya greeted with a broad smile, her presence catching me off guard. She looked stunning in her flowing maxi dress with denim jacket.

"Hi," I managed to reply, my astonishment evident. "How come you're here?" I asked, trying to make sense of the unexpected encounter.

"Lily called me to come here, and then we ran into Rishika," Aliya explained, still beaming.

Turning to Lily, I greeted her, "Hey, Lily, it's been a while since our first encounter."

"Yeah, I've been pretty busy lately," Lily replied.

As I glanced at Aliya, I noticed her smiling at me, her gaze fixed on mine. Rishika, too, seemed to notice Aliya's attention.

"Okay, enough staring for now. Let's head inside and grab something to eat. I'm starving," Rishika declared, breaking the moment, and she led the way into the food court.

With exchanged smiles, then followed Rishika inside, ready to satisfy our hunger.

The food court was bustling with people, and after a bit of searching, we managed to find a free table at the far end.

"I can't seem to find any waiters around," I remarked, scanning the area for service.

"Waiters? Forget about them. If we want anything, we have to go and get it ourselves. Look, there are plenty of food shops over there," Lily pointed out, gesturing towards the various food outlets.

"Did you guys notice that every dress shop has a fifty percent off sale?" Rishika observed.

"Yeah, I noticed. I'm actually thinking of buying some new dresses," Aliya chimed in.

"I was thinking the same thing," Rishika added, confirming my suspicions.

Realizing where this was headed, I decided to take charge. "Guys, I'll go and fetch some food," I announced, excusing myself from the conversation.

Heading straight to a nearby McDonald's, I placed our order for two pizzas, four burgers with extra cheese, four Pepsi drinks, and a full grilled chicken. After paying the bill, I was handed a piece of paper with our order typed on it.

"Come back after ten minutes," the staff informed me. I settled onto a chair in front of the shop, scrolling through Instagram reels to pass the time. After what felt like an eternity, but was likely just ten minutes, I retrieved our order in a large tray and made my way back to the table. Rishika's eyes lit up at the sight of the food.

Placing the tray on the table, I took a seat opposite Aliya. "Thank you for the food," the three of them chimed together before diving into the meal.

Aliya didn't eat much; instead, she kept her gaze fixed on me, a smile playing on her lips. It was unusual for her to be the one staring; usually, it was me who engaged in the staring business when we were together. I furrowed my eyebrows, silently questioning her about what was going on.

She simply shook her head, still smiling, as if to say that nothing was wrong.

After lunch, Lily and Rishika excused themselves to use the restroom, leaving Aliya and me alone in the lobby. With them out of sight, I turned to Aliya, unable to hide my curiosity.

"What's making you so happy today?" I asked, intrigued by her cheerful demeanour.

"It's nothing, really. I just think your girlfriend is very nice. You have a wonderful girlfriend, you know," she teased, her smile lighting up her face.

I felt a twinge of discomfort, unsure of how to respond. How could I explain to her that Rishika wasn't my girlfriend but my sister?

"You don't know her well enough to say she's wonderful," I replied awkwardly, trying to deflect her comment.

"I was wondering," Aliya began, her voice curious, "how come your name and your girlfriend's names are so matching, Rishab-Rishika?"

Her question caught me off guard, and I struggled to come up with a convincing response. Before I could formulate an answer, Rishika appeared beside me, saving me from my dilemma.

"It's just a coincidence," Rishika interjected, her tone casual as she addressed Aliya. "Isn't it, dear?" she added, turning to me for confirmation.

Caught in the moment, I simply nodded in agreement, relieved that Rishika had effortlessly diffused the situation.

Lily joined us too, and together we began our stroll towards the mall's exit. Despite the chatter around me, my mind remained fixated on Aliya's earlier observation. Did she suspect the truth about Rishika and me? The three girls engaged in lively conversation, and before I knew it, we were outside the mall.

"Well, let's meet again someday," Rishika said to Lily and Aliya.

"Of course," Aliya replied, turning to look at me. Her smile sent my heart racing, as we bid farewell to Lily and Aliya, I couldn't shake the lingering unease.

Once they were out of sight, I turned to Rishika with a sense of urgency.

"Did you tell her the truth?" I asked, my voice betraying my anxiety.

Rishika looked bewildered. "What truth?" she questioned, her expression one of genuine confusion.

"That we are brother and sister, not BF and GF," I clarified, hoping for reassurance.

"Of course not. Why would I want to tell her?" Rishika responded, her tone tinged with annoyance.

"Then why did Aliya ask about our matching names?" I pressed further.

Rishika brushed off the question with a dismissive wave. "Oh, never mind that," she said impatiently. "Can we go home now?"

Realizing I wouldn't get any answers, I acquiesced and went to retrieve my bike. As we rode back home, the question continued to plague my mind.

"Are you sure she didn't figure out our true identity?" I asked again, desperation creeping into my voice.

"Oh, for heaven's sake, can you please stop asking that stupid question?" Rishika snapped, her tone tinged with sarcasm.

"What if she did find out?" I persisted, unable to shake the feeling of apprehension.

Rishika let out an exasperated sigh. "Then she'll think you're single and probably propose to you," she replied, her words sending a flutter of excitement through my heart.

My heart leaped at the thought. Aliya proposing to me—it seemed like an impossible dream, yet one I couldn't help but entertain.

I didn't say anything after that. Once home, I resisted the urge to call Aliya, fearing she might become suspicious. Instead, I collapsed onto my bed and resumed watching the remaining half of the Game of Thrones episode.

However, my peace was interrupted by the ringing of my phone. Glancing at the screen, I saw it was Karthik calling.

"Rishab, I bought a brand new PS5. Come over, and we'll play whatever we want," he exclaimed eagerly.

His words sparked excitement within me. Playing on a PS5 had been a long-standing desire of mine, and now Karthik had one.

"Wait ten minutes, I'll be at your place. Bye," I replied enthusiastically, already eager to experience the thrill of gaming on the new console.

It was another boring lecture from Dubey sir, just like always. Neither Karthi nor I were paying attention to what he was teaching. Karthi was busy with his phone, probably scrolling through social media or playing a game. I, on the other hand, was watching Aliya from behind.

Aliya sat a few rows ahead of me. Her hair shone under the classroom lights, and every now and then, she would tuck a loose strand behind her ear. We talked a lot, walked together between classes, and spent a lot of time just looking at each other. But I still couldn't gather the courage to tell her how I felt.

I didn't know why I couldn't confess my feelings to her. Maybe it was because I was scared she would say no. Or maybe I was waiting for the perfect moment, which never seemed to come. If I could just find one good chance, I would definitely tell her.

Finally, the bell rang, signalling the end of class. Everyone was excited and quickly started packing up their things. The room was filled with chatter and laughter as students got ready to leave. I never thought Dubey sir's class could be so lively, seeing my classmates so happy to be done with it.

Anika, Varun, Seema, and Adhi gathered around Karthi and me, laughing and joking. I joined in their conversation, but my mind was still on Aliya. She was nearby, laughing with her friends, her smile brightening up the room. For a moment, our eyes met, and she smiled at me. That smile made my heart flutter.

I knew I had to tell her how I felt soon. The next time I got a chance to be alone with her, I promised myself I would definitely confess my feelings to her.

"Did you guys hear what Dubey sir just said? I've been waiting for this moment for so long!" Varun exclaimed, his eyes shining with excitement.

I looked around, confused. Everyone seemed to be buzzing with joy, but I had no idea why. "What did Dubey sir say? Why is everyone so happy?" I asked, hoping someone would fill me in.

"What? You didn't hear what Dubey sir said?" they all said at once, looking at me in surprise.

"Sorry, I wasn't paying attention to Dubey sir's words," I admitted sheepishly.

Seema gave me a playful nudge on the shoulder. "Of course you weren't paying attention when your attention was on someone else," she teased, winking at me.

"I never said my attention was on someone else," I protested, feeling a bit embarrassed.

"Stop pretending. Sometimes we notice things too, mister," Adhi said with a knowing smile.

"Okay, okay, you win," I said, raising my hands in surrender. "Now, can you guys please tell me what Dubey sir said?" I asked, my impatience showing.

"Our college trip will be conducted within ten days. The places aren't fixed yet, though. That's why he said the trip will be planned within ten days," Varun said.

"Listen, guys, I have a brilliant plan," Anika chimed in. "What if we bunk the boring college trip and make our own trip somewhere else, somewhere we've never been before? How does that sound?"

"Oh, that sounds great!" Seema said, beaming with excitement. "We never thought about going on our own trip. I'm totally in!"

Everyone started thinking about the plan. After discussing it and considering the options, we all agreed. We decided to skip the college trip and go on our own adventure instead.

Among all this excitement, my mind was still focused on how to propose to Aliya.

"Rishab, you seem lost in thought... Is something bothering you?" Anika asked, noticing my distraction.

Her voice jolted me back to reality. "Oh, it's nothing," I lied, not wanting to share my concerns.

"It's okay. You can tell us," Seema said, her tone reassuring.

"Yeah, if something's bothering you, we'll figure out a way to fix it," Karthi said, giving me a supportive pat on the shoulder.

"Alright, it's about Aliya," I said quietly, feeling a bit embarrassed.

"What about Aliya?" Anika asked, leaning in.

"Stop acting like you don't know. You all know that I love Aliya more than anything else. Even now, I can't stop thinking about her," I said

"If you love her that much, why can't you express your feelings to her?" Karthi asked. "And you know she's single, right?"

"There's a problem," I said, my voice filled with concern. "I haven't got a proper chance to propose to Aliya yet, and I don't know if that moment will ever come."

Everyone thought for a moment, brainstorming ideas. After a brief pause, Seema's face lit up with an idea. "Listen, we're going on our own trip, right? Ask Aliya to join us. Then we can pick the right spot where you can propose to her. How does that sound?"

"That sounds great!" everyone agreed with Seema's suggestion.

"Yeah, that's a fantastic plan. Thank you so much!" I said, relieved and grateful.

"Not so fast. Since I've shared my plan, you have to treat us to a meal at the Arabian Hotel," Seema demanded.

"What? The Arabian Hotel? Are you crazy? That's a five-star hotel! There's no way I can afford that," I protested.

"Then we won't help you," Seema said firmly.

"That's not fair at all," I said, feeling frustrated.

"You can't say no. You know that," Seema added.

"Alright, you win," I said, defeated but resigned to the situation.

"Okay then, what are we waiting for? Let's get going!" Karthi said, excitedly.

"And while we're at it, we can start planning where to go on the trip. Rishab, make sure to bring Aliya along," Seema said, standing up and stretching.

"You guys go ahead; I'll bring Aliya, and don't forget to reserve a table." I'll join you soon, I said.

Everyone stood up and headed out of the classroom. I glanced over at Aliya, who was chatting with some other girls. I took out my mobile and dialled her number. As the phone rang, I noticed Aliya shifting uncomfortably in her seat, glancing around.

"Why are you calling when you're just a few steps away?" she asked.

"Okay, then I'll come to you," I said, hanging up the call. I walked straight to where she was sitting.

"Hey, Karthi is giving us a treat at the Arabian Hotel. Do you want to skip the afternoon classes and join us?" I asked her.

"There's no way I'm going to skip class," she said firmly.

"If she doesn't come, she won't be joining us on the trip. That's unfortunate," I thought.

"I guess I should go with another girl then," I said, glancing around at the other girls in the class, though my eyes kept returning to Aliya.

"What? Why go with another girl? There's no need for that. I'll come with you," quickly she said, hearing I was thinking of going with another girl.

"But you said you didn't want to skip class," I reminded her.

"Never mind what I said. Come on, let's go or we'll be late," she said, pulling me out of the classroom. "See that was easy to convince her," my rational mind said triumphantly.

Once we were out of the class, I went to get my bike while Aliya was standing. She hopped onto the back seat without saying a word.

She held my shoulder and said, "Okay, let's go."

Her touch felt like a flowing current, travelling through my whole body.

After a few minutes of riding, we arrived at the Arabian Hotel. This was my first-time experience in a five-star hotel.

Everyone was seated at the window-side table, waiting for Aliya and me.

"Is there anything special today?" Aliya asked, noticing everyone at the table.

"Nothing special, but we're here to discuss a plan," I said.

"What plan?" she asked, looking surprised.

"You'll understand soon enough. Now, come on, let's join them," I said, leading the way toward my friends.

"Sorry if we're late," I said as I took a seat next to Karthi. Aliya sat opposite to me.

"Did you guys order anything or not?" I asked.

"Be patient, the food is on the way," Anika said.

"Okay, back to business. Where are we planning to go?" Seema asked, thinking deeply.

"Switzerland!" Aadhi blurted out instantly.

"Oh, hello, mister! It's a one-week trip, not one month. Don't suggest nonsense like that," Anika said.

"I just thought it would be fun to travel abroad," Aadhi said, looking disappointed.

"Sorry to interrupt, but can I ask what's going on?" Aliya asked, confused by our conversation.

"Ah, we forgot to tell you. We're bunking the college trip and going on our own trip," Karthi explained.

Aliya looked at me, surprised. I winked at her.

"Aliya, don't even think about telling us you're not coming with us," Seema said firmly, pointing a finger at Aliya.

"But is it okay to take a step that far?" Aliya asked.

"What are we, some primary school children? We're in college, Aliya. It's natural to enjoy ourselves with our friends. Right guys?" I said.

Everyone nodded in agreement.

"Okay then, I'm in," Aliya said happily.

"Now that's the spirit," Anika said.

"We're getting off track. Where should we go then?" Karthi said, reminding us why we were here in the first place.

"How about Kashmir?" Varun suggested.

"That would be too far for us. Remember, we only have one week," Karthi said.

"Can anyone think of a place that wouldn't be too far and full of vibe?" Seema asked.

"How about Goa?" Aliya and I both blurted out at the same time.

"You two have quite the same taste," Anika teased us.

"No, we don't," Aliya said, embarrassed.

"Same taste or not, think about that later. How about Goa?" I said. "I think it's the perfect place for a one-week trip, and we can enjoy ourselves without any restrictions."

"Yeah, it will be fun if we go to Goa," Seema agreed.

"Then it's Goa, right?" Aliya asked.

"Count me in," Aadhi said.

"Me too," Varun added.

"Don't forget about me. I'm in too," Anika said.

"Sorry for the delay. Here is your order," said the waiter, placing the food on the table.

"If you need anything, please give me a call. I'll be at your service," the waiter said before leaving.

I couldn't believe my eyes. The table was filled with so many different dishes that I couldn't even count them all. I knew this month's pocket money would be wiped out today.

"Thank you for the treat, Rishab," everyone said as they began to dig in. While everyone started to eat, Aliya looked at me, and I gave her a subtle nod. I then turned my attention to the delicious spread before me and began to enjoy the food.

"By the way, guys, our college's anniversary is next month," Anika said, her mouth full of hamburger.

"Wow, I didn't know we had a college anniversary too," I said, surprised.

"Same here," Karthi agreed.

"You just wait. This year's anniversary will be greater than last year's. It's going to be so much fun," Aadhi said.

"After we come back from the trip, the preparations will start, and we'll get free periods all day," Seema said enthusiastically.

"If all the periods are free after the college trip, then we can stay in Goa for longer than one week," I suggested.

"If we have enough budget, we can think about it," Aadhi said.

"While we're in Goa, there will be a special day for a special person," Karthi said.

I instantly stomped him under the table, and everyone laughed except Aliya, who, of course, didn't know what was going on.

"Yeah, how could we forget about that?" Varun said.

"What's so special about that day?" Aliya asked, looking confused.

"You'll see for yourself. Until then, you'll have to wait," Anika said.

"Come on, guys, that's not fair. Everyone knows about it, so why shouldn't I?" Aliya asked.

"Not everyone—I don't know either," I lied quickly. If she knew the plan, it wouldn't be a surprise.

Aliya looked at me, her hazel eyes searching for an answer. I couldn't bear to look at her; she looked so innocent, like a baby. So, I looked away.

When we came out of the hotel, the sun was setting behind the horizon, casting a warm glow over everything. Everyone else had left, except Aliya. Since I had brought her here, it was my responsibility to drop her back home.

"You wait here; I'll go get my bike," I said.

"I'll come with you," she said.

"I promise I won't run away and leave you here," I said with a smile, and headed to fetch my bike. I returned quickly. "See? I didn't run away," I said, pulling up in front of her.

"I never thought you would. And even if you did, I know the way back to my home," she replied with a slight smile.

"Well, if you're so confident, maybe I should just leave you here," I teased, looking into her eyes.

Her expression softened, turning a bit shy. Her hazel eyes looked so innocent, and in that moment, she seemed even cuter than before.

"I didn't mean it like that," she murmured in a small, almost childlike voice.

Seeing her like that tugged at my heart. "Hey, relax, Aliya. I was just joking. Come on, hop on. Let's get going before it gets too late," I said, trying to ease the mood.

As she hopped onto the back seat, she asked, "By the way, Rishi, I've been meaning to ask you. You've spent every evening this past week with me. Isn't your girlfriend angry with you for not spending time with her?"

Why is she obsessed with asking about my girlfriend, I wondered. Did she know I was pretending to be committed to Rishika?

"Actually, she's out of town for some work," I lied smoothly.

"Oh, I see. Well, shall we get going?" she said, thankfully not pressing further.

I started the bike and headed towards her house. After a half-hour drive, we arrived in front of her cozy little home.

She climbed off the bike and turned to face me, her eyes locking onto mine. "Rishi, can I ask you something?" she said, her voice soft and hesitant.

"Of course, go on," I replied, trying to keep my voice steady.

"Why are you spending so much time with me, even though you have a girlfriend?" she asked, her gaze unwavering.

I took a deep breath, "It's because I care for you," I said, trying to keep my emotions in check.

"Is that all?" she pressed, looking disappointed as her expression fell.

Why is she asking this now? I felt a surge of panic. If I stayed here any longer, I might say something I'd regret. I needed to leave before I lost control.

"I should get going; it's getting late," I said hurriedly, forcing a smile. "Bye."

Without waiting for her response, I accelerated the bike and sped away.

My mind was filled with thoughts of Aliya, and before I knew it, I had reached home. "I'm back," I said, stepping inside. I went straight to my room and tossed myself on the bed, my mind swirling with the question of how and where to propose to Aliya in Goa.

I pulled out my phone and opened Google, searching for the best couple spots in Goa. The results were disappointing—just beaches and more beaches. Frustrated, I tossed my phone aside and closed my eyes. I had no plan and no idea about the perfect place to propose.

"Rishab...," Rishika called out as she entered my room. "Did something happen?" she asked, noticing me sprawled on the bed.

"Not really," I said, sitting up.

"Come on, Rishi, you can tell me what's going on," she insisted.

"Alright, listen. Our college is organizing a trip, but my friends and I decided to go on our own trip to Goa," I explained.

"That's great! But I don't see any problems with that," she said.

"The thing is, everyone told me to propose Aliya while we're in Goa."

"That's even more wonderful! But again, what's the problem?"

The problem is, "I don't know where to propose to Aliya or how," I said with a deep sigh.

"Is that your problem? You can simply search on Google for the best spots," she suggested.

"I tried, but it only shows beaches and more beaches nothing else," I said, handing my phone to her.

She started scrolling and tapping continuously. After a few minutes, she finally stopped. "I think your problem is solved," she said, looking at me.

"Did you find something?" I asked, intrigued.

"Yeah, well, you see, it's not exactly a place I found."

"Then what did you find?" I asked impatiently.

"Propose in the sky," she said.

"What do you mean, 'in the sky'?" I asked, bewildered.

"I mean in a hot air balloon during sunset. How's that sound?" she asked.

"Wow, that's something new. I didn't know people could propose in a hot air balloon. That sounds wonderful! Thank you, Rishika. I don't know how I would have come up with this plan without you," I said gratefully.

"Thank you is not enough," she demanded.

"What, you need something for your suggestion now?" I asked.

"It's not like I want something..."

"Then what do you need?" I asked.

"I want to come with you on that trip to Goa," she said.

"No... not happening."

"If you don't agree, I'll spoil the entire plan," she threatened.

"What...? Come on, Rishika, you can't do that," I protested.

"If you don't want me to spoil the plan, then you should allow me to accompany you on that trip," she demanded.

Now, I didn't have any other option but to accept her coming with me to Goa. "Okay, fine then," I agreed.

"Yeah... you're the best brother in the whole world," she jumped with excitement and kissed me on the cheek.

"Ewww... gross... disgusting," I exclaimed, wiping my cheek.

"If you don't like it, I can give you another one," she said and kissed me again on the cheek, despite my hard attempts to push her away.

"If you kiss me again, I'll definitely slap you," I warned, half-joking.

She sent a flying kiss towards me. I rose from the bed to catch her, but she ran downstairs laughing, her laughter filling the room. I couldn't stop myself from smiling.

"Silly girl," I whispered, shaking my head.

"Do you have any plan on how to propose to Aliya?" Seema asked.

We were all gathered in the canteen, except for Aliya. If she found out about our plans, our efforts would be ruined.

"My sister suggested a really unique idea. She said I should propose during a hot air balloon ride at sunset," I explained, sharing Rishika's suggestion.

Karthi's eyes widened with surprise. "I didn't know people actually proposed in hot air balloons. That sounds pretty amazing."

"That's exactly what I thought when I first heard it. But do you guys like the plan or not?" I asked.

"It sounds great!" Anika said, and everyone nodded in agreement.

"It will be a unique way to express your feelings to Aliya. Believe me, she'll love it," Aadhi added.

"And Rishab, make sure you take a beautiful ring with you," Seema suggested.

"I was thinking about that too," I said.

"Do you guys have any information about the college trip?" Karthi asked.

"It's in three days," Varun answered.

"How do you know it's in three days? Are you sure?" I asked, intrigued.

"Seniors were talking about it. I overheard them," Varun explained.

Just then, the bell rang, signaling the end of our lunch break and the start of the afternoon classes. We all reluctantly prepared to head to our next classes.

We left the canteen and headed back to our classroom. We settled into our respective seats, and a few minutes later, Dubey Sir entered the room.

Everyone was shocked to see him. It wasn't his period, so why was he here? A few students stood up to protest, but they didn't get the chance.

"Please sit down, my dear students. I'm not here to take any classes. I'm here to inform you that the trip will be in three days from now. What day is today?" he asked.

"Friday!" everyone exclaimed with excitement.

"So, we will be leaving on Monday morning at seven o'clock. So be on time," he said, and then left.

Once Dubey Sir was out of sight, everyone jumped from their seats with joy. The classroom buzzed with chatter about the trip, but in my mind, something else was forming—the day I would propose to Aliya in a hot air balloon, the day we would be in each other's arms.

"Did you hear it, Rishab? The trip is on Monday!" Karthi said with excitement.

Aliya, Seema, Anika, Aadhi, and Varun gathered around me and Karthi.

"When do you guys think we should go to Goa?" Aadhi asked.

"How about Sunday night?" Anika suggested.

"I think we should head to Goa on Sunday morning. That way, we should be able to reach Goa by night. We can book a hotel for our stay, and the next morning we can explore the city," Aliya said.

"Okay then. So everyone should be at the central railway station on Sunday morning at sharp ten o'clock," Seema said.

Everyone agreed with Aliya's plan to go on Sunday. But then, the sir came in to start the period, putting an end to both our conversation and excitement.

"Hurry up, Rishika! What's taking you so long?" I shouted, waiting for her in the hall.

"Have a little patience, Rishi. Why are you rushing? Have some coffee," Mom said, handing me a cup.

It was Sunday morning, and just as planned, my friends and I were heading to Goa. For me, it was more than just a trip; it was the day I'd finally propose to Aliya, the love of my life.

"Okay, I'm ready. We can go now," Rishika said, emerging from her room with a large trolley.

"What's taking you so long? Were you getting ready for your marriage or something?" I teased.

"None of your concern," she replied, ignoring me completely.

A message popped up on my phone, indicating that our Uber had arrived.

"Come on, let's go. The Uber is waiting outside," I said, placing my empty coffee cup on the table and grabbing my small trolley. I couldn't help but wonder why girls always seem to bring so many clothes, but that's a question no man has ever been able to answer.

"Bye, Mom, we're leaving," I called out.

"Be careful out there and look after Rishika, okay?" Mom shouted from the kitchen.

"Yeah, yeah, of course," I replied.

We settled into the backseat of the Uber, and the car roared to life. Within minutes, we arrived at Mumbai Central Railway Station.

As we arrived at Mumbai Central Railway Station, the place was buzzing with activity. People hurried by, pulling heavy bags and chatting excitedly. The air was filled with the sounds of train announcements and the enticing aroma of street food from nearby stalls. The station was a whirlwind of commotion, with travelers rushing to catch their trains and vendors calling out their wares.

We finally reached where my friends were waiting. "Sorry for the delay, guys," I said as we approached them.

"It's okay, 'magar ye sundar kanya kon hai tumhare saath?'" Aadhi asked, noticing Rishika beside me.

"Abhe pagal behen hai meri," I said, lightly punching him in the stomach.

"Hi everyone," Rishika greeted with a smile.

"Wow, I didn't know you had a sister," Seema said, surprised.

"Rishika, this is Seema. Next to her is Anika, then Varun, Aadhi, and this is Karthi," I introduced her to my friends. "Guys, this is my sister, Rishika."

"By the way, Rishi, where's Aliya? I don't see her anywhere," Rishika said, scanning the crowd.

"Aliya is on the way. She should be here any moment now," Anika said.

"Before Aliya arrives, I need to tell you something," I said, drawing everyone's attention.

"Yeah, go on," Anika said.

"Aliya thinks that Rishika is my girlfriend, not my sister. If she finds out the truth, my entire plan could be ruined before I even propose to her. So, please act like you think Rishika is my girlfriend, okay?"

Everyone nodded in agreement.

"How on the earth did you manage to tell Aliya that Rishika is your girlfriend?" Varun asked, still shocked.

"Please, don't ask. It's a long story," I said, trying to avoid further questions.

"Am I too late?" I heard Aliya's voice from behind.

"Of course not, you're right on time," Seema said.

"Hey, Aliya, long time no see!" Rishika said, stepping forward.

Aliya's eyes widened in surprise when she saw Rishika with us. "Oh! Rishika, I didn't know you were coming too," she said, a hint of disappointment in her voice.

The train approached with a loud, clattering noise. "Here comes the train, guys!" Karthi said excitedly as the train screeched to a halt in front of us.

"Goa, here we come!" Seema shouted, leading the way as we boarded the sleeper coach.

The space inside was narrow, with beds stacked in tiers. The coach buzzed with the hum of the engine and the chatter of passengers. Aadhi, who was in charge of our expenses and tickets, looked at the slips of paper in his hand. "Guys, we have berths twenty-five to thirty-two," he said, pointing out our seats.

Karthi, curious as always, climbed up to check out the upper berths. "I want this one," he shouted, dropping his backpack onto the bed to claim it.

Seema and Anika chose the lower berths on the other side. They put their bags underneath and got ready with their headphones and playlists for the journey. Aliya stretched out on a middle berth and immediately settled in.

Rishika and I took the lower berths across from each other. Varun pulled out a deck of cards. "We need something to do," he said, shuffling them expertly.

As the train started moving towards the beaches of Goa, we watched the cityscape give way to the countryside. The journey began with us playing card games and sharing stories. Despite the fun, I noticed Aliya looking pale and sad. She was probably thinking about Rishika, still unaware of the real truth about our relationship.

She would definitely be angry when she found out. I knew she'd probably slap me for hiding the truth with her and making her for wait so long.

In the afternoon, everyone started to feel tired. After lunch, most of us settled down for a nap. I wasn't sleepy, though, so I scrolled through reels on my phone. I didn't even realize when my phone slipped from my hand or when I drifted off to sleep.

"Rishab... Rishab..." Rishika woke me up. Drowsily, I sat up on the bed, rubbing my eyes.

"What happened?" I asked, yawning.

"Nothing happened. We reached Goa. Come on, hurry up, let's go outside. Everyone is waiting for us," she said, her voice filled with excitement.

"We already reached Goa?" I said, surprised.

"Do you even know what time it is now? It's half past ten. Now, are you coming or not?" she asked impatiently.

I was shocked to hear the time. This was the first time I had overslept on a journey. I stepped off the bed, grabbed my trolley, and walked behind Rishika towards the exit.

Everyone was drinking tea at a small tea stall. "Finally, you woke up. How long have you been sleeping?" Karthi said, noticing me.

I ignored him and went straight to the washroom. After using the toilet and washing my face, I returned to them. "Bhaiya, ek chai," I said, sitting on a stool next to Karthi.

The station was bustling with people at night too. The chaiwala handed me the chai, and I took a quick sip. The taste of the chai made me fully awake.

"Don't forget, guys, we need to find a hotel first," Anika reminded us.

"Don't worry about that. I already booked a hotel a few kilometers away from here," Aadhi said.

After paying the bill, we walked out of the station. The cool night breeze embraced us, making all of us chill. The sky was dotted with twinkling stars, and in the distance, we could hear the soothing sounds of waves crashing against the shore.

We hailed two taxis, since there were eight of us, and went straight to the hotel. A few minutes later, the driver stopped the car in front of the Ocean View Hotel. After settling the bill with the driver, we all went inside the hotel.

"Guys, I only booked two rooms: one for the boys and another for the girls. Is that okay?" Aadhi asked.

"More than okay. Now can you go and fetch the keys, please?" Karthi said.

Aadhi went to get the keys. The receptionist greeted him with a warm smile and handed him the keys, but he never came back. But instead of returning, Aadhi began flirting with the receptionist. We tried to call him, but he didn't listen, so Varun had to go and drag him away. When he returned, he handed Seema a key and said, "Room no. 023, next to ours."

We headed straight to our rooms. As Aadhi opened the door to our room, a wave of fresh fragrance greeted us. The room had two king-size beds, two chairs, and a TV. The walls were perfectly squared, and a beautiful mattress lay on the floor. The bathroom was spotlessly clean, The room looked cozy but comfortable, and it had a balcony too.

Karthi, Varun, and Aadhi started to unpack their bags. I too started to unpack my trolley. Once we were settled, we all collapsed onto the well - organized bed, ready to relax and enjoy our time in Goa.

The first ray of sunlight hit my face, gently waking me. Slowly, I opened my eyes and sat up in bed. Glancing at the clock, I saw it was seven AM. I decided to take in the morning view and stepped out onto the balcony. The beach before me looked stunning, bathed in the soft glow of dawn. A few people were already playing on the shore, and the gentle sound of waves crashing against the sand soothed my entire body.

Feeling the urge to take a stroll along the shore, I freshened up in the bathroom. Afterward, I headed out, welcomed by the cool morning breeze. I walked barefoot, feeling the soft, warm sand under my feet.

Looking across the vast ocean, I was amazed by the endless stretch of blue water reaching the horizon. The sky was a perfect, clear blue, which made the scene even more serene. I found a spot and sat down on the sand, taking in the calm beauty of the sea. The peaceful atmosphere filled me with a sense of calm and contentment, making it a perfect way to start the day.

It looks like I wasn't the only one who woke up early. I heard Seema's voice from behind. She walked over and sat down beside me on the soft sand.

"Beautiful, isn't it?" I said, still gazing out at the sea.

"Yep, it's really peaceful out here," she replied,

"Do you always wake up this early?" I asked her.

"No, actually, this is the first time I've been up this early," she said.

"What about you? Do you wake up early often?"

"Sometimes," I said with a shrug. "Did Aliya wake up too?"

"No, she's still sleeping. By the way, Rishab, when are you planning to propose to her?" Seema asked, her tone turning serious.

"I'm not really sure when. I didn't even bring a ring with me. I'm feeling a bit lost about it," I admitted, feeling a twinge of anxiety.

"Don't worry about it. We're all here to help you," she said reassuringly. "You can count on us. And I'll handle getting a ring—don't stress about that. I'll pick out the beautiful one."

"Thank you so much, Seema. I really appreciate it. When do you think would be the best time to propose?" I asked.

"Let's see...We need to find a place where hot air balloons are available, and you still need a ring. How about proposing tomorrow evening? That way, we have time to sort everything out and still enjoy the day," she suggested thoughtfully.

"That sounds great to me," I said, feeling relieved and excited at the same time.

"And for now, we should head back to the hotel and wake up everyone. If we don't, they'll end up sleeping all day," Seema said, standing up and brushing the sand off her clothes.

"Yeah, we should definitely head back," I agreed, standing up alongside her.

Once we were back at the hotel, Seema went to her room while I headed to mine. As soon as I walked in, I was surprised to find Karthi, Varun, and Aadhi already awake and engrossed in their phones.

"Where did you go so early?" Varun asked, glancing up from his screen.

"Just took a stroll along the shore," I replied.

"So, what's the plan for today?" Karthi asked, putting his phone down.

"First, we should all get ready and have breakfast. Then we can figure out what to do next," Aadhi suggested.

Within a few minutes, everyone was ready, and we set out for our first day of exploring Goa.

Aadhi had ordered breakfast for both boys and girls separately. A few minutes later, a tray filled with Goan cutlet pao and coffee for all four of us arrived at our doorstep. The delicious aroma of the food quickly filled the room.

After finishing our breakfast, we headed to the hotel lobby, where the girls were already waiting for us.

"So, where are we going first?" Anika asked eagerly.

"First, we'll head to Miramar Beach. After that, we'll visit Calangute Beach for some parasailing and jet skiing. Lastly, we'll go to Anjuna Beach, which is famous for its flea market. We can shop for anything we might want there. After that, we'll come back to the hotel," Aadhi explained.

"Why are we focusing only on beaches?" Rishika asked.

"Because these are some of the most famous beaches in Goa. Plus, tomorrow, we're going to explore an island," Aadhi said.

"Wow, you've really done your research. That's awesome!" Karthi said, impressed.

"Now, let's go. Our taxi is waiting for us outside," Aadhi said, leading the way.

We all gathered our things and headed out, excited to start our adventure.

We all jumped into the taxi, and the excitement was palpable as we headed towards our first destination, Miramar Beach. The morning sun was warm, and the sea breeze filled the air, making it a perfect day for exploring.

Our first stop was Miramar Beach. When we arrived, we saw a long stretch of golden sand and blue water that sparkled in the sun. The beach was lively but not too crowded, which was perfect for us.

We spread out our beach mats and enjoyed the sun. Aliya was excited to explore and started collecting seashells and colorful pebbles along the shore. Seema and Anika joined her, and they all admired their finds, sharing their favorites with each other.

Meanwhile, Karthi, Varun, and Aadhi jumped into a game of beach volleyball with some local kids. They were having a lot of fun, and Seema and Anika cheered them on, clapping and shouting encouragement.

Rishika and I walked along the shoreline with Aliya. We dipped our toes in the water and talked about what we wanted to do for the rest of the day. Aliya was really happy and her smile made everyone else smile too. We agreed that Miramar Beach was a great start to our Goa trip.

After a while, we decided it was time to move on to the next beach. We gathered our things, and the taxi took us to Calangute Beach.

Calangute Beach was busier than Miramar Beach. There were lots of tourists and vendors selling all kinds of things. The sound of laughter and the sight of colorful parasails in the sky made it feel very lively.

We headed to the parasailing booths and took turns soaring high above the water. It was thrilling to see the beach and ocean from up high. Aliya was excited and had a blast, her face full of joy as she floated in the air.

Next, we rented jet skis and had a blast speeding across the waves. Karthi, Varun, Aadhi and I had a friendly race, while Seema and Anika enjoyed a more relaxed ride. Aliya and Rishika teamed up on a jet ski, laughing and having a great time as they zoomed across the waves.

After a few hours of fun, we decided to head to our final beach of the day—Anjuna Beach.

Anjuna Beach had a relaxed atmosphere and was known for its flea market. We wandered through the market, which was full of colorful stalls selling everything from jewelry to souvenirs.

Aliya found a beautiful, handwoven scarf and some lovely handcrafted earrings. Seema bought a pretty necklace, and Anika picked out a vibrant sarong. And Rishika chose a cute, hand-painted bag.

As the sun began to set, we decided to head back to the hotel. The day had been filled with laughter, adventure, and relaxation. We were all tired but happy, with a sense of accomplishment and contentment.

We returned to the hotel room late at night, completely exhausted but thrilled from our adventures. After a satisfying dinner, everyone went straight to bed, but I couldn't sleep. I lay on the bed, staring at the ceiling, my mind racing with thoughts of tomorrow.

Tomorrow, I'm going to propose to Aliya. Will she say yes? Of course she will—why wouldn't she? Whenever I look into her twinkling hazel eyes, I see something special. There's a kind of affection there, something she might struggle to put into words.

I can't help but notice the way she looks at me when I'm chatting with Rishika. There's a hint of sadness in her eyes, as if she feels she's missing something or losing someone. And I want to change that.

Tomorrow, everything will be different. I'll be standing beside her, holding her hand, taking care of her, and showing her how much I love her. I want to be the one who makes her smile and feel cherished, now and forever.

As I thought about these things, a sense of calm washed over me. I knew tomorrow would be special, and I couldn't wait to see the look on Aliya's face when she realized how much she means to me.

I tried to push thoughts of Aliya out of my mind and fall asleep, but it was impossible. I was too excited about proposing to her. All night, my mind was filled with images of her—her cuteness, her adorable face, everything about her. I tossed and turned, unable to stop thinking about her.

Before I knew it, dawn had arrived. I got out of bed, grabbed a towel, and headed to the bathroom for a shower. By the time I came back, Anika had already woken everyone up.

After breakfast, I went straight to Seema. "Did you bring the ring?" I asked, my voice filled with anticipation.

"Yeah, it's in my handbag," she replied with a confident smile. "Believe me, Aliya will love it."

As we gathered together, Anika turned to Aadhi and asked, "Where are we going today?"

"Today, we're heading to Chorao Island," Aadhi announced, excitement in his voice.

We all gathered in the hotel lobby, ready for another day of adventure. After a short taxi ride, we arrived at the ferry terminal. The ferry ride to Chorao Island was a pleasant experience, with cool breezes and scenic views of the surrounding water. As we approached the island, we could see the lush greenery and the quaint, picturesque houses dotting the landscape.

Once we docked, we started exploring the island. The first place we visited was the Salim Ali Bird Sanctuary, named after the famous ornithologist. The sanctuary was a beautiful, tranquil place, filled with the sounds of chirping birds and rustling leaves. We walked along the wooden pathways, trying to spot different bird species. Varun, who had a keen interest in photography, was busy snapping pictures of the colorful birds and the vibrant flora around us.

Aliya seemed particularly fascinated by the birds. She stood by the railing, watching them intently as they flitted from tree to tree. I couldn't help but smile as I watched her, thinking about how perfect she looked in the moment.

After spending a good amount of time at the bird sanctuary, we decided to explore the rest of the island. We rented bicycles and rode along the narrow, winding roads, passing by small villages and paddy fields. The island's rustic charm was captivating, with its old churches and traditional Goan houses.

We stopped for lunch at a local eatery, where we indulged in some delicious Goan cuisine. The spicy seafood dishes were a hit with everyone, especially Karthi, who couldn't stop praising the food. Rishika, meanwhile, was busy chatting with Seema and Anika, probably about the upcoming proposal.

After lunch, we continued our exploration. We visited a few historic churches and spent some time at a quiet beach. The beach was secluded, with clear waters and soft, golden sand. We all took a dip in the water, splashing around and having fun.

In the evening, we found ourselves at the hot air balloon flying zone. My heart was pounding like a drum, echoing in my chest. Rishika, sensing my hesitation, nudged me impatiently.

"What are you doing, Rishi? You idiot, go and ask Aliya to come with you on a ride in the hot air balloon!" she urged.

"Okay, okay... Give me a second, would you?" I replied, trying to sound cool, though inside I was shaking badly.

As the sun began its descent behind the horizon, I glanced over at Aliya. She stood gazing at the sky, her eyes fixed on the balloons floating gracefully above. In that moment, she looked more beautiful and enchanting than ever.

Gathering my courage, I walked towards her. Everyone behind me cheered, boosting my confidence. "Aliya," I called her name, and she turned to face me with a curious expression.

"Huh?" she responded.

"Do you want to come with me on that thing?" I asked, pointing towards the hot air balloon.

Her face fell slightly as she replied, "I wish I could come with you, but I can't. Rishika would definitely get angry at me."

"Is that a reason not to come with me? Wait a minute," I said, turning back to Rishika. "Hey, Rishika! Aliya wants to go on a ride with me in the hot air balloon. Do you have any problem with that?" I called out loudly.

"Why in the world would I have a problem with that? If she wants to go on a ride with you, then take her already, you moron!" Rishika shouted back, a hint of laughter in her voice.

"See?" I said, turning back to Aliya, who looked both shocked and delighted. "Now, what do you say? Do you want to go on that thing or not?" I asked again.

A bright smile spread across her face as she replied, "I would love to come with you."

We walked towards the nearest balloon, which was tethered to the ground. I helped Aliya climb into the basket, and just as I was about to join her, Seema came over and slipped something into my pocket. I knew what it was. I looked at her and smiled.

"Good luck," she whispered.

As I climbed into the basket, the balloon began its slow ascent into the sky. I stole a glance at Aliya, whose eyes were wide with excitement. She was smiling, her face glowing with joy.

The setting sun bathed the world in a golden hue, casting long shadows that danced across the landscape. The view was breath-taking, and the atmosphere felt almost magical.

"Wow, Rishi, I can't believe this. It's so beautiful. Thank you for taking me with you," Aliya said, her voice brimming with excitement and gratitude.

We floated higher and higher, the world below us shrinking as we ascended. The moment felt surreal, and I knew it would be one of those memories we would both cherish forever.

"Do it now, Rishab, it's the moment. Propose to her," my rational mind urged me. I took a deep breath and started, "Aliya... Eh... I've been wanting to say something for a very long time."

She turned to me, looking confused, her hair gently tousled by the cool breeze. I took her hand in mine; it was as soft as fabric, her soft, gentle hands fit perfectly in mine.

"Listen, Aliya, I'm not good at this kind of thing, but I'll try my best to express it to you. The thing is, ever since I met you for the first time in that club, I knew you were different. You're not like other girls. There's something special about you. When I see other girls, I don't feel anything, but when I look at you, there's something that stirs inside me. At first, I thought it was normal to have feelings like that for someone, but I was wrong. The more time we spent together, the stronger those feelings grew. Now, they're so strong that I can't control them anymore.

"Aliya, I've waited for this moment for a long time, and now it's the perfect opportunity to tell you how I feel."

I paused, taking a deep breath for the final step. Letting go of her hand, I dropped to one knee on the small wicker basket and pulled out a small velvet box. But before I could open it, she interrupted.

"Rishi... oh, Rishi... I can't.... I can't accept this. You already have a girlfriend, and I don't want you to cheat on her for me," she said, tears streaming down her cheeks.

For a moment, I was stunned. Then it hit me—I hadn't told her the truth about Rishika.

"Rishika is my sister," I said quickly.

She looked at me, bewildered. "What... did you just say?" she asked in shock.

"You heard me right. Rishika is my sister, not my girlfriend," I clarified.

She was speechless, clearly trying to process the revelation. "All this time, you were acting like you had a girlfriend?" she asked.

I nodded. "I'm sorry about that, Aliya. I wanted to tell you the truth, but it was Rishika's plan to reveal everything when I proposed to you."

"Oh my god, I thought you were already taken!"

"Forget all about that," I said, wincing as my knee started to hurt. "Let me finish what I started." I opened the velvet box, revealing a ring inside. Aliya's eyes filled with tears as she looked at the ring.

She looked into my eyes, her face radiant with happiness.

"Aliya, I love you. I always have, and I always will. Maybe it's too soon to ask, and maybe we're just college students, but I don't care about any of that. I still want to ask you—will you marry me?"

"Yes, Rishi, yes... a thousand times yes," she whispered her voice barely a whisper.

Gently, I took her hand and slipped the ring onto her finger. It fit perfectly, just like our hands did when we held each other. My knee was hurting badly, so I stood up. Instantly, she clung to me, holding me tightly. I could feel the warmth of her body against mine, and it was enough to make me forget all about the pain in my knee.

The sun dipped below the horizon, painting the sky in hues of pink and purple. It was a breath-taking backdrop for what was to come. Finally, I pulled her away slightly, Aliya smiled at me with a joy that made my heart swell. I moved closer, taking her hand in mine, she stepped nearer as well. We locked eyes, lost in the moment, as the space between us slowly vanished. Her lips were just an inch away from mine.

I gently cupped her cheeks, she leaned into my hand, closing her eyes. Our breaths mingled, and before I knew it, we kissed. Our lips met, her lips felt soft, gentle and tentative yet full of emotion. She wrapped her arms around my shoulders, and I placed my hands on her waist, pulling her closer. The kiss deepened, the time seemed to stand still. We were lost in our own world, savoring the tender moment.

Her grip tightened on my shoulders as if she never wanted to let me go. My hands tangled to her soft hair, and I felt her warmth against me. The kiss felt like an eternity and a fleeting second all at once. When we finally parted, we were both breathless. She rested her forehead against mine, her eyes closed, breathing heavily. I could still taste her on my lips, and the sensation was wonderful.

Looking at her, I noticed her cheeks were flushed, making her look even more beautiful. My love for her grew even stronger in that instant. She opened her eyes, which were glistening with tears of happiness.

"Thank you, Rishi," she whispered, her voice filled with emotion. "I never expected you would do all this for me."

I smiled, feeling an overwhelming sense of happiness. "I always aim for the stars when it comes to making you happy," I said softly.

She smiled back, and at that moment, everything felt perfect. We had shared something beautiful, a moment that would be cherished forever.

"Congrats, you two!" Rishika, Seema, Anika, Varun, Karthi, and Aadhi shouted in unison. Aliya and I jumped in surprise, not even realizing we had already landed. It felt like we were still up in the sky, lost in our moment.

"It looks like they finally got committed," Seema said, noticing the ring on Aliya's finger.

Aliya and I exchanged smiles, still feeling the joy of the moment.

"Come on, you two, don't just stand there smiling. You both are committed now. We need a treat from you two," Varun said, grinning.

Aliya and I glanced at each other, chuckling.

"You could have just told me Rishika that this idiot is your brother," Aliya said, giving me a playful punch on the stomach.

"Ouch... That hurts, Aliya," I laughed, rubbing my stomach.

Rishika grinned sheepishly. "I just wanted to have a little fun with you. Sorry for making you wait."

Aliya laughed softly, still holding my hand. "You know guys, when he proposed, I almost rejected him, thinking he already had Rishika. In my mind, he was already taken. Now it feels like my wish has finally come true."

Karthi's stomach growled loudly, breaking the sentimental moment. "Are we going to stand here all night or what? I'm starving!"

Everyone burst into laughter. "Yeah, we should head back," Varun agreed. "It's getting dark."

"But first, we need to find a place to eat," Karthi insisted, rubbing his stomach.

"I heard there's a shack not too far from here that serves the best seafood and desserts," Aadhi suggested. "Can we go?"

"Lead the way already! What are you waiting for?" Karthi urged impatiently, causing another round of laughter.

Aadhi led the way to the shack, with Aliya and I trailing behind, holding hands. Her hand felt soft and warm in mine. Within minutes, we reached the seafood-serving shack, the aroma of delicious food hitting our noses as we entered.

The shack was bustling with people, but we managed to find a free table at the center and quickly occupied it. A waiter approached us, handing over a menu card.

"What would you like to order, sir?" the waiter asked politely.

Karthi, without even glancing at the menu, boldly said, "Forget about the menu card. Bring us everything you've got."

The waiter blinked in shock, hesitating as he processed the request. "Everything, sir?" he clarified, looking around at the group for confirmation.

"Yep, everything!" Karthi reiterated, leaning back with a satisfied smirk.

Everyone else, including the waiter, looked stunned by his audacity. "What are we going to do with all that food?" I asked, bewildered.

Karthi chuckled, rubbing his hands together. "I'm going to eat it all!" he announced confidently, drawing laughs and incredulous looks from around the table. The waiter nodded, still a bit unsure, and headed off to fulfill the unusual order.

Three waiters approached our table, balancing a dizzying array of dishes. Within seconds, the table was a feast of seafood—grilled fish, prawns, calamari, and more. The enticing aroma made our mouths water.

Varun couldn't resist teasing Karthi. "Hey, Karthi, if you eat all this, your stomach will tear apart! Let us help you with it," he joked, already filling his plate with a variety of seafood dishes.

Everyone laughed and eagerly dug in, piling their plates high. We enjoyed every bite, savoring the delicious flavors, but the sheer amount of food seemed never-ending. Eventually, we all reached our limit, pushing back our plates in defeat.

Except for Karthi. He kept going, determined to finish everything. We watched in amazement as he ate every last bit, not leaving a single piece behind. Finally, he finished all the food with a big smile on his face.

"Guys, I need to use the toilet," Karthi said, standing up from his chair.

"I need to go too; I'll come with you," Varun added, getting up as well. They both headed to the restroom, leaving the table.

"I'll go grab something to drink. Wait here," Seema said, standing up.

"Let me accompany you," Anika offered. The two of them walked off to get some drinks.

"We're almost done here, so I'll call the taxi driver. Give me a second," Aadhi said, stepping outside to make the call.

That left just me, Aliya, and Rishika at the table. Before I could say anything, Rishika's phone rang. "Rishi, Mom's calling. Excuse me," she said, getting up and heading out to take the call.

Now, it was just me and Aliya, sitting at the table amidst the busy chatter and laughter of the shack. The moment felt intimate and special, I looked at her, and she smiled back, her eyes twinkling with happiness.

Aliya and I were finally alone. She sat across from me, her hands resting on the table. She looked at me expectantly, as if waiting for something. Feeling a surge of confidence, I reached across and placed my hands on hers. She smiled warmly and squeezed my hands.

But just as the moment felt perfect, the waiter appeared and placed the bill on the table. Aliya quickly pulled her hands back, and I couldn't help but silently curse the waiter's timing for ruining the moment.

"Where is everyone?" Aliya asked, glancing around the emptying restaurant.

I shrugged and picked up the bill. My eyes widened in shock—it totaled twenty thousand and one rupee. It hit me then that our friends had left us alone not for privacy, but to stick us with the bill.

"What happened, Rishi?" Aliya asked, noticing my stunned expression.

Without a word, I handed her the bill. Her eyes widened as she scanned the amount. "So that's why they haven't come back. It was all pre-planned," she said, shaking her head in disbelief.

I sighed, feeling a mix of frustration and resignation. "I guess there's no choice but to pay it. Let's go," I said, standing up.

Aliya looked concerned. "What are we going to do? I have some savings, but it's not enough to cover all of this."

I felt a rush of gratitude for her willingness to help. "Don't worry about it. I'll take care of it," I reassured her. "Now, let's just get out of here."

I took the bill from Aliya and walked to the counter, handing it over to the cashier. His eyes widened in surprise as he glanced at the total amount.

"How would you like to pay, sir? Cash or..." he began.

"Online," I said, pulling out my phone.

"Here, scan this." He held up the scanner, and I quickly scanned the code and completed the payment. As I finished, I checked my bank balance, only to see there was just one rupee left.

When we stepped out of the shack, everyone suddenly screamed, "Surprise!" and burst into laughter.

"Damn you guys, you tricked us!" I said, though I couldn't help but laugh along.

Seema stepped forward, holding a small cake. "We couldn't resist celebrating," she said, her eyes twinkling. "Consider this our way of congratulating you both for becoming a couple."

"You all are the worst of the worst," Aliya said, laughing and shaking her head.

"When it comes to surprises, we're the best at being the worst," Varun chimed in with a grin.

"Now hurry up and cut the cake!" Seema urged.

Aliya and I sliced the cake into eight pieces, and shared it with everyone. However, Rishika snatched one of the remaining two pieces and ate it before I could react.

"Why did you eat that? It was supposed to be for Aliya and me," I said,

"Nah, nah, not quite. You two have to share that piece," Rishika replied with a mischievous smile.

Aliya blushed at the comment. "Yeah, feed Aliya," everyone teased, and I couldn't help but smile at how they were treating us.

I took the last piece of cake and said, "Say 'ah.'" Aliya opened her mouth, and I fed her, she took a small bite. Her cheeks turned even pinker as she took the cake, savoring it.

"Now you have to feed Rishab," everyone said to Aliya. She took the piece from me and gently fed it to me with her sweet, delicate hand.

Aliya took my hand in hers, and it always felt wonderful to feel her warmth. We were both glowing with happiness, but Seema suddenly said, "I think we're missing something here."

"How about a kiss?" Rishika suggested with a grin. "Rishab, Aliya, kiss each other!"

"What! Kiss? That too in front of everyone?" I protested, my face reddening. Aliya's cheeks were already pink, and she was looking down, feeling shy.

"You have to kiss her," Rishika said firmly, "Yeah, kiss her! Kiss her!" everyone chanted.

Feeling cornered but unable to resist, I turned to Aliya. "Is it okay if I kiss you?" I asked gently.

She nodded, still looking down, her face flushed with embarrassment. I stepped closer, my heart racing. Leaning in, I pressed a soft, quick peck on her lips.

I quickly stepped back. "I think we should head back to our rooms," I said, trying to shift the focus. "It's already midnight."

"Yeah, and it's getting chilly out here," Karthi agreed, rubbing his arms. "We should head back."

We hailed a taxi and, within half an hour, we arrived back at the hotel. Everyone headed inside, but Aliya and I stayed outside the room. She stood there quietly, looking at me with a mix of expectation and affection.

I was unsure of what to do—should I hug her, kiss her, or just say goodnight? My mind raced as I tried to figure out the right move.

Before I could make a decision, Aliya stepped closer, her eyes soft and warm. "You moron," she said with a playful smirk. Without another word, she leaned in and kissed me on the lips.

The kiss was gentle and sweet, and it left me momentarily stunned. "You're a fool, you know that?" she said, pulling back with a teasing glint in her eyes.

"What...?" I stammered,

"And that's what makes me love you even more. Good night, my love," she said with a final, loving glance before she turned and walked into the room.

I stood there for a few moments, completely taken aback by her boldness. Her kiss and words echoed in my mind, making me smile despite myself. I promised myself that next time, I'd be the one to make the first move.

When I finally went inside the boys' room, everyone was already fast asleep. I was exhausted, and the day's events had left me drained. I tossed myself onto my bed, and within moments, I drifted off into a deep, peaceful sleep.

The next morning, Seema and Anika burst into our room with a wild energy that jolted us awake. Their loud voices and laughter filled the room, making us spring up from our beds in alarm. I was half on the bed, half off, my heart racing as I tried to make sense of what was happening.

Seema and Anika were laughing uncontrollably, their amusement clear as they watched our startled reactions.

"You guys are such scaredy-cats!" Anika managed between fits of laughter, her eyes twinkling with mischief.

Seema was almost doubled over with laughter as she added, "We just came to wake you up and say good morning, but look at you too — terrified!"

Karthi, who was still groggy, grumbled from his bed, "Ridiculous. Is this how you wake someone up?"

Varun, rubbing the sleep from his eyes, tried to play it cool. "We're not scared. We were just having a little competition to see who would wake up first," he said,

Seema shook her head, still smiling. "Stop acting like you're not scared. Breakfast is ready, so come on!" She turned on her heel and headed out, Anika following closely behind, still chuckling.

After we all washed up and refreshed ourselves, we gathered around the breakfast table. The room was filled with the comforting aroma of freshly brewed coffee and a spread of delicious Goan breakfast dishes.

As we settled in, Rishika broke the silence, sipping her coffee. "So, what's the plan for today?"

Aadhi, who was busy spreading butter on his toast, looked up with a thoughtful expression. "We've seen the beaches, so how about some historic sightseeing?"

Anika's eyes brightened. "Sounds great!"

I glanced at Aliya, who was sitting beside me. Her face lit up with joy and excitement at the prospect of exploring new places.

Our first stop was the Basilica of Bom Jesus. As we walked through the ancient church, Aliya and I wandered off from the group. The silence inside the church was mind relaxing.

"This place is beautiful," Aliya whispered, her fingers intertwined with mine.

"It is," I agreed, my eyes lingering on her face rather than the architecture. "But not as beautiful as you."

She blushed, nudging me playfully. "You're such a charmer."

We gathered in front of the church, posing for a group photo with its grand architecture as our backdrop. After capturing the moment, we continued our tour, visiting the Se Cathedral and the Church of St. Cajetan. Each site left us in awe, marveling at the intricate details and the impressive structure of the buildings. We made sure to take group photos at every spot, preserving the memories of our adventure.

After a delicious lunch, we headed to Fontainhas, the Latin Quarter of Goa. The vibrant colors of the houses and the narrow, winding streets made it a photographer's paradise. We spent hours wandering the area, soaking in

the rich culture and charming ambiance. I couldn't resist taking countless pictures of Aliya, her beauty perfectly complementing the vibrant surroundings. My phone's storage was nearly full, bursting with photos of her.

"How many photos are you going to take of me?" Aliya asked, striking a pose in front of a beautiful fountain.

"I don't know, maybe I should buy a new camera just to capture all your pictures," I replied, snapping yet another shot. She blushed, her cheeks matching the rosy hue of the sunset.

Rishika, feeling left out, and chimed in, "How many times are you going to take her photo? Did you even take one of me?"

"I don't want a virus on my phone," I teased, scrolling through the gallery of Aliya's photos.

Rishika gave me a sharp pinch, making me yelp, "Ouch! Ouch! Stop it, it's hurting!"

"Now tell me, who's the virus?" she demanded, still holding on.

"Okay, okay, I'm the virus! I'm sorry!" I said, wincing in pain.

Everyone burst into laughter. "You two are the perfect siblings," Aliya teased, her eyes twinkling with amusement.

"That's what you get for insulting your sister," Rishika said, feeling victorious.

"You're the worst sibling in the whole world," I retorted, trying to sound annoyed. She lunged to pinch me again, but I quickly darted behind Aliya, using her as a shield.

"You moron, stop hiding behind Aliya!" Rishika called out, trying to reach around her.

Everyone was laughing, enjoying the light-hearted moment. Finally, Aliya stepped in, "Okay, okay, enough you two," she said, playfully pushing us apart. The tension melted away, replaced with smiles and good spirits. We continued exploring Fontainhas, the laughter and joy of our group filling the colorful streets.

"Guys, our cab has arrived! Come on, let's go! Our next stop is Aguada Fort. Hurry up, everyone," Aadhi called out, urging us to gather our things and head out.

As we reached Aguada Fort, the sun was beginning its descent, painting the sky with shades of orange and pink. We quickly took a group photo in front of the fort, capturing the beautiful sunset as our backdrop. Then, we set off to explore the fort's historic grounds. We found a guide who shared the fascinating history of Aguada Fort, explaining its strategic importance in defending against the Dutch and British forces.

After thoroughly exploring the fort, we ventured to a peaceful spot at the far end of the fort to relax. Rishika, Anika, and Seema settled on a stone, gazing out at the vast Arabian Sea, while Karthi stretched out on the soft grass. Varun and Aadhi were engrossed in scrolling through the photos they had taken, reminiscing about the day's adventures.

Aliya stood at the edge of the plain, her hair flowing freely in the wind. The setting sun cast a golden glow on her, making her look even more radiant. I walked up behind her and gently wrapped my arms around her waist.

"Wow, Rishi, this place is beautiful," she whispered, her voice filled with awe. "Look at the sun going down. Thank you, Rishi, thank you for all this," she said, holding my hand.

I smiled and replied, "No, don't thank only me. Thank everyone, including yourself. It's all because we came here together."

She turned to face me, her eyes glistening with emotion. "Even though, you're the one who completed my incomplete world. If you hadn't come into my life, I don't know where I'd be right now. You're the reason for all the happiness in my life," she said, her voice sincere. She hugged me tightly, and I embraced her, savoring the warmth of the moment.

"Aww, how cute! Look at those two lovebirds," Rishika teased from a distance.

"Don't try to ruin the moment!" I shouted back playfully, still holding Aliya close. The gentle waves crashed against the rocks below, and the world seemed to stand still as we shared that tender embrace. The sunset, the sea, and the laughter of our friends created a perfect ending to a beautiful day.

The evening was perfect, filled with laughter and unforgettable moments. We returned to our rooms around eight o'clock at night, tired but content. After a quick dinner, everyone decided to go to bed early, eager to rest and recharge for the next day's adventures.

Just like the night before, after everyone went inside their rooms, Aliya lingered behind. She leaned in and gave me a quick peck on the lips.

"Do couples always have to kiss before going to bed?" I asked, a playful grin on my face.

"Maybe," she replied with a smile, her eyes twinkling. "But think of it as a goodnight kiss."

With that, she turned and went into her room, leaving me with a warm feeling and a smile on my face. As I made my way to my own room, I couldn't help but feel grateful for the sweet moments we were sharing.

The next morning, we all woke up feeling refreshed and ready for another adventure. After a hearty breakfast together, Karthi stretched lazily and asked, "Where to today?"

"We've already seen beaches and historic sites," Aadhi said thoughtfully. "How about exploring some of the beautiful waterfalls in Goa?"

"Great idea!" Seema exclaimed, and the rest of us nodded in agreement. We were all excited to explore the natural beauty of Goa's waterfalls.

We quickly got ready and set out for the day. Our first stop was Dudhsagar Falls, one of the tallest waterfalls in India. The journey there was an adventure in itself, with a bumpy jeep ride through the dense forest. The lush greenery and wildlife along the way made the ride even more thrilling. As we approached the falls, we could hear the roar of the water long before we saw it.

When we finally reached Dudhsagar Falls, the sight was breathtaking. The water cascaded down from a great height, resembling a sea of milk, which is how the falls got their name. We stood there in awe, soaking in the majestic beauty of the falls. Some of us couldn't resist the urge to take a dip in the cool, refreshing water. Aliya and I splashed around, enjoying the mist that enveloped us. Karthi, always the adventurous one, swam closer to the falls, laughing as the water pounded down around him.

After spending a good amount of time at Dudhsagar Falls, we decided to explore another waterfall. Our next destination was Arvalem Falls, also known as Harvalem Falls. This waterfall, though smaller than Dudhsagar, had its own charm. The water flowed gracefully over a rocky cliff into a pool below, surrounded by lush greenery. We took some more group photos, capturing the serene beauty of the place.

We hiked a short trail that led us to the base of the falls, where we sat on the rocks, dipping our feet in the cool water. The sound of the cascading water was soothing, and we enjoyed the tranquility of the place. Anika and Rishika were busy taking pictures, trying to capture the perfect shot, while Aadhi and Varun shared stories about their previous adventures.

For our final stop, we headed to Tambdi Surla Waterfall, tucked away in the heart of the forest. The hike to the falls was a bit challenging but rewarding, as we walked through dense foliage and crossed small streams. The waterfall was a hidden gem, less crowded and untouched. The water fell in a gentle, steady stream, creating a serene atmosphere. We spent a quiet moment there, simply enjoying the beauty of nature.

As the day came to an end, we sat by the falls, sharing snacks and reminiscing about our trip so far. The experience of exploring the waterfalls of Goa brought us all closer together, creating memories we knew we would cherish forever.

With the sun setting, we made our way back to the hotel, tired but happy. The day had been filled with laughter, adventure, and the stunning beauty of Goa's waterfalls.

The next morning, I woke up early, feeling refreshed and energized. I decided to take a stroll along the seashore, enjoying the peaceful morning air. Barefoot, I walked on the soft sand, the cool water gently lapping at my feet. Eventually, I found a spot and sat down, facing the calm, lovely beach.

"Wow! I didn't know my boyfriend would wake up early in the morning," came a familiar voice from behind. I turned to see Aliya approaching, a broad smile on her face. She was still in her nightgown, her hair slightly tousled from sleep. Seeing her sweet face brought a smile to mine.

"Good morning, darling," she said, sitting down close to me.

"Good morning. Did you sleep well last night?" I asked.

"Yep, and I had a lovely dream too," she replied, her eyes twinkling with excitement.

"Really? Can I ask what you dreamed about?" I inquired, curious.

"I'm not going to tell you. You'll definitely laugh at me if I do," she said, looking shy.

"Come on, Aliya. You can tell me. I promise I won't laugh," I insisted.

She hesitated for a moment, then extended her palm. "Okay, but promise me you won't tell anyone."

"Fine," I agreed, placing my hand on hers. I could see her cheeks turning a lovely shade of red.

"I dreamed that we were married and had a beautiful little baby girl," she began, her face glowing with happiness. "We named her after the first two letters of your name and the last two of mine."

"My first two letters are 'R' and 'I,' and your last two letters are 'Y' and 'A,' which means we named our baby 'Riya,' right?" I said, thinking aloud.

Aliya nodded, her smile broadening. "Imagine a life with just the three of us—me, you, and our symbol of love, Riya—living peacefully. Isn't it beautiful?"

I grinned, playing along. "And what if our baby turns out to be a boy, not a girl?"

"No way, it will be a girl. I can bet on it," she said confidently.

"It'll be a boy," I teased.

"No, a girl," she insisted.

"Boy."

"No, I want a girl," she argued back, adamant.

"If you want a baby that badly, I can put you through one," I said playfully, pulling her closer to me.

"What are you doing, darling?" she giggled.

Instead of answering, I leaned in and kissed her. Her lips felt soft and tender, and she kissed me back. But then, suddenly, she pushed me away.

"What are you doing? What if someone sees us?" she said, looking around nervously.

"It's too late for that. We already saw everything," Seema's voice came from behind us. We turned to see all our friends standing there, grinning mischievously.

"How long have you been spying on us?" I asked, feeling a bit caught off guard.

"Since you two got married and had a baby girl," Rishika teased.

Aliya's face flushed bright pink. "Stop it, guys, it's embarrassing," she pleaded.

"Oh, look! Someone got embarrassed real quick," Anika teased, and everyone burst into laughter.

"You guys sure love to tease us whenever we're together, don't you?" I said, shaking my head with a smile.

"Of course we do! How can we pass up a golden opportunity to tease our friends?" Seema said, laughing.

"You all are the worst friends I have," I said, still smiling.

"And you're the worst we have!" everyone chorused, and we all laughed together, our laughter echoing in the morning air.

"Okay, guys, we should hurry. It's our last day in Goa, and we should explore the city as much as we can. Come on, let's head back to our rooms and get ready," Aadhi urged, bringing us back to reality.

We all agreed, still chuckling as we made our way back to the hotel to prepare for another day of adventure.

Once we were back in our respective rooms, we refreshed ourselves and gathered for breakfast together.

"So, where are we going today?" Rishika asked, her eyes twinkling with curiosity.

"Today, we're exploring the streets of Goa," Aadhi announced. "You can buy anything you want—souvenirs, presents, whatever catches your eye."

Karthi sighed, "Once we board the train back to Mumbai, I'm going to miss this place."

"Now isn't the time to talk about that," Aadhi interjected. "If we get late, we'll miss out on some spots for sure. So, come on, everyone, Let's get going!" He rushed us all, eager to make the most of our final day in Goa.

With excitement in the air, we quickly finished our breakfast and headed out. The streets of Goa were vibrant and full of life. We wandered through the bustling markets, filled with colorful stalls selling everything from handmade jewelry and clothes to spices and trinkets.

Aliya and I held hands as we explored, stopping at different stalls to admire the beautiful items. She picked up a delicate anklet, and I could see the sparkle in her eyes as she tried it on. I knew right then I had to buy it for her.

"You like it?" I asked, smiling at her.

"It's beautiful," she replied, blushing slightly.

"Then it's yours," I said, paying the vendor.

Aliya smiled shyly, the anklet jingling softly as she moved. It was a simple, beautiful moment that added to the magic of the day. As we continued exploring, our friends found their own treasures. Seema and Anika spent time trying on colorful saris, each one more vibrant than the last. They giggled and spun around, admiring themselves in small hand mirrors provided by the vendor.

Karthi, always the foodie, was drawn to a stall selling traditional Goan sweets. He bought a box of bebinca and dodol, insisting we all try them. "These are amazing! You have to try them," he said, offering a piece to Varun, who eagerly took a bite.

"Delicious!" Varun exclaimed, taking a bite.

We continued our exploration, taking in the sights, sounds, and smells of Goa. The aroma of street food wafted through the air, making our mouths water. We stopped at a food stall to try some local delicacies. The spicy and flavorful dishes were a delight to our taste buds.

As we moved from one stall to another, we picked up souvenirs for our friends and family. Each item we bought carried a piece of Goa's charm and beauty.

"Look at this beautiful scarf," Seema said, showing us a vibrant, hand-woven piece.

"It's perfect for your mom," Anika suggested.

"You're right. She'll love it," Seema agreed, purchasing the scarf.

We spent hours wandering the streets, laughing, shopping, and creating memories. By the time we were done, our bags were full of treasures, and our hearts were full of joy.

As the sun began to set, we headed back to our hotel room, our feet tired but our spirits high. It was a day well spent, and we knew these moments would stay with us forever.

As we sat around in the room, the atmosphere was a mix of fatigue and melancholy. The reality of leaving Goa was sinking in, and it was clear we all felt the weight of it. The vibrant city, the stunning beaches, the historic sites, and the lively markets had given us memories we would cherish forever.

"Can you believe it's all coming to an end?" Aliya said softly, running her fingers through my hair as I lay on her lap. I looked up at her and saw the sadness in her eyes.

"I know," I sighed, feeling the same tug in my chest. "This place has been incredible. I wish we could stay longer."

"But we can't," Aadhi reminded us. "We're out of time and money, unfortunately."

Seema nodded, a wistful look on her face. "We've had such an amazing time here. It's hard to leave."

Varun stretched out on the bed, staring at the ceiling. "We'll definitely miss this place. The freedom, the beauty, everything. But we have to get back to reality."

Aadhi stood up, trying to rally everyone. "Alright, guys. No time for naps now. We've got to check out and pack up."

Reluctantly, I got up from Aliya's lap. We all started gathering our things, packing up the souvenirs, and making sure nothing was left behind. There was a quietness in the room as we folded clothes and zipped up suitcases, each of us lost in our own thoughts about the trip.

Once our bags were packed and we had checked the room one last time, and decided to have dinner before heading to the train station, but none of us felt like eating much. The energy and excitement from the trip had faded, and we were all a bit down.

After dinner, we went back to the hotel lobby to wait for our cab. The lobby was quiet, with only the sounds of our soft conversations and the rustling of bags. It was sinking in that our trip was really over, and we were all dealing with the emotions that came with it.

"We'll come back someday," Karthi said, trying to cheer us up.

"Yeah, definitely," Seema agreed. "Next time, we'll plan to stay longer."

As we loaded our bags into the cab, we took one last look at the hotel. We felt like we were leaving a part of ourselves behind in Goa. The trip had been everything we hoped for, and it was hard to say goodbye.

Half an hour later, we were all standing on the railway station platform, waiting for our train back to Mumbai. There was a sense of unease in the air, as we were all anxious about leaving Goa. The excitement of the trip was winding down, and the reality of returning to our daily lives was sinking in.

Seema, sensing the mood, tried to lift our spirits. "Hey guys, how about one last group photo to remember Goa?" she suggested, holding up her phone for a selfie. Her idea worked perfectly. and we all gathered around, squeezing into the frame. As Seema snapped the picture, our laughter echoed through the station, momentarily pushing away the sadness of leaving.

Just then, our train pulled into the station, signaling the end of our laughter and the start of our journey back home. We quickly gathered our belongings and climbed aboard, finding our assigned berths. Aliya and I ended up with seats opposite each other, and as we settled in, Varun pulled out a deck of cards.

"How about a game to pass the time?" he suggested, shuffling the cards with a grin.

We all agreed, eager to keep the fun going for a little longer. We played card games for hours, enjoying each other's company and the friendly competition. After we finished the games, the conversation turned more personal. We began sharing stories from our lives, deepening our bonds as friends.

When it was Aliya's turn, she shared her story of losing her parents at a young age and the challenges she faced growing up without them. The compartment grew quiet as everyone listened intently. Anika was the first to speak, her voice filled with admiration. "Wow, you're brave, Aliya. I can't imagine what you've been through. If it was for me I don't know how I'd cope without my parents."

Aliya smiled softly, looking down at her hands. "It wasn't easy, but I had to be strong. I had to keep going."

I reached across and took her hand, squeezing it gently. "She won't have to face anything alone anymore. I'll be by her side, no matter what," I said, my voice firm and reassuring.

Everyone smiled at that, touched by the sincerity of the moment. Aliya looked at me with teary eyes, her expression full of gratitude. "Thank you, Rishi. That means a lot to me," she said, leaning over to kiss my hand. I smiled back at her, feeling a deep warmth in my heart. It was a tender moment, and one that underscored the closeness we'd all developed during the trip.

As the train rumbled along the tracks, taking us closer to Mumbai, we continued sharing stories and memories. The sadness of leaving

Goa lingered, but we knew that the friendships and the experiences we shared would stay with us, no matter where we were.

Eventually, everyone settled into their berths, ready to sleep. But I found myself unable to drift off. The gentle sway of the train and the rhythmic clatter of the tracks kept me awake. I gazed out the window, captivated by the night sky. Millions of stars twinkled against the inky blackness, each one seeming to tell its own story. I didn't know how long I sat there, lost in the vastness of the universe.

Suddenly, I heard a soft voice beside me. "Not feeling sleepy?" Aliya asked, slipping into next to me. She had a gentle smile on her face, and her eyes shone in the dim light of the compartment.

I smiled back at her. "Not at all."

She studied my face for a moment. "You look anxious. Is it because we're leaving Goa?" she asked, her voice soft and understanding.

I sighed, turning my gaze back to the stars. "It's not just that. I mean, I'll definitely miss Goa, more than anyone else. After all, this is the place that brought us together," I said, looking back into her eyes.

She smiled warmly and rested her head on my shoulder, her hand gently taking mine and wrapping it around her. "The days we spent here, the stories we shared, and most of all, the day you proposed to me... I'll remember everything for the rest of my life," she whispered.

"Me too," I replied, kissing the top of her head. The moment felt perfect, filled with quiet intimacy.

We both looked up at the starry sky, the train rumbling softly beneath us. "Look at all those stars. Aren't they beautiful?" she murmured, her voice filled with wonder.

"Yeah, they are," I agreed, glancing down at her. "But not as beautiful as you. You're the most beautiful thing in the whole world," I said,

She chuckled softly. "You haven't changed a bit. You're as flirtatious as ever," she teased.

We both laughed quietly, the sound mixing with the hum of the train. Then, we fell into a comfortable silence, simply enjoying the peaceful moment together. We continued to gaze at the twinkling stars, feeling connected to something much bigger than ourselves.

"Darling," she began, her tone suddenly serious.

"Huh?" I looked at her, curious.

"Can I ask you something?" she asked, her voice soft but earnest.

"Of course you can," I replied.

She hesitated for a moment, gathering her thoughts. "You know, you're the first person I've felt so close to, the first person I love more than anyone else, even more than my late parents. I can't imagine a life without you. Promise me you won't leave me alone," she said, sitting up straight and looking deeply into my eyes.

"Where did all this seriousness come from?" I asked, trying to lighten the mood.

"Just promise me, Rishi, that you won't leave me alone," she repeated, extending her hand toward me.

Without thinking, I kissed her forehead. "Do you know, before my family and I moved to Mumbai, I was constantly arguing with my parents, trying to stay in Kalyan. I did everything I could to prevent the move, but in the end, we came to Mumbai. After we shifted to Mumbai, I was very anxious about it. Until a certain day when I felt really happy about the move. Do you know why?"

"Why?" she asked, her eyes searching mine.

"Because of you," I continued. "The day we first met at the club, I knew that if I was going to fall for someone, it would be you. After our first encounter, I couldn't stop thinking about you. Whether it was fate or not, I ended up in the same college, the same class. Our bond grew stronger every day, and I couldn't help but think of you all the time. Even if my parents abandoned me, I could somehow manage without them. But if you abandoned me, I can't even imagine living without you. I'd be shattered into pieces. You mean so much to me, more than you could ever imagine. As for your promise, not even death itself could take you away from me. I won't let that happen. If I were ever separated from you, it would only be by death."

Before I could finish my sentence, Aliya pressed her lips against mine in a deep, emotional kiss. Her emotions poured out, and I held her tightly, feeling her warmth.

"Shh... stop it. Don't say stuff like that," she whispered, pulling back slightly. "Even if death came to take you away from me, I'd happily go with you."

I smiled at her, gently brushing a strand of hair away from her face. "I will never, ever leave you, Aliya. It's not just a sentence; it's a promise."

"I know, darling. I know you'd never abandon me," she said, smiling through her teary eyes.

"Oh, I almost forgot. Where's my goodnight kiss?" I asked, grinning.

"You already got one, darling, and I'm not giving you another one," she teased.

"Come on, baby, that doesn't count as a goodnight kiss," I protested.

"Please don't call me baby," she said, a blush creeping up her cheeks.

"Oh, so you can call me darling, but I can't call you baby? How's that fair?" I joked.

"It embarrasses me," she admitted shyly.

"If you don't give me a goodnight kiss, I'll shout that you're my baby," I threatened playfully.

"Stop, don't shout. Fine, I'll give you one," she said, leaning in and giving me a quick peck on the lips.

Before I could protest that it wasn't the kiss I wanted, she hugged me tightly. I thought about complaining but decided to let it go, enjoying the warmth of her embrace.

"Darling," she began again.

"Huh?"

"Can I sleep holding onto you?" she asked, her voice softer than ever.

"Yeah," I replied, pulling her close. The warmth of her body soothed me, and suddenly I felt sleepy. I shut my eyes and quickly drifted off into a peaceful sleep, holding her close.

"Hey, you lovebirds, wake up! We reached Mumbai," Rishika said, gently shaking Aliya and me awake.

"What?! We already reached Mumbai?" Aliya said, quickly sitting up and looking around in surprise.

"That's right. We're at Mumbai Central Railway Station," Seema confirmed, grinning.

My whole body felt numb from Aliya sleeping on me all night. I stretched, trying to get the blood flowing again.

"Wow, Aliya, when did you end up sleeping over with Rishab? I have to admit, you two are quite the romantic pair," Seema teased, her eyes twinkling with mischief.

"Did you guys just cuddle, or did something happen between you two?" Anika asked, nudging Aliya playfully.

Aliya's face turned a deep shade of pink. "Stop it, guys. Nothing happened between us. We just slept together, that's all," she said, her voice a mix of embarrassment and firmness.

"Yeah, yeah, like we believe you," Rishika said, rolling her eyes.

"Come on, Rishi, let's go out," Aliya said, ignoring Rishika's comment and grabbing her luggage.

I stood up, grabbed my bag, and followed Aliya. "Where are Karthi and the others?" I asked, looking around.

"They are waiting for us outside," Anika replied.

As we made our way through the bustling station, the cold Mumbai breeze welcomed us, bringing a sense of familiarity and a reminder that our vacation had come to an end.

"Hey, Rishab, have you already done it?" Seema whispered to me, making sure no one else could hear.

"Done what?" I asked, not sure what she meant.

"Oh, you fool, have you had sex? What else?" she clarified, smirking.

I was utterly baffled. "What? Sex on a train? No way, Seema. How can you even think something like that when everyone is around on the train?" I said, shaking my head in disbelief.

"So, you haven't done anything yet," she said, almost disappointed.

"Of course not. It's the least thing I want to do on a train," I replied firmly.

"Hey, guys, how about a cup of coffee?" Aadhi called out as we reached them. We all agreed and sat together, drinking hot coffee and enjoying our last moments together before heading back to our routine lives.

After finishing our coffee, we gathered our things and stepped outside the station, where our taxi was waiting. The excitement of the trip was now replaced with a sense of nostalgia and the reality of returning to our daily lives. But the memories we made would stay with us forever, a treasure trove of moments to look back on fondly.

As we waited for the taxi, I felt a tug on my sleeve. I turned to see Seema grinning at me. "Hey, Rishab, seriously though, you guys are adorable. Just promise me one thing."

"What's that?" I asked, curious.

"Never let go of what you have with Aliya. It's something special," she said, her voice sincere.

I smiled and nodded. "I won't. I promise."

"Okay, guys, let's meet at the college then. Bye, see you soon," Seema said as she climbed into a taxi, with Anika joining her. One by one, everyone left until it was just me, Rishika, and Aliya.

"Aren't you going home?" I asked Aliya.

"I want to stay with you," she replied, her tone sweet and sincere.

I couldn't help but smile at her. "It's not like we'll never see each other again if we go home. We're in the same class at the same college, and you can call me whenever you want," I assured her.

"Hey, Rishi, are you done with your babu shona talk? If you are, can we go home?" Rishika said, already hopping into a taxi.

"Yeah, yeah, coming. Just give me a second," I said. I kissed Aliya on her forehead and helped her with her luggage to climb into another taxi heading to her home. She waved goodbye, and the taxi roared to life, driving away.

I then climbed into the taxi Rishika had hailed, and we headed to our home. "I can't believe it, Rishi. Aliya is really addicted to you. And don't even try to cheat on her," she said, a warning in her eyes.

"You know I would never do that to her," I assured her, meeting her gaze.

The ride to home was quiet, the events of our trip replaying in my mind. Despite the return to our daily routines, the memories of our time in Goa would remain with us, and I was grateful for every moment spent with Aliya and our friends.

Dear Rishi,
DAY-78

I'm so sorry, Rishi. I haven't written in you for a while, and I truly apologize for that. You see, I went on a trip to Goa with my friends, and everything was so overwhelming that I couldn't find the time to sit down and pour my thoughts into you. But I'm back now, and there's something I have to tell you—I feel like the luckiest person on earth right now!

Do you want to know why? Well, let me tell you... I'm finally committed. Yes, you heard that right! And do you know who it is? It's Rishab! I still can't believe it, even now as I'm writing this. After longing for him for so many days, he's finally mine.

I know I mentioned that I went on a trip to Goa with my friends. Well, after we arrived in Goa and had a day of fun, Rishab proposed to me. But it wasn't just any proposal—it was magical, like something out of a movie. We were up in a hot air balloon, floating above the world, and that's when he asked me to be his forever. Can you believe it? I still get chills thinking about it. It was the most unbelievable moment of my life, but it's true!

And then... we kissed. It was my first kiss, and it was with the love of my life, Rishab. That kiss... it was like nothing I've ever experienced before. It was full of passion and warmth, and it felt like our souls were intertwining. Even now, as I write this, I can still feel his lips on mine, that sensation of being completely lost in the moment, as if time had stopped just for us.

Oh, Rishi, my heart is still racing, and I can't stop smiling. Everything just feels perfect.

I guess that's all for now. I should get some sleep before this wonderful feeling keeps me up all night. But I'll be back soon, I promise. Until then, Rishi, keep these memories safe for me, will you? I can't wait to write in you again.

Goodnight, Rishi.

"Darling, can we bunk class and go out somewhere? I want to spend time with you alone," Aliya said, her voice sweet but insistent.

"What?! You want to bunk class again? Not again, Aliya. We've been skipping classes for the last four days, and now you want to go out again?" I replied, trying to sound stern, but I knew she could see through me.

It had been a week since we returned from our Goa trip and settled back into our routine. Our classes had resumed, but because the college anniversary was approaching, many of our periods were free as the staff was busy with preparations. Aliya had taken full advantage of this, insisting that we skip the afternoon classes to spend time together. And whenever I refused, she'd make that "I'm not talking to you" face, which I just couldn't handle. So, naturally, I'd end up going wherever she wanted.

"Are we going or not?" she asked, raising an eyebrow.

"I haven't even submitted the assignment Dubey sir gave us. Can we go out next time?" I tried reasoning with her.

"So you won't come? Alright then," she said, turning away with a pout, her expression resembling an angry bird.

At that moment, I knew I had no other option. How could I say no to the love of my life, especially when I hated seeing her upset?

"Okay, okay, I'll come," I relented.

As soon as I said that, her face lit up with joy. "I knew you would come," she said with a broad smile that melted away any last bit of resistance I had.

"And you know the cost, right?" I said, grinning at her.

She nodded shyly, understanding the playful meaning behind my words.

"I need to use the restroom. You go ahead; I'll catch up with you at the entrance," she said.

"Alright, but please come fast, okay?" I replied.

She flashed me one more smile before hurrying off, leaving me standing there with a grin on my face. I knew I'd follow her anywhere, even if it meant bunking class yet again.

I grabbed my bag and headed out of the classroom, making my way down the corridor. As I walked, I spotted Seema, Anika, and Karthi chatting near the lockers.

"Where are you going, Rishab?" Karthi asked, noticing the bag slung over my shoulder.

"Where else? Going out with Aliya, right?" Anika chimed in with a knowing smile.

I nodded. "Yep."

"Man, she really loves to hang out with you alone, doesn't she?" Seema added with a teasing grin.

"No doubt about it," I said, unable to hide a small smile.

"Of course she does! After all, you two are the ultimate *Nibba-Nibbi* couple now," Karthi teased, causing Seema and Anika to burst into laughter.

I rolled my eyes and playfully punched Karthi in the stomach. "We're not like those *Nibba-Nibbi* couples you see all over Reels, man," I protested with a grin.

"If you're going out, where's Aliya?" Anika asked, glancing around as if expecting to see her.

"She went to use the restroom. I've got to go, guys. See you later," I said, starting to move past them. But just as I was about to walk away, my phone rang. I pulled it out and saw Aliya's name flashing on the screen. A sudden sense of urgency hit me—had she already reached the entrance?

I answered the call. "Rishi, where are you?" Aliya's voice came through, trembling with fear.

My heart skipped a beat. "Why? What happened? Are you okay? You sound tense," I said, my voice laced with concern.

"I'm in danger, Rishi. Vikram and his men are after me. Please come fast," she whispered, her voice shaking.

The mention of Vikram made my blood boil. I clenched my fist. That guy had been a troublemaker ever since college started, and now he was after Aliya?

"Is everything okay, Rishab?" Karthi asked, noticing the change in my expression.

I waved him off, signaling I needed a moment. "Tell me where you are right now," I asked urgently.

"I... I locked myself in the boys' toilet. They're trying to break down the door. Please hurry!" she cried out, her fear palpable through the phone.

"What?! What are you doing in the boys' toilet?" I asked, shocked.

"There's no time to explain. Just get here before they break the door!" she pleaded, her voice trembling with panic.

"Hold on, Aliya. I'm coming. Just stay safe for a little longer," I said, hanging up the call.

Seema's concerned voice cut through my thoughts as I stared at the phone. "What happened, Rishi?"

"Vikram's after Aliya. She's locked herself in the toilet, and they're trying to break the door," I said, my voice tense and impatient.

"Why are they always after Aliya?" Anika asked, frustration evident in her tone.

"They love to mess with her, but this time I'll make sure they end up in the hospital for the rest of their lives," I growled, storming off toward the boys' toilet. Karthi, Seema, and Anika followed close behind, their expressions a mix of concern and anger.

By the time we reached the toilet, it was already too late. The door was shattered, and Vikram had Aliya by her hair. She was struggling, trying desperately to free herself from his tight grip, tears in her eyes.

Vikram sneered as I entered. "And here comes the hero to save his girl," he mocked. Rahul, Arjun, and Raj laughed cruelly, their eyes glinting with malice.

My blood boiled with fury. "You'll regret if you even lay a hand on her," I said, my voice low and threatening.

Vikram's laugh echoed through the room. "Actually, you're the one who's going to regret it, for going against me."

I smiled coldly at him. "We'll see who regrets it."

"Stay still, you bitch!" Vikram snarled at Aliya and slapped her hard across the face. The sound echoed in the small room, and Aliya fell to the floor, clutching her cheek in pain.

I clenched my fists, my knuckles turning white. "Now you're dead for sure!" I shouted, unable to contain my rage any longer. I launched myself at Vikram, my body moving on its own, driven by pure instinct.

Vikram smirked and signaled his men. "Go, guys. Teach him a lesson. Show him what happens when someone tries to mess with us."

Rahul stepped forward, pulling out a nunchuck from behind his back, twirling them menacingly. "Oh, not that stupid thing again," I said, remembering the last time I faced off against Rahul and his stupid nunchucks. "You remember what happened last time, don't you?"

"Stop your nonsense! This time, I'll be the one teaching you a lesson," Rahul spat. And rushed at me, swinging the nunchuck with surprising speed.

I dodged every attack he threw at me, my mind analyzing his movements. They were the same as before—predictable and easy to read. I just needed to find an opening and land a hard blow. and I wasn't about to let some thug with a toy weapon take me down. After all, ten years of martial arts training had taught me well.

"At this rate, you can't even touch me," I taunted, dodging another wild swing. In frustration, Rahul pulled out a second nunchuck from nowhere, attacking with both at once. I managed to dodge the first strike, but the second one connected, landing hard on my face. I staggered back, momentarily disoriented.

"What do you say now?" Rahul grinned, confidence returning.

"Not bad," I admitted, wiping a bit of blood from my lip. "But it won't be enough to take me down." I retorted, charging at him. He swung both nunchucks again, but I caught them mid-air and yanked them out of his grip. Now, I was the one wielding the nunchucks. His face turned pale with shock. Without hesitation, I spun the nunchucks and struck him hard on the head. He crumpled to the floor, screaming in agony.

"One down," I said, tossing the nunchucks aside. "Who's next?"

Vikram's smirk faltered. "What are you waiting for? Take him down!" he yelled at Arjun and Raj.

They hesitated but eventually charged at me together. It took only two solid hits to knock them both out cold. Now, it was just Vikram left standing. Despite seeing his men defeated, he was still smiling, and that unsettled me. Something felt wrong. My instincts were screaming at me to stay on guard.

I stepped closer, Aliya still struggling in his grip. "Please, let go of me," she pleaded, her voice breaking.

"Let her go," I demanded, my voice like steel.

Vikram's smile widened. "As you wish," he said, shoving Aliya toward me with force. I caught her before she could fall, holding her tightly. And steadied her.

"Are you okay, sweetheart?" I asked gently, cradling Aliya's face. She nodded, but her eyes were filled with tears, and the red mark of Vikram's handprint was still fresh on her cheek. The sight of it made my blood boil even more.

Before I could say anything more, Vikram's voice cut through the air, dripping with malice. "Don't think it's over, Rishab. Now!"

"Look out, Rishi, behind you!" Aliya's scream pierced my ears.

I spun around, but it was too late—Rahul had already swung his nunchuck toward my head. Instinctively, I raised my arms to protect myself, and the nunchuck slammed into my forearm. Pain shot through my arm like lightning.

"Ouch... man, that hurts a lot," I muttered, rubbing my throbbing arms together to ease the pain. But there was no time to dwell on the pain. Rahul was coming at me again, swinging the nunchuck with all his might.

This time, I dodged his swing and delivered a hard punch to his stomach. He stumbled backward, but he quickly regained his footing and came at me again. This time, I landed a solid blow to his face and followed up with a powerful kick to his stomach. He crumpled to the floor, screaming in agony, completely incapacitated.

Now, only Vikram was left. I turned to face him, and for the first time, I saw fear in his eyes. I approached him slowly, each step deliberate, grabbing the hand that had dared to slap Aliya and twist it with all my strength. Vikram screamed in pain, his bravado crumbling.

"This is the hand that slapped Aliya, right?" I said coldly, twisting his wrist even harder. He let out another scream, louder this time.

"You scoundrel! I'll destroy your whole life!" Vikram spat, still writhing in pain.

I leaned in close, my voice steady and calm. "I'll look forward to it. This time, I'm letting you go. But if you ever try to hurt Aliya again, I won't hesitate to kill you." With that, I released his hand, disgusted by the sight of him. and he cradled it, whimpering.

I turned to leave, but something nagged at me. I mustered all the energy left in my right hand, turned back, and slapped Vikram across the face with all my strength. The force of the slap sent him reeling, his head smacking against the wall with a dull thud

"Now we're even," I said, though my hand throbbed painfully from the impact. I took Aliya's hand, leading her toward the exit. As we approached the doorway, I was taken aback by the sight before me—a crowd of students had gathered outside the toilet, their eyes wide with amazement.

Whispers spread through the crowd, and I could hear bits and pieces of their conversation.

"Did you see that? He took on all of them by himself!"

"Rishab really cares about Aliya... he didn't even hesitate to defend her."

Aliya squeezed my hand tightly, and I could feel her relief mixing with the remnants of fear. We walked past the crowd, ignoring the curious stares and whispers. All that mattered to me was that Aliya was safe.

I managed to navigate through the crowd, feeling their eyes on me and Aliya, as I made our way out with Aliya by my side. As we emerged, Karthi, Seema, Anika, Aadhi, and Varun rushed over, their faces filled with excitement and concern.

"Wow, Rishab, that was awesome! You really beat the hell out of them!" Seema exclaimed, her eyes wide with admiration.

The others chimed in, showering me with praise for standing up to Vikram and his goons. But as I looked at Aliya, I noticed that she seemed upset, her gaze unfocused. Something was clearly bothering her, and it was weighing heavily on her mind.

"Guys, I need to go somewhere else. Can we talk about this later?" I said abruptly, not waiting for their response. I gently took Aliya's hand and led her towards the parking area.

Once there, I climbed onto my bike and started the engine. "Come on, sit," I told Aliya. She silently hopped on, wrapping her arms around my waist as I accelerated the bike and we sped off.

We rode in silence for a few minutes, the wind whipping past us as I drove through the streets. I could feel Aliya's grip tightening as we approached her house. When I finally stopped the bike in front of her gate, I waited for her to climb off. But she didn't move.

"Aliya, we're at your house. Don't you want to go home?" I asked softly, glancing back at her.

"No... no... I don't want to go home. I want to stay with you," she said, her voice small and trembling as she hugged me tightly from behind.

I understood immediately. After everything that had happened, the last thing Aliya needed was to be alone. She was scared, shaken, and what she needed most right now was someone to be by her side, to comfort her, and make her feel safe.

"Okay, okay, I'll stay with you, but we can't just sit on the bike in the middle of the road," I said, trying to lighten the mood.

"Then come to my home," Aliya replied, climbing off the bike.

"You sure about that? I mean, you don't have any problem with me coming inside your house?" I asked, wanting to make sure she was comfortable with the idea.

"Why would I have a problem with you coming to my place?" she said, pulling my hand with a reassuring smile.

"Alright, if you say so," I agreed, climbing off the bike and following Aliya inside her house.

Her home was small but cozy, with an undeniable charm. The space was impeccably clean, and the walls were adorned with paintings that added a touch of warmth and personality. A beautiful mattress was spread across the floor, inviting and comfortable.

"Make yourself at home," she said, leading me to her bedroom. I took in the surroundings, noticing how her room was even more beautiful than the rest of the house. A shelf filled with books caught my eye, and a small bed was neatly made in the corner. I sat on the edge of the bed, feeling at ease in her space.

"It's beautiful," I said, still absorbing the details of the room.

"Thank you," she replied, a slight blush coloring her cheeks.

I noticed a photo of a small girl hanging on the wall. "Is that you?" I asked, pointing to it.

"Yes, when I was ten," she said, looking at the picture with a soft smile.

"I have to admit, you were beautiful back then too. And who's that?" I asked, pointing to the next photo frame.

"That's my mom and dad," she said in a small voice, the smile fading from her face. Seeing her like that made my heart ache.

"Come, sit," I said, tapping the bed beside me.

She sat close to me, and I wrapped my arm around her. She rested her head on my shoulder, and I could feel the tension in her body slowly dissipating.

"Now, tell me why you're so upset. Is it because of the fight back at college?" I asked gently.

She shook her head. "No."

"Then what's bothering you?" I asked softly.

"When I locked myself inside the toilet, Vikram said he would destroy our whole lives. He kept saying 'one month, one month' over and over again. I don't know what he meant by that," she said, her voice trembling slightly.

I couldn't help but laugh at the absurdity of Vikram's threat. "Why are you laughing, Rishi? It's not funny at all!" she said, looking at me with frustration.

"You're so gullible, sweetheart. I mean, someone says he'll destroy our life, and you believed him? Come on, Aliya, he's not some dangerous criminal; he's just a college student like us," I said, trying to reassure her.

"But he tried to harm me, and it's the third time," she said, her voice tinged with fear.

"Do you know why he wants to harm you?" I asked, tilting her chin up to make her look at me.

She shook her head, still avoiding my gaze.

"It's because you're the most beautiful woman in our college, more than anyone else. and he can't stand the fact that he doesn't have you. He's just jealous, Aliya. He can't handle your beauty," I said, my voice taking on a flirtatious tone.

She blushed, a small smile forming on her lips. "Stop your nonsense," she said, playfully punching my shoulder.

"Really, Aliya. Even I can't resist looking at you and admiring your beauty all day. And right now, I badly want to kiss you," I said, leaning in to kiss her on the cheek.

She giggled, her earlier sadness replaced with happiness and pure joy. "You sure know how to change a girl's mood anytime, don't you?" she teased.

"Not every girl, only you," I corrected her, smiling as I held her close.

"Oh... I almost forgot you're in my house, and I haven't even offered you anything to eat or drink. How about a cup of hot coffee?" Aliya said, standing up to fetch the coffee.

I quickly held her hand and pulled her back, making her sit on my lap. "All I want right now is you," I said softly, kissing her.

She smiled, and rested her head in my chest. "Being alone with you feels wonderful. I wish we could just sit like this forever—only you and me," she murmured, her voice full of contentment.

"I wish that too," I replied, "but I need to go home now." I gently tried to free myself from her embrace, but she refused to let go.

"No, don't go just yet. Stay a little bit longer, please," she pleaded, tightening her grip around me.

"But I need to go home, Aliya. Look at the time; it's already half past seven in the evening. If I get home late, my mom will shout at me," I said, hoping to reason with her.

"No... I won't let you leave," she insisted, holding me even tighter.

Sighing in defeat, I realized I didn't have much of a choice. "Alright, I'll stay for just half an hour, okay?" I said, trying to strike a compromise. But she didn't respond, still resting her head on my chest, holding on as if she never wanted to let go.

As time passed, I started to feel a dull ache in my back from sitting in the same position with Aliya on my lap. "Aliya, my back is starting to hurt. Can you sit aside for a moment?" I asked, trying to shift slightly to relieve the discomfort.

But she didn't respond. The pain in my back grew more intense, and finally, I couldn't hold the position any longer. I gently fell back onto Aliya's bed, letting out a sigh of relief as the pressure eased from my back. But Aliya was still on top of me,

Man... I can't understand this girl, I thought to myself as I placed my hand gently on her. Suddenly, she looked up, her expression unreadable.

"What... did something happen?" I asked, but she didn't respond. Instead, she slowly moved up to my level, her eyes locked onto mine. Her gaze was intense and searching, as if she was looking for something deep within me.

"Are you going to talk or not?" I said, feeling a bit uneasy with the silence. But instead of answering, she leaned in closer, her breath coming in heavy and warm against my skin.

"What are you doing, sweetheart?" I asked, my voice barely above a whisper.

She pressed a finger against my lips. "Shh... don't talk," she murmured and kissed me. The kiss was deep and passionate, more intense than anything we'd shared before. I cupped her cheeks with my hands, pulling her even closer as our breaths mingled and our hearts raced.

After a few minutes, she pulled away, both of us breathing heavily. She sat on top of me, her eyes locked onto mine with a look I'd never seen before. Slowly, she started unbuttoning my shirt. I caught her hand midway, searching her eyes for reassurance.

"Are you sure about this?" I asked, my voice laced with concern.

"I don't know," she whispered, but she gently removed my hand and continued to unbutton my shirt, her fingers tracing over my chest. She leaned in for another kiss, and just as our lips were about to meet, my phone suddenly rang, cutting through the moment like a jarring alarm.

Aliya jumped off the bed, startled, and I was just as surprised. I grabbed my phone and saw that it was my mom calling.

"Who is it?" Aliya asked, her voice tinged with disappointment.

"Mom," I replied, answering the call. "Where the hell are you?" my mom's voice erupted through the phone, full of frustration.

"Why are you shouting? What happened?" I asked, still trying to shake off the interruption.

"What happened? Look at the time! It's half past eight, and you're not home yet!" she yelled.

"Yeah, yeah, I know. I'm coming," I said, hanging up the call.

"Everything okay?" Aliya asked, her voice concerned.

"Yeah, yeah, it's always like this at my home," I replied, starting to button up my shirt.

"So, are you going then?" she asked, her voice dropping as if she already knew the answer.

"If I don't, Mom will kill me for sure," I said and kissed her forehead. "And one more thing—don't get depressed over nothing, okay?"

She nodded, and I could see a small smile tugging at the corners of her lips. I made my way to the exit, with Aliya following close behind.

"Bye, darling," I said, standing on the doorstep.

She leaned in and pecked me on the lips. "Today's goodnight kiss," she said, smiling warmly.

I returned the smile, feeling a warmth spread through my chest. "Goodnight," I whispered before climbing onto my bike. I waved at her as I started the engine, and she waved back, watching me as I rode off into the night.

After a few minutes of driving, I finally reached home. I parked the bike, took a deep breath, and prepared myself for the inevitable lecture from Mom. But even as I braced for it, I couldn't help but think back to Aliya and the moments we'd just shared, a soft smile lingering on my lips.

"I'm home," I called out as I stepped inside the house. The moment my mom heard my voice, she rushed toward me, her face a mix of worry and anger.

"Where have you been so late?" she demanded, her tone sharp.

"I was at a friend's house," I replied casually, walking past her and heading toward the living room. Dad was sitting there, focused on something on his laptop.

"You could have called to let me know you'd be late," Mom continued, clearly not ready to drop the subject.

"Don't make a fuss about it, Shanthi," Dad interjected, glancing up from his laptop. "If he doesn't hang out with his friends now, then when? After he becomes an old man?"

Mom shot Dad an angry look before stomping off to the kitchen, muttering something under her breath.

"Thanks, Dad," I said with a grin, sending him a playful flying kiss.

"You're most welcome, my dear son," he replied with a smile.

I made my way upstairs to my room, feeling the weight of the day suddenly settle on my shoulders. As soon as I entered, exhaustion hit me like a wave. I headed straight to my bed and tossed myself onto it. My thoughts drifted back to Aliya's house, and I couldn't help but wonder what might have happened if Mom hadn't called me at that moment. The thought lingered as I closed my eyes, the day's events replaying in my mind.

The ring of my phone snapped me back to reality. I glanced at the screen and saw Aliya's name. Without hesitation, I answered the call.

"Have you reached home yet?" she asked, her voice soft but curious.

"Yeah, I got home a little while ago," I replied.

"Did your mom scold you for being late?" she inquired.

"Not at all," I chuckled. "Dad came to my defense and handled it well."

"That means I was worried for nothing," she said, her voice relaxing.

"So, what are you doing now?" I asked.

"Me? I was just thinking about the wonderful evening we spent together. Even talking about it now sends chills through my whole body," she admitted.

"Really? I was thinking about that too," I said, my voice lowering as I added, "And I was wondering, if my mom hadn't interrupted us, what would've happened?"

"If you really want to know," she teased, "then you'll have to come to my house right now—and make sure your phone is turned off."

"You know I can't come over right now," I laughed. "Mom would kill me if she found out."

"You're bad," she teased back. "Better luck next time. And make sure next time, there's no one to interrupt us." Her voice carried a playful edge, leaving the promise of something more lingering in the air.

I smiled at her playful tone. "Next time, I'll make sure the phone is off, the doors are locked, and it's just you and me."

"Good," she said softly. "I like the sound of that."

There was a brief pause, the silence between us filled with unspoken thoughts. It was comforting, knowing we were both thinking about the same things, even if we weren't saying them out loud.

"Aliya," I started, breaking the quiet, "I want you to know that tonight meant a lot to me. Not just the... well, the close moments, but everything. Being with you, talking, just... being together."

"It meant a lot to me too," she replied, her voice tender. "I feel safe with you, darling. Like I can forget everything else when I'm with you."

"I'll always be here for you," I promised. "No matter what."

"I know," she said, a smile evident in her voice. "You always have been."

Just as I was about to say something else, I heard my mom's voice calling from downstairs. "Rishi! Dinner's ready! Come down before it gets cold!"

I sighed, a bit disappointed that our conversation was being interrupted. "Looks like I have to go. Mom's calling for dinner."

Aliya chuckled softly. "Alright, I guess you can't ignore that. Go eat, or she'll be yelling at you again."

"Yeah, she probably will," I said, smiling at the thought. "But I'll be thinking about you the whole time."

"Same here," she replied sweetly. "Go enjoy your dinner. We'll talk more tomorrow."

"Definitely," I said, reluctant to hang up. "Goodnight, Aliya."

"Goodnight, darling," she replied softly.

I ended the call and put my phone down, still feeling the warmth of our conversation. As I made my way downstairs, I couldn't help but smile, already looking forward to seeing her again tomorrow.

Our college festival was fast approaching, with only seven days left until the annual day. The entire campus was buzzing with excitement, and the best part was that most of our classes were being let out early as everyone, including the teachers, was caught up in preparations. Even Dubey sir, usually strict, was busy helping decorate the college.

The seven of us gathered in the canteen, enjoying our lunch together. Varun was the first to bring up the latest buzz. "I heard that celebrities are coming to visit our college on the annual day," he said, his eyes wide with excitement.

"That would be awesome!" Karthi added, clearly already imagining the possibility of meeting someone famous.

But then, Seema leaned in closer, her voice dropping to a more serious tone. "Guys, don't overthink what I'm about to say, but I heard a rumour that Vikram and his men are plotting something big for the festival."

The atmosphere at the table immediately shifted. Aliya turned to me, her eyes filled with worry. I could see the fear in them, the same fear that had haunted her since the last encounter.

"Come on, Seema," Varun chimed in, trying to lighten the mood. "Rishab already beat them twice. They're totally exposed now. How can they plot something after being utterly defeated by a mere junior?"

Anika nodded in agreement, trying to reassure Aliya. "Yeah, that's right. There's no way they can do anything with Rishab around."

But Aliya wasn't convinced. She was still tense, her hand gripping mine under the table. I squeezed it back, hoping to give her some comfort.

Sensing the growing unease, I decided to change the topic. "Guys, can we drop this subject and talk about something else?" I suggested, trying to steer the conversation away from anything that could worry Aliya more.

Everyone hesitated for a moment, then Karthi jumped in with a joke, and the conversation shifted to lighter topics, but I could still feel Aliya's gaze on me, her concern lingering in the background.

After our college ended, I was dropping Aliya back to her home. When I stopped the bike in front of her house, I waited for her to climb off, but she sat still.

"What happened now, darling?" I asked.

"You heard what Seema said, right?" she replied, her voice tinged with worry.

"And you heard what everyone else said after that, didn't you?" I said, trying to reassure her.

"It's not like that, Rishi. Why don't you try to understand?" she said impatiently as she climbed off the bike.

I noticed that whenever Aliya was angry or upset, she calls me by my name instead of "darling." It was a small thing, but it always let me know how she was feeling. I reached out and took her hand. "I understand your concern, Aliya. But sometimes, you don't have to trust everything you hear," I said, trying to calm her down.

"But he threatened our lives, Rishi. Why don't you get it? We should do something about him now," she insisted, her voice filled with frustration.

"Come closer," I said softly. She stepped closer, and I gently held her face, kissing her forehead. A small smile began to form on her lips. "Okay, fine, I get it. From now on, I'll be more alert than ever before. I won't leave your side for a single moment. Even if they come to destroy us, they'll have to face me first, and you know that's impossible. And one more thing, if they ever come again, I'll make sure to cut off Vikram's hands and legs so he won't get another chance to come between us," I said, my tone both serious and comforting.

She looked at me, her worry slowly melting away. "You seem confident. I wish you could really break his hands and legs," she said, smiling.

"If it comes to saving the love of my life, I'll destroy the whole world to protect you," I said with conviction.

She blushed, leaning in to kiss my hand. "I love you, darling," she whispered.

"Love you too," I replied, hoping she'd invite me inside like last time. "Wouldn't you invite me inside your home?"

"What... inside my house? No, no... not now. I'm working on something, I mean, my house is a total mess right now. You definitely don't want to see it like this," she said, hesitating and looking a bit flustered.

"Really? Okay, maybe next time then," I said, pretending to be disappointed.

"Yeah, next time," she agreed quickly. "Bye, darling. Let's meet tomorrow," she said as she turned to go inside.

"Wait a minute, don't you think you're missing something?" I called out after her.

"Missing something? No, I'm pretty sure I didn't miss anything," she said, turning back, confused.

"You're such a dunce," I teased. "Where's my goodbye kiss?"

She smiled and came back. "You sure don't want to miss a chance to kiss me, do you?" she said teasingly.

"Hurry up," I urged, grinning.

"Okay, okay..." she said, leaning in to kiss me. It always felt wonderful to kiss her, which is why I never wanted to miss a chance.

"Okay then, bye, darling," she said before finally heading inside. I watched her go, feeling delighted as I drove back to my house.

I was catching up on episodes of G.O.T, trying to make up for the ones I missed during our trip to Goa. Whenever I got some free time, I'd watch the series. My attention was glued to the screen when my mom entered the room, carrying a plate filled with halwa. She placed the plate on the bedside table and sat on the edge of the bed.

It was unusual—my mom never brought food to my room, and just by looking at her, I could tell she was happy about something. I continued watching the episode, trying not to acknowledge her right away.

"If you haven't noticed me, I'm here, Beta," my mom said, trying to get my attention.

"I know you're here, Mom," I replied, finally shifting my gaze to her.

"I made your favorite halwa, especially for you," she said, handing me the plate.

I took it and ate a quick bite. It was delicious, just like always. My mom's halwa is the best I've ever tasted.

"How does it taste? Good?" she asked, eager for my approval.

"You know what I'm going to say, Mom. It's the best halwa I've ever eaten," I praised her, smiling.

"Thank you, dear. So, tell me, how's college life going?" she asked, her tone casual but clearly leading somewhere.

Before answering, I looked at her suspiciously. "Why this sudden affection, Mom? You never usually ask about my college life. What's going on?"

"It's natural for a mother to love her child, isn't it? And as for your college life, it just came to mind, so I asked," she said, trying to sound nonchalant.

"Is that so? Okay, well, college life is going extraordinarily," I said, playing along.

"Did you make any new friends?" she continued.

"Yeah, lots of friends," I said, still focused on the halwa.

Does that mean girls too, right?" she asked, her tone shifting slightly.

"Of course, there are girls. Why do you ask?" I said, now genuinely confused.

"Do you have a liking for someone?" she asked, finally getting to the point.

Ah, now I understood. She wanted to know if I had a girlfriend. "In other words, you're asking if I have a girlfriend, aren't you?" I said, raising an eyebrow.

She smiled, not hiding her excitement. "Well, do you have one?" she asked eagerly.

"Yep, I have one," I admitted.

"Really?" she blurted out, her excitement clear. "Then why didn't you tell me earlier?"

"You see, Mom, I thought you might not approve, so I decided not to tell anyone except Rishika. She knows everything about my love life," I explained.

"What's her name? How does she look? Where does she live?" my mom asked, all in one breath.

"Wow, Mom, slow down! Don't rush like that," I said, laughing. "Anyway, her name is Aliya, and I don't have the words to describe her beauty. She's the most gorgeous among the gorgeous."

"Really? Is she that beautiful? Then show me her photo already!" my mom urged, clearly eager to see her.

I took out my phone and opened the gallery. It was filled with pictures of Aliya. I handed the phone to my mom, and she started scrolling through the photos, her eyes widening. "Wow, she's really a living goddess!" Mom exclaimed.

"Why didn't you bring her home yet?" she asked, still admiring Aliya's pictures.

"I'll talk to her about it," I said, smiling at my mom's enthusiasm.

"Shanthi, come here!" Dad called from downstairs.

"Coming!" she shouted back, then turned to me before leaving. "Make sure you take good care of her," she said with a warm smile and headed downstairs.

I couldn't help but smile at my mom's sudden interest in Aliya.

After finishing my dinner, I headed back to my room and resumed watching Game of Thrones. Determined to catch up on all the episodes I'd missed during our Goa trip, I kept my eyes glued to the screen.

By the time I finished, it was already half past twelve. I wrapped myself in a blanket and was about to drift off to sleep when my phone rang unexpectedly. It was unusual for anyone to call me at this hour. Curiosity and concern mixed together as I glanced at the screen and saw Aliya's name. I quickly answered the call.

"Rishi... Rishi! They are here!" Aliya's panicked voice came through, making my heart race.

Her distress in the dead of night jolted me awake. "Calm down, Aliya. Who's there?" I asked, trying to keep my voice steady despite my growing anxiety.

"Vikram's here... Please come fast, Rishi. I'm scared. They're knocking on the door continuously."

Vikram's name sent a shiver down my spine. Thoughts of Seema's warning about Vikram's plans and Aliya's fears of him destroying our lives flashed through my mind.

"Don't panic, Aliya. Lock yourself in your room and stay safe. I'm on my way. Just wait for five minutes," I said urgently before hanging up.

I barely had time to think. I grabbed my bike keys and hurried downstairs. Outside, the rain was pouring heavily. Damn, why the rain has to come now, that too out of nowhere. I didn't have the luxury to wait for it to stop. I climbed onto my bike, started the engine, and sped off into the downpour. The rain felt like sharp needles against my face, but I didn't slow down.

After what felt like an eternity, I finally arrived at Aliya's house. My clothes were drenched, and water droplets were dripping from my shirt. I barely took time to park the bike properly before rushing inside.

Her front door was already open, which sent a wave of panic through me. Had I arrived too late? Had Vikram already gotten to her? I dashed inside, noticing that the house was a total mess, with items scattered all over the floor.

"Aliya! Are you there? Aliya!" I shouted, my voice echoing in the silence. No response came. My whole body trembled, and my heart pounded furiously in my chest.

I moved further into the house. Her bedroom door was closed. Please be safe, Aliya, I prayed silently. With shaking hands, I slowly opened the bedroom door.

"SURPRISE!" Aliya shouted, her voice full of laughter.

I stood there, drenched and stunned, I blinked in disbelief. Aliya stood there with a big grin, her earlier fear replaced by excitement. I could hardly believe my eyes as I saw Aliya standing in front of me with a white rose in her hand. The shock of seeing her safe and sound took a few moments to sink in. I muttered "Thank God Aliya is okay" and sank to the floor, completely drained. The realization that Aliya had just pulled a prank on me was slowly hitting me.

Aliya rushed over to me, concern evident on her face. "Are you okay, darling?" she asked, holding my face gently.

But rage soon replaced my initial relief. I was furious that I had come here in the middle of the night, braving a heavy rainstorm, all for nothing. I pushed her hands away and stood up, my anger bubbling over.

"What's all this?" I demanded, my voice raised in frustration. "You know how scared I was. You called me in the middle of the night and said you were in danger. Do you have any idea how I got here? I came through the rain, drenched, because I thought something terrible had happened. Do you have any idea what I went through to get here? I could have been hurt in that storm, and for what? A prank?" And what if something had happened to you for real? I'd be devastated!"

Tears began to roll down Aliya's cheeks as she looked at me with a heartbroken expression. Her voice trembled as she spoke, "I'm so sorry, darling. I didn't mean to trouble you. It's just that today marks one month since we committed to each other, and I wanted to celebrate our special day with a surprise. I put all this together just for you-everything you see here is for our anniversary."

Her words were laced with sadness and regret, and I could see how much this meant to her. "If you don't want to celebrate or if you're upset, you can leave," she continued, her voice barely above a whisper. "I won't hold it against you. I just wanted to make this day memorable for us."

I could feel the weight of her disappointment and the effort she had put into creating this special moment for us. The realization hit me hard—she had put so much thought and care into this surprise, and my reaction had overshadowed all of her efforts.

Her words and tears made me reconsider everything. I took a deep breath and began to really look around the room. It was beautifully decorated for our special day.

The room was bathed in the soft, warm glow of fairy lights that Aliya had draped across the ceiling and walls. The lights flickered gently, casting a cozy ambiance over the space. From the ceiling hung a collection of photos of us together—each picture carefully pinned and arranged to create a collage of our cherished moments. The images swung slightly with every little breeze, reminding me of the beautiful times we'd shared.

On the table in the center of the room sat a small, elegantly decorated cake. It was adorned with a delicate swirl of frosting, and in the center, our names were written in intricate, cheerful script. The sight of it made my heart soften further.

Aliya stood there in a stunning pink saree with a matching blouse, her outfit shimmering softly in the ambient light. The saree was draped gracefully, and she had a little bhindi on her forehead that highlighted her beauty even more. She looked like an angel who had descended from the heavens, her appearance a perfect blend of elegance and charm.

The decorations, the cake, and her radiant outfit—all of it was a testament to her love and effort. Seeing it all, I realized how much she had invested in making this night special for us, and how my initial reaction had overshadowed the genuine warmth and affection she had put into this surprise.

I realized I had overreacted. Aliya had put so much effort into this surprise to show me her love. I felt regret for my harsh reaction and for not appreciating her efforts sooner. I had been too focused on my anger to see her love and dedication.

I walked over to her and took her hands gently. "Baby, look here," I said softly, trying to get her attention.

"Don't baby me," she replied, still turning her face away from me, her voice laced with hurt.

"Fine, how about 'darling'?" I said, hoping to reach her. When she stayed silent, I continued, "I didn't mean to hurt you," I said softly. "I was just worried about you. I can't bear the thought of losing you. That's why I reacted the way I did. I'm sorry if my words hurt you."

Aliya looked at me, her eyes red from crying. I wiped her tears away and said, "Now be a good girl and don't cry. I'm here with you."

Aliya hugged me, but then she pushed me away with a playful look. "Ewww, you're all wet!" she exclaimed.

I realized I was still drenched from the rain. "You need to change your clothes; otherwise, you'll catch a cold," she said. She went to her wardrobe and came back with a teddy bear-printed T-shirt and pink trousers.

"What? I have to wear this?" I asked, looking at the clothes in disbelief.

"Of course! I don't want my hot boyfriend catching a cold," she said with a grin. "Now, change while I grab a knife to cut the cake."

I quickly changed into the warm clothes she had picked out. When I emerged, Aliya laughed and said, "Wow, darling, you look cute in that outfit."

"Don't make fun of me," I said, feeling a bit self-conscious. "You're the one who told me to wear these clothes."

Aliya came closer and gave me a sweet kiss on the lips. "Well then, shall we cut the cake now?" she asked.

We cut the cake together, feeding each other slices. Aliya took a photo of me in her clothes—I probably looked like an absolute idiot, but I couldn't help but smile. She then played a romantic song and said, "Come on, darling, let's dance."

"If you watch me dance, you might never want me to dance again," I said, half-jokingly.

"If you don't know how to dance, that's okay. I can teach you," she said, pulling me closer.

She showed me a few dance steps, and I tried to follow along. I wasn't very coordinated, but Aliya was patient. After about half an hour of trying and failing to sync my moves with hers, she gave up on teaching me how to dance.

We both sat on the tiny floor rug in the tiny bedroom of her tiny house, exhausted. Despite everything, we were happy just being together, enjoying the surprise and each other's company.

"I should head back now," I said, looking at the clock. It was three in the morning.

"What... don't go... just yet. Stay here. You can go in the morning," Aliya pleaded.

"If my mom found out that I wasn't at home last night, she will definitely kill me," I said, getting up.

"But I was thinking of spending the rest of the night with you," she said, disappointed.

"Tomorrow is Sunday. We can go wherever you want, and I will spend the whole day with you, I promise. Please let me go now," I said.

"No... no... no... I won't let you go," she obstinately insisted.

"But listen, darling—" Before I could complete my sentence, our lips met. She kissed me deeply, her lips tender and moist. Something was building deep inside me; I didn't want to pause for a second. I held the back of her head with both hands, her hair feeling like pure fabric—soft and smooth.

"We can take a break to breathe," I said after five minutes. We both took deep breaths, but before I could say or do anything, she leaned in and kissed me again. Her lips were so soft that I couldn't resist biting them. She moaned a little.

She lifted my T-shirt to remove it, but I stopped her midway.

"Darling, are you sure about this?" I asked, looking into her eyes.

"One hundred percent," she said, her voice barely a whisper.

"I mean, I don't have a protection," I said.

"Don't concern yourself about that. Even if you had one, I wouldn't let you use it, because I want to feel you for real," she said, fully removing my T-shirt.

I kissed her and held her close, looking deep into her eyes.

"What?" she asked, a soft laugh escaping her lips.

"Just thinking," I said.

"About what?"

"About how incredibly lucky I am to have you," I replied.

She smiled, her eyes glowing with affection. "You always know what to say to make me blush."

"It's the truth," I said, brushing a strand of hair away from her face.

She leaned in. "And you make me feel like the most cherished person in the whole world."

"Because you are," I said and kissed her.

I held Aliya and made her sit on the bed. I kissed every part of her face—her eyebrows, cheeks, dimples, eyelids, forehead, and finally her lips.

She turned off the lights, and I undressed her saree; her skin literally glowed in the darkness. I could have spent the whole night just looking at her perfectly shaped body.

"Come here," she said, holding my hand and drawing me closer.

The delicate fabric of her tiny bed's canopy draped around us, creating a cocoon of intimacy. The sound of her breath and soft moans filled the room. I kept her fingers intertwined with mine, and our eyes locked as we made love. She bit my neck, making my whole body quiver.

When we reached our peak, her fingernails dug deep into my back—a sensation that sent waves of pleasure through me. We finished together, our breaths heavy and mingling, our hearts pounding in unison.

I fell into her arms, feeling exhausted but intensely happy. She clasped my hand, and I pulled her closer, wrapping my arms around her. Her eyes filled with tears.

"Does it hurt you?" I asked softly, gently wiping away her tears.

"No," she said, shaking her head. "It felt wonderful. I'm just overwhelmed, that's all."

I smiled, brushing a strand of hair away from her face. "Then we should go on another round," I teased.

She playfully punched my shoulder. "You're such a horny guy," she said, a laugh escaped her lips.

I smiled, leaning in to kiss her forehead. "You're amazing back there, you know that?"

She looked up at me, her eyes still a bit watery but with a soft smile forming on her lips. "You always know what to say to make me feel special."

"Wow... I didn't know I gave you a love bite," she said, rubbing the spot on my neck where she had left her mark.

"Seems like you've claimed your territory," I chuckled, pressing a kiss to her forehead.

She giggled softly, her face nestled against my chest. "I guess I have."

We lay there for a moment in comfortable silence, listening to the soft rhythm of each other's breathing. The room was warm, cocooned in the faint glow of the tiny bed's canopy.

"Do you think this will last forever?" she asked quietly, her voice almost a whisper.

I looked down at her, surprised by the sudden seriousness in her tone. "What do you mean?"

"Us," she said, her fingers tracing small circles on my chest. "This feeling... this happiness. Do you think it will last?"

I cupped her face, tilting her head up so she could look into my eyes. "Aliya, I can't predict the future. But I do know one thing—I'm going to do everything in my power to make this last. I want to be with you, to make you happy every single day."

Her eyes softened, and she smiled. "I believe you. You always know how to make me feel safe."

I pulled her closer, holding her tightly. "That's because I never want you to feel alone, not even for a second."

She snuggled against me, her body fitting perfectly against mine. "Do you ever think about the future? About where we'll be?"

"Sometimes," I admitted. "I think about us—about what it would be like to wake up next to you every morning, to share every moment with you. I imagine us building a life together."

She sighed contentedly. "That sounds perfect. I want that too."

I kissed the top of her head. "Then let's make it happen. No matter what comes our way, we'll face it together."

She lifted her head to look at me, her eyes shimmering with emotion. "You make me so happy, darling. I never thought I could feel this way about anyone."

"I feel the same way," I said, my voice full of sincerity. "You're everything I've ever wanted."

We stayed like that for a while, holding each other, lost in the comfort of each other's presence. The world outside didn't matter; all that existed was the two of us in this tiny room, wrapped in warmth and love.

"Do you remember the first time we met?" she asked suddenly, her voice tinged with nostalgia.

I smiled at the memory. "Of course. I was waiting for my drink at that club and out of nowhere you came and stood beside me, and I don't know how but I found myself staring at you."

She laughed softly. "I came to get a drink too and found you staring at me, and I remember thinking, 'wow! His blue eyes looks beautiful?'"

"I couldn't help it," I admitted, grinning. "You were the most beautiful girl I'd ever seen. I was completely mesmerized."

"And now look at us," she said, her voice filled with wonder. "Who would've thought we'd end up here, together?"

"I did," I said confidently. "From the moment I saw you, I knew I wanted to be with you."

She smiled, her eyes shining with affection. "You always know what to say to make me melt."

"It's not just words, Aliya. I mean every single one of them," I said, my voice soft but firm.

She gazed at me for a long moment, then leaned in to press a gentle kiss to my lips. "I love you, darling."

"I love you too, sweetheart. More than anything," I replied, kissing her back.

We stayed there, holding each other close, the world outside fading into nothingness. The night was quiet, with only the sound of our breathing and the occasional rustle of the bedsheets.

As the minutes passed, I could feel her body gradually relaxing against mine. Her eyelids grew heavy, and her breathing became slow and even. I knew she was drifting off to sleep, and I felt a deep sense of peace wash over me.

"Sleep, my love," I whispered, kissing her forehead one last time.

She murmured something incoherent, her voice filled with sleepiness, and then she was out, her body completely at ease in my arms. I held her for a while longer, basking in the warmth of our shared intimacy, before I, too, let sleep claim me.

And just like that, in the tiny bedroom of her tiny house, we both fell asleep, wrapped in each other's arms, feeling like I'm the luckiest person in the world right now.

When I woke up, I found Aliya lying beside me, her eyes glowing brightly in the soft morning light. She was already wide awake, watching me with a contented smile that seemed to light up her entire face.

"Good morning, darling," she cheered, her voice filled with warmth. She looked more alive than ever, and I couldn't help but wonder if it was because of the wonderful moments we shared last night.

"Good morning," I replied, sitting up on the bed, still a little groggy from sleep.

"I already made breakfast. Go freshen up, and then we can eat together," she said with a playful grin.

I nodded and made my way to the bathroom for a quick shower. When I returned, my clothes were already laid out, dried and neatly folded. I got dressed and headed to the kitchen, where the aroma of freshly made waffles filled the air. The table was set, and Aliya had arranged everything perfectly on the small round dining table. She sat opposite me, her eyes sparkling with a happiness that was almost contagious.

"You look so happy today," I said, unable to keep from smiling myself.

She didn't respond with words but simply smiled even wider. After a moment, she added, "Oh, by the way, your mom called you."

My heart skipped a beat. "Oh, crap... I'm dead! What's the time now?"

"It's half past ten," she said nonchalantly.

"What? It's already ten in the morning? I really should head back as soon as I can," I said, feeling a wave of panic rise inside me.

"Relax," she said with a reassuring tone. "I talked to your mom, so don't worry. She won't do anything."

"You... talked to my mom?" I repeated, still trying to process it.

"Yes," she nodded. "You see, she was calling you constantly, and I didn't want to disturb your peaceful sleep. So, I picked up the call and told her you were at my place, sleeping peacefully."

I stared at her in disbelief. "And what did my mom say?" I asked curiously, taking a bite of the waffle.

"At first, she was shocked, but then I explained everything—how you ended up sleeping at my house, except one thing, of course," she added with a shy smile playing on her lips.

I knew exactly what "one thing" she left out—the intimate experience we shared last night. I couldn't help but smile to myself at how smoothly Aliya handled the situation.

Taking another bite of the waffle, I glanced at my phone and saw the call history. My mom had called me twenty-three times, and to my surprise, Aliya had talked to her for almost an hour.

"Wow, Aliya! You talked with my mom for an hour? What were you two talking about?" I asked, my curiosity piqued.

"Ahh... nothing much, just some of these and some of that," she replied, her tone teasing.

I raised an eyebrow. "Some of these and some of that, huh? Sounds mysterious."

Aliya just winked and continued eating her breakfast.

As we enjoyed our meal, she suddenly asked, "By the way, darling, do you have any plans for our college's annual day?"

"Oh, I almost forgot about that! It's only two days away. I don't have any particular plans in mind, but I was thinking about introducing you to my family," I said as I finished my waffle.

Her eyes widened with excitement. "Really? That's wonderful! I'm looking forward to meeting your family," she said, practically beaming with joy.

I couldn't help but smile back. The thought of bringing Aliya into my family circle felt like another step toward something deeper and more meaningful between us.

"Where are you, Rishi? We're waiting for you," Seema's voice crackled through the phone.

"On the way, please wait for ten minutes," I replied, glancing at the traffic.

"Aliya is with you, right?" Seema asked.

"Yeah, we're coming together," I confirmed.

"Okay then, come fast," she said, and the line went dead.

Today was our college's annual day, and Aliya and I were on our way to the event. I was driving my bike, with Aliya sitting behind me.

"Did they already reach?" Aliya asked, leaning in to speak over the roar of the engine.

"Yeah, they're waiting for us," I replied, focusing on navigating through the busy road.

The sun was beginning to set, casting a golden hue over the streets. Despite the traffic, I was eager to get to the college and join the festivities. Aliya seemed excited too; she leaned in closer, her arms wrapped around me as we sped along.

When we finally reached the college, I couldn't believe my eyes. The parking lot was completely packed, vehicles lined up bumper to bumper, with hardly any space left. Realizing there was no way I could squeeze in, I decided to park the bike just outside the college gate.

As we walked into the college, we quickly spotted our friends—Karthi, Seema, Anika, Varun, and Aadhi—all standing together, waving energetically as they noticed us approaching.

"Finally, you guys made it!" Karthi exclaimed, flashing his signature grin.

"Sorry for the delay, guys," I apologized, rubbing the back of my neck sheepishly.

"We can't waste our time here. Come on, let's go inside and explore," Anika chimed in, her excitement evident.

We made our way through the bustling crowd. The college grounds were transformed into a vibrant, festive arena, adorned with colorful banners and streamers fluttering in the evening breeze. Stalls and stages were set up everywhere, and the air was filled with the sounds of laughter, music, and chatter.

"Let's check out the main stage first!" Aliya suggested, pointing towards the largest stage, where a live band was busy setting up their instruments.

"Food can wait, Karthi!" Seema teased, pulling him away as he eyed a nearby food stall longingly. "Let's catch the performance first."

We arrived at the main stage just as the band started playing. The crowd erupted in cheers, and we quickly joined in, clapping and singing along to the energetic beats. The band's performance was electric, setting the perfect tone for the evening. After they wrapped up, we decided to explore more of the event.

One of the smaller stages had a dance competition going on, with students showing off their best moves to the latest hits.

"Guys, wanna see my dance?" Karthi asked, his eyes sparkling with mischief.

"We'd love to!" everyone replied enthusiastically.

Karthi confidently made his way up to the stage. As the music started, he launched into his performance, moving like a pro. The crowd went wild when he nailed a perfect moonwalk, channeling his inner Michael Jackson. Cheers and applause filled the air as he finished with a flourish, bowing to his impressed audience.

"Wow, Karthi! We didn't know you were such a next-level dancer!" Varun said, clapping him on the back as he rejoined us.

"Did you like my performance?" Karthi asked, grinning widely.

"No way you're asking that question—we loved it!" Anika replied, her voice full of admiration.

We moved on to another stage, where a drama play was in progress. The actors were in colorful costumes, performing with passion and flair. The storyline was captivating, drawing us into the performance.

"The drama club has really outdone themselves this year," Aliya remarked, clearly impressed by the quality of the acting and stage design.

But it wasn't long before Karthi's impatience kicked in. "Guys, let's eat something already—I can't wait any longer," he said, practically drooling at the thought of food.

We headed to a nearby food stall where the aroma of sizzling street food filled the air. The menu had everything you could think of—pav bhaji, dabeli, frankies, and more. We ordered a bit of everything, and as soon as the food was served, we dug in eagerly. The flavors were rich and delicious, and we found ourselves humming in satisfaction with every bite.

"This pav bhaji is amazing!" Seema said, licking her fingers. "And this frankie... it's just the right balance of spicy and tangy!"

"I think the dabeli steals the show," Varun chimed in. "It's packed with flavor!"

After finishing our meal, we decided to continue exploring the event. Just then, my phone buzzed. It was my dad calling.

"Where are you, Rishi? We've reached," Dad said on the other end of the line.

"I'm inside the campus. Where are you guys? I'll come find you," I replied.

"We're at the college entrance," he informed me.

"Okay, wait there. I'm on my way," I said, hanging up the call.

"Guys, can you wait for me here? My mom and dad just arrived, so I'm going to fetch them," I told the group.

"Yeah, of course! We'll wait for you right here," they said.

Before I left, I looked over at Aliya. She seemed a bit nervous. I gave her a reassuring smile and headed towards the entrance to find my parents. weaving through the bustling crowd, my mind was already planning how to introduce Aliya to my parents.

I reached the entrance of the college and spotted my family—Mom, Dad, and even Rishika and Roshan had come along. "Mom, Dad, over here!" I called out as I approached them.

Mom was quick to ask, "Where's Ariya, Rishi?"

"Ariya? Who's Ariya?" Dad asked, looking puzzled.

"Mom, it's not Ariya—it's Aliya," I corrected her, shaking my head with a smile.

"Well then, where is she, Rishi? Mom pressed, clearly curious.

"you still haven't answered my question. Who's this Ariya, I mean Aliya?" dad asked, clearly confused.

"You'll see for yourself, Dad. Now, let's go inside," I said, trying to steer the conversation away as I led the way toward the event area.

Roshan, who was walking beside me, leaned in and whispered, "Don't tell me you have a girlfriend, Rishi."

"Yep, I do. If you don't believe me, you can ask Rishika about it," I replied, unable to hide the pride in my voice.

Rishika smirked and nodded, clearly enjoying the little secret she was already in on.

As we reached the spot where I'd left Aliya and the others, I looked around but couldn't find them. My heart sank a little. They were nowhere to be seen. I scanned the crowd, hoping to catch a glimpse of them, but there was no sign of anyone from our group.

"Where exactly are you taking us, Rishi?" Roshan asked, puzzled.

"I told my friends to wait here, but it seems like they went somewhere else," I explained, already pulling out my phone to call them.

Just as I was about to dial, my phone buzzed. It was Aliya calling. I instantly answered. "Where are you, Aliya?"

She stayed quiet for a moment, and after a brief pause, she finally said, "Rishi, can you come to the backyard of the college?"

The fact that she used my name instead of the usual playful nicknames immediately set off alarm bells in my head. Something wasn't right.

"Is everything okay?" I asked, concern lacing my voice. "And where's everyone else?"

"Everything's fine. Just hurry up and come to the backyard," she replied, but there was a note of hesitation in her voice that only made me worry more.

I knew something was wrong. "I'm really sorry, Mom, Dad — something urgent came up, and I have to go. You guys go ahead and explore the event. I'll catch up with you later," I said quickly and rushed toward the backyard without waiting for their response.

As I made my way through the bustling crowd, my mind raced with possibilities. Aliya sounded dead serious, and the unusual location she mentioned only fueled my anxiety. I hoped nothing bad had happened, but I couldn't shake off the uneasy feeling in my chest.

Unlike the front of the college, the backyard was dimly lit and eerily quiet. As I approached, I found Aliya and the others huddled together at the far end, their faces etched with fear. I couldn't understand why they had come here or what was going on.

As I approached them, the tension in the air was palpable. "What happened, guys? Why are you here?" I asked, but before anyone could respond, Vikram, Rahul, Arjun, Raj, and a few others I didn't recognize, but clearly weren't from our college, emerged from the shadows and positioned themselves between me and my friends. Vikram's cruel smile sent a shiver down my spine.

"Now let's see how you save your friends," Vikram said, his cruel smile cutting through the darkness.

"Galath wakth par galath jagah pahonch gaya hei tu." You've ended up in the wrong place at the wrong time. Remember, this time I won't show any mercy, I retorted, trying to hide my fear.

"Today, fate might be on my side," Rishab. This time, I'm the one who won't show any mercy," Vikram blurted back.

"After I take care of your men, we'll see whose side fate is on," I shot back defiantly.

One of the new faces stepped forward, ready to attack. Three of them came at me simultaneously. The first one swung a punch, but I dodged. The other two were faster, their blows landing hard and strong, sending me staggering backward.

Aliya and the others tried to intervene, but Rahul, Arjun, and Raj held them back. Vikram's malicious laughter filled the air. "Looks like someone's getting a proper beatdown," Vikram jeered.

"You managed to land a blow on me—impressive," I said, gritting my teeth.

My eyes caught sight of a wooden log lying on the ground. With a burst of adrenaline, I grabbed it. As one of them lunged at me again, I swung the log and hit him on the head. He collapsed, blood oozing from his wound, his screams of pain piercing the night.

"One down," I said, panting as I turned to face the other two. They charged at me together, but I used the log as a shield, deflecting their kicks. I quickly steadied myself and struck them both with the log. They fell to the ground, howling in agony.

"Go, you three! What are you waiting for?" Vikram shouted at his men.

"I don't want to get hospitalized," Rahul said, clearly frightened.

"Me neither," Arjun added.

"And you, Raj?" Vikram's voice was laced with frustration.

"I'm not going to the hospital!" Raj declared.

"You scaredy cats! You're all morons!" Vikram cursed, his anger boiling over.

He charged at me. I was ready to block his attack, but Vikram was quicker. He pulled out a canister and sprayed it directly into my eyes. The intense burning sensation told me it was pepper spray. I staggered back, rubbing my eyes desperately but unable to see clearly.

"Now attack!" Vikram yelled.

I struggled to see through the searing pain. Blinded and in pain, I stumbled, trying to regain my vision. I could barely make out a figure approaching me, but before I could react, he struck a metal rod hard on my head. I turned to face the attacker, but his face was obscured by a mask. The eyes peering out from behind the mask were filled with hatred—a look I felt I would never forget. The pain overwhelmed me, and I collapsed to the ground.

Amidst the chaos, I heard Aliya's panicked voice. "Catch her! Don't let her go!" Vikram ordered.

"Leave me, please! Let me go!" Aliya's voice pleaded.

"Beat him and kill the others. I want both of them alive," Vikram commanded.

I felt the blows landing on me, the pain becoming almost unbearable. My senses began to fail. I tried to focus, but the pain in my head and my blurring vision made it nearly impossible to focus. My friends' cries filled the air. The last thing I saw was a red substance—blood—flowing from my friends as they fell, and then everything went black.

I was unconscious...

Chapter Four

Endless Confinement

Present Moment:

The night's cool breeze brought me back to reality as I stood on the balcony, gazing across the vast city illuminated by countless lights. I had lost track of time, lost in memories I hadn't wanted to revisit. My body trembled as the cold air clung to me, reminding me I'd been out here for far too long.

I finally decided to head inside, shaking off the chill. When I glanced at the clock, I was shocked—it was already four in the morning. I couldn't believe I'd been standing there for hours, letting the past haunt me all over again.

I needed to get some sleep. I made my way to the bedroom, where Riya was still curled up on the bed, sleeping peacefully. Her gentle breathing and serene face brought a much-needed sense of calm. The sight of her made me smile; she looked so innocent and carefree, completely oblivious to the turmoil that had gripped me.

I brushed a strand of hair away from Riya's face and gently kissed her forehead. She sighed contentedly in her sleep, As I was about to nestle down beside her when I heard a sudden knocking on the front door. My heart immediately started to race, and the hairs on the back of my neck stood on end. Who would be knocking on someone else's door at four in the morning? This couldn't be good.

My mind immediately jumped to the worst-case scenario: did Vikram's men track us down here? No... that can't be possible. We had just managed to escape that dreadful life after so much struggle. They can't pull us back into that prison of fear. The idea of being dragged back into that nightmare was too horrifying to consider. They couldn't imprison us again.

I desperately wished the knocking would stop, but it only grew louder and more insistent. Riya stirred slightly in her sleep, as if disturbed by the noise. If this continued, she would wake up, and I didn't want her to be frightened. I had to face whoever was at the door before they broke it down.

Determined, and careful not to wake Riya, I quietly closed the bedroom door behind me, bolting it shut. I needed a weapon, something to defend us with. The only thing that came to mind was a knife. I rushed to the kitchen, frantically searching, and found one on the pantry.

With the knife in hand, I steeled myself for a confrontation and approached the front door. My heart thumped like a drum, my legs trembling as I reached for the doorknob. but the knocking continued relentlessly.

Gathering all the courage I could muster, I swung the door open, gripping the knife tightly in my hand. Without even looking to see who it was, I instinctively slashed the knife forward, fully expecting to hear screams of pain from Vikram's men if I managed to land a hit.

But instead of the expected screams from Vikram's men, I heard a woman's terrified shriek—a voice I recognized. Then, a familiar man's voice shouted, "What are you doing, Rishi?"

My heart dropped. I froze, my grip on the knife slackening as reality started to sink in. I blinked, my vision clearing as I realized who was standing before me. My breath catches in my throat. My jaw fell open as I recognized who they were. The knife slipped from my trembling hand, clattering loudly onto the floor.

"Thank God we dodged it in time," the woman said, her voice trembling slightly. "You could have killed us, Rishi!"

"I knew something like this would happen for sure," the male voice said with a laugh. "Anyway, how are you, buddy? It's been a long time."

The people standing before me were Karthik and Seema, my close friends. They were both grinning, with wide smiles lighting up their faces. For a moment, I just stood there, unable to process it. Then, suddenly, tears welled up in my eyes. Without thinking, I launched myself forward and hugged them tightly, clinging to them as if I never wanted to let go.

"Whoa, slow down, Rishi! Don't break our bones!" Seema exclaimed, laughing but sounding a bit strained.

"Yeah, we can't breathe, man! We're not running away—you can let us go," Karthik added, half-choking, half-laughing.

I pulled back just enough to look at their faces, "I can't believe it's really you guys," I said, tears rolling down my cheeks. "Do you know how much I've missed you?"

"We missed you too, Rishi," Seema said softly, her voice laced with emotion.

"Are we going to stand here all night, or are you going to invite us inside?" Karthik teased.

"Oh, sorry! Please, come in," I said, stepping aside to let them in.

As they entered, I could feel a warmth spreading through me, a sense of comfort I hadn't felt in a long time. My past might still haunt me, but having my friends here, right now, made everything feel a little bit lighter.

Karthik and Seema settled on the sofa while I took a chair opposite them. I could hardly believe what I was seeing. "I thought Vikram had killed you on that tragic day," I began. "Seeing you both alive... I just... I can't express it." I paused and "Where's everyone else? Why didn't you bring them with you?"

Karthik and Seema exchanged a glance. Karthik began, his voice somber, "You see, Rishi, on that day when Vikram had... us... he stabbed us all," he said, his voice trailing off. And he fell silent, the weight of the memory evident in his expression.

"Tell me, Karthik. What happened to everyone?" I pressed, though a part of me already feared the answer.

"Everyone died that day, except Karthik and me. We had severe injuries and were hospitalized for many months." Seema said, her voice was barely a whisper.

An uncomfortable silence hung between us.

"I'm so sorry," I said, my voice cracking. "I couldn't save you back then. It's all my fault. Aliya warned me so many times, but I refused to listen. I was a fool to ignore her. I failed to protect my own friends. If only I had been more cautious, this wouldn't have happened. We'd still be living peacefully, like we used to."

Stop it, Rishi. Enough," Seema interrupted, placing her hand on mine. "No more blaming yourself. It wasn't your fault. Vikram's the one to blame for our friends' deaths, not you. You fought bravely that day, risking your life to save everyone. You did more than anyone could ask for."

"Yeah, Seema's right," Karthik agreed reassuringly. "It's all Vikram's fault, not yours."

"Let's not dwell on that tragic day, please," Seema suggested, her voice pleading. "It's too painful."

"We should change the topic. Where's Aliya? Is she sleeping? And who is that child you're roaming with?" Karthik asked.

I hesitated. This was the one question I feared answering. How could I tell them that Aliya was gone, that she was dead? Even Riya doesn't know the full truth. The pain of that loss was still raw, and I wasn't ready to speak of it.

"Wait a minute, Karthik," Seema said, noticing something. "How did you know Rishi was back in Mumbai and with a child?"

Karthik took out his phone and played a news clip. The anchor was reporting about a dead body found outside the city—a man who had been shot with a Beretta M9A4. The victim was identified as a wanted criminal involved in kidnappings and murders. The video showed the lifeless body of Vikram lying on the ground.

"After seeing this news, "I was certain that only one man could have killed Vikram," Karthik explained. "That would be Rishi. And I started searching for you, both in Kashmir and Mumbai, but I couldn't find a trace. Two days ago, I was heading to America on a business trip and stopped by this hotel to say goodbye to a friend of mine who works here as a receptionist. She told me that you had been asking about me. I knew then it had to be you, so I tracked you down," Karthik explained.

"Anyway, tell us, Rishi—where's Aliya? And who is that child?" Karthik asked again, his voice more insistent.

I stayed silent

"Rishab, what happened?" Seema urged. "Why are you quiet all of a sudden? Tell us, where is Aliya? We want to see her."

Their eyes searched mine, desperate for an answer, but I couldn't find the words. The truth was too painful, too devastating to share. "I'm sorry, guys, but you can't see Aliya anymore," I finally said, my voice barely above a whisper.

"What do you mean by 'we can't see her anymore'?" Seema asked, her voice tinged with surprise and confusion.

I stayed quiet for a moment, struggling to find the right words. How could I explain the horrors that Aliya and I endured? How could I tell them about the life we were forced to live in that dreadful place, and how Aliya died giving birth to Riya? The weight of those memories bore down on me, making it difficult to speak.

"Why are you silent, Rishab? Say something! We have the right to know what happened to Aliya," Seema insisted, her impatience growing.

"Calm down, Seema. Go easy on him," Karthik interjected, his tone soothing. "He's been through a lot. We can't just force him to talk."

"No, Karthik," I interrupted. "You both deserve to know what happened. You need to understand what Aliya and I went through after Vikram kidnapped us, and why you can't see Aliya anymore." My voice cracked as I continued. "And as for the child you saw me with, well... then you have to listen to the whole story—our story of six years in confinement, and what happened after Vikram took us," I said, the weight of the past pressing down on my shoulders.

Seema and Karthik exchanged a glance, their expressions shifting from confusion to concern. "Go on, Rishi. We're ready to listen," Seema said softly.

I took a deep breath, feeling the memories surge up like a tidal wave. This was not just my story—it was Aliya's too. The story of our six years in hell, the pain, the loss, and the little light that came into our lives despite it all.

And so, I began to tell them everything.

When I woke up, everything was dark. My head throbbed with pain, the sharp ache reminding me of the metal rod that had struck me. I managed to push myself up to my feet, struggling to steady my balance. My senses were on high alert, but there was nothing to see—just pitch-black darkness. I stretched out my hands, blindly feeling around until my fingers brushed against cold, solid stone. The walls boxed me in on all sides, and the more I explored, the clearer it became—there was no door, no windows, no way out. I was trapped.

"Hello, is anyone there?" I shouted into the void. My voice echoed through the emptiness, bouncing back to me without a reply. I shouted again, louder this time, but there was nothing. No answer.

I stood there, trying to remember what happened before I blacked out. The fight with Vikram and his men flashed in my mind—the college backyard, Aliya, and the others. Someone hit me from behind. Who was it? I couldn't remember his face, but those eyes... those malicious eyes burned into my memory. There was something terrifying in them and

I'd never forget them. Who was he? And what happened to my friends? Where are they? And what happened to Aliya? Did Vikram take me alone, or did he capture my friends too?

I clenched my fists, anger and regret swirling inside me. I should've protected them better. I should've—

My thoughts were interrupted by muffled voices coming from somewhere outside. I immediately started shouting again, banging on the walls. "I'm in here! Can anyone hear me?" But there was no response—just silence.

Suddenly, there was a creaking sound above me. I froze, staring at the ceiling as tiny holes appeared, allowing slivers of sunlight to pierce through the darkness. The light was faint, but it was enough to reveal the dark room and its grim features.

A rickety wooden cot stood in one corner, and a nearby bucket and toilet hinted at the room's grim purpose. I felt an icy chill of realization—this was a prison—a place designed to hold me captive.

Then, a small rectangular hole appeared in the wall. "Hello, Rishab. You're awake. That's great," Vikram's voice came through the small hole, his tone dripping with malice. "I hope you're comfortable in your new home."

My instincts flared with anger and fear. "Why did you bring me here, Vikram? What is this place? Where are my friends? Aliya?"

"Oh, I forgot to mention," Vikram's voice was almost cheerful, "welcome to my secret base, far from any human reach. From now on, you'll live here, suffering with every breath you take and regretting every moment you dared to oppose me. As for your friends... they're all dead. I killed them all. And Aliya—she's still alive for now. You'll hear her voice in a few minutes, but you'll never be able to meet her or see her, even if she dies."

The shock of Vikram's words hit me like a sledgehammer. My heart pounded violently in my chest, and my breath caught in my throat. The realization that my friends were dead was unbearable. I couldn't comprehend the enormity of the loss. My mind reeled, and my whole body felt numb. I sank to the floor, my strength drained by the devastating news.

"Tell me this is a lie," I begged, my voice cracking with desperation. "Tell me it isn't true. Please, you bastard," I shouted.

"I wish I could," Vikram's tone was cold and dismissive. "But the truth must be told, right? Your friends are dead. That's the reality."

His words were like a cruel knife twisting in my heart. The grief was overwhelming. I felt as if the ground had been pulled out from beneath me, leaving me in a void of sorrow. Tears streamed down my face, and my body shook with silent sobs. The weight of the tragedy was crushing, and I felt an all-consuming despair. I lay there, paralyzed by the enormity of what I had just heard, my mind struggling to grasp the finality of it all.

"You won't get away with this, Vikram," I whispered, my voice barely audible, choked by my grief. "I swear, I'll make you pay for this."

Huh... whatever, but Before I leave, Vikram's voice was final and detached, "I want to make one thing clear—don't even think about trying to escape. No matter what you do, you won't be able to get out of this place. You're trapped here forever, in short, YOU CAN'T ESCAPE."

With that, his voice faded away, leaving me alone in the darkness. The silence that followed was deafening, filled only by my own ragged breaths and the overwhelming grief that threatened to consume me. I was alone, trapped in this dreadful place, and the loss of my friends weighed heavily on my heart.

I couldn't believe it. I couldn't even let the thought settle in—Karthi, Seema, Varun, Aadhi, and Anika... all of them, gone. Dead. My mind refused to accept it. I felt a scream building up inside me, but no sound came out. The grief was so heavy that it felt like it was crushing me from the inside. My chest tightened, and I could barely breathe. How could they all be dead? How could everything end like this?

Suddenly, a glimmer of hope sparked in my mind—I had my phone! Maybe, just maybe, there was still a chance to get out of here. My heart raced with a glimmer of hope as I frantically searched my pockets. But when my fingers reached into my pocket, all I found was emptiness. My phone was gone. Vikram must have taken it when they brought me here. My last hope of escape, of contacting anyone, was gone too. Vikram must have taken it from me when I was unconscious.

The hope that had briefly flickered vanished instantly. I was trapped, completely cut off from the outside world. I felt my heart sink as the realization hit me—I was alone in this hellish place with no way out.

"Leave me!" A scream pierced the silence, a voice filled with fear and desperation. My heart jumped—Aliya!

"Aliya! Are you there?" I shouted with all the strength I had left, my voice cracking with panic. "Aliya, can you hear me?"

"Rishi... Is that you?" Her voice came through, trembling and weak, but it was definitely her. "Oh my God... thank God you're alright!" She was crying, the relief in her voice mixed with overwhelming fear. The sound of her voice was so close—it must mean she was in the room next to mine.

"Are you alright, Aliya?" I asked urgently, desperate to know she was okay.

"I'm fine... I'm fine," she said, though her voice was shaky. I let out a sigh of relief. Knowing she was alive and safe brought some comfort, even if it was small.

But the thought of my friends still gnawed at me. I needed to know—were they really gone? "Do you know where everyone else is?" I asked, clinging to the hope that maybe, just maybe, they were alive somewhere.

There was a long silence. Then, suddenly, Aliya's sobbing grew louder, her cries filled with anguish. My heart raced as I pressed her for an answer. "Aliya, tell me they're okay! Please... tell me they're safe!"

Her sobs turned into broken words. "Vikram... he... he killed them... everyone... they're all dead..."

Her words shattered the last bit of hope I had. My legs gave way, and I fell to my knees. My friends—Karthi, Seema, Varun, Aadhi, and Anika—were really gone. I felt like the world was crumbling around me, and the pain of losing them was unbearable. Tears welled up in my eyes, but they felt pointless. No amount of crying would bring them back.

All I could do was sit there, overwhelmed by grief and helplessness, while Aliya's sobs echoed in the background. The reality of it all was sinking in—Vikram had taken everything from me.

I still couldn't accept it—couldn't wrap my mind around the fact that my friends were dead. The anger inside me began to swell, a burning fury that almost consumed the grief. In that moment, all I wanted was to get my hands on Vikram and tear him apart. I clenched my fists, trembling with rage, and slammed my hand against the wall with all the strength I had. The pain shot through my knuckles, but it didn't matter. Nothing compared to the pain of losing them. I felt sick with frustration and guilt. How could I have let this happen?

"If I'd just listened to you that day," I muttered bitterly, my voice shaking, "maybe our friends would still be alive. Maybe we wouldn't be trapped in this damn place. It's all my fault." My words were filled with self-loathing. I couldn't shake the regret gnawing at me—regret for not heeding Aliya's warnings back then. Maybe, if I had been more careful, they would still be with us, and we'd be laughing and celebrating at the college anniversary instead of rotting in this nightmare.

"No, Rishi, don't do this to yourself!" Aliya's voice was firm but trembling with emotion. "It's not your fault. It's Vikram—he's the one who killed them. He's the monster here, not you. You can't blame yourself for what he did. Don't take the weight of his sins on your shoulders."

"But still," I said, my voice cracking, "if I had been just a little more cautious, if I'd paid more attention, none of this would've happened. We might still be together, happy, enjoying our lives... if only I'd been more careful—"

"Stop it, Rishi! Just stop!" Aliya cut me off, her tone desperate yet pleading. "What's done is done. We can't change it now. Two days have passed since Vikram took us—two days, Rishi. It's over. We have to face reality."

Her words hit me like a ton of bricks. "Two days?" I repeated, stunned. I couldn't believe I'd been unconscious for that long. Two whole days lost, with no memory of what had happened. It felt like time had slipped through my fingers, leaving me even more disoriented. "I was out for two days?"

"Yeah..." Aliya's voice was quieter now, filled with exhaustion and sadness. "I was unconscious too. When I woke up, they were dragging me into this room. I have no idea where we are."

Hearing her helplessness made my heart ache. We were completely in the dark—trapped, isolated, and with no clue where we were or how to get out. The hopelessness of our situation weighed heavily on me, but I knew I couldn't let it break me. Not now. I had to stay strong, for Aliya's sake and for the memory of our friends. But the grief and guilt still clung to me like a dark cloud, refusing to let go.

Eventually, the sun began to set, its fading rays slowly retreating from the cracks above. The room, once again, was swallowed by darkness, leaving me in that suffocating void. The only sign of time passing was the gradual dimming of light until the room was pitch black. Just when I thought I would be left alone in the darkness, a small bulb flickered to life overhead, casting a weak glow that barely filled the space.

I leaned against the cold wall, still processing everything. My mind was restless, cycling between grief, anger, and desperation. I couldn't help but wonder if people were out there, searching for us. The thought gave me a small shred of hope, but I knew we were far from being rescued.

"Hey, Aliya..." I called out softly, breaking the silence. "Do you think everyone's worried and looking for us?"

"Of course," she replied, her voice sounding tired yet hopeful. "I'm sure the whole college knows by now—students, teachers... even your parents must be searching everywhere for us. They've probably contacted the police too. They won't stop until they find us."

I wanted to believe her, but Vikram's twisted plan made me doubt anyone could find this hidden hellhole. As I pondered our chances of rescue, I heard a faint scraping sound. Someone was sliding something through the small rectangular hole in the wall. I walked over and picked it up—a plastic bag. My stomach churned as I opened it, revealing two stale pieces of bread and a bottle of water. This was all they were giving us to survive.

"Aliya, did you get a packet too?" I asked, hoping at least she wasn't being deprived of basic necessities.

"Yeah," she answered with a sigh. "Two stale breads and a bottle of water."

"We don't have much of a choice," I muttered, trying to push away the disgust in my voice. "If we want to stay alive, we'll have to eat it."

We ate in silence, the taste of the bread dry and bitter in my mouth, but it was enough to keep the hunger at bay. Despite Aliya being so close—just on the other side of this wall—I felt the agonizing distance between us. I could hear her voice, but I couldn't see her, couldn't reach out and hold her. This damn wall stood between us like an unbreakable barrier. I clenched my fists in frustration, wishing I could tear it down and free us both. But there was nothing I could do, except sit there in the dim light, listening to her breathing and knowing we were both trapped in this nightmare.

After our unpleasant dinner, Aliya and I talked, our voices low and laced with uncertainty. I kept reassuring her—and maybe even myself—that no matter what, we would find a way to escape this place. I had to cling to that hope, even if it felt almost impossible in this situation. We didn't know how long we kept talking; the room had no clock, no way to tell time. But I felt that as long as we kept talking, we could hold onto some sense of sanity.

Eventually, exhaustion crept in, and I tried to lie down on the rickety wooden cot, but sleep wouldn't come. The bed was hard, creaking under every slight movement, but the real reason I couldn't sleep was my mind racing with dark thoughts. I couldn't stop thinking about Karthi, Seema, Anika, Varun, and Aadhi. Were they really dead? Did Vikram go that far just to punish me? The more I tried not to think about it, the more their faces haunted me. I shut my eyes tight, forcing myself to push those thoughts away. But every time I did, a pair of those malicious eyes flashed in my mind—the eyes of the man who hit me. If he hadn't struck me down that day, my friends might still be alive. Aliya and I wouldn't be trapped here, with no escape in sight. Rage bubbled up inside me as I clenched my fists. If I ever meet that man again, I swear it would be his last day on earth.

I don't know when I finally drifted off to sleep, but when I woke up the next morning, the dim light from the bulb was already flickering above me. Someone had already dropped the same miserable package as yesterday. My body ached from the uncomfortable cot, and I rubbed my eyes, trying to shake off the stiffness. I dragged myself over to the rusty tap to wash my face. The water was freezing cold, shocking me awake as I splashed it on my face. The chill reminded me that even the smallest comfort was out of reach in this place.

After freshening up, I picked up the packet they'd left. Again, there were two stale pieces of bread, tough and tasteless. I sighed and called out to Aliya, "Did you get the same package, Aliya?"

"Yeah... just two breads," she replied, her voice carrying the same frustration I felt.

It was the same miserable routine all over again, and I hated how quickly we were falling into it. But as much as I despised it, we had to eat. I forced down the bread, each bite feeling like it was scraping against my throat. But I knew we needed to keep our strength up if we ever had any hope of getting out of here.

As I sat back down, I couldn't shake the thought—if we stay trapped here much longer, will there even be any strength left to escape?

After finishing the stale bread, I leaned back against the cold wall, my mind spinning with thoughts of escape. But no matter how hard I tried to think of a plan, nothing made sense. The walls were solid stone, no windows, and only a single door that was hidden, with no sign of how it even opened. The only light came from the small holes in the ceiling that let in sunlight during the day and that single weak bulb at night. We were trapped in what felt like an underground tomb, completely cut off from the outside world.

The air was thick with the weight of our situation, with no sound except the occasional drip of water from the tap. Time moved slowly, each second dragging out like an eternity. We talked in bits and pieces, but mostly, we sat in silence, lost in our own thoughts.

Hours passed, or at least it felt that way. I tried not to think about my friends, but their faces kept flashing in my mind, along with the terrible image of Vikram smirking while he boasted about killing them. The anger inside me simmered, but it was mixed with helplessness. If I were free, I would make him pay. But here? I was just a prisoner, powerless.

Suddenly, Aliya's voice cut through the silence. "Rishi, do you think anyone's looking for us? Maybe the police?"

"I hope so," I said, trying to sound confident. "Our teachers, our classmates, my parents—they must be doing everything they can to find us. And knowing them, they won't stop until they do."

I could hear her holding back tears. The wall between us was more than just stone; it felt like it was separating us from everything and everyone we cared about. I wanted so badly to comfort her, but all I could do was speak through that cold, unfeeling wall.

A few more hours passed. We barely spoke, and the silence was suffocating. Then, just like the day before, another plastic bag was shoved through the small hole in the wall. I opened it and found more stale bread and a water bottle. The same miserable meal.

"Aliya, did you get yours?" I asked, trying to sound upbeat.

"Yeah... same as before," she replied, her voice flat and exhausted.

We ate in silence again. The bread was dry and tasteless, but we had no choice but to choke it down. I couldn't stop thinking about how pathetic it all was—barely surviving on scraps in this hellhole, while somewhere out there, Vikram was living comfortably, enjoying every moment of our suffering.

After we finished eating, I lay down on the cot, staring up at the ceiling. My mind drifted between anger, sadness, and exhaustion. I thought about how we used to laugh and joke around at college, about the plans we had for the future. It all seemed so distant now, like another lifetime.

Just as I was lost in thought, Aliya spoke up again. "Rishi... what if... what if we never get out of here?"

Her words hit me like a punch to the gut. I wanted to say something reassuring, to tell her everything would be okay, but the truth was I didn't know if we'd ever see the outside world again. For a moment, I felt like I couldn't breathe. The fear was suffocating.

But I couldn't let her hear that in my voice. "Don't think like that, Aliya. We'll get out of here. We just have to hold on a little longer. Someone's going to find us."

She didn't respond, but I could hear her quietly sobbing on the other side of the wall. It broke my heart, but there was nothing I could do except sit there and listen, feeling more helpless than ever.

The hours dragged on, and eventually, exhaustion took over. Despite the discomfort of the cot and the turmoil in my mind, I fell into a restless sleep. But even in my dreams, I couldn't escape the nightmare of this place.

Week 1:

The first week was a blur of shock and confusion. I still couldn't fully grasp what had happened. My mind kept playing tricks on me, making me believe that any moment someone would come bursting through the walls to rescue us. But the days dragged on, and the only thing that broke the silence was my own voice echoing back at me. The room was small and oppressive, with walls that seemed to close in every time I tried to sleep. I would talk to Aliya through the wall, trying to keep both of us sane. We kept reassuring each other that someone out there was looking for us, but deep down, I could hear the doubt creeping into both our voices. It was the hope that hurt the most—hope that maybe, just maybe, this was all a nightmare we'd wake up from.

The stale bread and cold water were barely enough to keep us alive. The first few days, we tried to ration it, but hunger made that impossible. We quickly realized this was all we were going to get. I would hold the bread in my mouth for a long time, trying to ignore how dry and tasteless it was. My stomach constantly growled, reminding me of how empty it was. The bread felt like chewing on cardboard, and the water tasted bitter. I started to feel weak, and even standing up took more energy than it should have. My body ached all over, and I could tell Aliya was suffering the same. We would share brief moments of silence after eating, both of us too drained to talk.

Every night was a struggle. The wooden cot creaked every time I moved, and the darkness was suffocating. I could hear every creak, every drop of water from the old tap in the corner. My mind wouldn't shut off, constantly replaying the fight with Vikram and his men. I could see the person's eyes, who hit me from behind, the malice and hatred in them. If I hadn't been hit, maybe we wouldn't be trapped here. I blamed myself for not being careful enough. Guilt gnawed at me, refusing to let me sleep. I kept thinking about my friends—Karthi, Seema, Anika, Varun, and Aadhi. Were they really dead? The thought was unbearable. I would clench my fists, feeling rage bubbling up inside, but there was no one to direct it at.

The loneliness was maddening. The only relief was talking to Aliya. I would ask her about the outside world, imagining what it was like while we were stuck in this miserable place. She tried to keep me hopeful, but I could hear the exhaustion in her voice. She was struggling just as much as I was. Sometimes, I could hear her crying softly at night, trying to hide it from me. I would press my ear against the wall, wishing I could reach out and comfort her, but there was nothing I could do. We were both trapped in our own versions of hell, separated by a thin wall.

By the end of the first week, the realization of our situation fully set in. No one was coming for us. I felt my hope crumbling bit by bit, replaced by despair. The room had no windows, no clock, no way to tell time. Day and night blended together into a never-ending stretch of darkness and silence. The only thing that marked time was the delivery of our meager meals. I started counting the seconds, just to keep my mind occupied. I lost track after a while. The monotony was unbearable. I found myself wishing for something—anything—to happen, just to break the silence.

Week 2:

The second week began with the harsh reality that this nightmare wasn't ending anytime soon. I was losing track of time, and the days blended together into one endless loop of suffering. My body was growing weaker, and even talking to Aliya became difficult. I noticed how both of our voices were losing energy, like we were slowly fading. The bread was getting staler by the day, harder to chew, and I had to force myself to swallow it down. Water was barely enough to wash away the taste. Hunger was a constant companion, gnawing at my insides and making it hard to think clearly. My stomach cramped from the lack of food, and I could feel my strength leaving me bit by bit.

The isolation was starting to mess with my mind. I would lie awake for hours, staring into the darkness, imagining sounds that weren't there. Sometimes, I thought I could hear footsteps outside or distant voices, but I knew it was just my mind playing tricks on me. I would sit there, trying to think of a way to escape, but the walls were solid, and the door was hidden somewhere I couldn't see. Frustration built up inside me, but I had nowhere to release it. I would punch the wall until my knuckles bled, just to feel something other than helplessness. It was all pointless.

Talking to Aliya was the only thing that kept me grounded. We would talk about everything and nothing—our past, our friends, our families. I could tell she was holding onto hope for both of us, even if it was fading. I would ask her over and over if she thought someone would find us, and she would always say yes, but I could hear the uncertainty in her voice. I tried to comfort her, but I felt like a hypocrite. How could I give her hope when I didn't have any left? Sometimes, she would cry, and I hated myself for not being able to protect her from this. I kept telling her that I'd find a way out, but those words felt hollow.

By midweek, my thoughts were consumed by guilt. I couldn't stop thinking about my friends. The image of them lying dead somewhere haunted me, replaying in my mind like a broken record. I kept thinking about how I failed them, how I should've been more careful. I should've listened to Aliya, taken her warnings seriously. If I had, maybe we wouldn't be here. The regret was suffocating. I would whisper apologies into the darkness, hoping that somehow they could hear me. I felt like I was losing pieces of myself every day.

As the week dragged on, I began to feel numb. My emotions were dulled, and everything felt distant. I stopped caring about time, stopped trying to keep track of the days. All that mattered was getting through each hour, surviving the next meal. I would force myself to eat the bread, even though it made me nauseous. I couldn't afford to let myself get any weaker. I kept telling myself that I had to stay strong, that I had to protect Aliya, but it was hard to believe those words when every day felt like a step closer to death.

Week 3:

By the third week, we had settled into a grim routine. The light filtering through the ceiling holes marked the only semblance of day, while the bulb's dim glow defined the night. Our conversations had grown shorter, more strained. We were running out of things to talk about, and neither of us wanted to acknowledge the growing despair. The silence between us became heavier. When we did speak, it was often just to reassure each other that we were still there, still alive. I could hear the exhaustion in Aliya's voice, and it scared me. She was always the optimistic one, the one who kept us both hopeful. But now, even she was struggling.

Eating had become a chore. The bread was harder than ever, and I could barely stomach it. I would tear off small pieces, chewing slowly to make it last longer, but it tasted like dust in my mouth. My body was getting weaker. I could feel my muscles wasting away, and my energy was draining fast. Even moving felt like a monumental effort. I was constantly cold, shivering under my thin clothes. The room's dampness seemed to seep into my bones. My joints ached, and my head throbbed from dehydration. Sleep was impossible—I would lie awake, staring at the ceiling, thinking of nothing and everything at once.

By this point, I had given up trying to make sense of time. Days and nights blended together into an endless cycle of monotony. I could barely keep my thoughts straight. I would drift in and out of consciousness, caught between sleep and waking. Sometimes, I would hear Aliya muttering to herself, as if trying to hold onto her sanity. I knew I was doing the same. We were both clinging to whatever we could—memories of better times, fantasies of escape—anything to distract ourselves from the reality of our situation. But the longer we stayed here, the harder it became to hold onto those thoughts.

The guilt was still there, gnawing at me every moment. I couldn't shake the feeling that I had failed everyone. I kept replaying that last fight in my head, wondering what I could have done differently. Maybe if I had been faster, if I hadn't let my guard down, things would be different. But there was no going back. My friends were dead, and I was trapped here, unable to do anything. The helplessness was unbearable. I wanted to scream, to break something, but I didn't even have the energy for that anymore. All I could do was sit there, staring at the wall, feeling the weight of my failure.

By the end of the third week, I was losing the will to keep going. The darkness felt endless, and the faint light from the bulb seemed like a cruel joke. Every day felt the same—endless hours of nothingness, punctuated only by the delivery of stale bread. The loneliness was eating away at me. Aliya was the only thing keeping me sane, but even our conversations had grown hollow. I could tell she was struggling, too. We were both barely holding on, just surviving from one moment to the next. But deep down, I knew we couldn't last much longer like this.

Week 4:

The fourth week was when the hopelessness really set in. The routine had become mind-numbing: wake up to the same dim light, force down the same stale bread, and talk to Aliya just to remind ourselves that we were still alive. Our voices had lost all energy. We spoke in whispers now, our words weighed down by exhaustion and despair. Every conversation felt like it could be our last. I could hear the cracks in Aliya's resolve, and it terrified me. If she gave up, I didn't know if I could keep going. I tried to stay strong for her, but it was getting harder to pretend.

My body was deteriorating rapidly. I had lost so much weight that my clothes hung loosely on me. My bones ached constantly, and I could feel my ribs pressing against my skin. The bread was practically inedible now, rock hard and tasteless. But we had no choice but to eat it. The water had a metallic taste, leaving a bitter aftertaste in my mouth. I was always thirsty, but drinking too much made me feel sick. I could barely stand without feeling dizzy, and every movement sent a jolt of pain through my body. I knew I was getting weaker by the day, and there was nothing I could do about it.

Sleep was a distant memory. Even when I managed to doze off, I was haunted by nightmares—visions of my friends' lifeless bodies, Vikram's mocking laughter, and the walls closing in on me. I would wake up in a cold sweat, my heart racing, but there was no escape. The room was a prison, both physically and mentally. I felt like I was losing my grip on reality. Time had lost all meaning, and the days stretched on endlessly. I couldn't tell if it had been hours or days since I last slept. The only thing that marked time was the arrival of the next meal, and even that had become a twisted form of torture.

Talking to Aliya had become painful. Every word felt like a struggle, and I could hear the despair in her voice. We tried to comfort each other, but there was nothing left to say. We were both trapped in our own minds, battling demons that neither of us could fully understand. I could hear her crying more often now, and it broke my heart. I felt like I had failed her, too. I was supposed to protect her, to keep her safe, but all I could do was listen as she suffered. The guilt was overwhelming. I would lie awake, staring at the wall, wishing for a way out, but there was none.

By the end of the fourth week, I had given up on hope entirely. The future seemed bleak—an endless stretch of suffering with no end in sight. I stopped caring about escape, stopped fantasizing about revenge. All that mattered was surviving the next day, the next meal. I had become numb to the pain, the hunger, the loneliness. I was just going through the motions, waiting for something to change, even if it was for the worse. The light in the room felt like a cruel reminder of the world outside—a world we might never see again. All that was left was the darkness, the silence, and the slow, creeping despair that filled every corner of the room.

Week 16:

It's been four months since we've been trapped in this dreadful place. Time has become a blur—days turning into nights with no real difference between them. I've lost count of how many times I've pleaded with Vikram to let us go, but he's as cold-hearted as ever. He visits every once in a while, just to gloat or check on us like we're some kind of prisoners he's proud to keep caged. Each time he leaves, I'm filled with more rage, but it's useless. I still have no idea where we are or how to escape from this nightmare.

The monotony of eating the same tasteless bread three times a day has worn us down. It's not even food anymore; it's just something to keep us from starving. Aliya tries her best to eat it, but I know she's struggling more than she lets on. We barely talk about the outside world anymore because it only makes this place feel more unbearable. The only thing we do now is survive, day by day, hoping that somehow, this torment will end. But hope is a dangerous thing—it makes you believe in miracles that never come.

Every once in a while, Aliya and I talk just to pass the time, pretending everything's fine when we both know it isn't. Today was no different, or so I thought. We were sitting there, lost in a conversation about nothing in particular, when suddenly she excused herself. Before I could say anything, I heard it again—her retching. This wasn't the first time I'd heard it either. I've noticed her vomiting a few times over the past couple of weeks. It's like her body is rejecting this place as much as her mind is. Each time it happens, it tears me apart because I know something's wrong, but she won't tell me what it is.

When she came back, I tried to ask her again, but she brushed it off, like always. "It's nothing to worry about," she said, "It's just the food. I think my stomach hasn't adjusted to it yet." I know she's lying, she's too stubborn to admit anything. Maybe she thinks she's protecting me by hiding it, or maybe she's just scared. Either way, it's killing me not knowing what's really going on with her.

"Aliya, why are you hiding things from me? Don't you trust me?" I asked, trying to keep my voice calm, though concern was rising in my chest.

"Who said I don't trust you? Of course, I trust you," she replied, her voice trying to sound casual, but the tremor in it gave her away.

"Then tell me what's really going on. Why are you keeping it from me?" I demanded, sensing there was more to her silence than just the awful food and this prison we were stuck in.

"I'm not hiding anything from you, Rishi. Why would I?" she insisted, but the shakiness in her voice made it clear that she was holding something back.

"Don't lie to me, Aliya. I know you too well. Even though I can't see you, I can hear it in your voice—you're hiding something. You can't keep it hidden forever. If not today, I'll find out tomorrow, so why not just tell me now?" I pushed, wanting to break down the barrier that was clearly weighing on her.

Silence fell between us, thick and tense. I waited, the seconds feeling like hours. Then, finally, her voice came, quieter than ever. "Promise me, darling, you won't get angry when I tell you this."

The word "darling" hit me differently this time. It reminded me of how close we used to be before all this, how we were so happy and carefree before Vikram turned our lives upside down. "I promise, Aliya. Whatever it is, I won't get angry. Just tell me," I urged her, bracing myself.

There was a long pause before she finally said it: "darling, I think I'm pregnant."

It took me a moment to fully grasp what she was saying. Pregnant? My mind raced back to that night, the last night we were together before all this chaos. The love we shared, the intimacy, and now this. "Aliya, are you sure?" I asked, still struggling to accept the reality of the situation.

"I think so... My periods are late, which has never happened before, and I've been feeling tired all the time. My body feels different—my breasts have changed, and the food they give us isn't enough for me anymore. I'm always hungry, even after I eat," she explained, her voice cracking as she listed her symptoms.

"Why didn't you tell me earlier, Aliya?" I asked, frustration and worry mixing in my chest.

"I was scared... I thought you'd be angry or blame yourself. I didn't want to upset you even more than you already are," she confessed, her voice small and afraid.

"Aliya, stop thinking like that. Why would I be angry at you? It's not your fault. If anything, it's mine. I dragged you into this mess, and now you're suffering because of it," I said, guilt seeping into every word.

"What do we do now, darling? I'm so scared... What's going to happen?" she asked, fear lacing her voice.

"Don't worry, Aliya. We'll figure it out, I promise. Just take care of yourself. No matter what, I'm right here with you. We'll face this together, step by step," I reassured her, even though deep inside, I was terrified. We were in the worst possible place for this, but I had to stay strong—for her, for us. There was no room for weakness, not now.

After some time, someone dropped the usual package through the small hole. I picked it up and stared at it, lost in thought. Aliya was pregnant now, and that changed everything. She needed more food, more nourishment—otherwise, she'd starve, and in her condition, that was dangerous. I wished desperately that I could somehow give her my share of food, but there was no way to get it to her through this damn wall.

For the first time in these four months, I didn't feel hungry at all. The sight of that stale bread, which we had forced ourselves to eat every day, now just made me feel sick. How had we ended up like this? Why was this happening to us? I clenched my fists in frustration. Aliya needed me now more than ever, and yet I was stuck here, unable to reach her, unable to hold her or comfort her when she was most vulnerable.

The helplessness weighed on me, pressing down like a heavy stone in my chest. I wanted to be near her, to reassure her that we'd get through this somehow. But all I could do was talk to her, and even that felt inadequate. Words felt so meaningless compared to what she was going through. She needed someone by her side, and all I could offer was a voice from the other side of the wall.

I stared at the package in my hands, feeling a bitter taste rise in my throat. How could I sit here and eat while she was probably starving? I knew she'd tell me she was fine, that I shouldn't worry, but I could hear the exhaustion in her voice. I could feel the strain in every word she spoke, and it tore me apart that I couldn't do anything for her.

Pushing the bread aside, I leaned back against the cold, hard wall. All I could do was make a silent promise to myself: no matter what, I would find a way out of here. For Aliya, for our future—whatever it took, I'd find a way.

As I sat in the dark room, lost in my thoughts, a voice suddenly broke the silence. "Hey, you! What's your name again? Ah, Rishab, right? Here, eat this," the voice said, and a small container clattered through the hole in the wall.

I froze, stunned. Who was this man, and why was he helping me? I leaned closer to the hole, trying to catch a glimpse of the person on the other side. It was a new face, someone I didn't recognize. My mind raced with suspicion and curiosity.

"Who are you?" I demanded, ignoring the container for now.

The man chuckled softly. "Oh, right. I forgot to introduce myself. Hi, I'm Nithin, Vikram's brother," he said casually.

Hearing Vikram's name sent a surge of rage through me. My fists clenched involuntarily. This man, standing in front of me, was related to the monster who ruined our lives. My voice came out cold and harsh. "What's in the container? And why are you giving it to me?"

Nithin didn't seem fazed by my tone. "I want to help you," he replied. "I figured you've had enough of eating the same tasteless bread day after day. So I brought you some real food."

I narrowed my eyes, still skeptical. "Why should I believe you? And if you really wanted to help me, why haven't you shown up earlier? Why now?"

He sighed, as if my questions were tedious to him. "Good question," he admitted. "I won't force you to trust me, but I felt sorry for you. You've been stuck here for more than four months. I tried to convince Vikram to let you guys go, but he won't listen. So I decided to help you behind his back. If he finds out, I'm a dead man."

"But still—" I began, but he cut me off before I could finish.

"Can you please stop asking questions? Hurry up and eat before any guards notice," he urged, glancing around nervously.

I hesitated, still unsure. Then, an idea struck me. I picked up the container and held it out toward the hole. "There's someone who needs this more than me. Please, give it to Aliya," I begged.

Nithin's expression softened, almost as if he was impressed. "You're really something, aren't you? But don't worry—I already gave her a container of food. So this one's for you."

"Really? You already gave Aliya food?" I asked, relief flooding through me. "Thank you... thank you so much."

He smiled faintly. "My pleasure. From now on, you don't have to eat that tasteless stale bread. I'll bring proper food for both of you."

For a moment, I felt a spark of hope. Maybe we weren't completely alone in this hell after all. But before I could say anything else, Nithin suddenly tensed. "Oh, crap, someone's coming. I've got to go. We'll meet again," he whispered hurriedly before disappearing into the darkness. I strained to hear his footsteps fading away, leaving me alone with a glimmer of hope and a thousand questions.

After Nithin left, I sat down on the cold floor, staring at the container in my hands. For the first time in months, it wasn't stale bread and water. The scent of actual food made my stomach twist in hunger. For the first time in what felt like forever, the smell of real food filled the small, suffocating room.

As I opened the container, the aroma hit me, instantly making my mouth water. It wasn't anything fancy—just a simple meal of rice and curry—but after months of eating stale bread, it felt like a luxury. I could barely remember the last time I'd had anything remotely appetizing. My hands trembled slightly as I picked up a spoonful, savoring the taste of something other than dry, tasteless bread. The warmth of the food brought a comfort I'd almost forgotten existed.

After taking a few bites, I realized I couldn't enjoy this without knowing if Aliya got her share. "Aliya?" I called out, my voice filled with concern. "Did you really get the food Nithin mentioned?"

"Yes, darling, I did," she responded, and I could hear the relief in her voice. "And, oh my god, it's so good! I almost cried when I tasted it. It feels like heaven compared to what we've been eating."

I couldn't help but smile at her words. Knowing that she was finally eating something decent made the meal even more satisfying for me. "It's incredible, isn't it? I forgot what real food tasted like," I said, taking another bite. "For a second, it almost feels like we're not trapped here, like everything's normal again."

"You're right, darling," she said warmly. "For the first time in months, I actually feel a bit of hope. This food, it's giving me strength I didn't know I had left."

We continued to talk, our conversation light for once. We weren't discussing escape plans, or mourning our lost friends, or dreading the next confrontation with Vikram. Instead, we were savoring the moment—savoring the small, unexpected blessing of a decent meal.

"I never thought I'd be so grateful for plain rice and curry," I said with a soft chuckle.

"Me neither, darling" she replied. "It's just food, but it feels like so much more. It feels like a lifeline, something to remind us that there's still kindness out there, even in the darkest of times."

The way she called me 'darling'—with such affection despite everything we were going through—made my heart ache in both good and bad ways. I couldn't see her, couldn't hold her, but knowing she was okay, knowing we were sharing this tiny victory together, was enough to keep me going.

For a few precious minutes, we forgot about the horrors surrounding us. We were just two people, sharing a meal, finding comfort in each other's voices. It was a fleeting moment of peace in a world that had been nothing but cruel for too long.

As we finished the meal, a rare moment of calm settled between us. the atmosphere between us lightened, a rare moment of normalcy in our grim reality. Aliya's voice broke the silence, tinged with a hint of vulnerability. "Darling," she began hesitantly, "if we ever manage to escape from this nightmare, will you still accept me the way I am now? Will you still be there for me?"

I was taken aback by her question, my mind racing to grasp the implication of her words. "What nonsense are you talking about, Aliya?" I said, my voice firm but concerned. "Have you lost your mind? There's no way I would ever abandon you. You became pregnant because of me, because of what we went through together. I'm just as responsible for that child in your belly as you are. I'm not going anywhere. If you ever talk about me abandoning you or getting angry at you again, I swear I'll break through this wall and slap some sense into you if I could, just to make you understand how ridiculous that thought is."

Aliya fell silent, her voice trembling as she spoke. "I'm sorry, darling. I should have known that would irritate you. I won't ask that stupid question again. I just... I needed to hear it from you."

Her apology, coupled with her soft-spoken words, tugged at my heart. Despite everything, she was still worried about how I felt about her, even now when we were in such dire circumstances. "It's alright, Aliya," I said, my tone gentler. "I understand why you might feel that way, but trust me, I'm not going anywhere. We're in this together, and we'll get through it together."

She sighed, and I could almost imagine her nodding as she spoke. "Thank you, darling. I needed to hear that."

We spent the rest of the time talking softly, discussing the food and the small moments of comfort it had brought us. Despite the dire situation, we found solace in each other's words, clinging to the hope that someday, somehow, we would escape this nightmare and face the world together.

As Nithin had promised, he returned later that night, bringing food along with him. I didn't know the exact time—it could've been the middle of the night for all I knew—but I was awake, waiting for him. When he dropped the food through the small hole, I caught it quickly, eager for any shred of normalcy in this miserable place.

"Good to see you again," he said, his voice barely above a whisper.

"Actually, I'm the one who should be saying that," I replied, trying to muster a smile despite everything. "Thank you for bringing the food, Nithin."

"No problem at all," he said, though I could sense a hint of unease in his tone.

After a moment of silence, I decided to take a chance. "Hey, Nithin, since you're helping us with food... could you please help us get out of this place? Please, I'm begging you."

Nithin didn't respond immediately. The pause between us stretched on, heavy with the weight of what I was asking. Finally, he sighed. "I'm sorry, Rishab. I won't be able to help you with that."

His words hit me like a punch to the gut. "But why? You're the only one who could help us. We don't want to rot in this dreadful place for the rest of our lives. Please, Nithin, you have to help us."

"It's not that simple," he said quietly. "Vikram's the only one who has the key to this door. He would never allow me to take it from him, and even if I tried, I have no idea where he's hidden it. And suppose I somehow got the key and opened the door—you wouldn't be able to escape from this base. It's like a maze, a bhool bhulaiya. Even if you found the way out, there are hundreds of guards armed with machine guns guarding the exits and entrances."

"Why are there so many people guarding this place?" I asked, shocked by what I was hearing. "Has Vikram become an international criminal or something?"

"What do you expect? Nithin replied, his voice tinged with frustration. "Killing five students and kidnapping two more... do you think the police are going to let Vikram walk around like an innocent man? The police are on high alert, searching everywhere for Vikram—and for both of you. which is why this place is locked down like a fortress.

Desperation clawed at my insides. I couldn't let this be the end. "Please, Nithin, you have to help us. If you can't help both of us escape, then at least help Aliya. She's... she's pregnant. She won't be able to deliver the baby in this hellhole. She needs proper attention. Please, I'm begging you."

Nithin's silence this time was even more agonizing. When he finally spoke, his voice was laced with regret. "Believe me, Rishab, if there was any way for me to help either of you escape, I wouldn't be sitting here doing nothing. But it's out of my reach. The most I can do is bring you food. Please try to understand. I have to go now—if anyone sees me, I'm dead for sure. I'll meet you in the morning."

And just like that, he was gone, his footsteps echoing in the distance as he hurried away. I stood there, staring at the food in my hands, my mind racing with fear and despair. The only hope we had of escaping this hellhole was Nithin, and now that hope was gone too. I didn't know what to do. How could I tell Aliya that our chances of getting out had just vanished? What were we supposed to do now?

"Aliya," I called out, my voice heavy with guilt. I began explaining everything that Nithin had said, but she cut me off.

"I heard everything, darling. You don't need to go through that conversation again," she said softly.

"I'm sorry, Aliya... I couldn't do anything," I said, my voice cracking under the weight of helplessness.

"Why are you sorry?" she asked, her tone gentle yet firm. "It's not your fault that Vikram captured us. There's no need to apologize for something you couldn't control."

"No, it is my fault," I insisted, the regret gnawing at me. "If I had listened to you back then, if I had taken action when I had the chance, none of this would've happened. If I had been more cautious, we wouldn't be here suffering, and our friends—Karthi, Seema, Anika, Varun, and Aadhi—would still be alive. It's all my fault... they died because of me. I'm the one responsible for their deaths."

"Stop it, Rishi. Just stop it," she said, her voice firm as she interrupted me. "How many times do I have to tell you that it's not your fault? Vikram captured us, and he's the one responsible for our friends' deaths, not you. Do you understand? Don't blame yourself for the sins that belong to Vikram."

I fell silent, the storm of guilt and anger swirling inside me. I wanted to argue, to protest, to wallow in my self-blame, but Aliya's words had a way of cutting through that dark cloud. She was right. I knew it deep down, but it was hard to let go of that crushing sense of responsibility. I just sat there, unable to find the words, feeling the weight of everything pressing down on us.

All I could think about was how much I wished things were different, how much I wanted to be free from this nightmare—to be out there in the world with Aliya, far away from this prison. But that seemed like an impossible dream now.

Vikram's malicious laughter suddenly filled the room, echoing off the cold walls like a haunting melody. "Looks like someone's blaming me, ha ha haaaa..." he taunted, his voice dripping with arrogance.

Instantly, every muscle in my body tensed. My instincts sharpened, and an overwhelming surge of anger coursed through me. "You bastard!" I shouted, my voice trembling with rage. "Just wait! Once I'm out of this place, the first thing I'll do is kill you with my bare hands!"

Vikram chuckled, a sinister edge in his voice. "Is that so?" Vikram taunted, his voice dripping with mockery. "I've already told you before, but it seems you've forgotten. Let me remind you once again: *You Can't Escape.*"

"You murdered my friends, Vikram! You won't get away with it! I won't let you!" I snarled, clenching my fists even though he couldn't see me.

"Ah, whatever," he said dismissively, as if our suffering was merely entertainment for him. "You'll never step out of this place, Rishab.

And one more thing... just stay alive, okay? I want to see you both suffering more and more every single day," he added, his voice laced with pure malice. He let out another twisted laugh before his footsteps faded away.

I stood there seething, my heart pounding against my chest, fists trembling with fury. Every fiber of my being wanted to tear him apart, to end this nightmare once and for all. But the walls around us were unbreakable,

"Vikrammm!......" I screamed at the top of my lungs, the sound echoing in the cold, suffocating room. Without thinking, I slammed my fist into the stone wall as hard as I could, the pain shooting up my arm but failing to drown out the rage burning inside me.

"Rishi, please..." Aliya's soft voice broke through the storm of emotions swirling in my mind. "Don't let hate consume you, darling. Remember, love and forgiveness are stronger than any darkness."

Her words hung in the air, trying to reach the part of me that still held onto hope. But it felt distant, almost out of reach, as I sank onto the rickety wooden cot, clenching and unclenching my fists. My knuckles throbbed, but the pain was nothing compared to the image burning in my mind—the day when Vikram would be on his knees, begging for his life in front of me.

I closed my eyes, struggling between the desire for revenge and the wisdom in Aliya's words. But it was hard to listen to reason when all I could see was that cruel smile, that mocking laughter as he took everything from me. The hatred clawed at me, relentless, but Aliya's voice was like a distant anchor trying to pull me back from the edge.

I took a deep breath, trying to calm the storm, but it was easier said than done. All I could do was wait, wait for the day when this nightmare would end—and I swore to myself that when that day came, Vikram would pay for every single second of suffering he'd caused us.

Week 32:

Eight months have dragged on since Vikram captured Aliya and me and locked us in this forsaken hellhole. Each day has been an endless stretch of darkness and dread. But amidst the bleakness, there's been a small glimmer of hope—Nithin. Over the past four months, he's been sneaking in delicious food for us. Thanks to him, we've finally been able to enjoy something other than that tasteless, stale bread we used to get.

Still, no amount of better food can ease the worry that gnaws at me. Aliya's belly has been growing bigger every day. It's a constant reminder that soon, she'll have to give birth in this wretched place. I can't help but feel helpless, knowing she'll be enduring labor with no proper medical care, no comfort, nothing but these cold stone walls. I wish I could be there with her, to support her and hold her hand, but that's beyond my reach.

One evening, as we were having dinner, Aliya's voice came through the wall. "Darling, I can feel the baby kicking inside my belly," she said, her voice a mix of excitement and fear.

I clenched my fists, my heart aching to be there with her. "I wish I could be there, Aliya... to feel it with you," I replied, my voice heavy with longing.

"It won't be long now," she said softly. "Soon, the baby will be here."

"And it'll be a boy, just like me," I said, trying to bring a bit of cheer to our conversation.

Aliya chuckled softly. "No way! I've told you a hundred times, darling—it's going to be a girl, a cute little one just like her mother. And we'll name her Riya."

I couldn't help but laugh at her insistence. For a moment, despite everything, we both laughed together. It was these brief moments of shared hope and laughter that kept us going, giving us strength to face another day in this nightmare.

But then Aliya's voice grew serious, and I could sense a shift in her tone. "Darling, can I ask you something?" she said, her voice trembling slightly.

"Of course," I replied, sensing her unease.

"Do you think we'll ever escape from this place?" she asked, her voice tinged with a mix of hope and doubt.

"Of course we can," I replied, trying to be as reassuring as possible. "I'll find a way out, no matter what it takes."

Aliya sighed softly. "I trust you, darling. But if I can't make it out with you... promise me you'll look after Riya."

Her words hit me like a cold wave. "What do you mean by 'couldn't make it out with me'?" I asked, confusion and dread rising in my chest.

She fell silent for a moment, and when she spoke again, her voice was barely a whisper. "Just promise me you'll take care of Riya."

"You haven't answered my question yet. What do you mean by that? Aliya, what are you talking about? You're not making any sense." I pressed, trying to understand the fear in her voice.

"Please, darling, don't get mad at me for what I'm about to say," she said, her voice cracking with fear.

"Go on," I urged, trying to stay calm.

"See, I have a strong feeling in my heart that I might not make it through giving birth to Riya," she confessed quietly, the fear in her words making my heart ache.

The words hit me like a punch to the gut. "Stop talking like that, Aliya! Don't say such things. If I'm going to escape, you're coming with me, that's all there is to it. Do you understand?" I said, my voice filled with determination and desperation.

"I'm not talking nonsense, dear," she said, her voice breaking. "Please promise me you'll look after Riya if... if something happens to me."

"I promise, Aliya," I said, my voice resolute but choked with emotion. "Once we get out of here, I will make sure Riya has a safe and secure future. I will look after both you and Riya. You have my word."

"Thank you, darling," she said with a sigh of relief. "That means a lot to me."

As I sank onto the rickety cot, my mind raced with the terrifying thought of losing her. I couldn't allow myself to believe it, couldn't accept that the woman I loved might not make it through this ordeal. But I also knew I had to keep my promise, no matter what the future held. After Aliya and I had exchanged our promises and fears, the silence returned, though it was now laced with a new layer of melancholy.

"Darling," Aliya's voice cut through the stillness, soft and tender. "Can you stay with me a little longer? I don't want to be alone with these thoughts."

"Of course," I replied, my voice steady despite the turmoil within me. "I'm here for you, always."

We continued to talk, our conversation meandering through memories and dreams of a future beyond these walls. We spoke about our past—moments of joy and laughter that now felt like distant echoes

As the hours passed, our voices grew quieter, our words less frequent. The exhaustion of our confinement and the weight of our fears began to take their toll. I could hear Aliya's breathing growing more rhythmic, a sign that she was drifting off to sleep.

"Goodnight, my love," she whispered, her voice barely audible.

"Goodnight, Aliya," I replied, my own voice thick with emotion. "Sleep well. We'll get through this."

I could feel the heaviness of sleep pulling at me as well, but I remained awake a little longer, listening to the faint sounds of her breathing and the occasional creak of the room. It was a small comfort to know that, despite everything, we had each other.

Eventually, sleep claimed me, too, pulling me into a fitful rest filled with dreams of freedom and a future where we could finally escape this nightmare.

The night had been quiet for a while, with both of us finally drifting off to sleep after our long conversation. But suddenly, I was jolted awake by Aliya's terrified screams echoing from the other room.

"Rishi! Rishi!" she screamed in panic. My heart raced, fear flooding my veins. I shot up from the bed, my mind already filled with dread.

"What happened, Aliya? Are you okay?" I called out, my voice shaking.

"It's the baby, Rishi! I think the baby is coming!" she cried out in pain, her voice filled with agony.

Panic seized me. This was the moment I had been dreading for months. Aliya was going into labor, and we were trapped in this hellhole with no doctors, no proper help—nothing but cold walls and darkness.

"Stay calm, Aliya. Please, just stay focused!" I shouted, trying to sound confident, though fear was gnawing at me. "I'm here! Everything will be okay, I promise. Just keep breathing and don't lose consciousness. You're strong, Aliya—you can do this!"

But she continued screaming in pain. "I can't, Rishi! I can't do this! It hurts so much!" Her voice was raw with desperation, and I could feel the helplessness rising inside me.

"You can do it, Aliya!" I shouted back, my voice laced with urgency. "Just try harder! You have to hold on for our baby—just push through the pain!" I was pacing back and forth in my room, hands twitching with anxiety, wishing desperately that I could be by her side, holding her hand and comforting her.

Every time she screamed, it felt like a knife twisting in my chest. I was powerless—there was nothing I could do but encourage her from this distance. The thought of her enduring this all alone, with only my voice to guide her, tore me apart.

I clenched my fists, biting down hard to keep from screaming myself. "Come on, Aliya! I know you're in pain, but you have to be strong. For Riya, for us!"

Minutes felt like hours as her screams continued, each one a stab of agony in my heart. My mind raced, trying to think of anything, anything I could do to make this easier for her. But all I had were words—words that felt so empty in the face of her suffering.

"Stay with me, Aliya," I said softly, more to myself than to her, hoping against hope that she could hear me, that somehow my voice could reach through the darkness and give her strength.

I kept telling her she was strong, that she could do it, but deep down, I was terrified of what might happen next.

The air was thick with tension, Aliya's agonizing screams piercing through the walls, echoing in my ears, and tearing at my soul. I was frantic, desperate, and completely helpless.

"Hello! Is anybody there? Please, someone help—get a doctor!" I shouted at the top of my lungs, my voice raw with desperation. But it was useless. The silence of the night swallowed my cries, and I knew everyone in this cursed place was likely asleep, unaware of the life-or-death struggle happening in this room.

Aliya's agonizing screams filled the air, each one tearing at my heart. I felt utterly helpless, unable to do anything but listen as she suffered on the other side of the wall.

"Rishab, what's happening? Why is Aliya screaming?" Nithin's voice suddenly came through the small hole in the wall, sounding concerned.

My heart leaped at the sound of his voice. "Oh, thank God you're here, Nithin! Aliya—she's in labor! The baby's coming, but she needs a doctor! Please, get help, quickly!" I pleaded, my words tumbling out in a rush of urgency.

Aliya's screams grew louder, more intense, and panic clawed at my insides. Nithin's voice broke through the tension. "Don't worry, Rishab. We have a doctor here. I'll get him right away!" he said before disappearing.

I could barely breathe, pacing around the room like a caged animal, my mind racing. Each scream from Aliya felt like a knife twisting in my chest. I kept muttering under my breath, willing the doctor to arrive, hoping and praying that everything would be okay.

After what felt like an eternity, Nithin's voice came back. "Rishab, don't worry. The doctor is with her now. She's going to be alright," he assured me.

I let out a shaky sigh of relief. "Thank you, Nithin. Thank you so much," I managed to say, my voice trembling with emotion.

But the tension wasn't over yet. I could still hear Aliya's cries as I paced the small room, every nerve in my body on edge. I was desperate to hear the baby's first cry, to know that both Aliya and our child were safe.

Then, suddenly, the screaming stopped. For a brief, terrifying moment, there was silence, and my heart froze. But then, as if in answer to my prayers, the sound of a new-born's cry filled the air.

Relief crashed over me like a tidal wave, and I felt my legs give out beneath me. I sank to the floor, completely drained, tears welling up in my eyes. The wait, the fear, the anguish—it was all over. Aliya had done it. Our child was finally here.

All I could do was close my eyes, let out a deep breath, and allow myself a moment of pure, unfiltered gratitude. Despite everything, in this hellhole, a small miracle had just happened.

"Thank God, Rishab. At last, the wait is over," Nithin said, his voice calm yet tinged with exhaustion.

"Yeah..." I whispered, barely nodding. My voice was hollow, drained from the worry and tension.

"Wait here. I'll go check if the baby is alright," Nithin added before turning to leave.

The way he said it—"Wait here, I'll check"—like I had anywhere else to go. Like I could just walk away from this cold, dark prison that had trapped us for eight long months. I didn't even bother responding. My mind was somewhere else, anxiously waiting for news of Aliya.

"Aliya? Are you alright?" I called out, hoping desperately to hear her voice.

There was no response. My heart started pounding faster. "Aliya? Please, say something!" I called again, louder this time. Still nothing.

Suddenly, for the first time in eight months, the door to my room creaked open. I blinked, trying to process what was happening as Nithin walked in, followed by two armed men with rifles. Their cold eyes scanned the room, and within seconds, they had their guns trained directly on me. My breath caught in my throat.

But all my attention shifted when I saw Nithin cradling a tiny bundle wrapped in a towel—a baby. My baby.

Nithin slowly stepped forward and handed her to me. My hands trembled as I held her for the first time. She was so small, so fragile. Her little eyes were squeezed shut, her face red from crying, but even through the tears, I could see it—she was Aliya's mirror image. The delicate curve of her nose, the soft contour of her cheeks... she was exactly how Aliya had described her—a perfect little girl.

Riya, I whispered, the name Aliya and I had chosen echoing in my mind. For a moment, I forgot everything else—the prison walls, the darkness around us, the coldness in my heart. I was holding a part of Aliya, a part of us, in my arms.

But then reality crashed back in. "How's Aliya?" I asked, my voice tight with anxiety. I glanced at Nithin, who was avoiding my eyes, his expression unreadable. "Nithin... how's Aliya?" I repeated, the words catching in my throat.

He hesitated, and that hesitation was all it took for my fear to deepen. He looked at the floor, then finally back at me, his eyes filled with regret.

Nithin didn't answer. He just stood there, silent, avoiding my eyes. My chest tightened, fear gnawing at me. Something was wrong. I could see it in his face, a shadow that darkened his expression.

"Nithin! What happened to Aliya? Is she okay?" I repeated, panic gripping me as I clutched Riya closer.

He finally met my eyes, but what I saw there sent a chill down my spine. There was sorrow, regret—something I didn't want to acknowledge. "Rishab... Aliya, she couldn't... she didn't make it. She was too weak... you see, she passed away giving birth to Riya," he said, his voice trailing off into a whisper.

The words hit me like a sledgehammer. My mind went blank. "No... no... that can't be true... she was just talking to me a few minutes ago!" I stammered, my voice breaking.

"It's the truth, Rishab... Aliya's gone... she's dead," Nithin said quietly, but his words felt like shards of ice stabbing into me.

Time seemed to stop. I stared at him, waiting for him to take back those words, to tell me it wasn't true. But the look on his face said it all.

"No... no, you're lying," I stammered, shaking my head in disbelief. "She was fine! Just minutes ago... she was talking to me! She can't be gone, Nithin, she can't be!"

But he just stood there, looking defeated. "She was too weak... she lost a lot of blood. There was nothing the doctor could do..."

The room spun around me. I felt the floor give way beneath my feet. "No... no, this can't be happening!" I screamed, my voice raw with grief. "Aliya... no... please..."

Riya started crying, her tiny wails breaking through my anguish. I looked down at her tear-streaked face, and my heart shattered into a thousand pieces. Aliya was gone, and this little girl—our Riya—would never know the warmth of her mother's embrace.

"Rishab, calm down... you're scaring the baby," Nithin said gently, taking her from my arms and cradling her.

But I couldn't calm down. I couldn't accept it. "Let me see her!" I shouted, pushing past Nithin in a desperate attempt to reach Aliya. But before I could take more than a step, one of the guards kicked me hard in the stomach. Pain exploded through my body as I doubled over, gasping for breath. I collapsed onto the cold floor, clutching my midsection.

"Don't even think about leaving this room," the man snarled, aiming his rifle directly at my head.

"Mind your actions, you pawns!" Put your weapons down!, Nithin barked at them, his voice laced with authority. The guards reluctantly obeyed, lowering their guns.

Ignoring the pain, I crawled forward, tears blurring my vision. "Please, Nithin... let me see her... just one last time," I begged, my voice barely a whisper, choked with sobs.

Nithin's eyes softened, but he shook his head. "I'm sorry, Rishab... she's already gone."

I broke down completely, sobbing uncontrollably. Aliya was gone, and I never even got to say goodbye. All I had left of her was this tiny, fragile life in Nithin's arms—a life that I had to protect at all costs.

The weight of those words crushed me. I collapsed back to the floor, my whole world shattering into a million pieces. Aliya, my love, my everything... was gone. And there was nothing I could do. Nothing but cry, drowning in the unbearable grief of losing the one person who meant everything to me.

The world outside that room might as well have disappeared. In that moment, nothing mattered except the emptiness in my heart, the unbearable pain of loss, and the tiny heartbeat of the baby who would never know her mother's love.

Nithin guided me to the wooden cot, gently pushing me to sit down. "You need to calm down, Rishab," he said softly, but his words felt like a distant echo, barely reaching me through the haze of grief that clouded my mind. "You need to calm down, Rishab. Aliya is gone for good. If nothing else, at least she won't have to suffer in this endless confinement anymore," he said softly, his voice tinged with sympathy.

His voice was steady, almost comforting, but it did nothing to ease the pain that ripped through my chest. The reality of his words was too much to bear. My eyes were locked on the ground, unable to process what had just happened. Aliya, my love, the mother of our child... was gone.

Nithin held Riya out to me, his voice softer now. "Here, take her... If Aliya were here, she would've told you the same. Please, look after this child. She's all that's left of her."

I hesitated, my hands trembling as I reached out and took Riya into my arms. The moment I held her close, she stopped crying. Her tiny chest rose and fell steadily, and she was sleeping peacefully, unaware of the tragedy that had just occurred. For a moment, the warmth of her little body against mine was the only thing that kept me anchored to this cruel reality.

I looked down at Riya, her tiny face serene, her breathing soft and steady as she slept. The tears in my eyes blurred her features, but even through the haze, I could see Aliya in her. The pain in my chest only grew, but somehow, holding Riya made me feel both closer to Aliya and a thousand miles away from her.

Nithin turned to the thugs, his tone sharp as he ordered, "Bring the cradle."

One of them grunted in acknowledgment and left the room. Minutes later, he returned with a small, makeshift cradle. Nithin looked at me, hesitating as if he wanted to say something more.

"Rishab..." he began, but I cut him off, I couldn't hear it—I didn't want to hear it.

"Leave me alone, Nithin," I muttered, my voice barely more than a whisper, but laced with a deep, raw pain.

Nithin fell silent, understanding in his eyes. He paused for a moment, as if weighing his next words. "As you wish," he finally said, turning to leave. But just as he reached the door, he stopped and looked back at me. His voice was low, almost a whisper, but filled with a quiet determination. "I'm sure one day, you'll find a way out of this place. You will escape from this room, Rishab. I believe that."

With that, the door clicked shut, leaving me alone with my thoughts, my grief, and the sleeping baby in my arms. The silence that followed was suffocating, but in that silence, the promise of escape—of a future for Riya—took root in my heart.

I looked at Riya, peacefully asleep, her tiny chest rising and falling rhythmically. She had no idea that her entrance into this world had come at the cost of her mother's life. My heart ached as I watched her sleep, so innocent, so unaware of the sacrifice that had brought her here.

Suddenly, my mind drifted back to my last conversation with Aliya. Her words echoed painfully in my head: *"Promise me you'll look after Riya, if I can't make it."* A chill ran down my spine as I realized the truth—Aliya knew. She knew that giving birth to Riya could be the end for her, and that's why she made me promise. The tears that had been welling up in my eyes finally broke free, streaming down my face uncontrollably.

"Why, Aliya? Why did you leave me alone in this hell?" I whispered, my voice trembling. "How am I supposed to live without you? How am I supposed to look after Riya if you're not with me?" My words came out choked and broken, every syllable laced with agony.

The room felt colder, darker. The weight of my grief was unbearable, and it quickly turned into rage. The source of all this suffering, all this loss was Vikram. If it weren't for him, if he hadn't captured us and locked us away in this nightmare, Aliya would still be alive. We'd be out there living our lives, surrounded by our friends, free from this misery. Instead, she's gone, and I'm left alone, with nothing but the memory of her and the responsibility of raising our daughter.

"You'll pay for this, Vikram," I muttered through gritted teeth, the words laced with venom. "I swear, I'll make you suffer for what you've done. I'll take revenge for Aliya."

But just as my thoughts spiraled deeper into hatred, I heard Aliya's voice again, faint and distant in my mind: *"Don't let hate consume you, darling. Remember, love and forgiveness are stronger than any darkness."*

My heart clenched. How could I forgive Vikram when I felt like there was no love left in me? I was consumed by grief, anger, and a hollow emptiness that I didn't know how to fill.

I gently placed Riya into the cradle and lowered myself to the floor beside it, leaning my head against the wooden bars. Memories flooded back—the last time I saw Aliya was at our college anniversary. I hadn't seen her face even once in the past year, and now, even after her death, I didn't get a chance to see her one last time. The regret and sorrow weighed heavily on my chest, crushing me from within.

"Vikram... I'll make sure your death is painful and cruel," I swore under my breath. "I'll make you feel the same agony I'm going through right now. I promise, I'll make you pay."

But as I sat there in the dim light, staring at the ceiling, I realized I was feeling something deeper than just anger. It was a sorrow so profound that I couldn't describe it—a sharp, relentless ache in my chest that felt like a void, consuming every part of me. Were this what people meant by grief? By the unbearable sorrow of losing someone you love?

I closed my eyes, letting the tears flow freely. My heart was torn between the desire for revenge and the faint voice of Aliya, urging me to find something greater than hate. But right now, all I could do was grieve for the love I'd lost and hold on to the fragile hope that I could give Riya the life Aliya would have wanted for her.

The darkness of the night felt endless as I remained there, broken and lost, clinging to the one small light left in my shattered world—my daughter, Riya.

The emptiness of the room seemed to press in from all sides. My mind replayed Aliya's last words over and over, haunting me with the reality I didn't want to accept. She was gone... and yet, a part of her was still here, lying in that cradle.

Dawn eventually broke, but sleep had eluded me the entire night. I sat there, hollow and exhausted, yet unable to close my eyes. The disbelief clung to me like a shadow—I kept waiting, hoping that, just like every morning, I'd hear her sweet voice saying, "*Good morning, darling.*" But the words never came. The silence was suffocating. The woman I loved, cherished, and cared for the most was gone, and I was left alone in this cold, heartless world. How could I accept that? How could I live with this emptiness?

My thoughts were interrupted by a voice from the other side of the wall. "Good morning, Rishab," Nithin called out softly. "How are you holding up?"

I couldn't muster a response. I just stared blankly at the wall, my mind drowning in sorrow. And what's the point? Words felt meaningless.

"I brought you some breakfast," he continued, sliding a container through the hole. A small nursing bottle followed behind it. "It's breast milk. If the baby starts crying, feed her with this. I'll bring more from time to time,"

"Nithin... please, let me see Aliya... just once. I'm begging you," I pleaded, my voice breaking.

Nithin sighed heavily. "I'm sorry, Rishab. I can't help you with that. Vikram's men already cremated her body a while ago."

A knot formed in my throat, and it became harder to breathe. The thought of Aliya's body turning to ashes—no, it couldn't be true. My mind refused to accept it.

My heart sank as the reality set in—Aliya was gone, turned into ashes without me even getting to say goodbye. My mind refused to accept it. *No... it can't be true... my Aliya, reduced to nothing but ashes?* The thought clawed at me, tearing my sanity apart.

"No!" I screamed, my voice filled with raw agony.

The sudden outburst startled Riya, and she began crying. Her cries echoed through the room, piercing my already shattered heart. In a panic, I grabbed the nursing bottle and fed her the milk. She quieted down, her tiny mouth latching onto the rubber nipple, sucking instinctively, unaware of the grief engulfing her father.

I stared at the bottle, my hands trembling as I fed her. Tears blurred my vision as the weight of this realization settled deep in my chest. *Aliya should have been the one holding you right now, Riya. She should have been the one to comfort you, to nourish you with her love.* But instead, it was me, holding a cold, artificial substitute for the real thing.

This small, lifeless bottle was now the only way Riya could be nourished, and it broke my heart. She would never know the warmth and comfort of being cradled against her mother's chest, never feel Aliya's loving touch as she fed her. The cruel reality that Riya would never experience the bond every child should have with their mother gnawed at my soul.

I could almost see the image in my mind—Aliya holding Riya close, her smile gentle and filled with love as she whispered soothing words to our daughter. But that vision was nothing more than a cruel illusion now, a scene that would never become a reality.

The thought tore at my heart. *This isn't how it's supposed to be,* I thought bitterly. Riya should've been nestled against her mother, feeling the warmth of Aliya's skin and hearing her soothing heartbeat. Instead, she was left in my trembling hands, with nothing

A lump formed in my throat as I watched Riya drink the milk with a nursing bottle, unaware of what she was missing. She drank quietly, content and innocent, oblivious to the tragedy that had marked her entrance into this world. *You deserve so much more, Riya. You deserve to be held by your mother, to feel her warmth and love surround you.* But all I could offer was this—this pale imitation of what should have been.

Just then, I heard a voice that made my blood run cold. "Oh, poor Rishab, look at the state you're in. Pretty messed up, huh?" Vikram's taunting voice oozed through the wall like poison. My whole body trembled with fury.

How dare he come here, taunting me in my darkest moment? Anger surged through me, making my hands shake as I held the nursing bottle. *Calm down, Rishab,* my mind tried to reason with me. *He's just trying to provoke you. Remember Aliya's words—love and forgiveness are stronger than any darkness. And don't forget, Riya is in your arms. Keep her safe.*

With a monumental effort, I forced myself to take deep breaths and steady my trembling hands. I looked down at Riya, trying to focus on the tiny life I was holding. I began to gently rock her, my heart aching for the mother who should have been here.

Vikram's voice continued, dripping with cruel satisfaction. "Wow, look at you, baby-sitting. Do you know what? It suits you. Seeing you suffer to get out of this place makes me so happy."

I gritted my teeth, trying to block out his taunts. Just then, I heard Nithin's voice interject, filled with concern. "Stop it, Vikram. Enough. He's already going through a lot. Please stop it for my sake."

"Ah, whatever," Vikram replied dismissively. I heard his footsteps fading away, his mocking laughter echoing as he left.

"I'm sorry, Rishab, if he made you angry," Nithin began, but I cut him off.

"Can you do me a favor?" I asked, my voice strained.

"Yeah, of course. Just tell me," Nithin responded.

"Just... leave me alone." I said, my voice breaking.

After a brief pause, Nithin replied, "Fine, if that's what you want." he said quietly before walking away. Leaving me alone with my thoughts and the baby in my arms.

I stared at Riya as she sucked from the nursing bottle, her tiny lips moving in rhythmic patterns. The sight of her so helpless and innocent was a painful reminder of what should have been. My heart ached with every gulp she took, knowing that this was not how it was supposed to be. Aliya should have been here, holding her, feeding her with her own warmth and love.

Tears welled up in my eyes as I watched Riya, the bottle a cold substitute for the nurturing care her mother would have given. My heart ached with the weight of this cruel reality, and a deep, hollow sorrow filled the space where joy should have been.

As I gently rocked Riya in my arms, the nursing bottle now empty, I couldn't stop the tears from falling. *Aliya, how am I supposed to do this without you? How can I be enough for her when she's lost the most important person in her life before she even knew who you were?* The grief was overwhelming, and I felt like I was drowning in it.

I carefully placed Riya back in the cradle, her tiny face peaceful and serene. She looked so much like Aliya, and it broke my heart all over again. I sat down beside her, resting my head against the side of the cradle, feeling utterly lost. *I'll do my best, Riya, I promise. But it will never be enough. I'll never be able to give you what Aliya would have given you.* The thought haunted me, and I could do nothing but sit there, consumed by my grief, as the darkness of the night slowly gave way to the light of dawn.

Week 33:

It's been one week since Aliya died, and I've been in a constant state of turmoil. Every day feels like a struggle to accept the harsh reality that she's gone. How could this happen to me? The question lingers, gnawing at my mind, leaving me feeling weak—both physically and mentally.

But despite the overwhelming grief, one thing has kept me going: Riya. Ever since that tragic day, I've taken on the responsibility of caring for her. And thanks to Nithin, who brings the breast milk regularly, I'm able to feed Riya and ensure she doesn't starve. Looking after Riya has become my sole priority, a mission that gives me purpose amidst the chaos.

I've realized that death is the only constant in life. What remains after someone is gone are the memories they leave behind and the lasting impact they had on us. Aliya may no longer be here physically, but she's alive in the moments we shared, in the love we had, and in the little things that made her who she was. I can still hear her laughter echoing in my mind, still see the way her eyes would light up when she was excited. Those memories have become my strength, a reminder that she's still with me in spirit. I won't let them fade, not now, not ever. I've made a promise to her, to keep those memories alive and honor what we had.

Grieving her loss has been the hardest thing I've ever faced, but I can't afford to crumble. I can't let myself be consumed by sorrow when Riya needs me to be strong. She's so small, so vulnerable, and yet she's the only light left in this darkness. I've decided that no matter how broken I feel inside, I won't let it affect my responsibility toward her. I've been teaching myself how to be a father—how to comfort her when she cries, how to soothe her when she's restless, and how to make her feel loved even in this cold, lifeless place.

So, I made a choice. I chose to be strong, not for myself, but for Riya. Every time I looked into her innocent eyes, I felt a surge of determination. *Aliya would have wanted this. She would have wanted me to protect our daughter, to give her the love and care that she herself could no longer provide.*

Slowly, I started to build a routine around Riya's needs. I learned to soothe her cries, to feed her, to change her. Each task, though simple, became a small victory—a step toward healing. Caring for Riya became my anchor, a way to channel my grief into something constructive, something that honored Aliya's memory.

The first few nights were the hardest. I would lay awake, listening to Riya's soft breaths, the silence of the room a stark contrast to the lively conversations I used to have with Aliya. The loneliness was suffocating. But I would remind myself that Riya needed me to be present, to be strong. And so, I kept going, one day at a time.

I began to talk to Riya about her mother, even though she couldn't understand me yet. I told her stories of Aliya, of how much she loved her before she was even born. I told her about the dreams we had for her, In these moments, I felt a connection with Aliya, as if she were still with us, watching over us.

As the days passed, I noticed a change in myself. The pain of losing Aliya was still there, but it wasn't as sharp, not as consuming. It was as if Riya's presence had softened the edges of my grief. Every time she smiled, every time she reached out for me, I felt a renewed sense of purpose. I realized that, in caring for Riya, I was also healing myself.

I've come to accept that I'll never fully get over Aliya's death. There will always be a part of me that aches for her, that wishes she were here to see our daughter grow up. But I've also learned that I can carry that pain with me without letting it destroy me. I can honor Aliya's memory by being the best father I can be to Riya, by ensuring that she grows up safe and healthy.

Aliya, the love we shared, the life we planned—it lives on in our daughter. I'll make sure that Riya knows how much you loved her, how much you wanted to be there for her. I'll protect her, guide her, and give her the life we both wanted for her. That's my promise to you, and I intend to keep it.

As I look at Riya now, sleeping peacefully in her cradle, I feel a sense of calm. I know the road ahead won't be easy, but I'm ready to face it. For her, for us, and for the memory of the woman I loved more than life itself.

The days turned into a weeks, and each day brought its own challenges. Raising Riya under these circumstances was anything but easy, but I had no choice. The room we were trapped in was cold, damp, and filled with shadows that stretched long into the corners. But in that darkness, Riya became my light.

Every morning, I woke up to the soft coos of Riya. Her tiny hands would reach out for warmth, her delicate fingers curling around my thumb as if seeking comfort. I would lift her gently and hold her close, feeling the rhythmic rise and fall of her tiny chest against mine. In those moments, I reminded myself that my strength was no longer just for me—it was for her.

Feeding Riya had become a routine, one that held a bittersweet edge. Each time I prepared the nursing bottle with the breast milk Nithin brought, I couldn't help but think of Aliya. This should've been her moment, not mine. Yet, despite the grief that always seemed to linger, I made sure that Riya was well-fed and comfortable. I would cradle her in my arms, her small lips latching onto the bottle as she sucked hungrily, her eyes half-closed in contentment. I'd talk to her softly, telling her stories, reassuring her that everything would be alright—even though I wasn't entirely sure myself.

The confinement was taking a toll on me, both mentally and physically, but I refused to let it affect how I cared for Riya. I made a point to keep her as clean as possible, using the limited resources available. Nithin, despite the grim circumstances, ensured we had just enough supplies to keep Riya healthy—diapers, wipes, and whatever little comfort he could provide us.

Every day, I would soak the cloths in the cold water, wring them out, and use them to wipe Riya down, making sure she stayed fresh and comfortable. The icy water would sting my hands, especially during the early mornings, but I pushed through it. I couldn't let Riya suffer just because of our situation. I would gently wipe her small face, arms, and legs, talking to her softly as I did. She would stare up at me with those innocent eyes, unaware of the hardships around us, and it gave me a sense of purpose.

When Riya cried, I would walk back and forth across the cramped room, humming lullabies I remembered from my childhood. Sometimes, I'd hum the songs Aliya used to sing when we were together, songs she wanted to sing for our child. As I held Riya close, I found solace in those small moments of tenderness. It was a reminder that even in this prison, love still existed—within me, within Riya, and in the memory of Aliya.

The nights were the hardest. I would lay Riya down in the cradle, watching over her as she slept. The room would become unbearably silent, leaving only the sound of my own thoughts, looping over and over. But I couldn't afford to break down—not now, not when Riya needed me. I had to stay focused, had to push aside the pain and find strength. I would often sit beside the cradle, whispering softly to Riya about her mother, telling her how Aliya's love was still with us, protecting us even in her absence.

Each day blurred into the next, but my resolve grew stronger. I began to see Riya's small victories as our victories. The way she started recognizing my voice, how she smiled whenever I spoke, how her grip tightened when I held her hand—it all gave me a sense of purpose. I had to keep going, had to be there for her, even if it meant pushing through the emotional and physical exhaustion.

In between feeding and caring for Riya, I thought constantly about how to escape. I was aware of the danger that lingered outside, the armed men who would shoot without hesitation, but I couldn't let that fear paralyze me. I needed to protect Riya, to find a way out of this nightmare. But for now, I focused on what I could control—ensuring that Riya felt safe and loved.

Three weeks had passed since Aliya's death, and while the grief was still raw, I noticed something within me was changing. The pain was there, but it was slowly being balanced by the responsibility I felt toward Riya. I realized that while I had lost Aliya, I still had a piece of her left in our daughter. Riya was her legacy, her final gift to me, and I owed it to both of them to keep going.

As I held Riya one night, her eyes fluttering shut as she drifted into sleep, I whispered a promise into the darkness. *"I will take care of you, Riya. I will keep you safe. For your mother. For us."*

In that moment, I felt a flicker of hope. The future was uncertain, and the odds were stacked against us, but I knew I would do whatever it took to give Riya the life she deserved—even if it meant fighting through every obstacle in our path. And with that, I closed my eyes, holding Riya close, ready to face another day with renewed strength.

Week 58:

Six months passed, and in that time, Riya grew before my eyes. The tiny, fragile baby I once held had begun to show signs of growth and development despite the grim environment we were trapped in. Her once small limbs had filled out, and her chubby cheeks now showed a healthy glow. Even in this bleak place, her presence brought a warmth that I clung to every single day.

Riya had become more active and curious. Her bright eyes followed every movement I made, and she'd often babble in her baby language, responding to my voice with giggles and coos. The confinement still weighed heavily on me, but watching Riya develop small milestones reminded me that life, in some ways, continued even in the darkest circumstances.

One day, while I was sitting on the floor, Riya was lying on her blanket a few feet away. Suddenly, I noticed her struggling, kicking her legs with determination. And then, to my surprise, she managed to roll over onto her stomach for the first time. A surge of pride and joy filled my heart, and I couldn't help but smile for what felt like the first time in ages.

"Look at you, Riya," I whispered, my voice filled with awe. "You're growing up so fast. Aliya would be so proud of you."

She looked up at me with wide, curious eyes, and though she couldn't understand my words, it was as if she knew she had done something special. I clapped softly, encouraging her. She responded with a big gummy smile, her tiny arms flailing as she tried to push herself up.

In this cold, desolate place, those little moments kept me going. Every time Riya reached a new milestone—whether it was rolling over, laughing, or simply grabbing onto my finger with surprising strength—

it felt like a victory, a defiance against the hopelessness surrounding us.

Nithin continued to bring in what little he could—food, diapers, and occasionally a few toys to keep Riya entertained. She had taken a liking to a small, stuffed animal and a small ball he had managed to find. It wasn't much, but she would clutch it close whenever she slept, her little companion in this cold, dark world.

Even in this confinement, I tried my best to engage her. I would sing soft lullabies, tell her stories about the world outside, and play little games that made her giggle. Despite everything, Riya was thriving, and it was my only solace. I knew I had to stay strong, not just for myself, but for her. She was innocent, unaware of the cruelty that had taken away her mother and confined her to this dark room. All she knew was that I was there with her, caring for her, loving her with every fiber of my being.

Six months in, and Riya was already my whole world. And in her presence, I found the strength to keep going, to hold onto hope that one day, we'd break free and give her the life she truly deserved. Until that day came, I was determined to be everything she needed—her protector, her caregiver, and the one who would show her love even in a place devoid of it.

Week 80

It's been one year since Aliya passed away, and in that time, Riya has grown so much. Even though she has never seen the outside world, she's growing strong and healthy. Riya had become more energetic, and now she could stand up on her tiny legs. Though she couldn't walk just yet, she kept trying. She would take a step or two, then stumble and fall onto the floor. But she doesn't give up—she's determined to figure it out, and watching her try brings a small sense of hope to my heart.

We spend most of our time playing together, and those moments with Riya are the best part of my day. Her laughter, her little smiles, they make the pain of losing Aliya just a little bit easier to bear. We have our own games that we've created with the few things we have. Sometimes, I'll bounce a small ball to her, and she'll try to catch it with her tiny hands.

Her favorite game was when I'd lift her up and spin her slowly, pretending she was flying. Her joyful squeals were like music, making the room feel less like a prison, even if just for a moment. Her laughter was infectious—it was the one sound that could momentarily lift the heavy burden I carried in my heart. Despite the pain of losing Aliya, Riya's presence gave me a reason to keep going. Her innocent joy made the dark room feel a little brighter.

We also had our quieter moments. Sometimes I would simply hold her and rock her gently as she leaned against my chest, humming a soft tune that Aliya used to sing. Riya's tiny hands would grab onto my shirt as if she never wanted to let go. In those moments, I felt like I was holding onto the last piece of Aliya. Riya's warmth, her softness—it all reminded me of the love I had lost, but it also gave me strength. Taking care of her became my purpose, and her company eased the loneliness that threatened to swallow me whole.

Nithin still brings us food, but whenever he comes, I make sure Riya is fast asleep. I don't want anyone else looking at her or talking to her, I know she can't talk back yet, but I just can't trust anyone, not even Nithin. Something deep inside me refused to let anyone else get close to her. Even though Nithin has helped us survive, I couldn't fully trust him. my heart tells me not to let my guard down. There's a part of me that can't shake the feeling that he's somehow connected to the tragedy that took away my friends and my Aliya. That's why I never let him see Riya awake. My gut told me to be cautious, so I never allowed him to ask too much about Riya. Whenever he inquired about her, I would simply say she was sleeping peacefully and leave it at that.

But when it was just Riya and me, everything felt different. She had a way of pulling me out of the darkness. Her small victories, like the day she stood on her own without falling, filled me with hope. Seeing her smile, hearing her laugh—it all gave me something to hold onto. Even though our world was limited to these four walls, Riya's presence made it bearable. She was a constant reminder that life, no matter how difficult, could still carry moments of joy.

Every day I promised myself that I would protect her, keep her safe, and give her all the love I could. She was all I had left, and I would never let anything happen to her. Raising Riya became the one thing that gave me purpose. As she grew, so did my determination to ensure that one day, she would experience the world beyond this room. Until then, I would make sure she was happy, loved, and cared for.

One day, Nithin slipped a small blade, a portable stone mortar and pestle, and a spoon through the hole in the wall. I looked at them, puzzled, and asked what they were for. Without saying much, he dropped a few apples inside and said, "Make applesauce for Riya." It was such a simple thing, yet it felt wonderful. In this dark, confined space, it gave me something meaningful to do—a way to take care of my daughter beyond just holding her or feeding her milk. It was a small step, but it felt like a big one.

The first time I tried making the applesauce, I felt an odd sense of excitement. I took one of the apples and washed it under the cold tap. The water was freezing, but it felt refreshing to do something so ordinary. With the small blade, I carefully peeled off the apple's skin. The blade wasn't sharp, so I had to work slowly, but I didn't mind. Each peel felt like I was doing something special, something nurturing, something that Aliya would've done if she were here.

After peeling the apple, I cut it into tiny pieces. The blade made it tricky, and the pieces weren't perfect, but I tried to make them small enough so they'd be easy to crush. I placed the chunks in the stone mortar and, with the pestle, began grinding them down. The process was slow and required effort, but I found a strange sense of joy in it. As I crushed the apple, it gradually turned into a smooth, juicy paste. I kept going until the consistency was just right—soft and a bit runny, perfect for Riya.

While I was making the applesauce, Riya was happily playing with her small toys on the wooden cot. She was lost in her little world, giggling and babbling to herself. I got so absorbed in preparing the applesauce that I didn't notice her slowly scooting to the edge of the cot. I was almost done when suddenly I heard a loud thud behind me. My heart stopped for a moment as I turned around to see Riya on the floor, crying. Panic shot through me as I rushed to her and scooped her up into my arms.

"Shhh... shhh... nothing happened, Riya. Everything's fine," I whispered soothingly, trying to calm her down. Her tiny cheeks had turned a bright pink from all the crying, which only made her look even cuter, though it broke my heart to see her in pain. Her cheeks always turned pink whenever she cried, making it impossible for me to stay upset even in such a moment.

"Look here, sweetheart," I said softly, holding up the bowl of applesauce. "Daddy made something special for you. I'm sure you want to eat it, don't you? Now say ahhh..." Her sobs slowly quieted as she saw the applesauce, her tears replaced with a look of curiosity and hunger. She leaned forward a bit, eager to taste it, and her little lips formed a smile.

I sat on the cold floor with her in my lap, gently feeding her spoonfuls of the applesauce. She eagerly took each bite, her eyes sparkling as she enjoyed the sweet taste. Seeing her so content brought a warmth to my chest. In moments like these, it felt like all the pain and despair melted away, if only for a while. Despite everything, there was still love and joy between us.

But just as I was beginning to relax, a chilling voice interrupted the peace. "Looks like someone's having a tough time babysitting," Vikram sneered from behind the door. My body tensed, every instinct going on high alert. The sound of his voice made my blood boil, but I bit down the rage rising within me. I had learned the hard way that responding to him only made things worse.

I kept quiet, focusing instead on Riya, who was happily munching away, unaware of the hatred I felt toward the man who had taken everything from us. I couldn't afford to let Riya see me lose control. If I got angry, she might get scared, and that was something I couldn't bear. I promised Aliya that I would protect Riya, not just from harm but from the darkness that this place held.

So, I swallowed my pride and ignored Vikram, knowing that silence was my best weapon. He always lost interest whenever I refused to give him the reaction he wanted. Eventually, he left, muttering under his breath. I had to admit, sometimes silence really was the best answer.

Once he was gone, I turned my full attention back to Riya. "There we go, sweetheart. Just us again," I murmured, smiling down at her. In her innocent gaze, I found the strength to keep going. Even in this dark world, Riya was my light, and nothing would take that away from us.

After one year, Riya was starting to speak in simple words. She can say basic things like "papa," "no," and "more." Her voice is small and sweet, bringing so much warmth to the cold prison. Though her vocabulary is limited, she uses gestures and sounds to express herself, pointing at things she wants or calling out to get my attention in the sweetest ways.

Her first word was "Papa," and it was a moment that will stay etched in my heart forever. It happened one quiet afternoon. I was sitting beside her, playing with her small toys while she tried to stack them. She was focused, her little brows furrowed in concentration. Suddenly, she looked up at me with those bright eyes and, out of nowhere, she said, "Papa."

I froze, my breath catching in my throat. For a second, I couldn't believe it. But she said it again, this time with a big smile, "Papa!" Her tiny voice was filled with so much warmth and love. It felt like my heart was going to burst out of my chest. I couldn't stop the tears from welling up in my eyes—tears of pure joy, something I hadn't felt in what seemed like an eternity.

"Riya, say it again, please," I urged, my voice trembling with emotion.

She giggled, enjoying the attention, and said it again, "Papa!" It was like she knew how much it meant to me. In that moment, all the pain, all the suffering seemed to melt away. Hearing her call me "Papa" made every struggle I'd faced feel worth it. It was like a piece of Aliya had come alive in her, a small but powerful reminder that love endures, even in the darkest places.

I scooped her up in my arms and spun her around, both of us laughing. "Yes, Riya, I'm your Papa! My sweet girl, you said it perfectly!" I couldn't stop smiling, and neither could she. It was such a simple word, but to me, it was everything.

In that tiny room, surrounded by nothing but cold walls and dim light, the sound of her voice saying "Papa" filled the space with warmth and hope. For the first time in a long while, I felt like I could breathe again. Riya had given me something no one else could—a reason to keep fighting, a reason to believe that we could make it out of this nightmare someday.

From that day on, whenever she saw me, she'd say "Papa" with the biggest smile, and each time, it filled my heart with an overwhelming sense of love and responsibility. No matter what happens, I knew that as long as I had Riya and she had me, we'd find a way to keep going. Hearing her call me "Papa" gave me the strength I needed to face whatever lay ahead.

Week 250:

It's been four years since Aliya passed away, and Riya is now four. She's grown up healthily and is full of life, a true reflection of her mother. Although she's a blend of both me and Aliya, it's Aliya's features that dominate. Riya's face mirrors Aliya's delicate beauty—her soft, smooth hair falls like silk, and whenever she laughs, those dimples light up her entire face, just like Aliya's used to. The only thing she inherited from me is my eyes. Those twinkling blue eyes of hers are just like mine, but they shine with a brightness and innocence that are all her own.

"Daddy, daddy, let's play home-home!" Riya exclaimed, bouncing excitedly around me. I was busy preparing her favorite applesauce. Even though she's four now, she still loves it as much as ever.

"Alright, alright," I said with a smile, "but first, you have to finish this applesauce." I stirred the mixture, making sure it was just right.

"Hmm, okay!" she nodded eagerly, her eyes wide with excitement. "If I eat all of it, will you really play with me? Pinky promise?"

"If you finish every bite, I'll play as long as you want," I assured her, holding out my pinky. She wrapped her tiny pinky around mine and grinned.

I sat on the floor, ready to feed her. "Yay! Daddy's gonna play with me!" she sang, spinning in circles and clapping her hands.

"Come here, silly girl, and eat this," I said, smiling at her joyful energy.

She ran over and climbed onto my lap, her favorite spot to eat. She always insisted on sitting on my lap whenever I fed her, a habit that warmed my heart every time. I started to feed her the applesauce, and she ate it eagerly, savoring every spoonful.

"Mmm, Daddy, it's so tasty!" she giggled, her mouth still full of applesauce.

She finished the applesauce completely, then pointed at her tiny belly and exclaimed, "Look, Daddy, my stomach is so big now!"

I couldn't help but laugh at her antics. Her laughter, her playfulness—it was all a source of light in this dark, confined world we were stuck in. I wiped her mouth gently and placed the empty bowl aside.

"Alright, now that your tummy is full, let's play!" I said, ready to give her all the attention she deserved.

But just as I was ready to play with her, a malicious voice cut through the moment. "Looks like someone is enjoying feeding her," came Vikram's voice, dripping with contempt.

The joy on Riya's face vanished instantly, her laughter extinguished, and the excitement that had filled the room just moments ago died away at the sound of Vikram's voice. I quickly scooped her up and sat on the rickety wooden cot, holding her close. Her little arms wrapped around my neck, clinging to me. I could feel her tiny heart beating fast against my chest.

"What's it to you if I enjoy myself or not, Vikram?" I responded, keeping my tone steady but laced with defiance. "You've tried and failed to make my life miserable for years, and yet here I am, happy with my daughter. I'd gladly spend the rest of my life in this room with Riya, and I'm not suffering one bit." I mocked him, hoping to shield Riya from the venom in his words.

"Don't think it's all over, Rishab," Vikram said, his voice sharp with irritation. "I have the power here. If I want, I can take that little Riya away from you forever." he threatened, his voice cold.

"Go on then, try it," I shot back, my voice calm but firm. "But remember, if you want to take Riya from me, you'll have to come inside this room. And if you do, I guarantee the only thing leaving here will be your lifeless body." I made sure my words carried an icy edge, letting him know I wouldn't hesitate to kill him to protect Riya.

There was a heavy silence, and I could almost hear him gritting his teeth. Then, after a tense moment, I heard his footsteps fading away, leaving us alone once more.

As the tension slowly ebbed, Riya clung tighter to me, burying her face in my chest. "It's okay, sweetheart," I whispered, stroking her hair gently. "He's gone now."

Riya looked up at me, her big blue eyes wide with a mixture of fear and confusion. I kissed the top of her head, trying to reassure her. "Daddy's here, and no one's going to take you away. I promise," I said softly.

As I held Riya close, she slowly calmed down, her little fingers fiddling with the edge of my shirt. Her curiosity starting to rise again. After a moment, she looked up at me with those big, innocent eyes that never failed to melt my heart.

"Daddy, why we stay here all the time?" she asked, her voice soft and filled with a child's innocent confusion. "Why we don't go outside like others?"

Her question hit me like a punch to the gut. How could I explain this cruel situation to her innocent mind? How could I make her understand that this tiny room was both our prison and our shelter from the danger lurking outside?

I took a deep breath, gently stroking her soft hair as I searched for the right words. "Riya, sweetheart, this room keeps us safe," I began softly. "Outside, there are people who don't want us to be happy. They aren't nice like the friends we talk about in our stories. They're not good people, and they can hurt us."

She blinked, her little forehead crinkling in confusion. "But why they not nice, Daddy? Did we do somethin' bad?"

I forced a smile, though it felt heavy. "No, my love, we didn't do anything wrong. Sometimes, people are mean and do bad things, even when others don't deserve it. But that's why we're here—because as long as we stay in this room, they can't hurt us. And as long as I'm with you, you'll always be safe."

Riya's face scrunched up in thought. "But... but I wanna go outside, Daddy... I wanna see the sky and the sun like in the stories...you told me"

Hearing those words crushed me. The one thing I couldn't give her—the freedom of the outside world. "I know, sweetheart. And one day, we will. We'll go outside, and you'll see the sky, the sun, and everything we dream about. But for now, we have to stay strong together, okay? We can still be happy here, just like when we play and laugh, right?"

She nodded slowly, still not fully understanding. "Okay, Daddy... but we go outside someday, 'kay? Promise?"

I kissed her forehead and gave her a reassuring smile. "I promise, Riya. One day, we'll go outside. But until then, we'll make the best of our little world here, just like we always do."

Week 313

"Rishab, I can't keep watching you and Riya suffer like this. It's been six years... six long years in this dreadful place. Honestly, I don't even know how you've survived this long, especially with a little girl like Riya. But she's growing up, and she needs to experience the outside world. It isn't right for a child to be trapped like this. She should be running, playing, learning—living." Nithin's voice broke through the silence, but this time there was something different in his tone—something serious.

His words hung heavy in the air. For a moment, I just stared at the wall, trying to process what he was saying. After all these years, after all the suffering, he was talking about escape? Was this for real?

He continued, his voice urgent yet filled with guilt. "I've been thinking about it for a long time, Rishab. I know I haven't been able to do much, and you probably don't fully trust me. But I can't bear to see Riya locked up like this anymore. I have a plan to get you both out of here. It's risky, but it's the only chance you've got."

I felt my heart race as I listened. Was this finally it? After all the hopeless days and nights, was there really a chance for freedom?

Riya was sleeping soundly on the cot, her little face peaceful and innocent. My gaze softened as I looked at her, thinking about all the moments she's missed out on. She's never seen a sunset, never felt the breeze on her face, never even run in a field like other kids. Nithin was right—she deserves more than this. "It's been five years since Aliya died," I muttered, more to myself than to Nithin. "And Riya... she's five now. She's growing up in this cage. She doesn't even know what the outside world looks like."

Nithin slipped something through the small opening in the wall. But it wasn't food this time. I looked down and saw two sets of clothes. My eyes widened as the reality of what he was proposing sank in. For the first time in years, hope flickered inside me, but it was clouded by fear and doubt.

Nithin spoke in a low, hurried voice. "I've been planning this for months, Rishab. I know the guards' schedules, and I've figured out a way to create a diversion. If we time it right, you and Riya can slip out unnoticed. You'll have to move quickly and stay silent, but it's possible."

I was silent, my mind racing with a mix of emotions—hope, fear, uncertainty. After so long in this hellhole, could we really escape? Could I really protect Riya and give her the life she deserved?

I stared at the clothes, my mind racing. Could we really escape after all these years? Could I risk everything for this one chance? Memories of the promise I made to Aliya flooded my thoughts. I had promised to protect Riya and give her a future. If I stayed here, I'd be breaking that promise. I'd be failing Aliya and, more importantly, Riya.

But the fear was still there. What if this was a trap? What if it all went wrong? I couldn't shake the uncertainty gnawing at me. I had lost so much already—my friends, my Aliya. Could I really let myself believe in hope again?

"But why now, Nithin?" I asked, my voice edged with suspicion. "Why help us now, after all these years?"

Nithin sighed heavily. "I should've done something sooner, Rishab, I was scared. But I can't live with myself if I let Riya keep growing up in this nightmare. She's innocent—she doesn't deserve this.

I looked back at Riya, still sleeping, her little chest rising and falling steadily. This wasn't just about me; this was about her. It's always been about her. I couldn't let her be caged anymore. She deserved a life outside these walls, a chance to live, to dream, to be free.

After what felt like an eternity, I finally spoke, my voice low but resolved. "Nithin... I'll do it. For Riya, I'll risk everything. Just help us get out of here."

Nithin sighed, relieved. "Thank you for trusting me, Rishab. I won't let you down. But listen carefully—tomorrow, I'll bring a sleeping pill for Riya. She can't be awake to witness what's going to happen. If Vikram finds out you've escaped, there'll be chaos. Once she's asleep, I'll unlock this door. But after that, you're on your own. I won't be able to help if things go wrong. You'll need to be ready for anything."

My heart skipped a beat at his words, but I knew there was no turning back. I had to take this chance. "Alright, I understand. I'll be ready."

"Good," Nithin replied. "Prepare yourself for tomorrow. It's going to be a mayhem. I'll leave now—get ready." With that, he slipped away, leaving me alone with my thoughts.

After he left, I stood there, still struggling to fully grasp what was happening. Were we really going to escape? Was this finally happening after all these years? A mix of hope and dread swirled inside me. I closed my eyes and whispered, "Aliya... please, watch over us as we try to get out of this place."

That night, sleep evaded me. I lay awake on the rickety wooden cot, unable to shake the memories of that tragic day six years ago—the day that changed everything. The day I lost my friends, my freedom, and everything I held dear. The events of that day replayed in my mind like a cruel, endless loop, filling me with a sense of despair and rage.

As I stared into the darkness, one image burned vividly in my memory: the man who struck me from behind on that fateful day during the college anniversary. His malicious eyes, gleaming with a cruel intent, haunted me. Those two eyes—I would never forget them. Rage engulfed me as I recalled his cold, unfeeling stare. I knew, even then, that those eyes belonged to someone who would bring nothing but pain and suffering.

If I came face to face with him tomorrow while trying to escape, I would tear his neck in two. I swear, I would. He was the sole reason Vikram captured us and forced us to live in this dreadful place for six long years. If that man hadn't interfered, Aliya would still be alive, and so would all my friends. The weight of that thought crushed me, fueling the fire of vengeance that burned within me.

The night dragged on, each passing moment only deepening my sense of unease. I hadn't slept at all. The thought of escaping from this nightmare still lingered in my mind, filling me with both hope and dread. Was this really the end of our endless confinement?

Nithin's plan played over and over in my head. Tomorrow, he would bring the sleeping pill for Riya. Tomorrow, we would try to break free. But I couldn't shake the fear that gripped me. What if something went wrong? What if we failed? And yet, I knew I had no choice. I had to try—for Riya, for the promise I made to Aliya, and for the chance to make those responsible pay for what they had done.

As I lay there, the memories of that tragic day and the prospect of what was to come tomorrow intertwined in my thoughts. Tomorrow could bring our freedom—or our doom. I prayed silently, "Aliya, please, watch over us."

But in the back of my mind, I knew that if I encountered the man with those malicious eyes, nothing could stop me from exacting my revenge. He would pay for everything—every tear, every loss, every moment of suffering. This was not just about escaping; it was about justice.

The next morning, Nithin arrived earlier than usual. His footsteps were almost silent, but the tension in the air was palpable. He spoke in a hushed tone, "Are you ready for the mayhem, Rishab?"

"Totally," I replied, though my voice trembled slightly. The gravity of what we were about to do was beginning to sink in.

"Good to know," he said, a hint of urgency in his voice. "Here, this is the sleeping pill that will put Riya into a deep sleep." He dropped the pill through the small hole in the wall, and I quickly caught it in my hand, my heart pounding in my chest.

"Thanks, Nithin," I said, trying to express my gratitude despite the fear creeping into my voice. "I don't know how to properly thank you enough..."

"Forget about that," he began, but suddenly he fell silent, his voice cutting off abruptly. After a tense pause, he whispered urgently, "Someone's coming. I need to go before they see me. Make sure to give Riya the pill."

Before I could respond, Nithin was gone, leaving me alone in the dim room. The small pill in my hand felt heavy with the weight of what was to come. I stared at it, knowing that once I gave it to Riya, there would be no turning back. The plan was in motion, and our fate was sealed.

Riya was still fast asleep, so I quickly grabbed the last three apples we had and washed them under the cold tap water. The small blade I used to peel the apples had grown dull after years of use, making the task slow and difficult. After spending about half an hour carefully peeling the apples, I cut them into small pieces and placed them in the mortar. Then, I opened the packet of the sleeping pill Nithin had given me and added it to the mortar. I began crushing everything together with the pestle. The entire time, my hands trembled slightly, the gravity of what I was about to do weighing heavily on my mind.

Just as I finished preparing the applesauce, Riya began to stir. Her tiny body shifted under the thin blanket, and soon her eyes fluttered open. "Good morning, sweetheart," I whispered, brushing a strand of hair away from her face. "Did you sleep well?"

"Mhm," she mumbled, rubbing her eyes with her tiny fists.

"Daddy already made you breakfast. Do you want to eat it?" I asked, trying to keep my voice cheerful, though my mind was weighed down by what I was about to do.

"Yes, yes!" she said, her voice bright and happy.

"But before that, you need to wash your face," I said, scooping her up into my arms. I carried her over to the tap and gently splashed cold water on her face.

"It's colddd, daddyyyy," she giggled, her laughter ringing out like music in this dark place.

After washing her face, I sat down and fed her the applesauce, just like I always did, with her sitting comfortably in my lap. She ate it happily, unaware of the pill mixed into it. When she finished, I wiped her mouth and hugged her close.

Soon, I noticed her beginning to yawn, a sign that the pill was taking effect. Within minutes, her eyelids grew heavy, and she drifted off into a deep sleep, her small body going limp in my arms. She had only just woken up, and now she was sleeping again. I felt a pang of guilt in my chest. "I'm really sorry, darling," I whispered, placing her gently on the cot. "But it's important for us to escape from this dreadful place."

With her sleeping peacefully, I quickly changed her clothes into the ones Nithin had slipped to me the day before. After dressing her, I changed my own clothes, preparing for what was to come.

As I finished, I glanced down at Riya, my little girl, my princess, my hope. Everything I was about to do was for her—for the life she deserved, beyond these cold, confining walls. This was our chance, and I couldn't afford to fail.

As I waited for Nithin to open the door, a sudden thought struck me— What if one of the guards came in my way? What if something went wrong? I had to be prepared, but I had nothing—no weapon to defend myself or protect Riya.

I looked around the room, scanning for anything that could be of useful. The mortar and pestle caught my eye, but I knew they wouldn't be much help in a fight. I needed something quick, sharp, and deadly. Apart from that, there were only some of Riya's toys and a small, rusted blade I'd used to peel apples.

A blade... Even though it was small and rusted, it could still be useful. Quickly, I picked it up. My heart pounded as I picked up the blade, feeling its cold, metal edge press against my palm. It was small—too small to be effective in a fight—but it was all I had.

But then, those two malicious eyes flashed in my mind—the eyes that had haunted me for so long. Why now? Why were they tormenting me at a time like this, just when we were about to escape this dreadful place? Damn him. If that man crossed my path again, I'd cut his throat with this rusted blade, I swore silently, my anger boiling inside me.

As I waited for Nithin to open the door, my heart pounded like a bullet train. I took a few deep breaths, trying to steady my nerves. This was it. The moment I had been waiting for. The moment to break free.

Finally, after what felt like an eternity, Nithin's voice broke through the silence. "Rishab, all ready? Did you give Riya the pill?" His voice sounded shaky, almost unsure.

"Yeah, I gave it to her a while ago. She's fast asleep now," I replied, trying to keep my voice steady.

"Good. I'll open the door then. Step back a bit," he instructed.

As I heard the clicking sound of the door unlocking, my heart raced even faster. The stone door, heavy and imposing, began to move aside, grinding against the floor with a low, ominous rumble. Light from the outside world—light I hadn't seen in years—began to pour into the room, blinding me for a moment. My grip on the blade tightened,

Nithin stepped forward, his silhouette framed by the harsh light. In that instant, I acted. My muscles tensed, and I gripped the blade tighter than ever before. With all the strength I could muster, I slashed the blade forward, aiming directly for his neck. The movement was quick, driven by a mix of rage and desperation. The blade, though small and rusted, sliced through his flesh. I felt a sickening resistance as it cut into him,

For a split second, time seemed to stand still. Then, Blood erupted from the wound, a dark crimson stream that spilled out like a waterfall. The warm, sticky liquid splattered onto my hand, and for a moment, I felt a sickening satisfaction as I watched it flow.

Nithin's eyes widened in shock, a look of betrayal and disbelief spreading across his face. He staggered back, clutching at his neck as blood gushed between his fingers. He hadn't expected this—hadn't expected me to turn on him like this. He had let his guard down, just like I did six years ago.

For a brief moment, Nithin just stood there, his mind struggling to process what had just happened. "Why, Rishab? I was trying to help you..." he whispered, his voice barely audible over the sound of his own blood dripping onto the cold, stone floor. His legs gave out, and he collapsed onto the ground, his body twitching as life began to drain from him.

I stood over him, my breath ragged, my heart still racing. The blade in my hand was now coated in his blood, the rust mixing with the fresh crimson. I looked down at him, my eyes locking onto his, those same malicious eyes I had seen six years ago.

"Why?" he repeated, his voice fading, his life slipping away with each word.

"Why?" I echoed, my voice cold and filled with the years of pain and rage I had harbored. "Do you really not know? You're asking why I did this? Did you think you had hidden your face properly six years ago when you struck me from behind?... at the college anniversary. Not really. Those eyes of yours—I still remember them. Those malicious eyes of yours. I knew I'd never forget them when I first saw them at the college backyard."

His eyes widened further, realization dawning on him as his blood continued to pool around him. His mouth opened to speak, but no sound came out. His strength was failing him, his body unable to keep up with the shock and blood loss.

I paused, watching as the life drained from his body, his blood pooling around him. "Do you know how I figured out it? That it was you who struck me from behind like a coward?... When Aliya died giving birth to Riya, and you brought Riya to me, I saw the real face behind those eyes. It was you, Nithin. You hit me from behind. If you hadn't interfered, all my friends would still be alive, and my Aliya would be still alive, living peacefully."

My voice grew darker, filled with years of pent-up rage. "You're the reason my friends are dead. You're the reason for Aliya's death. You're the reason we've been suffering in this dreadful place. And you're the reason Riya has lost her right to experience the outside world, to play, to explore the outside world."

I stepped closer, leaning over his dying form. "Do you know why I kept quiet all these years? Because I knew, one day, I would take my revenge. I knew this day would come—the day I've dreamed about. Today is that day, Nithin. Today, I escape this nightmare. And you... you will die for your sins.

Nithin's lips moved as if he wanted to speak, but no sound came out. His body was covered in blood, the floor beneath him a crimson pool. His eyes slowly shut, his body went still, and finally, Nithin was dead.

Finally, after what felt like an eternity, I stepped back, letting the blade fall from my hand. It clattered to the ground with a dull thud, now useless. I wiped the blood from my hands onto my clothes, the adrenaline slowly leaving my system, leaving me feeling drained but determined.

This was it. The first step toward freedom. The first step toward avenging Aliya, my friends, and Riya. I looked back at the cot where Riya slept peacefully, unaware of the chaos that had just unfolded. I had to get her out of here. This was our only chance. I turned back toward the open door, ready to face whatever came next.

Present Moment:

"Wow... Rishi, you really are something," Seema said, her voice filled with a mix of awe and disbelief. "All this time, you knew Nithin's true identity, yet you acted like you knew nothing, even after losing everything... If it were for me, I'd have shattered into pieces."

Karthik nodded in agreement, his eyes full of respect. "I knew you wouldn't let them walk free after everything they did to our friends," Karthik added, a note of respect in his tone. "You took revenge—for us, for our friends."

"And for my Aliya," I added, completing his thought. The mention of Aliya brought a soft, bittersweet smile to their faces.

They both smiled at me, though the sadness in their eyes was unmistakable. Seema's curiosity got the better of her. "What happened next? What did you do after killing Nithin?"

"After killing Nithin, I took Riya and, I somehow found the way out of that hellish base. But just when I thought we were safe, Vikram appeared with two of his guards. I managed to take down his guards and used him as a hostage to escape. Once I was out, I killed Vikram in an isolated area and then came to Mumbai as quickly as I could," I explained, my voice steady, but my heart still heavy with the memories.

Seema and Karthik were silent for a moment, absorbing everything I had just told them. "You really suffered a lot, Rishi," Karthik finally said, his voice thick with emotion. "The hardships you faced, the losses you bore—no one else could have endured that. Yet you did. We're proud to be your friends."

"I did it for a promise I made to Aliya before she died—to give Riya a safe and secure future. I never let despair consume me because of Riya. She's the light that brightened me when I was drowning in darkness. She became my strength, the only reason I was able to escape that dreadful place," I said, feeling a warmth in my chest at the thought of my little girl.

"The way you talk about Riya... Hearing you, I want to see her badly. Where is she, Rishi? I can't see her anywhere," Seema asked, looking around.

"Yeah, me too. Where is she, anyway?" Karthik added, glancing around the hall.

Before I could answer, Riya's voice echoed from inside the room. "Daddy... Daddy... where are you?" she called out, her small fists knocking on the door.

It suddenly hit me—I had bolted the door from the outside. "Wait here for a moment. I'll be back soon," I told them and rushed to the room.

As I opened the door, Riya immediately clung to my legs, her tiny arms wrapping around them as tightly as she could.

I immediately lifted her up, noticing her tear-filled eyes. "Why are you crying, baby? Daddy's here, no need to cry," I said softly, gently wiping her tears away.

"Where did you go, Daddy? I was scared," she said, her voice trembling as she clung to me even tighter.

"I didn't go anywhere. I'm here," I reassured her, holding her close. "Do you know someone came to meet you? Do you want to see them?" I said, to make her feel safe and comfortable.

Instantly Her curiosity piqued, and she nodded eagerly. "Yes... Yes!" she said, her earlier fear replaced with excitement.

"But first, let's wash your face. Then you can meet them," I said, carrying her to the attached bathroom. As I splashed cold water on her face, she giggled, the sound filling the room with warmth.

"It's cold, Daddy!" she laughed, her tiny hands trying to splash water back at me.

After washing her face, I gently wiped her face with a towel. "Now you're perfect," I said, cupping her face and giving her a reassuring smile.

Hand in hand, we walked out of the room. Seema and Karthik were looking at her with wide eyes, amazed by how much she resembled Aliya.

"Wow, Rishi... She's such a cutie!" Seema squealed, unable to contain her excitement as we approached them.

"I can't believe it, Rishab," Karthik said, still staring at her in awe. "She's the mirror image of Aliya. She looks just like her."

"Guys, this is Riya, my princess, my little daughter. And darling, these are Seema and Karthik, Daddy's friends," I said, properly introducing them. My heart swelling with pride.

Seema couldn't resist any longer. She quickly scooped Riya into her arms, planting a deep kiss on her cheek. At first, Riya was startled by Seema's sudden action, her body tensing up. But within moments, she relaxed, sensing the warmth in Seema's embrace. A shy smile crept onto her face, and soon, she was giggling, playing with Seema's hair and enjoying the attention.

Karthik watched them with a smile, and I couldn't help but feel a deep sense of gratitude. Despite everything, we were here, together, and for the first time in years, I felt a glimmer of hope for the future.

But as I remembered the need to find my family, a wave of urgency washed over me. I turned to Karthik, hoping for some clarity.

"Karthi, do you know where my family is living right now?" I asked, my voice tinged with the anxiety of years spent in uncertainty.

Karthik nodded. "Of course I do, Rishi. After Vikram took you, your mom, dad, your brother Roshan, and your sister Rishika—they all searched everywhere for you. They even filed a FIR, pushing the police repeatedly, but they couldn't find you. Five years ago, your family shifted back to Kalyan, the same house where they lived before moving to Mumbai six years ago." But still they haven't overcome with your disappearance, your mom is still struggling to cope with it.

a wave of relief washed over me, knowing they were safe. But a heavy sense of urgency also filled me; I needed to see them, especially my mother, who still hadn't fully recovered from my disappearance.

"Yeah," I agreed, the thought of seeing them filling me with a bittersweet longing. "I should go and meet them as soon as I can."

Karthik glanced at the clock on the wall. "But first, let's have breakfast. It's already half past nine in the morning. You'll need your strength before you head to Kalyan."

I nodded in agreement. We all decided to head downstairs to the hotel's dining area. As we made our way down, Seema carried Riya in her arms. Riya, who had quickly warmed up to Seema, was playing with her hair, twirling the strands between her small fingers and giggling.

Once we were seated in the dining area, Seema sat Riya on her lap, her arms securely around the little one. The atmosphere was calm, filled with the comforting clatter of breakfast being served around us. The sunlight filtered through the large windows, casting a warm glow over everything.

The server brought out a platter of assorted breakfast items, but it was the stack of pancakes that caught Riya's eye. Her eyes lit up at the sight, and Seema noticed immediately.

"I know these are your favorite, princess," Seema said softly, her voice filled with affection.

Seema carefully cut the pancakes into small pieces, then began feeding Riya. With each bite, Riya's face lit up, a smile spreading across her lips. She would occasionally reach for Seema's hair, playing with it as she ate. Seema didn't mind; in fact, she seemed to enjoy it, smiling warmly each time Riya's tiny hands tugged at her strands.

Karthik and I ate our breakfast quietly, exchanging occasional glances and small smiles as we watched the interaction between Seema and Riya. There was a sense of normalcy in this moment that I hadn't felt in a long time, a brief reprieve from all the darkness that had consumed my life.

The pancakes were fluffy and warm, drizzled with syrup that added just the right amount of sweetness. I ate slowly, savoring each bite, though my mind was already on the next steps—going to Kalyan and reuniting with my family.

Seema continued to feed Riya until the plate was almost empty. When Riya's small hand reached for the last piece, Seema guided it to her mouth, laughing softly as Riya gave a satisfied hum. Once Riya was done, Seema gently wiped her mouth with a napkin, planting a light kiss on her cheek afterward.

Also she couldn't resist herself doting on Riya, her laughter filling the room as Riya giggled, delighted by the attention. Even Karthik, found himself drawn into their playful exchange, occasionally reaching over to tickle Riya's tiny feet, eliciting more laughter.

"She's a little angel," Seema remarked, her voice filled with warmth as she looked at Riya, who was now leaning against her, clearly content.

I couldn't help but smile at the sight. "She's my strength," I said quietly, more to myself than to anyone else. "She's the reason I survived."

Karthik reached over and placed a reassuring hand on my shoulder. "And now, it's time for you to reunite with your family. They need to see you, Rishi. They need to know you're okay."

I nodded, feeling a deep sense of gratitude for my friends. This breakfast, though simple, felt like the first step toward reclaiming my life. Once we finished eating, I knew the next step would be to finally reunite with the people who had been waiting for me all this time.

After breakfast, the comforting warmth of the meal settled in, giving me the strength to face the next steps. Seema gently placed Riya down, and the little one clung to her hand, her eyes bright and curious.

As we made our way back to the room to gather our things, I couldn't help but feel the weight of the moment. It had been years since I had last seen my family, and the thought of reuniting with them brought a mix of emotions—excitement, fear, and anticipation.

Karthik noticed my silence and placed a reassuring hand on my shoulder as we walked. "You'll be fine, Rishi. They'll be overjoyed to see you."

I nodded, trying to push away the anxiety gnawing at me. "I know. I just hope they're ready for this, for everything that's happened."

"They'll understand," Seema chimed in, her voice gentle yet firm. "They've missed you, Rishi. Your return will be the best thing that's happened to them in years."

We reached the room, and I quickly gathered the few belongings I and Riya had. My hands were slightly shaky as I packed, but I took a deep breath, reminding myself that this was what I had fought so hard for—Riya's future and the chance to see my family again.

Once everything was packed, I picked up Riya, who had been quietly playing with one of her toys. She looked up at me with those big, innocent eyes, and I felt a surge of love and determination. This was for her. Everything I had done was to give her the life she deserved.

"Ready to go meet your grandparents, baby?" I asked softly, smoothing down her hair.

She nodded enthusiastically, though I knew she didn't fully understand what was happening. But that was okay. She would know soon enough.

After packing our things, we headed downstairs and checked out of the hotel. The air outside was crisp and cool, carrying the morning's freshness as we approached Karthik's car. Seema quickly took the front seat, and I settled into the back with Riya. She immediately nestled into my lap, her tiny hands gripping my shirt, her eyes wide with wonder as she peered out the window. Every passing building, every tree, and every person on the street seemed to captivate her attention, her innocence a stark contrast to the turmoil brewing in my mind.

As we began our journey to Kalyan, I found myself staring out at the blur of the city passing by, my thoughts heavy. Would my parents believe the unbelievable story I had to tell? How could they possibly understand where I had been and the horrors I had endured? The years that had slipped away from us couldn't be regained, and I feared that the truth might only bring them more pain.

And then there was Riya. How would they react to her? Would they accept her, love her, the way I did? She was a living reminder of everything that had happened—of Aliya, of the suffering, and yet she was also the light that had kept me going, my reason for survival. Would they see that, or would she be a painful reminder of the years lost?

The weight of these thoughts pressed down on me, swirling together in a storm of uncertainty. My heart ached with a mix of hope and fear, the unknown stretching out before me like a vast, uncharted sea. I tightened my hold on Riya, drawing comfort from her warmth. She was my anchor in this storm, the one thing that kept me grounded.

As the car continued to wind its way through the city streets, I forced myself to take a deep breath. Whatever happened, I would face it head-on. I had come too far, endured too much, to let fear control me now. My family deserved to know the truth, and Riya deserved to be loved and cherished, not just by me but by everyone in her life.

I glanced down at Riya, who was now pointing excitedly at something outside the window, her innocent joy cutting through the darkness of my thoughts. I smiled, brushing a strand of hair from her face. No matter what awaited us in Kalyan, we would face it together.

After two long hours on the road, we finally arrived in Kalyan. My heart began to race as the familiar sights of the town came into view. It had been six years since I last set foot here after shifting to Mumbai, yet everything seemed almost frozen in time. The streets, the shops, even the air felt unchanged, as if waiting for my return.

As Karthik drove us closer to my home, my anticipation grew with every passing moment. When he finally pulled up in front of a familiar house, a wave of emotions crashed over me. The house looked exactly as I remembered—its white walls, the neatly kept garden, even the same old mailbox at the gate. Nothing had changed at all, it felt like time had barely moved. The house stood as it always had, unchanged, as if waiting for us to return.

This was it. After years of being held captive, the day I had dreamed about was finally here—the day I would see my parents again. The thought both exhilarated and terrified me. I took a deep breath, trying to steady my nerves as I opened the car door. The crisp air filled my lungs as I stepped out, and I quickly helped Riya out of the car as well. She looked up at the house with curiosity, her small hand clutching mine tightly. Karthik and Seema joined us, their supportive presence grounding me in this moment.

The first thing that caught my eye was my old bike, leaning against the side of the house. The sight of it unleashed a flood of memories—

the day my dad surprised me with it. The memory was so vivid, I could almost feel the joy and excitement of that moment. The bike looked a bit worn, but it still stood proudly as a reminder of a life that once was.

For a moment, I stood there, lost in the past. The memories were overwhelming, and I felt the sting of tears behind my eyes. This was the home I had left behind, the life that had been ripped away from me. But now, I was back. I had survived, and I had brought Riya with me.

I glanced down at her, her wide eyes taking in the surroundings with innocent curiosity. She was the new chapter of my life, the bridge between the past and the future. I squeezed her hand gently, drawing

strength from her presence. I had come back not just for myself, but for her—for the promise I made to Aliya to give our daughter a safe and happy life.

"Go on, Rishi. What are you waiting for?" Seema's voice broke through my swirling thoughts, pulling me back to reality.

Slowly, I made my way to the door, Riya walking beside me, her tiny hand holding mine tightly. Karthik and Seema stood behind, offering silent support as I approached the front door, my heart pounded in my chest, a mix of excitement and fear gripping me.

My hand trembled slightly as I reached out to ring the doorbell. The sound echoed through the house, and for a moment, everything was still. I held my breath, every second feeling like an eternity.

Footsteps approached, and the door slowly creaked open. It was Rishika. She just stood there, staring at me, her eyes wide with shock. Her mouth opened, but no words came out. Then, in a move so familiar it almost made me smile, she reached out and pinched me—hard, like she always did whenever I teased her.

"Ouch, that hurts, Rishika," I said, rubbing the spot where she pinched me.

Oh... my God! Rishab, it's really you! she exclaimed, her voice trembling with disbelief. Her hands flew to her mouth, tears welling up in her eyes.

"Yeah, it's me," I replied, my voice thick with emotion.

Without wasting a second, Rishika turned and shouted, Mom! Dad! Look who's here! Her voice was loud, filled with excitement and disbelief.

From inside, I heard my dad's voice, followed by my mom's. "Why are you shouting, Rishika? Who's here?" they asked as they hurried to the door.

But as they reached the doorway and saw me standing there with Riya, they both froze. Their eyes widened in shock, their expressions a mirror of Rishika's disbelief.

My mom was the first to move. Slowly, she stepped forward, still in shock. "Rishab..." she whispered, her voice breaking. Her hands trembled as she reached out to touch my face, as if needing to confirm that I was really there, that I wasn't just a figment of her imagination.

Mom, I whispered back, my own voice shaking. "I'm home."

With those words, she pulled me into a tight embrace, her sobs breaking the silence. I held her close, feeling her tears soak into my shirt. The warmth of her hug, the scent of home—it was overwhelming, and for the first time in years, I felt a sense of peace wash over me.

My dad stood there, his eyes glistening with tears that he didn't bother to hide. He reached out, placing a hand on my shoulder, squeezing it gently. Rishab... my boy... you're really back, he said, his voice choked with emotion.

Rishika joined in, wrapping her arms around both me and Mom, her tears mixing with our own. We stood there, a tangle of arms and emotions, all the pain and suffering of the past years melting away in that moment of reunion.

Mom... where are you, came Roshan searching for her, but as he appeared from behind. He just stood there, completely frozen like everyone else, his eyes wide and filled with shock. He seemed unable to move, his gaze locked on me as if he couldn't believe what he was seeing. The disbelief on his face mirrored that of my parents, and for a moment, none of us moved.

At that moment Roshan looked like he was seeing a ghost. He stepped closer, pulling me into a hug. "I can't believe it's really you, bro. We missed you so much," he said, his voice cracking with emotion.

I held onto him, feeling the warmth and strength of his embrace. The hug was filled with a mixture of relief, joy, "Roshan," I whispered, my voice choked with emotion. "I missed you too. I missed all of you."

For that brief moment, All the pain, all the suffering, and all the loss—it was still there, lingering in the background. But it was overshadowed by the overwhelming love and joy of this reunion. In that embrace, everything else faded away, and all that mattered was that I was finally home, surrounded by the family I had fought so hard to return to.

Dad looked at me, his expression a mix of confusion and disbelief. "Where were you, Rishab? All these years? Do you have any idea how much we searched for you?" His voice was thick with emotion, his eyes searching mine for answers.

"It's a long story," I said, my mind drifting back to the dreadful place where I had been held captive. The memories were still fresh and painful, but I pushed them aside, focusing on the present moment.

"And who's this cute little child with you?" mom asked, her curiosity piqued as she looked at Riya with gentle eyes.

"This is your granddaughter," I said, bringing Riya forward and gently placing her in front of my parents. Her small frame seemed to shine with innocence as she looked up at them with wide, curious eyes.

All four of them—Mom, Dad, Roshan, and Rishika—stared at Riya, their expressions a mix of bewilderment and awe. They looked back at me, still struggling to grasp the reality of the situation.

"What do you mean by she's our granddaughter?" Dad asked, his voice filled with surprise. "How can that be?"

"Didn't you get it?" I replied, trying to steady my voice. "If she's your granddaughter, then it means she's my daughter."

The realization seemed to hit them all at once. Mom's hand flew to her mouth, and Dad's eyes widened in shock. Rishika and Roshan exchanged looks of disbelief, their faces mirroring the same stunned reaction.

"But... but how?" Mom finally managed to ask, her voice trembling. "How did this happen?"

As the gravity of the situation sank in, Riya, sensing the intensity of the moment, grew shy. Her small hands tightened around the hem of my shirt, and she took a step closer to me, hiding a bit behind my leg. Her big eyes, still filled with curiosity, darted from one face to another, clearly feeling the weight of the unfamiliar situation.

Seeing her shyness, Mom's expression softened. She reached out with a gentle, reassuring smile. "Come here, sweetie," she said softly, her voice warm and inviting. "It's okay, we're just surprised. We're happy to meet you."

Riya studied her for a moment, then looked up at me for reassurance. I gave her a small nod and a comforting smile, and that seemed to be enough. With a small, tentative step forward, Riya released my leg and allowed my mother to take her hand.

The moment my mom gently squeezed her little hand, Riya's nervousness finally gave way. She offered a shy, but sweet smile, and my mom's eyes filled with even more tears as she carefully pulled Riya into a warm hug. Riya, now feeling more secure, started to relax completely. She let out a small giggle as my mom smoothed her hair

"I know, Mom, Dad, you're all confused," I began, trying to keep my tone light despite the weight of everything I needed to say. "I'll explain everything—where I've been all these years, what happened—but first, can we please go inside? I don't want to stand out here all day," I added with a small smile, hoping to ease the tension a bit.

Mom's eyes softened, and a small smile tugged on her lips. "Oh, really sorry, beta," Mom said, quickly stepping aside. "Come inside."

Rishika, who was still in shock but quickly warming up to the situation, gently took Riya's hand and guided her into the house. The sight of my sister leading Riya inside made my heart swell with a mix of relief and gratitude. At least Riya was being welcomed with open arms.

Before stepping in, I turned back to where Karthi and Seema stood by the car. They had been my pillars of support through everything, I gave them a grateful smile, knowing how much their support meant to me. "Thank you," I mouthed, not trusting my voice at that moment.

"Don't just stand there—go inside," Seema called out, her voice tinged with that familiar warmth that always made me feel like everything would be okay.

Karthi nodded, "Yeah, we'll be around and in touch. Take care, Rishab." he said, smiling back at me.

I gave them one last grateful look, feeling a deep sense of appreciation for their friendship and support. Then, with a deep breath, I turned and walked into the house—the house that held so many memories, and now, a new chapter of my life.

As I crossed the threshold, I could feel the weight of the past few years slowly lifting off my shoulders, even if just a little. I was home, and I was finally ready to share my story with the people who mattered the most.

Everyone settled in the living room, surrounding me, their eyes filled with concern and curiosity. They were all waiting for me to speak, to explain everything about my disappearance and about Riya. The weight of their expectations was heavy, but I knew I had to be strong and tell them the truth.

I glanced over at Rishika, who was playing with Riya, her laughter filling the room with a lightness that contrasted with the tension. Thanks to her, I could gather the courage to explain everything to my family. I didn't want Riya to know the truth about her mother's death—not yet. She was still so small, so innocent. She needed time to grow, to understand, before she could bear the weight of that loss.

"Okay, here's what happened," I began, "It's a long story, but I'll try to make it as clear as I can."

Taking a deep breath, I began. For the next hour, I recounted every painful detail of what had happened to Aliya and me after Vikram kidnapped us. I told them about the endless suffering we endured, the isolation, and the fear. I described how Aliya, even in her final moments, fought to bring Riya into this world, how she passed away, leaving me alone in that dreadful place.

As I spoke, I could see the pain in my family's eyes. They listened carefully, not interrupting, just absorbing the horrors I had lived through. The room grew silent as I finished, the weight of my story hanging in the air.

For a moment, no one spoke. The look on their faces told me everything—they were heartbroken, devastated by what they had heard. My mom's eyes were filled with tears, my dad looked like he was struggling to hold back his emotions, and Roshan's fists were clenched, his face a mask of anger and sorrow.

But in that silence, I also saw something else—a deep sense of relief that I was finally home, that I had survived. Even though my story was one of pain and loss, the fact that I was sitting there with them, alive, gave them hope. And in that moment, I realized that together, we would begin to heal.

Mom was the first to break the silence. Her hand reached out, gently touching my arm, as if seeking to anchor me to the present. Tears streamed down her face, her eyes swollen from hours of holding back emotions.

"Oh, my dear Rishab... what you went through... We'll get through this together, Rishi," she whispered between her sobs, stroking my back like she did when I was a child. I could feel her trembling, as if she was trying to absorb some of my pain into herself.

My dad nodded in agreement, though his expression remained tense. "We missed you so much, son. I can't imagine the pain you went through, but you're not alone anymore. We're here for you and Riya."

Roshan, who had been quiet since I finished speaking, finally spoke up. His voice was thick with emotion. "I'm sorry, Rishab. I'm sorry we couldn't find you. I should have done more—"

"Roshan, don't blame yourself," I interrupted, my voice firm. "There was nothing anyone could have done. Vikram was ruthless, and he made sure no one would find us. What matters is that we're here now, together."

He nodded, though the guilt in his eyes didn't fully fade. "I just... I'm so glad you're back, bro. I missed you so much."

Before I could respond, Riya's laughter broke the heavy atmosphere. She was sitting on Rishika's lap, giggling as Rishika tickled her sides. The sound was like a balm to our wounded hearts, bringing a small smile to my face.

My mom's gaze shifted to Riya, her eyes softening as she watched her. "She's beautiful, Rishab," she whispered, her voice filled with awe. "Aliya would be so proud of her."

"Yeah," I replied, my voice thick with emotion. "She's all I have left of Aliya. I'll do everything I can to protect her, to make sure she has a better life."

"We'll all protect her," my dad said, his voice resolute. "She's our family now, and we'll make sure she knows how much she's loved."

Riya, sensing the attention on her, looked up at us with wide, curious eyes. "Daddy?" she called out, reaching her arms toward me.

I leaned forward and lifted her into my arms, holding her close. "I'm here, princess," I whispered, pressing a kiss to her forehead. "I'm not going anywhere."

My mom wiped away her tears and smiled softly. "Let's not dwell on the past anymore. You're home now, and we'll build a new future together."

Rishika, who had been holding back her emotions, finally let out a small sob and leaned into Roshan's shoulder. He wrapped an arm around her, offering comfort, while my dad placed a reassuring hand on my shoulder.

"We'll take it one step at a time," my dad said, his voice steady. "You've been through enough, Rishab. It's time to focus on healing and moving forward."

I nodded, feeling a sense of relief wash over me. For the first time in years, I felt like I was where I belonged—surrounded by the people who loved me, who would help me carry the burden of my past.

We spent the next few hours talking, not just about the past, but about the future. My family asked questions about Riya, about her likes and dislikes, and I found myself smiling as I shared small stories about her.

Riya, tired from all the excitement, eventually fell asleep in my arms. I looked down at her peaceful face, feeling a deep sense of gratitude that she was here with me, safe and loved.

I gently handed Riya to Rishika, making sure not to wake her up. The moment felt right—too perfect. I knew I had to go now, while Riya was fast asleep.

"Mom, where's my bike key?" I asked, standing up from the couch.

She looked at me, concern etched on her face. "Why? Where are you going, Rishi?" Her voice trembled with worry and fear.

"Yeah, you should rest first, son. You've been through a lot. There's no need to rush," my dad added, his tone gentle yet firm.

I shook my head, feeling a sense of urgency. "No, Dad. I need to go now. It's the perfect moment—Riya's asleep. If she wakes up, I might never get the chance. Please, try to understand," I urged, my voice filled with determination.

"But listen, beta—" Mom began, her voice pleading, but I cut her off gently.

"Please, Mom, I need to do this. Trust me, I'll be back before nightfall. I promise," I insisted, hoping she could see how important this was to me.

She hesitated for a moment, the worry still clear in her eyes, but she sighed and nodded. "Fine, if you say so." She disappeared inside for a moment, then returned with the key, handing it to me with a lingering reluctance.

"Be careful, beta," she said softly as I stepped out of the house, her voice filled with both love and concern.

"I will, Mom," I shouted back, already feeling the thrill of anticipation building up inside me.

After six long years, I was finally riding my bike again. As I climbed onto it and started the ignition, the engine roared to life, as if celebrating the return of its old owner. Slowly, I accelerated, feeling a deep sense of joy and freedom. The sensation of navigating through the busy streets was exhilarating, a welcome change after all those years in captivity.

Hours passed as I drove, my thoughts a mix of past memories and the present journey. Finally, I stopped in front of Aliya's small house. I parked the bike and dismounted, taking in the sight before me. The house that had once been so beautiful and full of life now looked abandoned, almost like a haunted house, with dust and cobwebs covering everything.

I expected the front door to be locked, but when I pushed it, it slowly opened with a loud creak. The sound echoed through the stillness, adding to the eerie atmosphere. The house was shrouded in darkness, I pulled out my phone and turned on the flashlight, stepping cautiously inside.

As soon as I took a step forward, a spider web brushed against my face. I grimaced, brushing it away as I took in the state of the place. Aliya's home was now a shadow of its former self, filled with dust and cobwebs. Yet, despite the decay, everything was still in its place, as if waiting for her to return. I remembered how Aliya had decorated the walls with paintings and photo frames. It was now just a sad memory, buried under dust and webs.

Ignoring the state of the living room, I headed straight for her bedroom. The moment I stepped inside, I was hit with a wave of nostalgia. The room, too, was coated in dust and cobwebs, but I could still see the remnants of the love and warmth it once held. I stood in the center, taking it all in—the memories flooding back. I vividly remembered the day Aliya and I celebrated our one-month anniversary here. She had decorated the entire room with lights and photos of us, creating a magical atmosphere that I could never forget.

Six years had passed since that wonderful day, yet all the photos of me and Aliya were still hanging from the ceiling, untouched. My gaze shifted to her tiny bed, the very same bed where we had shared our first night of intimacy, where we had cuddled together until morning. The memory brought a bittersweet smile to my face, mixing the joy of our love with the sorrow of her loss.

Determined to preserve her memory, I sprang into action. I carefully took down all of Aliya's photos, cleaning them and stacking them neatly on the table next to her bed. I had no photos of her with me—the last time I saw her was on that tragic day in the college backyard. After that, I never saw her beautiful face again, not even once. These photos were all I had left of her, and I wanted to keep them close, to remember her as she was.

Though she died five years ago, I would not let her memories fade. I would cherish them for the rest of my life. I found an old, dusty bag in the corner of the room and cleaned it as best I could. Then, I began to place Aliya's photos inside, carefully packing away these precious remnants of our time together.

As I was doing so, while I was packing the photos, a diary fell from the table and landed on the floor. My eyes caught sight of it, and I picked it up, curious. To my surprise, it was Aliya's personal diary. I opened the first page and was shocked to see that she had named the diary after me. My name, written in her delicate handwriting, brought a lump to my throat.

I sat down on a chair, which creaked under my weight, and started to read. Aliya had started writing in it after I had saved her for the first time at the club, from Vikram. From that moment on, she had written in it regularly, documenting her thoughts and feelings.

I spent the next hour absorbed in Aliya's diary, unable to tear my eyes away from the pages. I couldn't believe it—she had written every single day, documenting her thoughts and feelings, all centered around me, capturing her emotions from before I joined the college, right up to the moment I proposed to her. It was clear that she had fallen for me the very first time she saw me, just as I had fallen for her— a true love at first sight.

She had detailed everything—the moment I proposed to her on the hot air balloon, our first kiss, and how it felt to her. Every single detail was captured in her handwriting, a testament to the love we shared. The last time she had written in the diary was from the night we made love, two days before our college anniversary.

When I reached the final, unfinished pages, my eyes welled up with tears. The diary, a testament to our love, had ended abruptly, leaving gaps where our life together should have continued.

I found a pen on the table and picked it up. I doubted it would work after all these years, but to my surprise, it worked perfectly. Aliya hadn't completed the diary—she had died before she could. But now, I will finish it for her. I began to write, pouring out everything that had happened since our college anniversary—the nightmare that started when Vikram kidnapped us, the years of suffering, and finally, how Aliya died giving birth to Riya, and how I and Riya escaped from that dreadful place taking revenge with Vikram by his death.

As I wrote, I felt a sense of closure, as if I were keeping a promise to her, honoring her memory by telling our story. When I reached the end, I wrote:

My beloved Aliya,

Sometimes love is meant to sacrifice themselves for others' happiness, and that is exactly what you did. You sacrificed yourself for Riya's future and her happiness. I promise, from the depths of my heart, that I will ensure she receives the happiness and love you would have given her.

Even though you are gone, Aliya, I still love you, and I always will. The moments we shared, every single one of them, I will cherish them for the rest of my life, until the day I die. No one can ever take your place in my heart. It is forever reserved for you and only you. I Love You, ALIYA, now and always.

With that final promise written, I gently closed the diary. feeling a mix of sorrow and peace. The pain of losing her would never go away, but I knew that she would always be with me—in the memories we made, in the love we shared, and in our beautiful daughter, Riya.

With the diary and Aliya's photos safely packed, I took one last look around the house. The dust-covered remnants of our past were a poignant reminder of the life we once shared. I knew that as I walked out, I was leaving behind a part of my heart but taking with me the strength to honor Aliya's memory.

As I stepped out into the fading light of the day, the sun setting in hues of orange and pink, it felt like a gentle farewell from Aliya herself. The sky seemed to embrace me, and a soft breeze caressed my face, as if she was whispering her love and encouragement.

I mounted my bike and revved the engine, feeling a surge of hope and determination. The road ahead was uncertain, but it was mine to travel, carrying with me the love and promise I had made to Aliya.

As I rode away from the house and into the twilight, I looked back one last time. The house stood silent, a guardian of our past, while I moved forward into a future shaped by our love. The journey would be long, but I was ready. With Aliya's memory in my heart and Riya's future ahead, I felt a renewed sense of purpose.

The road stretched out before me, and as the night enveloped the world, I rode on, carrying her love with me always, forever.

www.ingramcontent.com/pod-product-compliance
Lightning Source LLC
LaVergne TN
LVHW091659070526
838199LV00050B/2207